Is This Tomorrow

Also by Caroline Leavitt

Pictures of You
Girls in Trouble
Coming Back to Me
Living Other Lives
Into Thin Air
Family
Jealousies
Lifelines
Meeting Rozzy Halfway

✳✳✳✳✳✳✳✳✳✳✳✳

Is This Tomorrow

✳✳✳✳✳✳✳✳✳✳✳✳

a novel

CAROLINE LEAVITT

ALGONQUIN BOOKS OF CHAPEL HILL

2013

Published by
ALGONQUIN BOOKS OF CHAPEL HILL
Post Office Box 2225
Chapel Hill, North Carolina 27515-2225

a division of
Workman Publishing
225 Varick Street
New York, New York 10014

A portion of this work appeared, in very different form, in *Five Points,* 2006.

This is a work of fiction. While, as in all fiction, the literary perceptions and insights are based on experience, all names, characters, places, and incidents either are products of the author's imagination or are used fictitiously.

Library of Congress Cataloging-in-Publication Data
Leavitt, Caroline.
Is this tomorrow : a novel / by Caroline Leavitt.—First edition.
pages cm
ISBN 978-1-61620-054-1
1. Divorced mothers—Fiction. 2. Children—Crimes
against—Fiction. 3. Suburbs—Massachusetts—Boston—History—
20th century—Fiction. 4. Domestic fiction. I. Title.
PS3562.E261718 2013
813'.54—dc23   2012051162

10 9 8 7 6 5 4 3 2 1
First Edition

For Jeff and Max, with love

Part One

1956

❖ Chapter One ❖

She came home to find him in her kitchen. She was in no mood, having spent the whole morning arguing with a lawyer, but there he was, her son's best friend, Jimmy Rearson, a twelve-year-old kid home from school at three on a Wednesday afternoon with too-long hair and a crush on her, reading all the ingredients on the back of a Duncan Hines Lemon Supreme cake mix, tapping the box with a finger. "Adjust temperature for high altitudes," he said, as if it really mattered. She felt a pang for him, a boy so lonely he feigned interest in how many eggs and how much sugar a cake might need. He leaned over unabashedly and turned on her radio, and there was Elvis crooning "Heartbreak Hotel," the words splashing into the kitchen.

"How'd you get in here?" Ava asked, reaching over to turn down the music. No one, except for her, locked doors in the neighborhood. She had her kid wearing a key around his neck like an amulet. Other kids were allowed to run free to wander in and out of everyone else's houses, something Ava never could quite get used to. It wasn't that she had anything to steal—truthfully, she had so much less now—but still, there was Brian, miles away, breathing down her neck with a custody threat, telling her he got a lawyer and she'd better get one, too, because he was going to file to revisit their agreement. But, in fact, she had started locking her doors the moment the movers left, two years ago, and maybe that was what made the neighborhood suspicious. "Don't you like kids?

What's the matter, do you think they're going to wreck your house?" a neighbor asked, but how could she explain what she was afraid of?

"Your lock is easy," Jimmy said. "All it took was a bit of wire."

"Don't break into my house again," she said. She didn't know if she was angry or not, but she didn't like the way it sounded. *Easy to break into.*

"Lewis is at the dentist," she said. She had given Lewis money to take a cab (it wouldn't cost much), and by the time Lewis was finished and safely home, Ava would be at work.

"I know. He told me at school. I'm meeting him at my house later."

She nodded at the box in his hands, and then glanced at her watch. No matter what kind she bought, the mixes never turned out right. Quick and easy, the labels always said, but the cakes were always dry and powdery, and what good was quick if it was also tasteless? Well, baking was something to do, and they had some time. She didn't have to be at the plumbing company until five today. It was her day off, but she took an emergency evening shift she couldn't afford to turn down, not if she didn't want to go back to retail, which paid less, gave her fewer hours, and had no chance of advancement. It was only for an hour tonight, too, typing letters about 14K gold toilets and colored tubs that Richard, her boss, said had to be ready to go first thing in the morning, but even the small extra pay would be something she could tuck in the bank. "Want to bake?" she said, and he looked at her. "Boys don't cook," he said, abandoning the box on the counter. "Can we play checkers instead?"

"Sure. Why not," she said.

She set up the board on her dining room table, giving him the red pieces. She didn't really like checkers all that much, but she always seemed to be playing it with the kids. She would make sure they beat her so they'd feel good. Today, though, she wanted to take her mind off her problems, so she concentrated and without really meaning to, she won the game.

"Well, what do you know!" she said. She looked over at Jimmy, and then, shocked, saw that he was blinking back tears.

"Why, what's this?" she asked. "It's just a game. And you beat me every other time." She handed him a handkerchief she kept in her pocket.

He rubbed fiercely at his eyes. "I always win," he said. "I've never, ever lost."

Ava leaned forward on her elbows. "You can't win all the time," she said. "I wish you could." She thought of Brian, saw him moving on a checkerboard toward her. "King me," he'd say.

"Don't tell anyone I cried."

"Who cried? Did someone cry here?" She got up, smoothing her dress. "I have to get to work," she told him. "And you have to scoot."

They put the pieces back in the box, and then he waited at the table for her to get ready. He was in his red jersey and green plaid shorts, his Keds scribbled over with Magic Marker. He watched as she rustled around the living room, looking for her purse and the little veiled hat she sometimes wore because she thought it made her look more professional. Sweat beaded along her back. She'd wasted her whole morning and some of her afternoon running to a lawyer to talk about Brian's custody threat. It was five years since Brian had left them, barely sending money, barely calling, and even though the divorce had been his idea, all of a sudden he was telling her that *she* now posed a psychological and physical danger to their son. She had had to scramble to find a lawyer she could afford, a man whose name was actually, ridiculously, John Smith. He worked out of a tiny overheated office, without even a secretary, and he seemed so indifferent she wanted to shake him. "This is just nonsense, isn't it?" she said to the lawyer.

"The law is never nonsense," John Smith said.

She told the lawyer how Brian used to have a drinking problem, one that started after he left her, and that he had called her drunk a few times. She talked about how he'd abandoned his son—and her—after things at his job went bad. He hadn't even seen Lewis in nearly five years, so how could he possibly think about wanting custody now? She spilled all the details of her life, and the whole time, John Smith didn't say a thing. He just leaned back in his chair, making a tent of his fingers, waiting until she was finished, and then he shrugged.

"Circumstances change," he said. "And so do people. You said he has a full-time job, but you only work part-time, which puts him in a more stable financial situation than you. It could look like a better environment for a kid."

"You're joking. My environment is just fine."

"Is it?" He rolled his pen between his fingers. "You said he thinks you have a lot of men coming over. Can you prove you don't? Can you show that your bills are paid right on time?"

Ava thought of all the bills she kept in a shoebox, the careful way she went through them every month. She had a whole separate bank account of money she was saving so she could buy her house instead of rent it, and she made sure to put something in it every week, even if it was only ten dollars. "I have savings. I have a house."

"Correction: you rent the house. You don't own it. And banks don't like giving mortgages to women."

"But I will own it," Ava said stiffly. She thought of how hard it had been to convince the realtor to rent her the house, how he kept asking her if there was a man who could cosign the lease. She might have to fight to get a bank to give her a mortgage, but fight she would.

"But you don't own it now. And if you can't prove your finances are sound, we may have a problem. How's your son doing? Does he have friends? Is he doing all right in school?" He shuffled papers on his desk, waiting for her response, but she knew, suddenly, that he wasn't going to be able to help her, and she knew she was still going to have to pay him for his time. "You want to think about all this, Mrs. Lark," he said.

She came home, feeling sick, her head splitting like a seam. Jimmy had distracted her, but now she had to get to work, and worry hung on her like a too-heavy winter coat.

"Ava," Jimmy said, and she snapped back toward him. She felt his eyes on her, trailing her as she grabbed up her purse.

"Call me Mrs. Lark, Jimmy."

"Mrs. Lark," he said, even though they both knew there wasn't a husband around, that she was no more a Mrs. than he was. She waved her hand. "I have to get to work," she repeated.

She knew what she had to do. She had to make that company think she was good enough to hire her full-time at regular hours, with benefits, instead of just three days a week or whenever they needed her. She had to pay the bills, including the useless lawyer's bill, and the rent on this little house. It was the only one in the neighborhood that was a rental, smaller and older looking than the other homes, an anomaly that hadn't been razed when the new development had sprung up (Brookstone Family Homes!) because the owner refused to move, and by the time he died, the other houses were all built and occupied and the Brookstone company was long gone. If it hadn't been a rental and in bad shape, she'd never have been able to afford it, but because it was, she could never feel quite secure.

Ava passed by Jimmy to get to the card table, where she opened the top drawer and retrieved some of the extra pin money she kept for gas. She pocketed the money and rubbed at a smear of dirt on the wall with her thumb. Until she could afford paint, soap and water would have to do.

"Mrs. Lark." She looked over and Jimmy was shifting his weight from foot to foot, staring at her again. She was a grown woman with grown-up problems and suddenly she was in no mood for Jimmy's quiet devotion, for the way his eyes followed her around the room.

"Lewis will be home soon from the dentist," she said. "You can wait for him at your house."

Jimmy's nails were bitten and raw and she wanted to brush his hair back with her hands, wash his face with a cloth. She wanted to bend down and tie his sneaker laces tight, and wash the Magic Marker from them, bleaching the shoes until they were white again. She could see some of what he had written on his shoe: *Hep cat. Cool.* He was too young to be either. She pointed at his laces and watched while he did the job himself, making tight little double loops like rabbit ears.

The lawyer had asked her if Lewis had friends. Most of the other kids kept their distance, but maybe that was because Lewis was so smart. He could have been skipped ahead two grades if he didn't keep bringing home bad marks in school. The teachers kept telling her how he wasn't living up to his potential, that he kept disrupting the class with his questions. "Aren't you supposed to ask questions?" Ava had asked, and Lewis's teacher had sighed. "His job is to listen," she had told Ava.

From the time he was little, Ava had tried to make sure Lewis would be successful in life, buying him books, reading to him, teaching him to read when he was three. Education could prepare you for anything, she thought. But when she sent him off to kindergarten, it wasn't long before she got a call from his teacher. "He knows how to read," the teacher accused. She told Ava to cut it out, that Lewis being so far ahead of the other kids was bad for both him and the other students. "Everyone should be on the same page," the teacher insisted. Ava disagreed. The more you knew, the better things would be for you. She kept taking him to the library and encouraging him, and Brian even bought him a set of *Collier's Encyclopedia*. Every night, Lewis looked at the pictures in a volume, and read what he could. She still remembered the look on his face when, shortly before Brian had left them, and Lewis was just in first grade, Brian gave him one of his old briefcases so Lewis could carry a volume to school with him. Lewis was so proud, so excited, about learning! But she was no match for that school, or for his new school when they moved to Waltham. "The teacher told me to just do the work she gives me," Lewis said miserably. Lewis entered second grade and then third, and the teachers were calling her not because Lewis was so far ahead, but because he was behind. She had to sign his failed science paper on the solar system. "But you knew all this," she said astonished.

"You told me last night what all the planets were made of," and Lewis stayed silent. She began to find half-done homework crumpled on his desk in his room, which she would carefully smooth out and put in a folder. How could he be reading *The Odyssey* from the library and get a D on a multiple choice test about *Huck Finn?* How could he read the encyclopedia every night, marking off the sections when he was done with them, regaling Ava with facts at breakfast about how there were three different kinds of volcanic eruptions and you could tell which was which just by the lava, and still fail science? It made her feel panicked, because what would become of him if he couldn't get to college? There was no family business for Lewis to go into, no money to cushion him. The thought of him having to nickel-and-dime it the way she did made her want to weep and she'd be damned if she let him join the army. With college, he could have a profession. He could be someone.

At least Jimmy and Rose seemed smart, too, and she hoped they might influence him in a good way. Lewis and Jimmy did homework together all the time, the two of them sprawling on the floor of his room. She heard him excitedly talking to Rose about *The Wizard of Oz,* a book they both loved. But still, Lewis brought home report cards peppered with Cs.

He had good friends, Jimmy and Rose. That was something, wasn't it? The Three Mouseketeers, they called themselves, the moniker from that Mickey Mouse Club program they all watched some days at five on her temperamental little black and white Zenith, banging on the top of the set to stop the vertical hold from swimming. Rose was the odd girl out, in more ways than one, pale as paper while the boys tanned like peanuts, her hair a pour of ink down her back, while the boys' shaggy cuts were sandy brown. Jimmy and Lewis were now in Miss Calisi's sixth-grade class at Northeast Elementary. Rose, at thirteen, went to MacArthur Junior High on Lexington Street, but different schools didn't stop them from playing together. They were always riding their bikes around the neighborhood, vinyl strips streaming out from the handlebars, a few of Ava's old playing cards snapping along the spokes. They walked to the Star Market to check out the magazines and toys. They wasted time at Brigham's, sugaring up on raspberry lime rickeys. It was a relief because she had worried so much about Lewis finding friends. "You know this isn't a Jewish neighborhood," the realtor had told Ava when he first showed her the rental house. He had tried to show her all these crummy little apartments, but she had moved twice already from apartments in Watertown. She wanted something that felt like home, something that felt like hers. She wanted a house.

She was so thrilled when Lewis had found Jimmy and Rose. Of course, they would be together, the only kids on the block without fathers and with single mothers. Ava was grateful, too, that Dot Rearson was so open-minded, and they were actually good enough friends to talk over a cup of coffee every once in a while. Dot didn't share the same prejudices as some of the other parents. Oh, Ava had heard the remarks. *Divorced and Jewish, what a combo platter.* "You killed Christ," one neighborhood kid had told her matter-of-factly as he ran across her front lawn, and Ava had stood there, shaken. It was awful enough that Lewis had to say the Lord's Prayer in school every morning ("Just fold your hands and shut your eyes and think about what you want to do later," she advised him), but when Lewis was in third grade, he had come home with an F on a test, and she was about to yell at him when she saw all the questions were about Christmas—about Mary, Jesus, and Joseph. *Who was Jesus's mother?* She had gone up to talk to Mr. Powers, the principal, but all he said to her was, "I understand your peoples' sensitivity," like it was her fault.

Well, these kids were lucky to have one another. You didn't have to be a genius to see Rose was besotted with Lewis. Ava couldn't remember how she had felt about love at thirteen, if love had ever unspooled her the way it seemed to be doing with Rose. How could you possibly feel so much when so young? Rose followed Lewis around, her head cocked as if she were waiting for him to say something to her. She looked at him as if she were breathing him in, her shoulders rising and falling. Ava knew Rose went into her room and daubed her mouth with Ava's old DuBarry lipsticks, that Rose dotted Ava's Wind Song perfume on her wrists, but Rose didn't know that Ava set them out deliberately to make them easier for Rose to find. Once, Ava had seen Rose slide up behind Lewis while he was painting a model airplane. Rose lifted up her hand and held it just above his hair, as if she were blessing him, her eyes hidden beneath the palm frond of her bangs. He hadn't noticed a thing. Ava, though, had watched and all she could think was, *You poor darling.*

She whisked into the den for her white gloves. Jimmy trailed after her, nearly bumping into her when she came back out again. "Jimmy," she said and he grinned at her. Look at all of them, this round of wrong-headed love. Jimmy in love with her and Rose in love with Lewis. Lewis yearning for his father, and Brian in love with himself. Only Ava couldn't imagine ever being that lucky again, to have the kind of innocent crushes these kids had, or what she most wanted, a love that might last. *You have all those men,* Brian had accused. He heard them in the background when he called, he insisted. He said someone he knew from Boston had seen Ava out on the town one too many times, dressed skimpily, with her shoulders and her bosom hanging out, and was that a way for a mother to act? "My pal said you looked drunk," Brian had insisted.

Ava didn't drink. And if she had men, she usually had them only for weeks at a time. It wasn't long before they realized that Lewis was part of the deal and they didn't want to be a father to someone else's kid. They soon learned that despite her curvy hips ("Maybe you should wear a cowbell on them so we can hear you coming," one man, an accountant who had asked her to dinner, had joked when he watched Ava walking), Ava wasn't advertising anything but her heart, and the kind of relationship she was looking for was one that would end up with a ring on her finger.

A headache pulsed over her right eye. "Can you grab me a glass of water?" she asked Jimmy. He glided into the kitchen. Tonight, she'd come home and she wouldn't think about how she hated and needed her job. She would put the lawyer out of her mind, and she would forget about Brian, looming like a storm.

Tonight, her latest boyfriend, Jake, was coming over. He was going to take Lewis and her to Brigham's for ice cream, and she was thrilled about it. It was a school night, so Lewis had to be in bed by ten, but Ava thought a short first meeting might be just the thing for the first time the two guys in her life would meet. She didn't give a damn what Brian thought, because this was something. They'd been dating three months already. Still, she had told Jake not to expect much, because when she had told Lewis about meeting Jake, he brought up his father, as if she and Brian were still married and what she was doing was a crime, and then he had gone into his room and shut the door. "We'll get along fine," Jake had said. She had never let Lewis meet the men she dated because she had never felt sure about them. But Jake was different. She thought that maybe this time, this one might last. He was the polar opposite of Brian, which had drawn her to him. Maybe he didn't look as good on paper because he was a musician and he didn't have the steady job Brian had had, the money, but he was easygoing. Kind. He actually seemed to like and appreciate her just the way she was.

She'd let Lewis get a double-decker cone, and while she wouldn't let him actually ride Jake's motorcycle, how could he turn his nose up at getting to sit on it?

"Maybe we could play checkers again tomorrow," Jimmy said. "I know what I did wrong. I shouldn't have moved so you could double jump me." He handed her the water, in a purple steel tumbler the guy from the Esso station had given her as a promotion even though she didn't have the money to fill her tank all the way. She glanced at Jimmy. How could she not understand such loneliness when she felt it herself? "Is your mother at home? Who's watching you?" she asked and he shrugged, a little offended. "I can watch out for myself," he said. "I'm not some little kid. I'm twelve." He stood up, stretching. "Anyway, she's going to the church carnival after the beauty parlor."

The beauty parlor. Ava remembered when she could afford to spend a whole afternoon being pampered, getting her curly hair permed so it wouldn't look so untamed, adding highlights so it would glint in the sun, and adorning her toes with polish with names like Rosy Rapture or Midnight Plum. The beauty shop women used to fuss all over her, asking endless questions about Brian, the one they were really interested in because he was so handsome, so charming to all of them when he came to pick her up at the shop. He's a salesman, she wanted to remind them. He can sell anything to anyone, including himself. She ought to know. Now, she trimmed her own hair at home, pin-curled it herself, following the complicated diagrams in *Ladies' Home Journal,* and made dates with Lady Clairol (*Does she or doesn't she?* Well Ava certainly did, later scrubbing the dye spatters out of the tub with a stiff brush.)

"If you give me a moment, I can walk you home," she said, glancing at her watch. It was nearly four. It would take her forty-five minutes to drive into Boston to work because of the traffic. She reached for her newspaper, glancing at the headlines. Communists and the pale baked-potato face of Eisenhower warning everyone about nuclear disaster. *We have to be safe, we have to be safe.* Over and over like a drumroll. She had seen Khrushchev on the TV news ranting about Stalin and all she had thought of was Lewis when he was five and how he had had a tantrum in the middle of Better Dresses in Filene's because he was tired of shopping and wanted to go home. The kids had duck-and-cover drills at school, curling up under their desks, their hands over their heads, waiting out a fake nuclear attack until the teachers gave the all-clear signal, and Ava couldn't see how anyone would know it was all clear when radiation was invisible, and anyway, couldn't it chew right through a desk, let alone a person?

Jimmy looked out the window. "I can make it home myself." He had the same rangy build that Lewis did. Both boys could use some meat on their bones. He sighed, as if he were humoring her. "You can watch me from the window. I'll be fine," he said.

"You just be careful," she said. "And wait a minute. I'll walk out with you." Last week, she was running catty-corner across the street to borrow some eggs from Jimmy's mother, Dot, when she had heard the neighborhood women gossiping about a man hanging around the playground at school, staring so intently at the kids that a teacher had strode over to find out what he wanted, but the man had sprinted into the woods. The week before, the *Waltham News Tribune* had reported a car had swerved onto a curb in Belmont and frightened a little girl. A man had tried to grab her, but she ran away. The kids seemed riled up by the news, especially Jimmy, who kept asking Ava how much faster could a man run than a child? "What if the man was in a car? What do they do to you when they have you?" Jimmy persisted.

"That's not going to happen, so don't you even think it," Ava told him.

"We should watch our kids better," Ava had insisted to the other neighbors, but one of the neighborhood women had narrowed her eyes at Ava. "It wasn't one of your boyfriends looking for you, was it, Ava?"

"That's not what her boyfriends are after," someone had smirked and they had all laughed, except for Ava.

Well, things had calmed down. This is a safe neighborhood, people said, a good neighborhood. There had been no more reports, and if she still felt uneasy it was probably because all the gossip always seemed to lead to yours truly, Ava Lark, no thank you very much.

Ava grabbed her things, ferreting out her lipstick and swiping it on her lips. She held up one finger, to tell Jimmy to wait, and then she called Jake, just to make sure they were still on for tonight. "You bet, baby," he said, "See you at eight," and hearing his voice, rich as maple syrup, she pressed the receiver hard against her temple, and then she turned and saw Jimmy was watching her. "Come on, out we go," she said. She led him outside, and then she locked up the house. (Fine! Let her be the only one to lock her door!)

It was so unseasonably hot. Everything looked wilted and spoiled in the heat. The tarry road buckled from the sun. Her car was dirty but she didn't want to spend money to have it washed. Maybe it was something she could do with Lewis, or with Jimmy and Rose, too. Make it fun, washing her car.

Jimmy was the only other kid who just had a mom, but Dot was widowed, and Ava knew that that was considered a step up from divorce, since it couldn't be Dot's fault that her husband had keeled over from a heart attack while mowing the lawn. Rose was only three and Jimmy barely two when it happened. Dot had told her that her husband had had an insurance policy so large that she would never have to work. The neighbors had brought casseroles and flowers for weeks, and they still invited Dot and her kids to dinner and to backyard barbecues and parties. But when they found out Ava was divorced, they didn't invite her to any of their soirees, not even to the Tupperware events, which maybe wasn't such a terrible thing since Ava didn't have extra money to spend. The women saw their husbands' eyes following Ava, and they noticed the way the men talked to her as if she were as exotic as a South American parrot. They were always asking her if she needed them to fix her gutters or take out her trash. "Anything I can do," one of the men said meaningfully.

"Where is everyone?" Ava wondered aloud. Why was everything so empty and still, as if the air itself had stopped in place?

"Our Lady's, probably," Jimmy said. "I told you. The church carnival. Same as my mom. You couldn't get me there if you stuck bamboo shoots under my fingernails. The rides are junky and the hot dogs taste like rubber." And then Ava remembered driving by the little parking lot by the church over on Trapelo, seeing how crowded with people and tables it was. "My mom won't be back until after the church supper."

Jimmy stared into the street for a moment. "Bye!" he said, and then he ran, all arms and pumping legs, her son's best friend in the world. She was shamed to think that sometimes he was the best company she had. She watched Jimmy sprint out of her house. He tore out across her lawn, crossed the street, and veered to the left toward his home, two houses down, a yellow ranch house with white shutters. When he got to the door, he turned and waved with both hands, grinning.

Later, that's what she told the police. How happy he was. How he smiled.

❖ Chapter Two ❖

Ava hurried herself into the office for the evening shift. She moved past the big green Perkin's Plumbing sign (WE PLUMB NEW DEPTHS OF GREAT DESIGN!) to the small gray room that housed the three other women in the typing pool besides Ava, all of them in their twenties, younger than Ava by a decade. Traffic had indeed been terrible, stalled for miles, and it was now five on the dot. The other women had been here since nine in the morning, and they were done for the day, cleaning their workstations, draping their typewriters with plastic covers. Richard's office was already dark, the door closed, which was a relief because it meant she wouldn't have to talk to him. Betty frowned over her glasses at Ava. She took off her smock, thoroughly stained with carbon. Charmaine and Cathy were already putting on their coats

"Well, look who's here," Cathy said.

Ava sat at her desk, taking off the cover on her typewriter, reaching for one of the papers in her overfilled in-box, which even so, looked like a smaller pile than those of the other women's. Each invoice she had to type was more mind-numbingly boring than the next. Her lightning typing was a curse because the faster she got a job done, the more work Richard gave her, and the less the other typists seemed to like her.

Maybe it was because she was older than they were. Betty, Cathy, and Charmaine were just working until they could get married and take on their brand-new lives, something they talked about incessantly. Cathy and Betty shared apartments with other young working women, and Charmaine lived with her mother, whom she treated like a girlfriend, calling her several times a day to ask for advice or just to say hello. They had friends and pets (Betty had once brought her new kitten Fluffy to work, hiding it in the file cabinet until Richard heard the meowing and made her take it home.) They all worked full-time, with paid vacation and job security. Betty had been there for five years already, and Cathy and Charmaine for only a little less.

She wasn't sure why the women didn't like her. Ava had tried so hard when she had started, bringing in a Whitman's Sampler of candy to share, trying to make conversation. At first the women were friendly. They wanted to know everything about her. Betty admired the framed photo of Lewis that Ava had brought in. "You got one of his dad?" Charmaine asked. "I'm divorced," Ava said quietly, and then the women stopped fluttering around her. They began to look at her as if there were something wrong with her, something they didn't want to catch.

On her first day, when Richard had called from his office, "I need coffee in here," Ava got up, thinking she'd make the other women's lives easier, but Cathy quickly stood, nudging past Ava. "That's my job," she said curtly. Ava watched Cathy sweetly handing Richard his coffee, lowering her head so her curls dipped down onto her face, and when Cathy came back to her desk, she gave Ava a hard, triumphant smile.

Ava still tried, but she kept getting off on the wrong foot. Betty organized all the office parties for birthdays and engagements, and she took offense when Ava didn't decorate her desk for Christmas the way the other women did. "I'm Jewish," Ava had said. "Well, pardon me for trying to make things festive," Betty had replied.

Coming in to work had begun to make Ava feel like she was walking across a field full of hidden explosives, so she kept to herself, because it just felt safer. She watched the women laughing and listened to them talking to each other over her head, as if she weren't there. But she felt compassion, too. When Charmaine called her mother, she always seemed to be soothing her. "Mom, stop crying. I'll be home soon and I'll help you figure it out," Charmaine said. Cathy was clearly smitten with Richard, but he ignored her even more than he ignored Ava, and Betty spent hours planning the office parties, buying decorations with petty cash and excitedly adorning one of the conference rooms, but unless it was to celebrate one of the secretaries or typists, she herself couldn't attend any of the very events she had so carefully organized. She had to walk past the party and wistfully glance inside at her own handiwork.

Ava sat at her desk and studied the pile she had to type, a mix of invoices and letters. She was lucky, really. It was easy work and it paid the bills. She still felt wired from talking with the lawyer. She told herself to just think about all the good things that were in her life now, to block out Brian's threats. Think about Lewis. Think about Jake. Her mouth curved upward.

"Is that finally a smile on your face or gas?" Betty said and Cathy laughed. Ava blushed with shame, as if she had been caught putting on her panties in public, but she kept silent.

"I don't want to go to Rudy's again tonight," Cathy said to Charmaine. "The guys are just scouting good times and divorcées."

Ava tried to keep her hands steady as she turned the scroll of her typewriter and quickly began typing.

"Want to invite Barb from accounting?" Charmaine said. "She's fun."

Ava finished the first invoice and reached for another. She thought she was fun, but they never asked her to join them. In a flurry of coats and laughter, they were gone. She had to admit she liked the office when no one was there. She worked in a narrow pool of light, and sometimes she brought in a little transistor, propping it on her desk so she could listen to the radio while she worked. She picked up another invoice. Plaid sinks. Who would want plaid sinks?

She glanced at her watch. Tonight she'd see Jake. She couldn't stop thinking about him. Jake was a jazz saxophone player and her relationship with him was the longest she had had with a man since her ex-husband had left.

She'd met him one night when Lewis was at a sleepover at Jimmy's and she had gone into Boston by herself. She'd wandered into a smoky little jazz club on Tremont Street and sat at the front table. He was alone on the stage, lean and tall, with a shock of black hair. When he played, it was as if the only thing that existed in the room was him and his music. He swayed with each note, smiling to himself as if he had a secret. Ava couldn't look away from him. She felt as if he and his music had gotten into her blood and were coursing through her. Jake's eyes were shut the whole time he was playing, but when he finished, she saw how pale and blue they were, like ice floes. He looked as if he were hypnotized with joy, and she couldn't help but feel a flicker of envy.

Afterward, he came down into the audience. Several women flocked to him, but Ava saw him looking at her, and then he came over, the women trailing him. "You remind me of James Dean," a blonde said, sliding up against Jake's shoulder. "That kind of smart, burning sexy glow."

"What about you?" he said suddenly to Ava. "Did you like the set?"

"You remind me of Charlie Parker," Ava said. She cleared her throat and said it again. She spoke louder so he could hear her over the din, so he would understand that the music was the only reason she was here. "You've got some blues in with the jazz," she told him. Jake looked at her with new interest. He brushed the blonde away. "You like Charlie Parker?" he said, but she knew he was really asking another question.

He rested one hand on her table, leaning toward her. "Let me take you to dinner," he said impulsively. "Whenever you want."

"You don't even know me," she said. She watched him carefully, wondering what he'd think if he knew who she really was. "I'm divorced," she said. "I have a son. I'm Jewish." He pulled out a chair and sat down next to her. "I like kids," he said. "I teach a little. Kids are my favorite students."

"Aren't you on the road all the time?" she asked, beginning to relax. "How does that work with teaching?" She knew the stories about musicians, how you couldn't depend on them, how they had lots of women, how they drank or took drugs. You'd have to be crazy to want to be with someone like that. Then she thought of Brian, how even with his steady job, he always was running off to sales conferences, coming home with awards or, once, an oversized star sprinkled with glitter that spelled out his name for the top salesman. She remembered, too, how lonely she had felt.

"Not me," he said. "Rooted like a green plant. I have a steady gig here and a few other places around town." He smiled encouragingly at her.

"Really?"

He leaned closer to her. "I even own a house."

A mortgage. He paid a mortgage. She felt something unfolding within her. A thrill. She thought again of how he had sounded on stage, lost in a kind of zone, delirious with happiness. "So when can we have dinner?" he said. "Anytime you like. Anywhere you want."

"My choice?"

"Totally up to you."

She wasn't sure how to answer. Brian had always planned everything for them. He would take her to the best restaurants in Boston, but he always ordered for the two of them. He'd take her to shows, but he'd decide what they were seeing. When she tried to talk to other women about wanting to have a say in things, they laughed. "At least he takes you out," one woman told Ava. "Count your blessings." And fool that she was, Ava had.

Smoke clouded around them and she felt as if she were seeing Jake through a haze. She blinked, trying to clear her vision and figure out if this was a good move for her or not, and then he started to get up, still smiling at her, and she reached for him. When he took her outstretched hand in his, a jolt of heat ran through her. "Thursday," she said. "How about Thursday?"

That Thursday, a night when Lewis was staying at Jimmy's again, Ava went to meet Jake at the restaurant she had chosen, despite his offer to pick her up at home. Instead of taking her car, which would be impossible to park, she took the bus, which left her off in front, and when she looked up, he was already there, standing at the door.

They sat at a table in the back, next to a potted tree that smelled faintly of jasmine. He rolled up the sleeves of his white shirt and leaned toward her and she could smell him, like pine and grasses. She knew you were supposed to ask men about themselves, but he said, "Tell me about Ava," and as she did, she realized just how much had been bottled up, all the stories she hadn't been able to share with the neighbors or her coworkers. He didn't seem to care that she had been married or that she had a son or that she was Jewish. When she told him about Brian, how he had cheated on her, running off with a woman who came with a business attached to her, he just shook his head. "What a jerk," he said. "It was smart of you to get a divorce." No one had ever said that to her. He didn't look at her with pity, or wonder what she had done to make Brian leave her. She reached out and touched Jake's fingers, one at a time, making him laugh.

When he asked to drive her home, Ava didn't think twice about it. But when they got outside the restaurant, she stared in wonder at his motorcycle. "This thing safe?" she asked.

"With me driving, it is."

She didn't know what to do, but he was patiently waiting for her, and so she popped on the heavy helmet he gave her and hooped one leg over the seat. She held on tight, her head against his back, her eyes wide open as the streets flew by. The wind bit at her cheeks and flung her skirt up over her knees, but she didn't loosen her grip. When he peeled into the neighborhood, she saw the curtains in the house across the street fluttering open, and for a moment she worried how this wonderful night might end up in neighborhood gossip.

She got off the bike, her legs wobbly. "Gotta get your sea legs," Jake laughed and he held out his hand to gently steady her. Jake walked her to her door, polite. He didn't try anything, not a kiss, not asking if he could come in. Instead, he walked his fingers up her arm as if he were playing notes, making her laugh. "We're like jazz," he told her, "we go together." And then he said, "I'll see you, kiddo."

The very next afternoon, Jake had called and suddenly they were seeing each other as if it were the most natural thing in the world. He understood why she didn't want him meeting Lewis just yet, how you'd need to prepare a kid for something like that, and he was fine about her keeping things quiet. He appreciated, too, that she cared about how the neighbors saw her, and he was careful to arrive late at night when everyone was asleep, and only on nights when Lewis was at Jimmy's. "We'll improvise," he laughed. It was always an odd hour when she saw him. Friday after midnight. Wednesday morning after Lewis went to school. He called her blue note, bebop, but never honey, and every time he left, after she heard his motorcycle rumbling away into the distance, she had to stop herself from running after him.

At night, by herself, she sometimes worried. Jake didn't have the things she had told herself she wanted. He did have a mortgage, but it was in Cambridgeport, which was sort of a hardscrabble part of the city, looping around the river, an area where everything was dirt cheap. He didn't have a full-time job or a lot of money. It made her scared. One night, she told herself this was too crazy, too difficult, that it didn't have a future. She'd have to break it off. Then he came over at two in the morning with his sax. He was keyed up after his set, and before she could open her mouth, he said, "Listen to this." He took his sax and began playing something for her, a melody so haunting and moody, she was hypnotized. She couldn't help it. She walked over to him, rested her head along his back, and she swore she could feel the music coming through her, like a vibration, almost as if she were a part of the melody. She shivered and shut her eyes. "I'm so glad you're here," she told him.

She knew what a big a step it was, Jake meeting Lewis, how it turned their relationship into something new. He had been the one who had suggested it, which seemed an even bigger deal to her. They were in bed when he had asked, the fan on them, filmed in sweat. "Wait," Jake said, and then he vanished. She thought he was just going to get a drink or to the bathroom, but he came back with a glass of water. Laughing, he sprinkled it over her curves until she couldn't help herself. She shut her eyes. She felt him leaning over her. "Ava," he said. "You should let me meet your son now."

She liked the way he put it, like she was in control, like it was up to her. *You should let me.* She threaded her fingers at the back of his head, pulling him closer so she could kiss his mouth.

Now, she glanced at the clock. Five more minutes and she could go home and get ready.

IN PREPARATION FOR her date, she showered in lilac soap. She stood in a cloud of Tabu perfume, a sample they had handed out at Grover Cronin's, and pulled on a new dress, red, with a low neckline. This was the start of a whole new phase of their relationship. She knew it. As soon as you got your child involved, you couldn't be casual. And he had suggested it, not her, and maybe that was why her heart was hurtling. She kept going over and over in her mind how the evening might go. She didn't do more than sip wine, but Jake liked a glass, and she had bought a bottle of red that the man in the wine store assured her was delicious, even at such a low price. She picked daisies and put them in a vase on the table, and even set out some Charlie Parker records.

Ava paced the house, waiting for Lewis. She wasn't sure how he'd act tonight, if he'd be nice and give this guy a chance. When Lewis wasn't home yet and it was seven, she began to get annoyed. She wanted him to put on good pants and a nice shirt, to wet a comb and rake it through his hair, straighten up his room.

She walked from room to room, obsessing, trying to see if her house looked presentable. Her mind churned. She moved back into the living room and sat on the couch. It felt like two different days, the worry about Brian and the joy about Jake. But it was important to remember that she deserved happiness and had worked hard for it. They were two very different people, Brian and Jake. History didn't have to do any repeating.

She got up and brushed some dust off the edge of the couch, then she glanced at her watch. Seven thirty. How did it get to be so late? Where was Lewis? She looked outside, at the waning light splashing across the neighborhood.

Jimmy had said his mom was at the Our Lady's carnival, but when she spotted a light across the street, she called Dot, who sounded exasperated. "Jimmy's not home, either," Dot said.

"Those boys," Ava said, relieved. Lewis wasn't alone then.

"And girl. Count Rose in, too." Dot sighed. "At least they're together, having fun," she said.

"The Three Mouseketeers," Ava said, and Dot laughed.

"They're good kids," Dot said. "We're lucky they have each other."

Ava didn't want to spoil her good mood by yelling at Lewis when he got home, nor did she want to risk making him surly and silent when Jake got there. No, she'd rise above it, the way she did at work when Richard decided he needed to throw his weight around as the boss and stood in front of the whole typing pool and blamed her for botching a sale of the new turquoise sinks they were pushing, when she and everyone else knew all Ava did was type invoices and letters, and the real reason they hadn't sold was because the sinks were so ugly no one wanted them. The other women had looked at her as if she were to blame, too, or maybe they were just glad she was the one being chewed out, instead of them.

No, she'd bide her time. She'd talk to Lewis later about responsibility and considering other people. He'd bow his head as if he were praying, but she knew him: he acted like he didn't care sometimes, but he was a sensitive kid. He'd take it to heart.

She glanced out the big picture window. Some of the neighbors were walking home with their kids, holding on to balloons and stuffed animals from the carnival, carrying covered aluminum dishes of food. She saw wives greeting their men, already home from work, flinging their arms around them, talking and laughing. By eight o'clock, she was furious, wondering if Lewis was doing this deliberately. Jake would be here soon. Her good mood, her joy, wilted. The daisies in the glass now looked faded, her dress felt wrinkled, and the jazz albums she had put out casually on the table seemed suddenly forced and stupid, so she got up and put them back in the album rack. What was she supposed to tell Jake when he showed up and there was this silent spot where her son was supposed to be? How would the evening go now?

She walked to the kitchen, knocking her hip against the edge of the table, placing one hand over the jab of pain, and then she reached toward the phone, about to call Dot again, when it rang. Lewis, she bet. At the Wal-Lex bowling alley or the skating rink, his voice hushed with apology. At the library. All the places he usually went to and she wouldn't have been so angry if it hadn't been this one special night for her. If it hadn't meant so much.

"I don't know where Jimmy and Rose are," Dot said, "And frankly I'm beginning to worry." Ava leaned against the kitchen wall, shutting her eyes. She wasn't afraid. Not then.

"Those kids are so irresponsible," Ava said. "They all have watches— why can't they learn to use them?" She thought of Lewis's Superman watch, red and bright yellow. She had scoured all of Boston for it for Lewis's birthday, wrapping the timepiece up, buying a card, and forging Brian's name, so he'd think his father had remembered him. Lewis never took it off. He even slept with it on. When people asked him who gave it to him, he always said, "My dad."

The roar of a motorcycle split the air. "What's that?" Dot said alarmed.

"I have to go," Ava said.

There were neighbors outside, in a group, studying Jake as he parked. Ava felt their eyes on her as she walked toward him in her heels, sinking a bit in the soft grass. She heard someone say, "That's what she's wearing?" The comment felt aimed at her like a barbed arrow, and she self-consciously smoothed down the front of her dress. Jake was in a suit, and he held a small wrapped package. He smiled when he saw her, and when she told him about Lewis, he shrugged

"Kids," he said. "I'd be pissed off, too, if I thought someone was courting my mama."

Courting. He said courting.

He bent and kissed her. "We have time." He held up the package. "You told me he liked magic, so I bought him a kit." He unpeeled some of the tape on the wrapping, opening one side carefully to show her, and she felt a pulse of warmth. It was such a sweet gesture. Then she studied the glossy cover of the kit and her heart sank a little when she saw the silly-looking rabbit popping out of a hat, the cartoony magician holding the animal by the ears. She could tell that it was a kit for a younger kid, and even worse, right there in shiny red letters on the bottom it said "for ages 4–6." Lewis would be insulted. He read adult-level books. He'd no more want this kit than he would want a pacifier, but she could only hope that Lewis would be polite.

Ava and Jake sat in her living room and had a glass of the burgundy, but she couldn't relax, not without Lewis being there. She kept checking her watch, and every time she saw the time, she felt a little sicker. After half a glass of wine, she felt faintly buzzed, as if there were a scrim over the room. They played a game of gin, but in the back of her mind, she thought of what she was going to do and say when Lewis sauntered in. She'd wait to see if he apologized, and if he did, the evening still might be salvaged, but if he didn't, she might explode. She was going to ground Lewis. She was going to set down new and clear rules around the house that he had to obey. She was furious with him for being so inconsiderate. Kids. They ran away, they did stupid things, they came home tired and dirty and full of excuses and you didn't know whether to yell at them or hold them close.

By ten, she was frantic. He had never stayed out this late before, even when he was with Jimmy and Rose. She looked out the window and saw how dark it was.

"We need to go look for him," she told Jake, and he nodded and stood up, just as the phone rang, startling her.

"I called the police," Dot's voice was strained. "They're coming over."

The cops arrived within ten minutes, pulling up to Dot, who was standing in the street, her face pale of her usual makeup, her I Love Lucy curls limply held back by her kerchief. Ava and Jake came out to join her, but Dot looked at them as if they were strangers, instead grabbing for the first cop who got out of the car, an older beefy guy who absently patted her hand. The second cop sauntered out, young and thin, and then the other neighbors came out of their houses to find out what was going on. Ava, tight with fear, didn't care that the neighbors were watching her, that they were drinking Jake in. Lewis. Where was Lewis?

"Where could they be?" Dot cried.

Ava thought of the map that had been in her son's room for a week before it went back to Jimmy's, all those pushpins tacked to the places that he and Jimmy were going to visit when they were older, a cross-country trip they thought would be an adventure. She dropped Jake's hand. "They were planning this trip—" she said. "There's a map."

"The map's for fun, it doesn't mean anything!" Dot said. "And they're happy kids, why would they run away?"

"You don't know that they were running away," Ava said, her voice sharpening. She tried to imagine Lewis on the road and felt sickened. Lewis had no sense of direction. He had once left their table at a restaurant to go to the men's room, and on the way back, he had gotten lost. He wouldn't ask any of the waiters for help, and she had finally gotten up to look for him and found him wandering in another room by a tropical fish tank. She had tried to teach him how to find his way, from home to the school, from the Star Market to home. "Pick out signposts," she had told him. "Look for trees, a white house, a mark on the wall." She thought of Lewis out somewhere in the dark and she braced one hand against Jake's arm.

"Who saw the kids last?" one of the cops asked.

"Jimmy came to my house this afternoon," Ava said, and as soon as she said it, the cop looked at her with interest. "Lewis was at the dentist."

"Again at your house?" Dot said. "Again?" Her voice slid up an octave.

"What do you mean, again? Of course at my house. The kids are always at my house. He was waiting for Lewis. I don't like kids being in my house without me so I shooed him out so I could get to work. He went right home. I saw him."

"Who were these kids' other friends?" the cop asked. "Did they have any enemies? What do they do to blow off steam?"

Ava told them everything she remembered. How Jimmy had looked standing on his front porch, the day shiny with heat. How Lewis had promised to be home by six. A metallic taste filled her throat and her heart was beating so hard she felt it pushing against her skin.

She watched one of the cops writing something down. And then, like a mirage, in the distance, she saw Lewis and Rose stumbling toward them, in a gold halo of streetlight.

❖ *Chapter Three* ❖

At four o'clock, earlier that day, after the dentist cleaned his teeth ("You need to brush better," the dentist had scolded Lewis, smacking a new red toothbrush onto Lewis's palm), Lewis walked to the library to pick up a book he needed for school. He was supposed to meet Jimmy at his house, something they'd planned earlier at school, and though Lewis had sort of wanted to check out the carnival, Jimmy wouldn't even consider it. "Bunch of junk and parents," Jimmy said.

Sometimes Lewis wondered if Jimmy only hung around him because of Ava, which was an absolutely creepy thought. "Is your mom going to be home?" Jimmy had asked this morning, which irritated Lewis. "What if she isn't?" he had asked and Jimmy just shrugged. "I have to go to the dentist, but I'll meet you at your house around four," Lewis told him. Then later, at lunch in the cafeteria, when two of the rougher boys, Billy D'Adario and Tommy Scanell, had pried Lewis's sandwich from his hands to show there was no filling in the middle, to laugh ("Haw! A bread sandwich!" Tommy had said), Jimmy had just sat there. Billy flung a handful of rusty pennies on the table. "You're a Jew, pick them up," he said, and for one horrible moment Lewis had wanted to, because he could have used those pennies. There were enough there so he could have put the coins in his pocket, along with the cab money Ava had given him, adding it all to the stash he was saving for his trip across the country with Jimmy when they were older. Instead, he did what his mother had told him to do. He turned away. He pretended it didn't hurt, looked bored, and the boys scattered.

"Why didn't you stand up for me?" Lewis asked Jimmy.

"You can't win with those guys," Jimmy said. He sipped grape juice from a plaid thermos.

"You're just scared," Lewis muttered, and Jimmy flushed, which meant that Lewis was right. But Lewis was scared, too. He stared down at his bread sandwich, manhandled by the boys, and shoved it aside. He saw the pennies were still there, but he wouldn't touch them, either.

That had been earlier, but he was still upset about it at the dentist, and even here in the library. He wandered into the main room, which was cool and dark, and as soon as he saw the stacks of books, he felt a little better. He traced his fingers along the spines of the novels (his favorite section), and pulled out *The Great Gatsby*. Maybe it would be good. He turned right and then left until he was in biographies. The titles winked out at him. He was supposed to find a biography of a famous person to do a report for sixth-grade finals, but none of these names spoke to him. Benjamin Franklin was boring and fat and greasy looking, Clara Barton had a mean face, and no way was he going to do Davy Crockett like every other kid in school because they all thought it might be a good excuse to buy those stupid furry hats.

He wished he didn't have to go to school. Every grade was more boring than the last. He could read already in kindergarten because Ava had taught him, making a big deal of getting him a library card as soon as he could scribble his name. "If you want to be someone, you have to be educated," she told him. Every Friday, she took him to the library, letting him sprawl in the kids' room for hours, choosing as many books as he could carry to take home. Before his father had left, he had bought him the absolute best birthday present in the world, a set of *Collier's Encyclopedia*. "Everything you want to know is in there," his dad told him. Whenever Lewis could tell his dad a new fact, Brian would ruffle his hair and hug him. The week his father left, Lewis began systematically reading them, starting at *A*. He kept imagining how proud his father would be when he came back and Lewis could tell him all about the atomic bomb or how fire was produced. Every time he was given any toy, from plastic dinosaurs to a deck of cards, he looked it up in his *Collier's* to find out everything he could about it.

But school was different. Knowing more than the other kids meant he had to sit around listening to everyone struggling to figure out colors, and later, to sound out "Run, Sally, run," in their *Dick and Jane* books. But it wasn't just reading that was easy for him. Math was pretty simple. He often completed his work early, and then there was nothing else to do but sit around waiting for the rest of the class to finish. Even if he asked, his teacher never gave him anything extra to do.

It didn't take him long to realize that he knew more than some of the teachers did and that, to his shock, they didn't like him for it. Every new grade, he started out thinking it might be different, but as soon as he began to ask questions, his teachers would say, "Let's have somebody else speak up for a change." When they were studying civil rights, Lewis remembered the Milks, a Negro family that was supposed to move onto their block, but all the neighbors had started up a petition to stop them. Only his mother had refused to sign. In the end, the house sold to another white family. "How come there are no Negro kids in our school?" he asked and the teacher said, "They go to other schools," and when Lewis asked what those schools were, his teacher told him not to be so smart. When they were studying American Indians in fifth grade, his teacher brought in pictures of teepees. Lewis raised his hand and she sighed. "Yes, Lewis?" she said, and he told her that the Indians didn't just live in teepees, that they actually had many kinds of houses depending on where they were. "Where it was warm, they had grass houses," he said. "They had wood and adobe, too."

"Yes, but the teepee was the most prominent," she said.

"Just for the Plains Indians," Lewis added.

"Let's move on," his teacher said, dismissing him with a frown.

Sixth grade with Miss Calisi was no better. She talked a lot to the class about how she square-danced and why rock and roll was responsible for juvenile delinquency, and she smelled like old socks. Lewis had felt a spark of hope when he started her grade and she had announced, "I'm a really tough teacher. You're all going to work really hard," but instead, it was the same easy work, the same admonitions not to ask so many questions, and after that, Lewis just stopped trying in school and busied himself thinking about what he wanted to learn. He kept quiet and filled his notebook with things they weren't doing in class, plans on how to build a ham radio, facts about ten different kinds of whales. One day, he was working on a drawing, comparing a beluga whale with a blue whale, when a shadow fell across his paper. He looked up and Miss Calisi's brow was buckled in anger. "I asked you a question and you didn't even hear me," she said. "What are you doing?" She lifted up his notebook and peered at the page in astonishment. Lewis hunkered down in his seat. "This has nothing to do with long division," she said curtly. She flipped some of the pages and then tucked the notebook under her arm, making him worry he wasn't going to get it back. He watched her at her desk, scribbling something, while the other kids twisted in their seats to stare at him. Then she came down the row and handed him a note. "I want your mother to sign this," she said. "Now open your arithmetic book." She stood over him, waiting until he did. He sat there, listening to her drone on about long division, and in his mind, he heard humpback whales singing mournfully.

There was no way he would give this note to his mother. His mother was always telling him how important it was that he do well in school, that he had to get good grades because that was how he'd get a scholarship to college. But he couldn't see what was so important about college. He made a list of everyone famous who had never gone to college: Henry Ford. Andrew Jackson—and he became president. George Washington. Gandhi. Hitler. He crossed out Hitler because that seemed like an argument for why you should go, so you wouldn't be like him. He ticked off all the different politicians, leaders, inventors. You could do anything. He had a whole notebook of things he himself wanted to do. Be a doctor. Study animals. Maybe be a scientist. And he could figure out how to do it without this dopey school. Anything he needed to learn was right here in the library. His dad had been like that. "I'm a self-made man," Brian had always told Lewis, and he had won all these trophies and prizes for being the best salesman to prove it.

He'd sign his mother's name on the paper.

Now, Lewis wandered the library stacks. The biography he really wanted was Houdini. Harry Houdini was Jewish like he was, and he was cool and the one thing Lewis wanted to do tonight, rather than meet his mother's boyfriend Jake, was to disappear. Jake. What a name. Like jerk. Like stupid. Like stay out of my life.

His mother had told him that Jake was going to take them both out for ice cream, a special treat on a school night. "He's a friend. We'll have a great time," she had insisted. Lewis had asked her, well, what about his father? How about what Mr. Gallagher across the street had told him—that people were married forever in the sight of God, like he and his wife Tina were? A child, like their little Eddy, who was always swatting a baseball bat at the bushes, was the covenant. That was why divorce wasn't a real thing. Ava had narrowed her eyes at him. "Divorce is very real," she told him.

He hated thinking about his mother and this new guy. What if she really liked him? Every time he thought about it, he had to sit down and make lists. He thought of running away, but then where would he go? How would he live? If he could just find his father—but he hadn't been able to yet. He knew his father had had to leave because of his mom, because of the way they were fighting, and the few times his dad had called, Lewis could tell how happy Brian was to talk to him just by the sound of his voice. He didn't know why his dad didn't visit or call him, except that it had to have something to do with his mom and that was why Lewis had to be careful around her. She could make things worse. Especially with this Jake guy.

"Lewis." He turned around, startled. Mrs. Groth (the librarian, a spindly woman who didn't like it that he took books out from the adult section and always shooed him, as if he were a dog, back to the kids' room with all those dumb toys and miniature desks) glared at him. "Is this where you belong?" she asked pointedly. She stared at the book in his hand, *The Great Gatsby,* and took it from him. "This is too old for you," she said, as if she knew the slightest thing about him. She leafed through it, stopping at a page with a small rip. "And where did this come from?" she demanded, fingering the page.

Lewis stared at the tear, a fingernail of paper. "It was there when I took the book."

Her mouth pinched like his mother's change purse. "I see," she said. She walked to her desk and then took a slip and wrote something on it and handed it to him. "You have to pay for what you destroy," she said.

"I didn't destroy anything," Lewis said. He stared down at the note. She had written "Two dollars: destruction of library property" in black ink and underlined it twice. The last time she had done this, he had told his mother when he got home and, to his surprise, Ava had driven all the way back to the library and marched right up to Mrs. Groth and told her that not only did she personally remember the rip ("I don't know why the library doesn't keep better care of their books," she had said) but she was tired of hearing comments about what books her son could take out. "I'm his mother and if he wants to read *Lady Chatterley's Lover,* he can," she had snapped. "What do you care, as long as he's reading?" Mrs. Groth had flushed. He had loved his mother intensely at that moment.

"You see that you pay for this," Mrs. Groth told him now.

Lewis stuffed the notice in his pocket. He waited for her to leave, and then he began roaming the adult stacks again. He knew if he asked, his mother would confront Mrs. Groth again. She'd never stand for any of this. Still, as grateful as he was, there were so many times he wished that his mom were different.

No one else's mother made sandwiches out of bagels or brought home foods like lox and chicken livers, and even worse, tongue. Even though Lewis liked bagels, he was embarrassed to be seen with them because kids made fun of them. "What's with the donut bread?" they mocked. Other children complained about having to go to church on Sundays, but Lewis's mom didn't even take him to temple. The only religious thing she did was light those stupid Sabbath candles on Friday nights when she remembered, which wasn't all that often. Every once in a while, she would talk to him about God, but it didn't sound anything like what the other kids talked about. "Everyone communes with God in his or her own way," she said. She didn't believe that one religion was better than another. "You find your own truth," she told him. She didn't look like anyone else's mother, either, not the suits she wore to work when all the other mothers were in housedresses, the tiny two-piece swimsuit she wore to get a tan, when everyone else's mother wore a skirted one-piece. The other mothers wore slacks, but Ava wore tight dungarees with the bottoms rolled into cuffs. "Why do you dress differently from everybody else?" he had asked. She had looked at him, surprised. "I do?" He noticed her watching the neighborhood women as if she were studying them. Two days later, she came home from shopping with a pair of slacks that zipped on the side and a housedress, but the pants were still tight and the dress was a shocking shade of orange.

And he remembered Jimmy's amazed reaction the first time he'd ever laid eyes on Ava. The two boys were walking past Lewis's house to Jimmy's when they saw Ava through the picture window, feather duster in her hand, dancing in their living room as she cleaned. She swooped the feather duster into lazy circles. Her hips snaked. "That's your mom?" Jimmy asked. The two boys stood on the sidewalk and Lewis watched his mother swaying, throwing her head back so her hair tossed in her eyes and you couldn't see her face. Her mouth moved, as if she were singing. Lewis could hear Jimmy's intake of breath and Lewis tried to will his mother to stop, to pull the curtains at least. Jimmy flapped his hands as if he were cooling the world down.

"Hubba-hubba," Jimmy said. "Va-va-va-voom." Lewis socked him in the arm. "Hey, I'm sorry, I'm sorry," Jimmy said, but his gaze stayed on Ava.

Lewis wasn't sure how he felt about his mother anymore. He didn't think he trusted her. She seemed full of secrets lately, and sometimes he swore he could hear them rattling around in her like marbles caught in a glass jar.

Last week, he was sleeping at Jimmy and Rose's, a special treat on a school night. He, Rose, and Jimmy had spent the evening playing Go to the Head of the Class. Later that night, Lewis was tucked into a sleeping bag on Jimmy's floor, sandwiched between Jimmy's bed and Rose's sleeping bag. Lewis felt woozy and achy. Sweat filmed his body, making his pajamas paste against his skin. "I want to go home," he told Jimmy. "I think I'm sick." Rose put one hand on his forehead. "You're boiling," she said.

They didn't want to wake Jimmy's mother, who got cranky if she had to lift her sleep mask or take her earplugs out, so Jimmy and Rose both put their coats over their pajamas, slid into their slippers, and walked Lewis to his house across the street. The night was still and cold and sparkling with stars, but every step Lewis took, he felt sicker and sicker. The houses seemed to be moving. The ground felt soft and sticky, as if he might sink into it. Rose's hand drifted across his back and he leaned into it, feeling a pulse of heat.

At his door, he heard music. Frank Sinatra. One of the albums his mother liked. Lewis could see his breath in the air. He could feel the sweat trickling along his back. Rose shut her eyes for a moment, swaying to the music. "Your mom is some smoothy," she said. "Music past midnight! My mom doesn't even have a record player. When she hums, she hums Speedy Alka-Selzer commercials."

Jimmy tilted his head up to the window and then stopped. He put one hand out in front of Lewis, the way Lewis's mother did when she was driving and she had to stop short, keeping Lewis from banging into the glove compartment or going through the windshield. Lewis stumbled, and then he looked at the window, at the shadows through the curtains. They all saw his mother standing up, her head resting on someone's shoulder, slow dancing, moving into one dramatic dip. Rose sucked in a breath.

Lewis froze. His mother's shadow kissed the other shadow and he turned away.

"I feel okay now," he said stiffly. He turned and faced the dark street. "Let's go back to your house."

Jimmy and Rose were just standing there, staring at him.

"C'mon, I'm okay. I feel fine now," Lewis said. "I want to go back to your house."

Rose tugged his arm and Lewis pulled it roughly away. Then he started walking away, and every step he took, the music grew fainter and fainter, the image of his mother and the man blurred, and he felt so weak and dizzy he could have lain down in the middle of the road. He didn't turn around to see if Rose and Jimmy were following, but he heard the scuff of their slippers, and he was grateful for their silence.

They all went back inside, removed their coats, shuffled off their slippers, and got back under the covers. Lewis stayed awake, staring at the ceiling, trying not to cry. The room reeled around him. He heard Jimmy beginning to snore and he felt more alone than he had ever felt in his life.

Then he heard Rose, the rustle of her sleeping bag. She got up and left the room and a few minutes later, he heard her bare feet on the floor. He heard her coming closer to him, as if she were about to tell him a great secret.

A cloth, stunningly cool, pressed along his forehead. He shut his eyes, sighing. She tapped his shoulder and his eyes flew open again and he saw her, blurry, hovering over him. "Lewis, take this," she said, and she held out her palm with two aspirins resting in the center. He saw the glass of water she held in her hand. He couldn't see her eyes, hidden under her bangs, long as sable paintbrushes. When she leaned over, one of her braids dusted against his chest, rising and falling as if it were alive and breathing along with him.

Rose sat on the edge of his sleeping bag. She waited for him to take the aspirin and drink the water. "Lie back down," she whispered. But she didn't move and he didn't really want her to. Every time he drifted off to sleep, his eyes would flutter open, and he would see her again, so calm and still. It made him feel better. He sensed her there, and gradually, he rolled into sleep.

When he thought about it now, he bet anything that shadow they had all seen through the window was this Jake person. Well, forget Jake. Forget his mother. Forget tonight. He was done with his dentist appointment, finished with the library. He was going to hang out with Jimmy and who knew what they might do, what plans they might devise? Lewis left the library, surprised at how the day had grown so hot and muggy. He paid attention to the buildings along Lexington Street so he wouldn't get lost, something that often happened, leaving him tense and disoriented as if the world had changed shape without his knowing it. There was the church on his right, the gas station on his left. Over there was the huge maple tree.

A car passed, honking at him, making him leap closer to the inner side of the sidewalk, and for a moment, he thought the man driving might be his father. Wouldn't that be perfect? If it was his dad, he wouldn't have to meet stupid Jake tonight, and neither would his mom. If it was his dad, everything could go back to normal.

When his father left abruptly just after Lewis's seventh birthday, without even saying good-bye, the whole world had changed. Things didn't taste right. Lewis would eat a bite of cereal and it would taste like steak. His potato at dinner would taste like metal and he'd have to spit it out into his napkin. It was as if the world had gone suddenly crazy. Lewis and his mother couldn't afford the big Back Bay townhouse on their own, and had to move out of Boston to one tiny apartment after another, and finally to the suburb in Waltham and the only thing good about it was that it was a house and he had a backyard. "Does Dad know we're here?" Lewis kept asking

"Of course he does," his mother said, but she looked suddenly smaller to him.

"How does he know?" Lewis thought of ham radios, of smoke signals, of the way a voice could travel on a phone line

"He knows," his mother said.

His father was even supposed to visit him once. He had called shortly after Lewis's eighth birthday, just like a sudden snap of fingers, and when Lewis heard his voice, he started to cry.

"Hey, what's that crying?" His father's voice was jovial, teasing. He was slurring his words in a funny way. "That couldn't be my Lewis crying, could it? My Lewis doesn't cry."

Lewis snuffled. "I'm not crying," he insisted, swiping at his eyes. "Where do you live? How can I find you?"

His father cleared his throat. "Well, right now, you can't really visit me. I'm living out of a suitcase, but maybe later. In the meantime, I can visit you."

"When?"

"Well, I don't know, sport. Maybe next weekend, how about that?" He could hear his father's breathing, deep and even on the phone.

"I'll be better," Lewis said. "I'll be quiet in school. I'll get good grades."

The silence hummed through the wires.

"I miss you," Lewis said. "I'll wait out front for you," and then his mother was taking the phone out of his hands and hanging it up. "He's coming to see me next week," Lewis said, but his mother walked over to the sink and began clattering dishes under the water.

That weekend, Lewis waited out front on the porch, though Ava tried to get him to come inside. Every time a car passed, Lewis jumped up, but then the car sped by. When Ava came out to say she was going grocery shopping and would he like to come, he shook his head no.

Later, when Ava pulled up and saw Lewis sitting there, she didn't move for a moment. Then she got out of the car and handed him a package of cookies from the grocery bag, Fudge Stripes, his favorite, and sat beside him. "I'm sorry," she said. She ripped open the cellophane bag and even though it was before dinner, they both sat there, eating cookies and not talking, ruining their appetites and not even caring.

Another car passed and then another, but of course none of them was his father. Lewis rested his chin on his knees. Why didn't his father come see him? If he split himself into two columns, it felt like he had more pluses than minuses. He saw it, so why didn't his father? Why didn't he know what he had done wrong?

"I love you," his mom told him, but how could he be sure? "You're my best friend," Jimmy assured him, but Lewis wasn't always convinced Jimmy really meant it. He had to keep replaying how Rose and Jimmy always sought him out, how they didn't want to hang out with anyone but him. "Hey, worrywart," Rose teased. "Keep looking like that and your face will freeze." She was smiling when she said it.

Houdini used to say that people saw what they wanted to see, they imagined it to be true, and maybe that was what Lewis was doing. But then again, Jimmy and Rose really did seem like real friends, the realest Lewis had ever had. They were plotting their future together, he and Jimmy. As soon as they were old enough, they were going to buy a car and drive cross-country into new lives. He and Jimmy had pooled their money and bought a big huge map and taped it to Jimmy's wall. For every place they wanted to go—and it had to be a place that had meaning to them—they stuck in a pushpin. Lewis thrilled every time he saw the map, but it was something that Rose was miffed about because she wasn't a part of their plan.

"It's a boy thing," Lewis told her.

"You can come visit," Jimmy assured her. "We'll keep an extra room for you."

"Sure, we will," Lewis said. He liked Rose. When he practiced magic tricks, she was always willing to hold the top hat or be his guinea pig. She always acted surprised and pleased when Lewis told her about something he was reading—about space travel or carnivorous plants—and she always wanted to know more.

"I can get my own room," Rose said. "And I can leave before the two of you because I'm older. I'm going to plenty of important places myself."

He and Jimmy were going to Kentucky or Wyoming or California, where they would be chefs or doctors. Jimmy wanted to stop in Santa Fe because his favorite aunt lived there. He liked Los Angeles because there were movie stars and maybe he could see Natalie Wood, whom he sort of had a crush on. Lewis wanted to visit Springfield, Missouri, because he thought that was where *Father Knows Best* took place. He made sure to put a tack on the Mojave Desert, where Death Valley was, because he loved the show *Death Valley Days* and watched it all the time. They were going to be happy and famous, and he wouldn't have to think about his mother's boyfriends or the light not going on because the electricity bill hadn't been paid or getting secondhand bags of clothes from Morgan Memorial that he'd have to wear. He'd be so well-known that he'd get in the news or maybe be a star on TV and his father would read about him, and feel terrible, and call him instantly to make amends.

Lewis was walking from Main Street, winding in and out of the side roads of the neighborhoods because he was bored. He was on Chesterbrook Road when he saw the three kids hanging around the muddy empty lot. He knew them vaguely from the junior high crowd, their hair slicked back, two of them smoking cigarettes. They were all swigging bottles of soda. Joey Salvatore, the one with the curly dark hair, had once been at the same school bus stop as Lewis. Joey had taken a piece of chalk from his pocket and written PENIS and then VAGINA on the telephone pole, snickering and hooting when one of the girls glanced over and blushed. He once had grabbed another kid's gym suit and stuffed it into the mailbox, and when the kid had protested, Joey had kicked him hard enough to topple him to the ground.

Lewis had learned to steer clear from Joey and his crew, but now there was no escape. He felt the boys all looking at him.

"Hey, creep." Joey waved at him, casually. "Hey, I recognize that shirt."

Lewis glanced down at his shirt. Blue and red check, pulled from one of the Morgan Memorial bags. He hadn't given a thought whose shirt this might have been when he put it on. He only knew it wasn't his.

Joey snickered. "I threw up on it and that's why my mom gave it away."

Lewis kept walking, hoping to be ignored. He thought as soon as he got home, he'd throw this shirt out. He'd rather not have anything to wear than have to wear something that had been Joey Salvatore's. Suddenly, the boys were around him, grins stretched across their faces, eyes hard and gleaming. "Jewish Lewish," Joey said.

"So." Barney, one of the other boys, shoved him. "You hungry? Because we've got cookies." He held up a pack of Oreos, half of them gone. "You want one?"

"No," Lewis said.

"Oh, for crying out loud, don't be like that," Joey said, taking a drag on his cigarette, then chasing it with a big gulp of soda. "Thirsty, Lewis?" he asked. "I didn't spit in it. You can have a drink."

Lewis kept silent.

"Pull your pants down and you can have it," Joey said. He tossed his cigarette and teased a cookie out of the bag and waved it under Lewis's nose. "Mmmm, fresh, delicious cookie." The other boys laughed and Joey took a few steps closer until his nose could have touched Lewis's.

Joey grabbed the edge of Lewis's shirt. His smile widened. "No, I mean it," he said pleasantly. "Pull your pants down. I hear Jews' wieners are different and I want to see." Lewis could smell Joey's breath, sugary from the Oreos, sour from tobacco. He could see the other boys behind Joey, impatient, shifting their weight from one foot to another, waiting to see what was going to happen. Joey shook the soda bottle, making it fizz.

"Here, wet your whistle," Joey said, and then he heaved the soda towards Lewis, soaking his clothes. Barney bent and scooped up handfuls of mud, flinging them at Lewis, spattering his shirt and pants. "Aw, what a shame, but you're used to dirty clothes, aren't you?" he said.

Joey snickered and something snapped in Lewis. He sprang one fist back and grazed Joey's jaw, and Lewis didn't know who was more surprised, he or Joey. His knuckles throbbed. Numb with terror, he tried to swallow, but the lump in his throat refused to dislodge.

The other boys were frozen, but Joey's eyes gleamed. "You're dead," Joey said, rubbing his chin, and Lewis turned and broke into a run.

Lewis was faster than they were. He was horrible in gym, the last one ever picked on a team, but he could run when he wanted to, and now he sprinted, his breath in his ears. Huh huh huh, and when he ran onto Lexington Street, there was Rose, like a miracle, in a yellow dress, almost as if she had been waiting for him. She looked beyond him at the other boys and then she reached out and grabbed his hand as he ran past. "Run," she said.

They both ran, hearing the boys shouting after them. "Always remember, the toughest people are cowards," his father had once told him, but these kids were still running. They weren't giving up. The clap of their sneakers quickened. "This way," Rose said, tugging him. "We have to hide." They ran up to the pathway for Green Acres Day Camp, sprinting into the woods. He followed her deep into the forest, brushing aside the bushes, until all they could hear was their own breaths. They stopped, and Lewis looked around.

The sun dappled through the trees. The ground was soft with moss, and Rose was standing so close to him that he could smell her hair, like wet wood and cherries. He didn't hear footsteps or voices. Rose touched him and he jolted. "You're shivering," she said. "You're completely soaked and covered in mud." She stepped closer and then, before he could stop himself, he was crying. It wasn't just about being chased or shamed, there was Jake, his father, everything was wrong.

"I bet your clothes will dry in the sun." She pointed to a patch of bright light, a clearing. "We can brush the mud off then."

He squinted at her.

"I'll shut my eyes. Your clothes are wet. It's only me."

His clothes—Joey's clothes—were damp and sticky and caked with dirt. If he could have burned them, he would have.

"I have a younger brother, remember? It's nothing I haven't seen before." Her eyes were clear and gray and serious. "I won't tell anyone," she said. "Not even Jimmy." Lewis thought of the boys jeering, *I want to see. I hear Jews' wieners are different.* The whole time he had known her she had never teased him, even when he and Jimmy had ganged up on her and tickled her or hid her diary or threatened to read it. She had never snapped at him when he and Jimmy shut her out of Jimmy's room, when they wanted it to be just boys. Sometimes Rose ignored them, too, when she wanted to be alone to read.

Jimmy wasn't much of a reader, but Rose read so intently, you could shout in her ear and she wouldn't lift herself up out of the story. You had to shake her, and then she'd look at you, dazed, as if she couldn't believe she was no longer in the story. And best of all, she talked to Lewis about what she was reading. She was the one who put *A High Wind in Jamaica* into his hands and insisted he read it. She gave him *A Tree Grows in Brooklyn* and *The Catcher in the Rye.* He held her dog-eared copies in his hands, reading at night in his bed. He read the notes she wrote in the margins. *I feel like that. I love the pirates!* And once, *What are we all to do?* It was as if she were reading the books with him, talking with him on every page.

"Come on," Rose said now.

He felt clammy, but it wasn't as if he'd be naked. He still had his gym shorts under his pants because his mother hadn't done laundry and there wasn't anything else.

He stepped out of his clothes, glancing at his watch. He was late to meet Jimmy. Then he had to meet Jake, but how could he do either when he felt as if he were breaking apart?

"It'll be really warm in the sun over there. Your clothes will dry. We can just brush the mud off," she repeated. When he didn't move, she gave him a look of great pity. "It's all right," she said. "Everything is all right." She put her hands over her eyes and carefully lay down on the ground in the patch of sunlight. Then he took off his pants and his shirt, stretching them out in the sun. He lay down beside her, the two of them not moving. Lewis didn't dare look at her, and Rose's eyes were still covered. "We'll just lay here," she said.

He listened to her breathing, and then his own, almost as if it were a conversation, her quick, short breaths, and his longer ones. "Jimmy's going to be so mad," he said.

"He could never be mad at *us*," Rose said.

Lewis couldn't deny it. He had never had a friend like Jimmy or like Rose, people who made him feel anchored to the world. When he and his mother had lived in an apartment in Watertown, before they moved here, he had hung out with a boy in his third grade named Don, but although Don was funny and liked to ride bikes and play Go to the Head of the Class as much as Lewis did, the person he really loved was Don's father, a big, burly man who always lighted up when he saw Lewis. "There's my other boy!" he said. He was always taking the two boys places, the movies, the museum, the theater, and when Don took his dad's hand, and Lewis shied, Don's father laughed and grabbed Lewis's fingers. Don's father spoiled Don, buying him games and books and toys. All Don had to do was look at something and his dad would buy it for him, and if Lewis was tagging along, Don's dad would buy one for Lewis, too. Lewis loved it when they all would go out for ice cream and the lady who served the cones said, "What two fine boys you have!" and Don's father didn't correct her. Instead, Don's father just smiled and the whole world seemed to fit into place.

A few months later, Don's father got a job in Texas and the whole family moved away. Lewis, frantic, ran to the house, watching the moving truck. "I'll write you every day!" Don promised, but how could Lewis tell him that it wasn't Don that he was going to miss? He hugged Don's father, shutting his eyes so the tears wouldn't come, and Don's father stroked his hair. Lewis was just figuring out how he could stow away, when his mother came over and put her arm around him. "Come on, honey," she said quietly. "It's time to go home."

He had found Jimmy the first day of fourth grade, shortly after they moved to Waltham, zooming in on him in art class when they were doing family portraits, and Lewis quickly saw that Jimmy was the only other boy without a father. "I'm Jewish," Lewis said defiantly, because he wanted to get it over with, the weird looks, the questions ("So do you hate Christ?" some kid had actually asked him at his old school), but Jimmy had actually looked impressed. "You lucky duck, you don't have to go to church on Sunday," Jimmy said. Lewis met Jimmy's sister Rose, who offered to teach Lewis how to play Chinese checkers, and had one whole wall of her bedroom filled with books that she said he could borrow. Soon, they all began to hang out together, forming their own little family. They never talked about their missing fathers, but they didn't have to. When the kids had to make presents for Father's Day at school, Jimmy and he spent the time looking up information on all the places they were going to go to when they were older. Lewis carefully wrote all the facts into one of his notebooks. "Madison, Wisconsin, has great cheese," Jimmy informed Lewis. "Write that down. Write down they have rodeos there." When they saw fathers playing ball with their sons in the neighborhood, the three of them hightailed it to the schoolyard where it was empty and quiet and they could play ball on their own without the distraction of fathers.

Now, lying next to Rose, his lids heavy, he wanted to reach out and touch her shoulder, to make sure she was really there. Her eyes were open and she was watching the sky. The air felt hot, like a blanket thrown over the world, and the more he listened to Rose's breathing, the more tired he felt. Slowly, so gently that he didn't feel it at first, she curled against him, resting her head on his shoulder. "Rose," he started to say, and then he thought about Jimmy, waiting for him, he thought about their plans, and how he needed to get home, and then he was drifting, falling deeper and deeper into sleep while Rose was whispering something in his ear, the beginning of a story that he couldn't quite hear.

IT WAS DARK when Lewis jolted awake. The woods seemed to be moving around them. He turned to Rose, who was sleeping, one arm thrown over his chest. As soon as he moved, her eyes flew open. She jolted up and started brushing the twigs from her skirt. "Hurry," he said. He was suddenly embarrassed and grabbed for his shirt, his pants. They were dry, though still sticky and caked with mud. He tried to brush the mud off, but all it did was smear on the cloth. He threw on his shirt and stepped into his pants. Rose was hurriedly combing her hair with her fingers. She wouldn't look at him. "My mother's going to kill me," she said.

"Mine, too."

Jimmy. He glanced at his watch, shocked. Ten thirty at night now. Jimmy would never forgive him. And his mother—she'd be furious that he hadn't come home to meet Jake. She might think he had done it on purpose.

The whole way home, picking their way through the twigs and the rocks and the dark, they tried to come up with a story. "We could tell the truth," Rose said, and Lewis glowered at her.

"My mother would call their mothers," he said and Rose's face fell.

"We can't do that, then."

They tested out other stories. Rose's mom had been at the Our Lady carnival, so they couldn't say they had gone there, because she'd know they were lying. Brigham's was open late, filled with high school kids. Maybe they could say they had gone there. "But what about Jimmy? I was supposed to meet him at your house. And what about the time?"

"Say you forgot," Rose said. "That we both forgot the time."

"That'd really bug Jimmy." He thought of how Jimmy hadn't stood up for him in the cafeteria. Too bad, he thought. Too bad if it bugged him.

Rose held her finger up. "I know. Say I was upset, then. That I was crying about school and you had to calm me down." She looked at him hopefully. Rose was a girl who almost never cried. "You can blame me," she insisted. He tried to think and then they were on pavement, walking down Lexington Street to Trapelo Road, over to Warwick Avenue.

The first thing he saw was the police car, white and black with a revolving gumball light on the roof, and he stopped walking, stunned. "We weren't gone that long," he said. The doors of the police car were open, like a mouth. There were two cops, one with his hands on his hips, and there, in a group, was his mother and Dot, and some of the neighbors.

Lewis saw his mother pointing to him, calling out to him. "Lewis!" she cried and there was something strange and stretched in her voice that made him uncomfortable. "Lewis!"

Rose and Lewis walked toward the group. When he got close to his mother, she grabbed his shoulders. "Where were you kids?" Ava cried. "It's past ten o'clock!" She shook him and then she hugged him so tightly he could barely breathe. "Don't do that again," she said. "Don't ever do that!" Lewis saw a man standing beside her, narrowing his eyes, as if he were drinking Lewis in, considering him. Jake, he thought. That must be Jake. For a moment he thought, I've ruined their date, and he felt a skip of glee.

Ava pulled away and then stared at him. "What happened to your clothes? What's that all over you, mud? What have you been doing?"

"Do you know how worried we were?" Dot said to Rose. "I drove around looking for you! I called everyone I could think of!" Dot put both her hands on the sides of Rose's arms, making Rose stiffen.

"What's the matter with you?" Ava asked Lewis. "Do you have any idea how scared I was?" Lewis hung his head.

"It's my fault," Rose blurted.

"Where were you two?" Dot asked. "What were you thinking?"

"We went to a movie," Lewis lied. "We sat on a bench and fell asleep."

"What? You did what?" Ava looked at him as if she didn't know him. "Where did you get the money for a movie? Why didn't you call?"

Lewis wouldn't meet her eyes. Instead, he kept glancing over at Rose, who quietly shook her head. *No. Don't tell.* When Ava looked at Rose, Rose looked away, panicked and moved closer to Lewis. "What's going on here?" Ava said. She tried to pin Lewis in place with her gaze.

The cops seemed to relax. "Kids," he said. One of them started writing something on a pad, while the other went to sit in the police car, to message something in. The man Lewis thought must be Jake walked over and wound one arm about his mother's waist. He nodded at Lewis, but he didn't say anything. Instead, he lowered his head, whispering to Ava and she nodded. Lewis stepped back, not wanting to have to speak to Jake, relieved, in a way, that Jake was there, because then he wouldn't get punished. At least not for a while.

Dot let go of Rose, who rubbed her arms as if Dot's hold had bruised them. Dot circled away from the group of people. She arched her neck as if she were looking over a great height. She put her hands to her forehead, rubbing the skin over her eyes, squinting. Then she turned to Rose.

"Where's your brother?" she said.

❖ Chapter Four ❖

"Jimmy's not here?" Lewis said. Ava stared at him, incredulous. His hair was awry and there was some sort of muddy stain splashed across his shirt and pants.

"Weren't you with your brother?" Dot cried, and Rose looked down at the ground. "Where is he?"

Ava felt Jake's hand against the small of her back. She thought of Jimmy, crying because he had lost at checkers. She saw him standing at his doorstep, waving at her, his chin tilted up. Jimmy, she thought. Oh Jesus, Jimmy.

The cops milled around, asking questions. "We should do a search," one of the neighbors said, and a cop lifted one hand. "Now, just settle down and let us do our job," he snapped. "Things need to be done quickly and in the right way and you can do more harm than good if you interfere."

Bob Gallagher shook his head. "Size 12 shoe and size 5 hat. That's the way they want them in the force. Brawny and stupid," he muttered.

"Bob," said Tina, his wife, putting one hand on his elbow. Her big silvery hoop earrings swung against her cheek.

"You say something?" one of the cops said.

"Not me, Officer," said Bob Gallagher.

"Kids, come here," one of the cops said. He crouched down so his face was level with theirs. "What kind of places did your friend Jimmy like to go?"

Lewis stared blankly. He bit on his lower lip, trying to think, but it felt as if a cloud had settled in his head.

"Look in everyone's basements," one of the neighbors said.

"He didn't like the dark," Lewis blurted. "He'd never go in any basement."

"Oh no?" the cop said. "Where'd he like to go?"

It was warm out, but Rose was shivering and when the cop looked at her, her whole body seemed to shake. "He liked climbing trees," she said. "He liked wide open places. He liked the Wal-Lex!" Her voice cracked.

"Don't forget Brigham's," Bob Gallagher said. "All the kids hang out there. My Eddy loves it there." There were the swings in the Northeast Elementary playground, the Embassy theater.

"Who were his other friends?" the cop asked.

"Us. Just us," Rose said.

One of the neighbors started talking about an abandoned refrigerator over by the Star Market, and one of the cops wrote that in a notebook.

"He'd never go in a refrigerator!" Rose said, but the cop kept writing.

"What about Brigham's?" Bob Gallagher said again.

"I didn't see him at the church carnival," Tina Gallagher said.

"Jimmy wouldn't go to the carnival," Rose insisted.

The cops wanted Dot and Rose to come with them, to call out to Jimmy from different locations. Ava and Lewis were told to go with another officer and drive around in a patrol car. "Something might jar your memory," the cop told Lewis. Jake stood there, his hands in his pockets. Ava turned to him, trying to read him. "I don't know what to do," she said.

"Go," Jake urged. "You need to go with Lewis." She wanted to lean over and kiss him, touch his face, his hair, but she felt the neighbors watching, so she headed for the cop car instead, staring at him through the smeary window.

The patrol cars took off in different directions to cover more ground. Ava turned around in the car and saw her neighbors spreading out over the neighborhood like a lengthening shadow.

AT NIGHT, WALTHAM was dark and uninviting. The church parking lot was empty and silent, the carnival completely gone, the church closed up. The cop drove by, not stopping. "My partner will go talk to them," he told Ava. "I'm just double-checking." The two-way radio in the car spit static and the police officer muttered under his breath. "Jesus, give me a break here," he said. The streets were empty except for a few students from Brandeis wandering around, young couples holding hands. The front windows of Grover Cronin's were covered with brown paper while they were being redesigned. To Ava, everything had a dangerous edge to it, nothing looked familiar.

Jimmy wasn't at Wal-Lex. He wasn't bowling or at Brigham's. They drove up to the schoolyard and all tumbled out. Lewis lagged behind, muddying his shoes as he walked through the dirt by the playground, his small face pinched in misery. Ava glanced at her watch and saw that it was nearly midnight. Lewis was asleep on his feet. She touched the cop's arm and nodded at her son. "It's really late," she said. "I need to get my son home."

"We'll wrap it up," the cop said.

They got back in the car with Ava and Lewis in the back. Every time Ava glanced at the rearview mirror, she saw the cop watching her.

"Is it possible Jimmy tried to get back inside the school?" the cop asked.

"Why would he do that?" Lewis said.

"Did he have a girlfriend?"

"We're twelve. No one has girlfriends."

"He might have. It's possible, isn't it?"

Lewis shook his head. "We hung out with Rose," he said. "His sister. And I would have known if he had a girl."

"Where could he have gone?" Ava asked, and Lewis moved closer to the door, as if any minute he might push open the handle and tumble out into the night.

"Honey," she said. "Jimmy said he was going to meet you at his house. Why didn't you meet him?"

"I just didn't."

"But why not, honey—"

The cop cleared his throat. "How did your clothes get so muddy?" he said and Lewis stiffened. "I fell," he said.

"How?"

"I don't know. I just fell!"

"Where were you, really?"

"I told you—with Rose. We were walking around!" He pressed his body close to the door. "Why don't you believe me? I was with Rose!" He looked at Ava pleadingly. She reached across the seat to touch his shoulder, and then she sat up straighter.

"Stop," Ava said fiercely. "No more questions tonight."

The two-way radio crackled again and a voice snapped, "What the hell are you doing, Maroni?" He stiffened and picked up the phone. "What do you think I'm doing?" he snapped. "Trying to find the boy. We're out looking right now. I got someone from the neighborhood. The kid's best friend and his mother." The static jumped.

"In the squad car? Are you crazy? Take them home immediately and you get back to the station," the voice said. The cop hung up. "Whatever you goddamned say," he said under his breath, turning the car around. The car was silent after that. Ava wished she could see Lewis's face, but his head was lowered. She stared out at the street, as if any moment she would see Jimmy darting out from the bushes.

When they got back, the neighborhood was dark. If you didn't know what had happened, you'd think that nothing had. The lights were off, the front doors shut, except there was a cop car in front of Dot's that made her feel as if her bones had turned to water. "Call me if you think of anything else," the cop said, and he gave her a card, his name on it in tiny block letters. Detective Hank Maroni. "Usually, they just send regular officers first," he told her. "But I came along."

Lewis spilled out of the car, and Ava followed. Then she saw Jake, sitting on her front porch. He had stayed. As soon as he saw them, he stood up and started walking toward them.

"I couldn't leave," he said, and she nodded. "Lot of commotion. A few more cops showed up and they were canvassing the neighborhood. Talking to everyone, writing everything down. A TV crew showed up. I talked to some of the other neighbors, then I sat out here and watched the stars." He touched her shoulder. "Do they know anything?" He looked so concerned, she felt herself listing toward him.

"No, nothing."

Jake sighed. "Then I'm sorry." He stood so close, it felt comforting, then he glanced over at Lewis. "Hey." Jake held out the present to Lewis, who stared at it. "It's for you," Jake said. "I hope you like it. Your mother says you might."

Lewis took it without looking at it. "Thank you," he mumbled, his face lowered. He walked past Jake to the house, his shoulders hunched. "It was nice of you to stay," Ava said.

"I just wanted to make sure you were okay. It was quite a scene here."

Ava glanced at Lewis, letting himself into the house with his key. "It's his best friend. He's upset."

"I get that."

She leaned her head against his shoulder. She wanted to ask him to come inside and sit with her. To lie beside her and just hold her so she wouldn't feel so small and alone. She wanted to get out of the neighborhood and take Lewis and go to his place, but he had never invited her over. She had driven past, wanting to see. It was a great old house, pale yellow with flowers lining the walk, and big picture windows and, for a moment, she imagined herself inside. She had no idea what he did when he wasn't with her, if he puttered in the garden the way she did or sat for hours reading. She tried to remember if he had ever asked her what she wanted in life, but all she could remember was the way he kissed the inside of her elbow, the way he stroked her hip.

"We'll do this another time," he told her. Jake leaned in and kissed her, as brief as a quarter note, and then was gone before she realized he hadn't said when he would call, or when she would see him next.

When she got inside, the house was quiet. "Lewis?" she called, winding her way to the den where he was staring at the magic kit Jake had given him, the wrapping torn into strips. He blinked at the picture of the grinning man, at the thought bubble that said "Abracadabra!" "This is for a little kid," Lewis said, but when he got up from the table, he took the magic kit with him, tucked under his arm, and she could hear the slam of his door.

She fell onto her own bed, but couldn't sleep. She worried about how little sleep Lewis would have for school the next day. She thought of having to go to work tomorrow and pressed the pillow over her head. She could call Richard and tell him she needed to be home because she didn't want her son staying alone in an empty house after what happened. But she knew he'd say, "This isn't a half day, Ava. You're either here when we need you, or you're not." She had already seen Richard fire one of the typists for coming to work a half hour late, and when the poor girl tried to explain, he had said, "I don't care if it was the atom bomb." Without a job, she didn't stand a chance of keeping custody of Lewis. She could ask one of the other neighbors if Lewis could go over there, just until she was home from work, or at least to just keep an eye out on the house, but would they do it? If he stayed inside, Lewis would be safe.

Her mind tumbled from one scenario to another. Where in God's name was Jimmy? She got up and went outside. The police had told her they had checked, but she searched her whole backyard again. She remembered one night, when she had woken with a headache, worrying about bills and Brian and custody, she had stood out at the kitchen window and she had seen Jimmy sprawled on her lawn in his pajamas, his eyes closed. She had gone outside in her robe and nightgown, not relaxing until she had seen his shoulders moving up and down with breath. He was sleeping, that was all. Just sleeping. Why had she even thought otherwise? "Jimmy," she had said, and his eyes had fluttered open and he had given her a big, drowsy smile. His feet curled in the dewy grass, a dandelion caught between his toes.

"What are you doing here?" she had whispered.

He had sat up, rubbing at his eyes. "I couldn't sleep." His pajamas were printed with space ships on green cotton and he suddenly looked about ten years old to her.

"Oh, sweetie," she had said, with deep pity. She had made him promise that he'd never do anything like that again, and then she had walked him back home and waited to make sure he was in his house again.

So he had promised her, but here she was again in the backyard, looking for him, the grass cool against her bare feet. She was half sure she might find him, because what kid ever really listened to an adult? She parted the overgrown rhododendron bushes with her hands, looked around the side of the house, and then, defeated, she came back inside. She went to Lewis's room and cracked open his door so she could see him sleeping, his shoulders under the covers moving up and down, his nose poking out. She felt a flood of love. What would she do if Lewis was missing? How would she manage? And how would he?

Lewis was afraid of so many things. Bugs, dogs, birds, even the jungle gym in the park that the other kids climbed all over. It broke her heart. "There's nothing to be afraid of," she kept telling him, urging him to try the rope ladder, to kick high on the swings, but he shook her off, turning away. "Be a man!" Brian used to tell him when he was little, which was no help at all. "My Lewis doesn't cry," Brian would say when Lewis scraped his knees trying to play basketball with his dad.

Lewis was twelve now, and without her even realizing it, he was growing up. He'd begun to read by himself in bed, falling asleep with a book and not coming out to kiss her good-night. "I forgot," he'd tell her in the morning, but he forgot to kiss her more and more, and she found herself collecting those losses like debts that might never be paid. When she went to check on him at night now, he looked suddenly so much older that she felt discombobulated. He holed up in his room alone, or with Jimmy and Rose, and when she came with cookies for them, the conversation abruptly stopped, not starting up again until after she was gone. "Close the door, Mom," he said. Mom. Not Mommy anymore, but a truncated syllable, like the bang of a screen door. Mom.

Ava had started to realize how much she was going to miss the boy that he was. Well, twelve was still a child, wasn't it? She still had a few more years with him before he would be gone from the house.

She made her way deeper into his room. When he was at school, she often wandered in here, not snooping—never snooping—but just wanting to be around him, trying to learn all the things about her son that she could. Now, she crept to his bed and leaned down, inhaling the scent of his hair, which was like green leaves, and he woke, startled. He sat up in bed.

"Mom, what are you doing?" He rubbed his eyes.

"Nothing, honey," she said. He squinted at her and then rolled back down on the bed, asleep again. He wouldn't remember this moment, but she would never forget it.

❖ Chapter Five ❖

As soon as Ava left his bedroom, Lewis threw back the covers. He was still in his clothes and all his senses were ramped up to alert, as if he were wired for an emergency. Every noise, every feeling, could mean Jimmy was near. He hadn't put on his pajamas because he might have to leave the house any moment, and he'd need his clothes and shoes, so he could move fast. His thoughts kept roller-coastering. How could Jimmy be gone? He dug his fingers into his arms. *It should have been me.*

He could hear his mother clattering pots, moving about the house cleaning, the way she always did when she was upset. She wasn't sleeping, either.

"Jimmy." Now he said his name out loud as if he were calling him. Jimmy had been in his room just the day before and right now Lewis could be breathing in the same air that Jimmy had breathed. He traced his hand along the bedspread because he had read that cells slough off all the time and maybe he was touching Jimmy's. He thought of how weird it was that when people left, the world didn't come spilling in to fill up the hole where they had been, the empty space just stayed there. When his father left, he had first told himself his father was just away at one of his sales conferences, and that he'd be back, with a trophy and little gifts for both Ava and Lewis, cups with the name of the city on them, or snow domes, which Lewis kept on a shelf in his room. He didn't know where his father was now or why he wasn't coming back, except that somehow it must be his fault. Just like Jimmy was.

Who's next? That was what one of the neighbors had said, her hand fanned across her mouth as if she didn't want the words to escape. Are any of our children safe?

The house was quiet. His mother must have stopped cleaning and gone back to bed. Lewis couldn't breathe. He threw the covers off, sweating. Shadows crowded his room. He went to the window and looked out at Rose and Jimmy's house across the street. All the lights were on, but he couldn't see anyone.

He hadn't liked it when Ava had hovered over him, but that was because he didn't want her asking him about Jimmy, finding out that Lewis hadn't met him when he was supposed to. But he didn't want to be alone in this room, either. Shivering, he padded to Ava's room, opening her door. She was sleeping, the covers curved over her head. He lay on the floor beside her bed, on the rug, facing her, so he could see her chest rise and fall with breath. He had read that the moments before sleep were like hypnosis and you could give yourself a command. He told himself he would wake at six, before she was up. She would be the first thing he saw when he opened his eyes, and then he could quietly get up and leave before she even knew he had been there.

THE NEXT DAY, he was already at the breakfast table, pouring Sugar Frosted Flakes into a bowl when Ava came in, dressed in a suit. He looked at her, surprised. "You're going to work?"

"Yup, and you're going to school," she said. She opened the blinds to the windows so dust sparkled in the light stream. "I can't not go. I can't afford to make them think they can do without me." She peered out the window. "I want you to walk to school with a group of the other kids, though. Don't go by yourself."

"I'll wait for Rose," Lewis said. "She can walk with me part of the way."

"Honey, she's probably not going to school today," Ava said.

"I should go talk to her," he said.

"Let her alone right now," Ava said. "There's still police at the house now, and you need to get to school, just like I need to get to work."

He wasn't hungry, but Lewis ate the cereal because otherwise his mom would nag him about waste, and then he walked outside with her. She turned to him. "Lewis," she said slowly. "You have to walk with a group to and from school. I want you to come home and lock the door. Don't go outside."

"Mom," he said, but she shook her head. "You lock that door," she repeated. "That's where you'll be the safest, right in this house with the door locked." Ava's anxiety seemed to spark off her like static. She scanned the street. The parents were all outside with the kids, forming them into groups, smaller kids together, then older kids. She put one arm about Lewis's shoulder. "Come with me," she told him, and they walked over to Mrs. Hill, who was holding on to Barbara, her kinder-gartner's hand, while herding the other kids into a line.

"Are you walking the kids to school?" Ava's voice was tight as a wire.

"I most certainly am." Mrs. Hill nodded at Lewis. "Lewis, would you like to walk with us?"

"And will you walk him home, too?" Ava said.

"As long as he's waiting out front of the school with the other kids."

Ava took her arm off Lewis's shoulder. "Thank you," she said. "Thank you." Then she turned back to Lewis. "Come right home after school," she told him. "If anyone calls, tell them I'm home but I have to call them right back. Don't answer the door. I'll call you from work."

Usually, he wouldn't let her kiss him good-bye in front of anyone, but today, he reached for her. He held on. "I'll see you later," she said, like it was a promise.

He watched her leaving, getting into the car. Another neighbor, Mrs. Carter, came over to talk to Mrs. Hill, and though they were stand-ing away from him, he could see how they were watching his mother, shaking their heads. "A woman just shouldn't be alone," said Mrs. Hill. "Something terrible can happen."

Mrs. Carter looked over at Dot's house. "Something terrible already did," she said.

It was strange going to school without Jimmy. Lewis walked in the group, not saying anything, but no one else was talking, either, not even Mrs. Hill, who kept staring into space, frowning. When he got inside the school, he walked by Jimmy's classroom and when he saw Jimmy's empty desk, he shut his eyes. That day the school had an assembly in the gym and Mr. Girard, the assistant principal, told them what to do if someone came near them, how to act. You were supposed to kick, especially in the groin. You could also try to gouge out an eye. "If you're stuck in a car trunk, kick out the back lights," he said, and Lewis felt a bolt of terror, imagining Jimmy in a trunk, and then himself. How would you know what the lights looked like? How would you know how much air there was to breathe? He tried to calculate it in his head, but his mind went blank. It was the first time Lewis paid attention in an assembly, the first time he thought this might be something he could learn. "If you see a strange car, get the license plate number. Be smart," said Mr. Girard.

But being smart had never done Lewis any favors. Plus, what kind of knowledge could possibly save you against someone who was twice your size and three times as strong, or someone with a gun? The more he thought about it, the sicker he felt.

The school made all the kids sign in and out on a big pad of paper, one for each grade. Everyone had to have someone walking them home. Mrs. Hill was standing outside waiting, a group of kids already around her. When she saw Lewis, Mrs. Hill waved. "Will your mother be home from work when we get there?" she asked. "Because I don't think you should stay in the house alone. Not with all this going on." She peered at him so intently, Lewis felt a flash of shame. "She's there," he lied.

They walked down Putney Lane, shaded by the thick rows of trees along the path. None of the kids were speaking. "Isn't this a pretty day?" Mrs. Hill said brightly. She kept up a patter about the weather until they turned right onto Warwick. Then, she began leaving kids off at their doorsteps, waiting until she saw them safely inside.

By the time she got to Lewis's house, there were only a few kids left. Mrs. Hill turned to Lewis. "Okay, then, we'll see you tomorrow morning," she said. He felt her watching him enter his house.

Lewis used to love coming home to an empty house on the days Ava was working. He could do whatever he wanted, although he never really did that much, just watch TV or read. But the whole house felt different when he was the only one in it, as if he were in charge. Today, he felt anxious. He ticked off in his mind the things that made him safe. Window locks and a deadbolt. His mom would call every hour. There was a squad car right outside Rose's house, but he kept worrying. What if someone had picked the lock and was hiding out in a closet? He turned on all the lights, and the radio, and the TV. Then he grabbed a baseball bat from his room and went slowly from one end of the house to another, checking under the beds, swallowing his fear to open the closets. When the phone rang, he grabbed for it.

"It's me. Everything okay?" Hearing her voice made him relax.

"Totally fine."

She called him two more times. He could hear typewriters clacking behind her, and once a man yelling, "If I wanted it a half hour late, I would have said a half hour late." As soon as she hung up, he wished she would call again.

He devised elaborate plans. If someone came in, he would run to his closet and hide behind the winter coats. If they smashed a window, he would head for one of the doors. He got out the J–K encyclopedia volume and read about jujitsu, trying a few kicks, slicing the air with his sneaker.

Ava was home by five, bustling into the house, calling "Lewis!" and he felt himself relax. She had a bag of groceries in her arm. "Come on," she said. "Keep me company."

That night after supper, they sat on the porch. The squad car was gone, and all the lights were on in Rose's house. Outside, some of the fathers, big, burly men towering over their kids, were watching them play outside, their arms folded as if they were standing guard. Lewis thought about what Mrs. Hill and Mrs. Carter had said, how terrible it was to be a woman alone. He had this horrible thought. A scary thing had happened and it had happened to the only other fatherless boy on the block.

"How tall was Dad?" he blurted.

His mother startled. "Why do you want to know that?"

"We should call him," he said, and she looked at him. "Why?" she asked.

"If he knew this was going on, I bet he'd come back."

Her mouth tightened, the way it always did when he mentioned his father. She stood up, brushing off her skirt. "We should get inside," she told him. "You have school tomorrow."

He got into his pajamas and brushed his teeth. He heard her in the kitchen, the whistle of the teakettle. Later, when he was in bed, he thought he heard her crying. He got out of bed and opened his door, but the house was quiet.

He missed Rose. He went to the window and stared down the street. She had the front bedroom, the same way he did, and her room faced his. Her blinds were drawn; everything looked dark.

❖ Chapter Six ❖

Friday, when Ava got up for work, she went out onto her porch to see if anything had changed at Dot's house. The squad car was there again, and she saw Hank Maroni strutting around, ordering people out of his way.

Mrs. Hill came into view, followed by a chain of children. "Lewis! Mrs. Hill's here!" Ava called through the front door. Lewis stumbled out onto the porch, his hair barely combed, his shirt misbuttoned. He was upset, anyone could see that. The more she tried to reassure him that Jimmy would be back, the more distant he got. Ava watched Lewis join the group, walking away from her, and for a moment she thought, What if I don't see him again? "Lewis!" she called, and he turned and then she smiled weakly. "Have a great day," she told him. She took a snapshot of him in her mind. His lashy eyes. The tilt of his nose. *I love you so much I don't know what to do with myself.*

She waited until he was gone from her sight and then walked down the driveway to her car. She was just about to get in when she saw one of the cops walking toward her. He smiled. "You're Ava Lark?" he asked and she nodded. He held out his hand. "Larry," he said. "Can I ask you some questions?" He had a notebook under his arm, and she looked past him to Dot's house.

"I already spoke to the police," she said.

He nodded casually. "Purely routine," he said. "We're talking more thoroughly now to all the neighbors. Thought we'd start with you since your son was Jimmy's best friend."

"I have to get to work," Ava said, and the officer nodded. She thought of how Richard, her boss, made it a point to walk the halls, snapping those damn suspenders of his, slicking back his hair, so greasy she bet his head would leave an imprint if he leaned against a window. He liked to make sure everyone in the typing pool was at her desk and working at nine sharp. "If I can get here on time, so can you," he said, though he lived five minutes away, while most of the typing pool had a long commute.

"I can't be late," she said and the cop looked at her with sympathy.

"I can call your boss for you, if you'd like. He's probably heard what happened on the news." The news. She hadn't turned on the radio or the TV, hadn't seen a paper. For a minute she didn't know what to do. Would it be worse for her to have the policeman call, like the parent of an errant child? At least Richard would have to believe her excuse then. Ava smoothed down the skirt of her dress, and when she bit down on her lip, she tasted the waxy pink of her lipstick. "Would you call?" she asked and he nodded. She touched his arm. "What are you going to tell him?

"That it's routine. That we're talking to everyone."

She relaxed. She let him inside, embarrassed by the dishes in her sink, gave him the number and listened, leaning against the refrigerator. His voice was pleasant, official. "Of course," he said, before hanging up.

"Was he mad?" Ava said and the cop frowned. "Why would he be?" he said. "Let's go sit down. This won't take long."

Up close, Ava saw he had a tiny little cluster of freckles on the bridge of his nose. He was so young, she thought. He couldn't have been more than twenty and here he was talking soothingly to her. She glanced at his hands. No wedding band. She didn't know why, but the phrase *fancy free,* like a sad refrain, flitted into her mind.

He sat in a kitchen chair, motioning for her to sit, too. "What can you tell us about Wednesday, Ava?" He said her name as if she were a friend.

"I already told the police—"

"Tell me again," he said, as if it were his shortcoming that he couldn't remember.

"I went to work at around four. I had to be there at five. When I got home, the kids weren't home yet." She heard her own breathing.

Larry nodded. "Tell me about Jimmy," he said. "I understand you were friends." He picked up his pen and tapped it on his yellow pad.

There. There it was. A lonely kid comes to her house and she had kept him company and suddenly she was guilty of something.

"He was my son's friend," she said. "He was always at our house."

"But sometimes he was at your house when your son wasn't here, isn't that right?"

Larry's gaze was impassive. "Lots of kids hang out in lots of houses," she said. "It's all open doors here."

"But not your door, I understand."

"I lived in the city, in the Back Bay," she said. "I'm used to locking my door." She saw the flicker of surprise, that someone who had lived in the Back Bay might be reduced to living in a shabby house like this one. "Sometimes he came over when Lewis wasn't home and he wanted to sit around and wait for him. I always said it was fine. Why wouldn't I?"

"Was it the way of the neighborhood to play games with the kids?" His face stayed friendly.

"Excuse me?"

"I'm asking because some of the mothers said they've seen you in the backyard playing cards with Jimmy. For hours, they said. Seems like a long time to be with someone else's kid."

"What mothers? Who did you talk to?" She tried to remember seeing speaking with a cop, but all she could remember was the chaos, the way everyone seemed to be running around.

He raised one brow. "Does it matter?"

"We both liked playing checkers. We both loved gin rummy." Ava tried to think of what the other women did. When she saw them, they were always spilling the kids out of their homes, urging them to go play, get outside, take their bikes. They took them back in to refuel them with Kool-Aid or Twinkies. They scrubbed dirty knees and put on Band-Aids, and then they sent them right out again, like their houses were one big revolving door.

"We all took care of the kids," Ava repeated. "We helped them with their homework, played games." She knew it wasn't really true. She didn't want to mention the time she had overheard two kids talking and one of them said she wasn't allowed to go to Ava's house because her mom thought it was dirty. "Plus she's divorced," the kids whispered. "You know what that means."

She knew the stories about her and they were all horribly exaggerated. Lewis had taken bread sandwiches to school once when she hadn't had time to go to the store, and suddenly he was a charity case. Yes, Lewis wore clothing from Morgan Memorial, but everything was cleaned and pressed, with every button sewn. What was so terrible about economizing, especially when she was trying to save enough to buy her house?

Who knew how stories got started? When she had begun to hear the rumors, she had felt sick. The mattresses in her house, which she knew were old, but were still clean, were supposedly stained with pee. As if she would have stood for that! Neighbors said there were roaches in her kitchen, though all she really had were the occasional ants and when she saw them she wiped every surface with white vinegar and water. She was a Jew and the neighbors said that all Jews had money, and if she seemed poor, it was because she must just be cheap, which was something else all Jews were.

"The neighbors say you keep to yourself," the cop said.

"That's right." Ava didn't tell him how hard she had tried to social-
ize. She had thrown a party the week she had moved in, making invita-
tions out of some of Lewis's colored construction paper and slipping
them in all the mail slots. As soon as the women arrived, in slacks and
casual dresses, Ava, in a shiny violet dress, perfume spritzed on her
pulse points and at the nape of her French twist, knew she had made a
mistake. She had decorated the backyard with candles and red Chinese
lanterns. "Isn't this different?" one of the neighbors said through a
forced smile, and Ava felt stung. She stacked up 45s on the record player
so people could dance, but the only person who asked her was one of
the husbands and when she felt his hand slide low along her hip, she
pulled away, leaving his hand in midair, and soon after that, his wife
was at his side, her eyes gleaming slits, and the party was over.

"Any reason you might know for Jimmy to run away?"

Ava shook her head. "He wouldn't run away."

The cop leaned forward. Here it comes, she thought. "Let me be
frank, Ava," he said, swirling her name around in his mouth like a cube
of sugar. "Some people have said you were a bit too close to Jimmy."

Ava frowned. "He's my son's best friend," she said. "My house was
his second home."

"Would you say that he's your friend, too?"

"He's a boy and I'm a grown woman. You can't possible think—"

"I don't think anything. I'm just asking questions." He scribbled
something on the pad. "Did he ever tell you about other grown-ups he
knew?"

"No," Ava said. "I don't know what other grown-ups he knew." She
felt sweat prickling down her back. "Why are you asking me these questions? Do you want to search my house?" Larry put the pad of paper
down and his gaze grew more intent.

Larry cleared his throat. "Ava," he said, and it suddenly bothered her
that he was calling her by her first name, that he wasn't giving her the

respect of calling her Mrs. Lark. "Of course you're not a suspect. But you've had boyfriends. A lot of different ones, people said. Who knows how well you really knew them?"

"I knew them. And they didn't come over during the day or when Lewis was home," Ava said, and then she flushed, realizing how that sounded. "I just didn't want my son to meet anyone until I knew it was going to be something," Ava said. "Some things didn't work out."

"I see," he said. "And you're divorced."

"That's not a crime. I'm allowed to date."

"So, these boyfriends, how many were there?" He tapped her arm with his pencil and her arm sprang back.

"None of them would have touched Jimmy."

"Did I say that?" He wrote something down again. "Mrs. Lark, could you get me the names and numbers of all your boyfriends? We just want to ask them some questions. Nothing major. Same as we did here with you. It would be really helpful."

He pushed the pad to her. "I don't remember the phone numbers," she said, "I'd have to look them up."

He nodded, still friendly. "That's okay. Just give me the names and we can find them." She hesitated and he nodded encouragingly. He rolled the pen across the table and when she picked it up, it still felt warm from his hand.

The faces swam up in her memory. Each name she wrote down conjured little bits of things, like different patches on one big quilt. Tom Sullivan. She had met him getting gas for her car. He had soft, pillowy lips that he would brush along her collarbone. Richard Meserve had been her accountant one year. He brought her flowers every date but then he yelled at a waitress for not bringing the water fast enough, and after that Ava didn't want to see him again. None of her relationships had lasted very long. Not when they found out Ava wasn't the good-time girl they expected. Ava wouldn't pack up and take off for a weekend away because she had a son. Ava wouldn't stay up drinking until two because she had to work. Ava wouldn't peel off her dress and get right down to her skivvies after a first date. Ava wasn't what they wanted, but they, too, had disappointed her.

"Did any of them ever meet Jimmy?"

"No. And they never met Lewis, either. Except for Jake, and that was after Jimmy was gone." She hated saying that: *gone.* She felt a pang, remembering Jake's dressy clothes, his gift. He had really tried. None of her other boyfriends had been terribly interested in Lewis as anything but a detriment.

There were five names, and then six. Three a year, that wasn't so many. She didn't feel a single thing about any of them until she got to Jake, and then she began to tremble. She wrote out his name and it was all she could do not to touch the letters with her fingers, not to rest her face along the page. She pushed the pad across the table to Larry.

He took it and studied the names. "That's quite a list." He stood up. "That's all, Mrs. Lark. Just call us if you have any news, or you think of anything that might help us."

She stood up, glancing at her watch. Nine thirty. She was a half hour late to work. Even though the cop had called, Richard might still be furious. How was she going to explain what had taken so long? She thought of her in-box with all the invoices about claw-footed tubs and pedestal sinks she had to type, and she felt exhausted. She'd have to stay late to make up the time.

AS SOON AS Ava walked into the office, Charmaine glanced at her. Betty tapped her watch. "I did some of your work," Betty said to Ava. "Richard wanted it right away." She held up the razor blade the women used to scratch mistakes from the carbons. "Lot of errors, Ava," she said. Ava couldn't tell if she was smirking or not. "Thank you," Ava said. "I had an appointment."

Betty shrugged. "No skin off my nose. Long as you're here now."

Richard hadn't told them, then. It was one less thing for them to gossip about in the break room and thank God for that. She took off her coat and hung it up. Just as she had thought, her in-box was piled with papers. There were scribbled notes on her desk of the things Richard needed her to do, some of them with sharp little exclamation points after them, like stab wounds. She uncovered her typewriter and sat down.

Then Cathy began talking about Maureen, a secretary in accounting who had run away and gotten married over the weekend and had called the office to announce she was quitting without notice. "Can you imagine?" Cathy marveled. "She said to just chuck her things."

"Why didn't she at least stay for a party?" Betty said.

"I'm so jealous of her I could spit," Charmaine said.

Ava kept silent. She couldn't imagine having that luxury of quitting. She put a piece of paper into the roller, and Richard appeared. The other women straightened up, and Cathy fluffed her hair. Ava's fingers froze on the keys. "Could you come into my office, please?" he said to Ava. He wasn't smiling. The other women were watching her. She felt their stares, like a film on her body she wanted to scrub off. She walked into Richard's office, sitting in the chair he pulled out for her.

"I'll work late to make up the hours," she said.

Richard waved his hand and sat down, putting his feet up on the desk. "First time in my life an officer of the law called me," he said.

"I'm sorry."

He waved his hand. "So what did they ask you?" His eyes were bright with interest. "What's going on in that neighborhood of yours, Ava, and why would they ever question you?"

"I'm not a suspect—"

He laughed. "Of course you aren't."

She didn't know what else to tell him. "They just asked me some questions," she said. She told him how she had driven around the other night in the cop car, helping to look for Jimmy, how everyone was worried. He listened, his eyes glazed with sympathy, but he didn't say, "You have a son, take the day off," or even, "If you need extra time, the break room is always open for you."

He let her go. She wound past him to the typing pool and sat down. "You get chewed out?" Betty asked, lowering her voice, not looking up from her typing. The return bell rang and she slammed the carriage back, frowning. Ava shook her head and stared at all the papers on her desk. She blinked hard, willing herself not to cry. She'd be lucky if she was able to leave by seven, let alone six, and she'd certainly have to work through lunch.

She put paper and a carbon into the typewriter, trying to be careful so it wouldn't smudge on her hands, and then her clothes. She should wear an apron, the way Betty did. The other women were busy typing. She put her hands on the keys.

By three, when Lewis should be home, she felt anxious. Ava wasn't supposed to make personal calls, so she waited until Richard was in a meeting and then dialed her home number. Lewis answered on the first ring. "Is your mother home?" she said, making her voice raspy, with a fake French accent she remembered from school, testing him.

"Mom, I know it's you," he said. "And I'm fine."

Ava returned to her work, feeling better having spoken to Lewis. He had told her how everyone at school was acting weird because of Jimmy. "I have to work late, honey. Make yourself spaghetti for dinner," she told him.

The rest of the afternoon glided by. The sound of the typewriter keys, the steady ding of the carriage return bell hypnotized her. At four, the other women got up to go to the snack room for break, but Ava never went with them, so no one thought it odd that she was working straight through. She could hear them laughing and talking about hope chests and dresses and what to have for dinner. Plumes of their cigarette smoke swept out into the hallway. She kept typing when the five o'clock bell rang and the other women covered their typewriters, got their coats, and filed out. She kept typing when Richard walked by in his topcoat and hat, and for a moment, when she heard him clear his throat, she expected him to say, "Just go home. You've had a rough day." Instead, he kept walking. The cleaning service came in, a woman who worked around her, and left quietly. She kept typing, only occasionally looking out one of the big windows that faced another building. She watched the other windows blink dark, one by one. A figure would move past her line of vision. A man in a coat. A woman in a beaded sweater and a fascinator, pulling on a pair of white gloves. She felt as if she were the only person left in the world.

By the time she left, she was exhausted. She drove home in the silence, parking in the shadows. Opening the door, she found Lewis asleep on the couch, a book spread on his chest. His mouth was half-open, his forehead damp. She gently shook him. "Honey," she said. "Go to bed." He looked at her as if he were a kitten. "What time is it?" he asked.

"It's late. Go to bed, sweetie. I'm right about to follow you."

She made him wash his face, brush his teeth, and she leaned against his door watching as he fell into bed. "Good-night, Mom," he murmured into his pillow.

THE FOLLOWING MORNING, Ava woke to find a green flyer under her door. MEETING AT THE HILLS, THE JIMMY REARSON CASE, it said, 8:00. Ava was surprised she had been invited. She knew how the neighbors felt about her, and that she was somehow suspect because of all the time Jimmy had spent at her house. She knew, too, that the cops didn't seem to appreciate the neighbors' self-appointed search. Tough, she thought. She was determined to go.

The Hills lived opposite Ava, but Ava had never been inside their house. She knocked on the door and Debbie ushered her in, as if seeing Ava was the most natural thing in the world. "We're in the rec room," she told Ava, showing her to the basement, which was so darkly wood-paneled it seemed to leach all the light from the room. A painting of a deer in the woods, carefully framed, gleamed above a wet bar. The deer looked so pained and startled that Ava wanted to tell it that she knew how it felt. A plaque hung beside the painting, festooned with a silly drawing of a man with his tongue lolling out, and a caption underneath: THIS PLACE RECOMMENDED BY DRUNKEN HINES.

"Come on, I'll get you seated," Debbie said. She led Ava to the six card tables in the back, each one already filled with neighbors munching on cookies and sipping from bright, sweating aluminum glasses. "God bless Green Stamps," Debbie said. "Those tumblers make even fruit punch look pretty."

Debbie's husband, Dick, walked over, his hands filled with fliers that he held against his burly belly. "Dick, look who's here," Debbie said, touching her husband's arm.

"Where's Lewis?" he asked. He nodded to all the kids scattered about the room, running around aimlessly or playing games. Ava had deliberately left Lewis at home because she didn't want to subject him to the neighbors' interest in what he might know.

"Safe at home," Ava said.

"Let's get you seated," Debbie said. She put Ava at a table with the Corcorans, who lived one block down on Greer and had a son, Stanley, a year older than Lewis. Bob Gallagher, beside Ted Corcoran, nodded pleasantly. "Ava," he said. Dick moved from table to table, handing out fliers. "We need to put these up everywhere," Dick said. "On the bottom is a checklist of all the places we've looked already."

"Aren't the police supposed to be doing this?" someone said, and Dick snorted. "Yeah. The police," he said. "Like they get everything right."

There were all sorts of rumors floating around. There had been a TV crew to interview Dot, who had wept and begged people to come forward. Dot had offered to sell the house for reward money. "Is Dot here?" Ava asked.

"Doesn't Dot have enough to think about?" Dick said. "We're doing this for her."

The flyer floated in Ava's hands. HAVE YOU SEEN THIS BOY? the flyers said, and there was Jimmy's grainy picture, reprinted from the *Waltham Tribune*. Ava touched his face. Below the picture was a hand-drawn set of eyes, the pupils dark so the eyes seemed to follow you. WE ARE WATCHING YOU, the signs said.

Frank Fitzgerald, the locksmith, stood up. "I want to put deadbolts on everyone's doors, free of charge," he said. Ted, who owned a toy store, handled out silver whistles on silver chains to all the kids, stopping to hand one to Ava. "Any car or person comes near you or your kid," he said, "you blow this like a hurricane." Someone blew the whistle so it sounded like a scream and then Ted clapped his hands to his ears. "I'd like to keep what's left of my hearing, if you don't mind," he said.

"Kids, if you ever need to, you bite," he said. "Kick them where it counts." He gestured to his groin and Ava turned away, her face hot with embarrassment. "Go for the throat, the eyes, anywhere tender," he insisted. The kids shuffled their feet and socked one another in the arm. "I'm carrying my Daisy rifle with me all the time," Stanley said.

"We could have seen him without even knowing it," one of the neighbors said. "We could have brushed right past him."

"How do we know it's a him?" Debbie asked, and Ava sipped her watery lime punch, and then set it down again.

"We don't. We don't know anything," said one of the mothers, but Dick snorted. "Women don't do things like that. They wouldn't know how."

"Things like this just don't happen," Ted said. Not in Belmont, not in Waltham, and certainly not in this new development where they lived, with rows of ranch houses and driveways and leafy backyards, an enclave where everyone knew everyone else, where every summer there were barbecues, the fathers in plaid shorts, the mothers in starchy cotton dresses, and the kids all got to stay up late and drink Shirley Temples in paper cups.

"How the hell could this have happened?" Ted said angrily. "A twelve-year-old boy."

"The cops swarmed over my place like bees," Bob Gallagher said. "I'm surprised they didn't want to look down my throat. Especially that Maroni guy."

"I told him we were doing this neighborhood patrol and you might have thought I told him we had an atom bomb in here," Ted said. "He told me it was a poor choice of time and resources, that speed was of the essence, but I don't see them having any success. Why shouldn't we look? Why shouldn't we do what we can?"

One of the other men handed out a list he had made of all the fathers who would scan the neighborhood every night, along with what things to watch out for. Unfamiliar cars. Strange people. "Stay in groups," one of the men advised. "Be on the lookout."

Other groups were going to go into the woods behind the Northeast Elementary School to see what they could find. "Didn't the cops look there already?" Debbie said. "We don't want to waste time here."

"They sure as hell did," someone said.

"Not very deep," Ava said and everyone turned and looked at her.

"Well, we'll go deeper then," Bob Gallagher said.

Debbie stood up, waving her hands as people began to get up. "Tomorrow night," she said. "We meet here at seven and we scout the area. We see what we can find."

"What exactly are we looking for?" Ava asked and Ted frowned.

"We'll know it when we see it," he said.

WHEN AVA GOT home, it was nearly ten and the house was quiet. Lewis's door was shut, but she cracked it open to check on him. He was sleeping. Then she walked back to the living room and stood at the picture window and watched the street, and the few times a car drove by, she tensed until she recognized a neighbor's sedan. She kept going over and over the day of Jimmy's disappearance in her mind, how Jimmy had looked, what he had said to her, and how quiet the neighborhood had been, and when she finally slunk down in a chair, her eyes wet, she was thinking about Lewis, too. You won't take him from me, she had told Brian.

She couldn't sleep. She watched a little TV, until the test pattern came on, and then she read *Marjorie Morningstar* until it was two in the morning and she had finished it. When she closed the book, she felt vague and uneasy, and annoyed with Marjorie's choices to give up her theater career, but what really could she have done differently? She was about to make some coffee when she heard a soft knock at her front door. For a moment she was scared. Who would be coming by so late? Was this danger or simply some bad news she didn't want to hear? Was it Jimmy? She cautiously parted the curtains, and there on the porch, his hands in his pockets, was Jake. He was never supposed to come at night when Lewis was there, but even so, she was so relieved to see him, she threw open the door. "I didn't even hear your bike," she said, but he stepped back from her, leaving her hands in midair, and then she saw how angry he was. "The cops visited me," he said.

She remembered Larry making her write down all those names. "Come inside," she whispered.

They sat in the living room. He told her how the police had come to the club. The cops approached him after his first set and wanted him to leave with them. "Can I finish my second set?" he asked politely, sure it was going to be okay, but the cops frowned.

"Now," one of them said.

What do I have to hide, he thought, but the manager of the club was annoyed. "They can't wait?" he asked Jake. "People came to see you play." Jake didn't like it, either, the way the cops escorted him out. They kept telling him it was no big deal, it was just routine questioning, but it was still pretty humiliating, especially when one cop automatically put one hand over Jake's head as he got into the backseat. "They asked me if I was a beatnik," he said wearily.

Ava tried to touch him, but he moved away. "They're asking everyone questions," she said.

"They asked me if I had ever touched Lewis."

Ava sat up. "That's a disgusting question."

"Yeah, well, they asked me. They wanted to know what games I played with Lewis, what we did together."

"You only met Lewis the other night."

"They asked me if I had ever talked to any of the kids. I told them that I came to see you late at night when Lewis was sleeping over at a friend's, so the neighborhood wouldn't talk, but he seemed to think that was even more suspicious. He kept asking me where I was that afternoon, if I could prove it." Then Jake stood up. "Jesus, Ava, I live alone. I play saxophone, I see you. That's my life."

She didn't ask him not to go. She walked with him outside, into the night, to his bike. The lights were still on at Dot's house, and she couldn't help it, she suddenly felt watched, and she folded her arms about her body. He tilted her head and kissed her briefly.

"Don't worry, I can handle it," he told her. He ran his fingers up her arm, the way he always did. Don't go, she wanted to tell him. Please don't go. She thought of how people always said the way you could tell how a couple was going to do was how they got through a bad time. It could make you closer, it could make you appreciate what you had.

"Can we try dinner again next week?" she said.

He shrugged. "I'll call you."

HE DIDN'T CALL for days, and then it was only to say a terse hello. Two weeks after Jimmy's disappearance, she heard that Jimmy's case was turned over to homicide, a word so chilling, it made Ava nauseous every time she heard one of the neighbors say it. Now when Hank Maroni came by, he was accompanied by another detective. Dot never came out of her house. The neighborhood grew tenser and people gathered at night to compare notes about what the detectives were asking them, how the questions were getting more personal, more disturbing. "How the hell do I remember what I last talked about with a kid?" Bob Gallagher said.

The other men Ava had dated began to call her. Their voices were raw and angry on the phone. Sometimes they didn't say their names right off, so she had to struggle to piece together who they were, picking out their identities by a twang in a voice, a figure of speech. "We didn't even get along," said one man, "Why would you have them call me?" They were angry that they had been contacted at work, that their girlfriends knew, the women who were now their wives. It was the sort of case where being questioned made people look at you differently. Ava remembered a teacher in Lewis's school who had been accused of molesting one of the kids. He had lost his job and had had to move away and then, four years later, the child had recanted. The boy said he had made it up because he was mad at the teacher for yelling at him in front of the class, that he had been with a cop in a room with no windows for what seemed like hours and he was scared and tired and all he wanted to do was say the things the cop seemed to want him to say.

"I'm sorry," Ava said. She let the men rant until their anger died down and then they hung up.

She had a terrible feeling that, on top of all of this, Brian might call again, asking about custody. What if he had heard what was going on here, what if that gave him more of a case against her?

◆ *Chapter* *Seven* ◆

The first time Ava had set eyes on Brian, she was nineteen years old and working behind the candy counter at a Woolworth's in Boston. Her parents lived in Chelsea, but she had left home as soon as she could, fleeing their relentless arguing to share a tiny Brookline apartment with a girlfriend. "A girl shouldn't leave her parents' home until she gets married," Ava's mother had told her. "It doesn't look right." Although Ava worried about the same thing, she had decided to take her chances.

From the time she was little, her parents had had screaming fights because her father was always at the racetrack, gambling away their money. He didn't always pay the bills, he didn't always go to work at his construction job, and all of his sure bets on horses with names like Lucky Thunder or Juliet's Romeo never panned out. Her father could be funny and charming, but you couldn't depend on him. He forgot Ava's tenth birthday party. He missed his wedding anniversary party at the house, and when he finally showed up, just as people were leaving, Ava's mother walloped him across the face. Ava still remembered how he had taken her to the movies, but right in the middle, just when Rin Tin Tin was about to save the day, he had gotten up. "Just be a minute," he whispered, touching her arm. She sat there, watching the movie alone, unable to concentrate, and every time she heard a noise, she kept craning her neck around, hoping it was him. When the movie was over, she didn't know what to do. She went to the front of the theater, and stood there, terrified, while people thronged around her. Her dad had driven her here and she had no idea how to get home and she knew if she called her mother from the pay phone inside the lobby, she would be the cause of another blistering battle. She was just about to burst into tears, when she saw him running up to her, grinning. He put his arm around her. "Thanks to your dad, we're all going out to a fancy meal tonight!" he said. He showed her a fan of bills, but all Ava could think about was how long she had been waiting and how scared she had been.

Her mother loved her father, but Ava saw how hard it was for her. Ava's mother might reach for her husband's hand and glow when he came home, but she never knew what kind of a mood he'd come home in, and he always took it out on her, egging her on until she shouted back. Ava's mother gave Ava a lot of advice. "Don't marry just for love," she told her. "You want a good provider who'll take care of you. Someone calm and kind who thinks about your needs and not just his. Someone with a steady job who doesn't gamble."

Ava listened. As soon as she started dating, she considered every boy husband material. She wouldn't date any man who didn't have a good job and some money in his pocket. He had to have a plan for his future and if a man so much as raised his voice at her, she was gone.

Marcy, a friend over in cosmetics, had offered to set her up on a blind date. Ava was reluctant until Marcy told her that, at twenty-two, Brian was already a sales manager at a car lot, and that he even had his own apartment in the Back Bay. "He's going places," Marcy said. "If I didn't have my Billy, I'd date him myself." Her friend nudged her. "Blue eyes. Blond hair. Dimples. Tall, too. Come on, you don't want to be standing behind the candy counter at Woolworth's forever, do you?"

So she said yes, and then Brian showed up at her door three nights later, and he wasn't just everything Marcy said, he was more. His teeth were perfect and dazzlingly white. His hair wasn't just golden, it had a wavy dip in it, and his lashes were as long as hers, and she used

Maybelline. He was in a dark suit, and he carried a bouquet of daisies in his hand.

"How did you know I loved daisies?" she asked, surprised.

"I asked Marcy," he said. "I try to find out what people like so I can give it to them." She felt a blush stain her cheeks.

He took her to a French restaurant in the Back Bay, with gold foil wallpaper and waiters in tuxedos and bow ties. Ava had never been to any place so fancy. The maitre d' smiled as soon as he saw Brian. "Mr. Lark," he said, "always a pleasure to see you," and Brian slid some money into the maitre d's hands, whispering something. They were instantly led to a table by the window, which impressed Ava even more. The menu was all in French and she looked helplessly at it, too embarrassed to admit she didn't understand what anything said, but Brian seemed to know she was struggling. He carefully took it out of her hands. "I'll order for both of us," he said.

All through dinner, he talked to her, carrying the conversation so she didn't have to. He told her his mother had died when he was a kid. His father was a retired surgeon who now lived in Florida, but they weren't close. When the waiter brought the wrong appetizer to him, smoked oysters instead of onion soup, he didn't get angry the way Ava's father would have. "No problem," he said easily, "I'll just have this." He told her he had gotten his third raise just this year alone and when he talked about the things he liked to do—fishing, bowling, going for drives—he didn't mention cards or the racetrack. By the end of meal, Ava was sure there was such a thing as love at first sight, because she could have sworn it had just happened to her.

THEY MARRIED THAT spring, she in a tea-length white dress with tiny cap sleeves, a bouquet of daisies in her hand, all his office-mates standing there cheering, their wives smiling at her, her friends from Woolworth's crying happily into their handkerchiefs. Brian's father was sick, and did not make it. After the ceremony, Ava's father hugged her and slid a fifty into her palm. Her mother took Ava aside. "You did good, honey," she said. "You picked a fine man." Ava beamed and hugged her.

They moved to Brian's apartment in Back Bay, a one-bedroom that looked out onto trees. He bought new venetian blinds for every room in the place, and a Danish Modern divan. When it came to the bedroom, he surprised Ava by ordering one big double bed instead of two twins, extra long both because he was tall, and because it was more luxurious. When she told him that her mother had always insisted couples should have twin beds, with a nightstand separating them, in case one of them had a cold, he laughed. "Whatever you have, I want, even a cold," he told her. Ava leaned her whole body up against his. "I fit perfectly here," she told him.

She quit her job, of course. "Your job is to run the house," Brian told her. She didn't miss the paltry paycheck she used to get because every week Brian gave her an allowance that was hers to use however she wanted. They had lots of money. She was a wife! Finally, a wife! She couldn't stop staring at her ring, flashing her hand so it caught the light and so everyone could see it. Every once in a while, they went out to dinner with her parents—Brian's treat—but with Brian beside her, it didn't bother her so much when her father got up to use the phone and didn't come back for twenty minutes. When her parents started arguing loudly as they left a restaurant, Brian took her arm and led her quietly away to their car. As soon as they were inside, he turned on the car radio and leaned over and kissed her and she felt the tension slide away.

She loved that everything was taken care of. He chose the restaurants they went out to, the movies, the shows in Boston. But what she loved even more was that there was no drama. He woke up in a sunny mood and stayed that way, and when Ava was upset, usually after calling her parents, he glided her onto his lap and rocked her.

"Life is golden," she told her mother, and it took her a while to see the miles and miles of tin.

IT TOOK HER two years to get pregnant, but when she finally was, she had the whole kit and caboodle. The early nausea turned into full-blown morning sickness and she was too exhausted to even straighten up the apartment.When she told Brian she was pregnant, he cried. He kneeled and kissed her belly. "Wait until you see the father I'm going to be!" he told her. By then, both her parents had died, one after the other, as though one didn't know what to do without the other. Brian only had his father in Florida, whom Ava had never even met, but Brian told her it didn't matter. "We have each other," he said. "The perfect family. That's all we need."

And oh, but he was a great father at first, and an even more wonderful husband. He doted on her during the pregnancy, rubbing her feet, sometimes even making dinner, nothing fancy, just Green Giant vegetables heated up and spaghetti with sauce from a jar, but to Ava, it tasted delicious because Brian had made it. When Lewis was born, and Ava was still groggy from the anesthesia, he stayed at her bedside the whole week she was in the hospital, telling her dirty jokes to make her laugh, charming all the nurses with boxes of chocolate. "That's for taking such good care of my little wife," he said. When she came home, he brought flowers for Ava and soft plush toys for the baby, a little basketball, a monkey, a whale. Sure, he wasn't always there because he was working, but he was already talking about buying a big house in the suburbs. Ava was thrilled. Though she loved the city, the suburbs were green and leafy, a paradise. She could just imagine it. A house! Maybe a little grassy backyard for Lewis to play in.

Sometimes when she missed him, she would put Lewis in her lap and spread Brian's clippings from the company newsletter all across the living room floor. There were the photos of him holding a trophy for generating more sales for the lot this year than any other salesman. He was smiling so hard his whole body seemed to gleam. There he was, caught in time, and still so beautiful, as supple and strong as a willow tree, that her breath skipped. "That's your daddy," she whispered. Lewis banged his rattle against her wrist.

Everything Lewis did fascinated her. She loved just watching him grow. Look at the way he lifted his head! Look at how he toddled around the house, and when he began speaking, all she wanted to do was scoop up every word. She was determined that he was going to have everything in life. College. A good job. A happy home.

She spent all her time with her son, reading him books, painstakingly teaching him his letters, making excursions to the park, but Lewis grew up worshipping his father. "He's your biggest fan," she told Brian, and for a while, it seemed to be mutual. Lewis couldn't wait to go bounce a ball around with his father, to go catch fish. When little Lewis was six, even taking a walk with his big, tall daddy was excitement for him, and Ava didn't mind. It gave her time to nap, or just sit in the apartment and read a magazine. How could life be any better?

But then Brian had a bad month at the lot. The cars weren't moving the way they should and he had to fire two of the salesmen, but the new hires didn't seem to be working out. The next month wasn't much better. Brian began to come home without flowers or toys. He didn't talk about a house in the suburbs anymore. They stopped going out to dinner because he said he was too tired, and when she tried to comfort him, he brushed her worries away. "It's all going to work out," he promised.

A few months later, she came home from the grocery store and there was Brian slumped on the couch, in the middle of the day. "I got let go," he said quietly.

She sat on the edge of the couch. "Fired? Just like that? But why?"

He put his head in his hands. She scooted over beside him, and when he cried against her, she stroked his hair. "It's going to be fine," she said. "You'll find another job. A man like you."

It didn't take him long, He looked great dressed up in his best suit, his handshake was firm, and in two weeks, he had a new position, working at Buxbaum Buick. "Didn't I tell you?" he told Ava, beaming. He said it didn't matter that it was a used car lot, rather than a new one. The fact that he wasn't a sales manager but only a salesman was no obstacle for him. "They'll see how good I am and move me up," Brian told Ava. The pay was much less, which made Ava worry, but Brian told her that wasn't an issue, either. "There's such a thing as raises," he said. If he had to be a salesperson for a while, well, then, he was going to be the best one on the lot.

He had trained enough salesmen in his old job to know there was a real art to it. You never sold a car to a person who shouldn't have it. You found out what the customer wanted and you found the car that would do the job for him.

Brian was surprised when Mike, his boss, gave him the traders and the beaters that would never make much money. How could he succeed with cars like these? He tried to think of a strategy, but he was used to taking his time to make a sale, and now Mike kept urging him to move faster. "You've got to go for the today deals," he said. "And no one but you wears a shirt and tie on the lot. Who do you think you are?" Brian cast a wider net for sales jobs, refusing to give up. "How would you feel about living in Chicago?" he said. "What about Detroit?" He was so radiant with hope that she dared to hope, too. She began imagining a bigger, burlier city than Boston, a life back on track, but none of his leads ever panned out.

By the time Lewis turned seven, Brian was almost always tense and defeated when he came home. No matter what Ava did, no matter how she took Lewis to the zoo, the circus, or the playground every day, he still scrambled toward his father, his face bright and expectant. "Want to shoot hoops?" Lewis asked. He lifted up one hand, twirling the ball clumsily on one finger. Lewis followed him around like a puppy.

"Not tonight," Brian said. Lewis let the ball fall from his fingers, watching it roll to the corner of the room. Brian put his hands in his pockets. Then he went to the table and began to write out notes for himself on lined pieces of paper, ignoring both her and Lewis, not speaking at dinner. Ava touched his sleeve, but Brian didn't even react to the warmth of her hand.

"Lewis told me something new and wonderful about Alaska today," she told him and Lewis perked up, sitting straighter in his chair, watching Brian expectantly, but Brian looked at her as if she had told him the moon was made of plaster. "I'm tired," he said. "I've had a long day."

Ava followed him into the kitchen, where he rummaged in the spice cupboard. She lowered her voice. "You have a son in there who needs you," she said. "And so do I."

He picked up a canister of salt, closing the cupboard, and then he set it down. "I'm not hungry," he said, and he went out of the apartment.

He didn't sleep nights. Ava heard him walking around the apartment and when she got up, she found him standing in the middle of the living room, gesturing, practicing a sales pitch about sedans. He blinked at her, and his hands fell to his sides. "Oh honey," she said, resting her head along his shoulder, but he didn't lift his hand to stroke her hair. He just stood there. "Go back to sleep," he said. "I'm not going to come to bed for a while."

He stopped doing anything with Lewis. One night, she urged him to at least help Lewis with his homework. "He needs you," she insisted. Lewis was at the dining room table, his science book spread around him, fiddling with a pen. Brian sat down beside Lewis. "So, what have we got here?" Brian said, and Lewis began explaining about the phases of the moon. "New moon, waxing crescent, first quarter," Lewis said. Ava saw the way Brian's smile began to fade. Lewis set out a sheet of paper with all the moon phases. "I have to label all of them," he said.

Lewis pointed to a slice of moon that looked like a fingernail. "What do you think that is?" Lewis said, his voice firming up as if he were a teacher, and Brian frowned, looking back at the book. "This is a little confusing," Brian said. "These diagrams sort of all look alike, don't they?"

"No, it isn't hard at all," Lewis said, his face brightening. "I can show you, Daddy. Look, this one is easy. It's a waning gibbous." Lewis pointed to another one, full except for a slice taken away. "Now, what's that?" Lewis asked in an authoritative voice. "Come on, you can do it, Daddy," Lewis said, and then Brian abruptly got up from the table, pushing the book away. "Why did you ask for my help if you didn't need it?" Brian snapped. "You know how to do this, so go do it."

Ava, startled by the force in Brian's voice, saw Lewis's eyes flood with tears, his pen gripped in his hand.

"Brian," she said, but he glared at her, as if it were her fault. "I'm taking a drive," he muttered. When he left, the door slammed and the sound traveled up her bones.

Ava noticed the house money Brian gave her every week was a little less. She was afraid to ask him why, because he was so edgy lately. He had snapped at her at breakfast because she had forgotten to buy the kind of orange juice he liked. At night, when she reached for him, he pulled away, so she lay on the bed staring into the darkness. He didn't even look the same. The sprinkle of gray in his temples was suddenly gone, and it wasn't until she discovered that her brand-new black mascara was dried up and there was a stain on his pillowcase, that she realized he must have been using it to color his hair to look younger.

She didn't have access to their bank statements or a checkbook of her own, because Brian handled all that, but she began to worry. Where was the money going? Panicked, she began doing her grocery shopping at the Thrift-T-Mart, which was cheaper than the Star Market. She bought dresses on sale rather than in the boutiques, and still, every month, the money he left her dwindled.

Then, there began to be phone calls with hang-ups, a trail of breath on the line. She couldn't stand it, and one night, when they were lying in bed, she asked him, "Are you seeing someone else?"

He sat up, the sheets bunching around him, and she wished suddenly that she hadn't asked at all. "Am I the kind of guy who would do that to you?" he said.

"Is it the job? You don't have to sell cars," she said. "You could do something else. Or, I could get a job."

"You're my wife. You don't work."

"We could get a smaller apartment."

"Things will work out," he said. "I promise you." He rolled over, pulling the blankets around him, tugging them so hard, she was left with only the sheet.

The next week, Ava was on her way to the grocery store when she passed a diner and happened to look in and there was Brian, waving his hands in conversation. She couldn't see the other person, so she moved closer, imagining it was a colleague from the car lot. Instead, though, it was an older woman with a sharp nose and dry-looking curls, in a dowdy gray suit and hat. Ava knew Brian tried to be innovative in the way he sold cars, so she thought maybe he had taken a customer to lunch to close the deal, but then Brian lifted one hand and placed it along the woman's cheek and Ava froze.

She forgot her errands and went right to the car, driving herself back home. Brian used to love to show Ava off. He encouraged her to buy new dresses, to get her hair done, because he said she was a reflection of him. So who was this older woman and why would he be with someone like her?

She hadn't bought the meat they needed, the vegetables, so she made spaghetti for dinner, but Brian didn't come home. When she called his office, no one answered. "Where's Daddy?" Lewis demanded and Ava forced a smile. "He's working late, honey," she lied.

When Lewis went to bed, Ava promised that she'd send Brian in to kiss him good-night, even if he was sleeping. She sat in the dim light of the living room, waiting for him. Brian had told her he always practiced his sales pitches so he'd feel more confident. She began to rehearse what she'd say to him. What's going on? What did I do? How can we make this better? She went into their bedroom and brushed her hair until it snapped with shine. She glossed on lipstick and put on one of his favorite dresses, and then she went back into the living room.

Around midnight, she heard his key in the lock and she stood up, flicking on the light. He looked at her, startled. She could smell alcohol on his breath. "I thought you'd be asleep," he said. "Long night at the office."

She forgot everything she had planned to say. "Please don't lie," she whispered. "I saw you with her today."

He sat down on the couch, breathing into his hands.

"She's older," Ava said in wonder. "Isn't she?"

Brian lowered his hands. "She's thirty-eight," he said finally.

"I don't understand—"

"She's a businesswoman. She works for her father's paper business in Cleveland."

"She works?" Ava thought of all the times she had begged Brian to let her go to work and he had taken offense. "Women don't work," he had insisted.

"Ava, please."

"Who is she?"

"Does it matter?" He got up and started to pace, the way he always did when he was nervous.

"How did you meet?"

"Ava—"

"No, tell me."

"She came to look at a car with her brother. Things just happened."

"What things?"

"Her father offered me a job as sales manager."

"What? Paper? You don't know anything about paper."

His eyes narrowed. "You think I can't do it? You don't have faith in me anymore? Well, she sure does. And so does her father. He's been looking for someone first-rate to eventually take the whole place over. That could be me, Ava."

"Do you love her?"

He wouldn't look at her, but threaded his hands together.

"How can you do this to us?" Ava's voice was a whisper. "This is so crazy."

"You can keep the furniture, the apartment, what's in the bank account. But you'll need a lawyer. I think this is going to be better for everyone," he said.

"Why? Why do you think that?" Of all the ways she thought they could fix their marriage, she had never considered that he would leave them. How could she manage? What would she do? Ava felt something breaking up inside of her, pop-pop-pop, as fragile as bubbles. "What about Lewis?" she asked.

"He has you," Brian said. "I'm gone all day anyway. He hardly sees me."

"Are you crazy? You're his father!" She heard the begging in her voice and tried to swallow it down. "Aren't you going to say good-bye to him?" she asked.

"Of course I will," he said. "As soon as I'm settled. I'll still see him."

"What about me?" she said. "How are we supposed to live without you here?"

"Ava," he said slowly. "You've been doing that for quite a while now." And then, just like that, he was gone and she still didn't really understand why.

❖ Chapter Eight ❖

Two weeks after Jimmy had vanished, when Rose finally went back to school, she was a celebrity. A picture of her and her mother had been in both the *Waltham Tribune* and the *Boston Globe,* a bad, blurry shot of her in a tired plaid dress and scuffed saddle shoes, her hair pulled back in a messy braid. Anyone glancing at that picture would think her mother was looking to her for support, the way her mother was clutching her arm, depending on her, the one child left, when in fact Rose was the one hanging on. She could feel her mother's rage like a force field, pushing her away. No one would know how angry Rose's mother had been at that moment. "Why weren't you watching out for your brother?" Dot had accused Rose, her voice a whisper.

Now every time Rose's mother noticed Rose, her eyes narrowed, as if she couldn't believe Rose was there in front of her and Jimmy was not. As if she were thinking: *They've taken the wrong child.* "First Benjamin and now this," she said.

Benjamin was Rose's father. Rose couldn't really remember him. She'd been only been three when he had died, and though she believed he was up in Heaven with the angels, her mother kept him alive in their home. She talked about him daily, as if he were still somehow there. "Oh Benjamin, how you'd love this program!" she said, when Jackie Gleason came on the television, making faces and pumping his arms. "Let's get a roast, your father's favorite," she'd say to Rose in the supermarket.

His clothes stayed in the closet, his desk wasn't touched, and there were photos of him hanging in every room. There they were on their wedding day, her mother in a soft satin dress with bridal point sleeves, her father, tall and beaming, his thick, dark hair in a brush cut, his mustache trim and dapper. There were a few photos of them on vacation, slick as seals at the beach, or the two of them in a canoe, Dot's tight red curls blowing back from her face, their eyes locked on each other as if they couldn't believe their luck. Her mother told her he had read her stories every night, that he made up silly songs and the two of them sang them together. "Oh hobbledee-hoy, it's time to buy you kids a new toy," Rose's mother sang. "You were Daddy's girl," her mother said, and Rose wanted to scream, *how?* How could she have been Daddy's girl if she couldn't remember any of it? What did a wonderful family life feel like? How could she miss it if she didn't know what it was?

When Rose plunked in front of the television, instead of just enjoying her favorite family shows, she studied them. She ached to be Kitten in *Father Knows Best*. She watched Katrin running into Papa's arms in *Mama,* and she started to cry out of yearning. What would it feel like to have that? Jimmy, a year younger, recalled nothing of their father, but she had one memory: her father handing her a teddy bear in a shoebox and showing her how to move it around the floor like the bear was in a boat. That was it. She had nothing else of her dad.

Jimmy had inherited his father's thick mass of hair, his cat-shaped eyes. His resemblance to their father was always the first thing anyone said when they met them, even after her father had died, and it always made Rose's mother beam. "It's such a blessing," she said. "It's like God made sure there was a piece of Benjamin left on earth." Her mother was always going on about Jimmy, how handsome he was, how all the teachers loved him. She put Jimmy's blue ribbon for baseball up on the kitchen wall, but when Rose brought home As on all her papers, her mother just leafed through them and said, "Keep it up."

Rose didn't really know her father's relatives. Dot had told her that the Rearsons, who lived in California, had never thought Dot was smart or cultured enough for their son. They put up with her once a year, inviting her to Thanksgiving dinner where everyone talked over her head about books she hadn't read or theater productions she hadn't seen, but they never bothered to ask her a single question. "That's just the way they are," Benjamin had tried to soothe her when she cried. "They take time to warm up." He insisted they would eventually love Dot, but even when Jimmy and Rose were born, they stayed distant, sending cards and sometimes gifts for the children, but rarely visiting. And when Benjamin died of a heart attack, they saw her at the funeral and then abandoned her altogether. "You marry a man, you marry his family," Dot told Rose. "Good or bad. You remember that. It's never just the two of you."

After Jimmy disappeared, everyone seemed to think Rose would want to stay at home, but Rose couldn't wait to get out of the house. She was glad to be back at school. She didn't want to be home, where her mother was either laying on her bed, staring at the ceiling, or putting the dishes away so hard she ended up smashing some of them. Rose hated going to church on Sunday, where her mother kept her head bent down in prayer, and when the priest mentioned Jimmy, Dot cried as if she would never stop. Rose hated having the detectives around the house. They kept asking her the same questions. They wanted her to stay inside, as if she were a hothouse flower. One detective, that Mr. Maroni guy, asked her if Ava ever walked around in front of them naked. "Are you crazy?" Rose asked. Just the thought of that made her so embarrassed she wanted to die. But most of all, she didn't like how being at home made her miss Jimmy even more.

Her mother wouldn't let her take the school bus and instead drove her to and from school every day. The first time she walked into her classroom, the kids stared at her as if they had never seen her before.

Miss Pizzi, the homeroom teacher, plucked at a button on her blouse and then called Rose over. "If you need to go home, or you want to stay in the art room, you just let me know," Miss Pizzi said meaningfully. Her frizzy brown hair was held back loosely with a rust-colored bobby pin Rose couldn't help wanting to touch. "I'm okay," Rose insisted. She wanted to poke Miss Pizzi's bobby pin back into place but she kept her hands at her side.

She kept hearing her name. "Rose," someone said, but when she looked around, she couldn't tell who had said it. A few kids shied away.

Night after night, she had lain in bed going over what had happened. At three o'clock, she had come home from school and Jimmy wasn't there. She decided not to do her math homework just yet, even though she could have polished it off in ten minutes. She just didn't feel like it. Something unsettling was swimming its way up inside of her. She kept walking around her room, annoyed that Jimmy had plans with Lewis that didn't include her. "No girls today," Jimmy had said that morning, and she had rolled her eyes, pretending she couldn't care less, that she had better things to do. Sometime around four, she was tired of watching the clock, of flopping on her bed trying to read or do anything but think about what she was missing. She felt that strange tingle in the air, as if something were about to happen, and she went outside. The neighborhood was hot and silent. Even her mother was at the stupid carnival, and Rose had had enough of church on Sundays without wanting to go today. The only other living thing on the street was Romeo, a white cat from down the block, that stared impassively at her while he licked his front paws.

She decided to walk into Waltham to kill some time, maybe try on dresses even though she couldn't afford them.

All she had to do was to change two seconds of her life, and everything might have gone differently. She might have realized that feeling meant she had to go find Jimmy. She could have stayed home. Maybe she'd have walked faster and missed Lewis altogether. Instead, as soon as she saw him, running onto Lexington Street, she felt dizzy with love, as if a thousand magnets were pulling inside of her and she was powerless to resist.

Lewis didn't know it, but if he had asked her to beat up all those boys who were after him, Rose would have done it, winding up her fists and kicking with everything she had. If he had asked her to sing in the middle of the road, her mouth would have opened and a tune would have flown free. She took his hand without thinking. "Run," she told him, but she meant with her.

She had been so busy tuning in to Lewis that she had jammed the station she kept for her own brother. She thought of how it had been, laying so close to Lewis, wanting to kiss him but being terrified, because what if he didn't love her back? What if he shoved her away? Or laughed at her? And all the while, Jimmy had been in trouble and she hadn't even known it.

Now, both she and Lewis were being kept close at home and they weren't even in the same school. The phone had to be left free because any moment Jimmy could call. There might be a voice, a clue, a sign. Sometimes she thought Lewis was just avoiding her. He could have come over to her house, couldn't he?

By lunchtime, at school, everyone seemed to be watching her. She was eating her baloney and cheese sandwich alone when Annie came over, plunking down in the seat opposite her. "I saw your picture in the paper," Annie said and Rose nodded.

"Now everyone knows who you are," Annie said.

"Is that good?"

Annie shrugged.

"Who am I, then?" Rose blurted and Annie laughed.

"You're a big dope," she said.

All that day, Rose felt as if she were sleepwalking, but she was in no hurry to go back home. She couldn't be there in her house without Jimmy. Rose had always felt that he had somehow belonged to her.

They played together and slept in the same room until Rose turned ten, when her mother told her "a young lady needs privacy" and gave her the front bedroom all to herself. But Rose missed sharing a room, and even though she was only a year older, had always felt that taking care of him was her job.

One day at school, she had felt a cloud darkening over her, and she just knew something wasn't right. She ran home, panting, and when she finally banged into the house, there was Jimmy sitting on a kitchen chair, his hand bandaged. "I burnt it on the stove," he told her. Another day, she felt a bright flash of joy, and as soon as she got home, Jimmy was crowing that he had won a marble tournament, holding up the green cat's-eye that was his prize. She wanted to be around him all the time, and they were, until he became friends with Lewis.

She went into Jimmy's room at night and stared at that stupid map that he and Lewis were using to plot out their lives, and every thumb-tack she saw pushed into a city hurt her. The blue tacks marked the places they were going: San Francisco and Chicago and Kansas. The red ones were the side trips like the Grand Canyon and Yellowstone Park, the places they didn't want to live but definitely wanted to visit. She pulled out the blue tacks in Los Angeles and Nashville and put them in her pocket. She moved the red tacks around, confusing their routes. If she could have, she would have spelled out her name right there on the map.

They never even thought to blame her, which somehow made it worse. "Jeeze Louise, what happened here," Lewis said, and the two of them spent an afternoon fixing the route, while Rose, flopped on Jimmy's bed, said nothing.

One afternoon she came into the room and Jimmy said, "We're busy here." They were poring over the map. "No girls allowed."

"That's too bad because I know a pool we can crash," she said.

"You do not," Jimmy said, but he looked at her with interest. "Where?" he asked.

She led them over to Trapelo Road and then to Lexington Street and over to Green Acres Day Camp and showed them how to climb over a big fence. The pool was clear and glossy and cool and they jumped in in their clothes, though Lewis stayed in the shallow end, wading. "How did you know about this?" Lewis asked, splashing her.

"I just know things," she said. The truth was she had heard a senior girl in school talking about how she and her boyfriend always came here, but she wanted the boys to think she had somehow known this magically. "Like Houdini," she said, "I can make things appear," and when he grinned, she felt something in her heart fluttering, like a bird's wing. She didn't tell him that she thought Houdini was a jerk, a man who could have lived if he had gotten medical attention, a man who promised his wife he would come back from death and then didn't.

"She does know things," Jimmy admitted to Lewis. "She showed me how to make phony phone calls. She knows how to get a burger at Brigham's and sneak out without paying."

Lewis looked at Rose as if she were a new page in a book. After that, they rarely excluded her, and if Lewis came over when Jimmy wasn't around, Lewis didn't turn and go home. He stayed and hung out with her. He didn't act as if she were second best, either. Lewis tested out his magic tricks on her. She gave him books she thought he should read, and she began to protect him, the way she had Jimmy when he was younger, only it felt weird and different with Lewis. She told herself she was brushing her hair a hundred times because there were knots in it, that she was wearing Ava's perfume not because of Lewis, who never noticed, but because didn't every girl want to smell good? Lewis looked her straight in the eyes when he talked to her, and every time he did, she felt herself listing. It was crazy. He was her brother's best friend. He was her friend. He was too young, just a kid. Girls her age were interested in eighth- or ninth-grade boys, not sixth graders, whom they viewed with disdain.

Now, there was nobody who wanted to be with Rose. She traced a line someone had dug into the desk. *Biff loves Tina Forever.* She wondered if he still did. She thought about what Lewis was doing now, where Jimmy might be. She knew she'd feel it in her body if Jimmy were gone. She'd somehow know it if he were being hurt in some way. Instead, she felt that same connection she had always had to her brother, as if nothing had changed. But things were hidden, like in one of Lewis's magic tricks, and she swore if she shut her eyes, if she listened, she could hear him whispering to her, telling her where he was, and why. One thing she had to believe: Jimmy was alive.

ONE AFTERNOON, SHE came out of school to find her mother waiting for her, dressed, with a little veiled hat on. "Come on," she said. "We're going someplace special." Rose got in the car. She didn't say a word, not even when her mother parked in front of a brown house, not even when a woman in a turquoise turban opened the door. "Ah, an old soul," she said, looking at Rose.

"I'm thirteen," Rose said.

"This is Miss Diane. She's a psychic," Rose's mother said. "She's going to help us find Jimmy."

The tight fist in Rose's chest loosened, becoming fingers against her ribs. She told herself it didn't matter that Miss Diane's turban was sort of hokey looking and had printed moons and stars all over it. Miss Diane led them deeper into the house. There were plastic slipcovers on the sofa, and a TV tray set up by the TV with a plate of what looked like macaroni and cheese. The house smelled sour, like milk curdling, and Rose noticed a litter box shoved in one corner and a white cat dumbly lying in the center of it. Miss Diane rested her hand on Rose's shoulder. "We shall see what we shall see," she said.

They all sat at a green leather card table. Dot handed Miss Diane two folded bills which Miss Diane discreetly tucked into her pocket. Then Miss Diane ordered everyone to hold hands. Rose didn't like the powdery feel of Miss Diane's hands, but when she tried to loosen her grip, Miss Diane's fingers tightened around hers. Miss Diane shut her eyes for a moment and then breathed noisily. She opened her eyes and, to Rose's relief, let go of everyone's hands. "I see water," she said. "Deep green water. I see him." She shook her head. "I see the letter *W*. Is there water near you with a *W*?"

"Walden Pond," said Rose's mother, her lips beginning to tremble.

"He's alive," Rose said. She dug her fingers into the spongy edges of the table.

"Walden Pond," Miss Diane said. "That's what I'm seeing." Miss Diane frowned and shut her eyes again, and in the silence, Rose could hear the creaks the floor made.

"He didn't like Walden Pond," Rose said. Every time he had to go to Walden with Rose and her mother, he sat on the shore. The water was too cold or there were too many people. He always had excuses.

"I see deep water," Miss Diane said. "And the name Jack. Does that mean anything to you?" When Rose's mother remained blank, Miss Diane said, "I see the name Thomas. And Martin. Do you know a Martin?" She folded her hands, threading the fingers together.

Rose's mother shook her head. "Who are they? Who's Martin?" She looked at Rose, frowning. "Do you know?" she begged.

"I'm seeing a Rodney," Miss Diane said. "It's definitely a man," she said.

"Is he coming back?" Rose's mother cried. "Is he alive?"

"He's alive—" Rose said again, but Miss Diane shrugged.

"I can know only what I'm shown."

Rose's mother grabbed Miss Diane's sleeve and when Miss Diane pulled away, she gripped it again, harder this time. "How can you not know? I just paid you forty dollars? How can you not know? What kind of person are you?" Her body began to shake and Rose peeled her mother's fingers free. "Mom," she said.

Miss Diane smoothed her dress. "There's nothing more to see today," she said. "Maybe another time. But at least now, you have information."

Then, she stood at the door, watching Rose and her mother get into the car and when Rose turned around, Miss Diane waved.

The whole ride home, all Rose could think about were the slipcovers, the smell of the house, and the litter box. She thought of how Miss Diane had only closed her eyes for two seconds. "She's a fake, Mom," Rose said. "I know he's alive." But her mother kept driving. "Let me concentrate on the road," she said.

As soon as they got home, Rose's mother called the police. Rose couldn't hear what they were saying, but she heard the way her mother kept insisting. "Please, I want you to do this," she said. "How far is Walden Pond? You can be there in five minutes. I don't know about the psychic, but it's one of the places he went to. Isn't it worth a look?"

An hour later, the phone rang. The detective told Rose's mother that there was nothing there. There were no clues. The lake was clear and didn't need to be drained. Nobody who worked there at the pond had seen anything and they didn't have time for any more wild-goose chases.

ROSE CAME HOME from school the next day to find her mother curled up on her bed, still in her nightgown, even though there were policemen in the house drinking coffee at the dining room table. "Mom?" Her mother beckoned Rose, patting the bed, and Rose, surprised, climbed up. Her mother hooped one arm about her, pinning her in place. "My girl," she said and Rose tried to shift position. Her mother's perfume smelled stale and vanilla, and she was holding Rose like a vise. When Rose tried to move, her mother held faster. "Stay," she said.

"Mom," Rose said. Her mouth felt as if she had swallowed a wash towel. "I know he's alive."

Her mother's arm loosened and she sat up. "Rose, please," she said.

"He is. I know it. I'd feel it if something happened—"

"That doesn't help." Her mother got up from the bed, grabbing for a robe, pulling it around her. She stared at herself in the mirror, and then turned away. Rose had always thought her mother was pretty, had always loved it when her mother came into her grade-school class to chaperone trips, wearing one of her flowery dresses with a full skirt, her high heels that clicked along the floor. But now, Rose's mother walked toward Rose like an old woman, and Rose suddenly wanted to fling herself into her mother's arms and beg, don't go, don't go away.

"I can find him," Rose said.

"You can find him, is that right?" her mother countered. "Well, then, you never should have lost him in the first place," she said, and walked away, leaving Rose sitting on the bed.

IT WAS AFTER school and Rose's mother had given her money to take a cab home, but instead Rose walked all the way back to the neighborhood, taking her time. She didn't want to go inside her house and be drenched by her mother's sorrow. When she got to Warwick Avenue, she saw Mrs. Hill dropping off Lewis at his house. Neither one of them spotted her, which was good because Mrs. Hill would probably yell at Rose for being on her own. She waited until Mrs. Hill was gone, and then she sprang over to Lewis.

She took his arm and gently tugged him aside. "What are you doing alone?" His voice sounded flattened, like a can.

"Jimmy's alive."

He grabbed her shoulders, his whole face lighting up. "He is? He's alive? Where is he?"

"I don't know where. I just know my brother and I know he's alive somewhere."

Lewis dug his hands into his pockets. His hair was falling in his face, his smile gone. He looked at her suspiciously. "How do you know that?"

"I just know. I feel it."

"Rose, feeling doesn't prove anything."

"I'm telling you, I feel it. I feel him." She grabbed his arm. "Who knows him better than we do? I have no one else but you. You were there for this. You have to help me. You have to. Remember Houdini? Things are not always the way they appear. We have to do something. We can't just sit around."

He looked past her, as if he were thinking. "What do you want to do?"

It was Rose's idea to buy special notebooks to keep track of things the way the cops were doing. "Every time I pass a place I have a feeling about, I'm going to write that place down and we can investigate it," Rose said.

"Maybe we can write down the descriptions of people who look suspicious," Lewis said. "Or the license numbers on cars. We can try to figure out where everyone was every hour of that day."

"We won't miss a thing," she told him. "And we shouldn't go anywhere without our notebooks. Not ever. We need to collect as much information as we can. Later, we can compare notes."

They walked down to the Star Market, even though they weren't supposed to, stopping only so Rose could call her mother from a pay phone and lie about the cab. "It was late, so I had to call again," she said, promising to be home soon.

The Star had all kinds of notebooks with movie stars' pictures on the covers. Lewis grabbed Tony Curtis, who had played Houdini in the movies, though Rose thought his hair was too greasy. Judy Garland looked insane to Rose, and in the end, Rose got Jimmy Stewart because she felt he had such a kind face, and because his name was Jimmy.

They went back to Rose's house and if Dot was surprised to see Lewis, she didn't say anything. They got to work immediately, quietly stepping into Jimmy's room, cataloging everything they found in their notebooks: a button in Jimmy's underwear drawer, a dark stain on a white T-shirt, and a portrait Jimmy had drawn of a man with the head of a growling lion and the body of a man. "What does it mean?" Lewis asked. "How is this supposed to help us?"

"I don't know. I just have a feeling about it. Write it down."

That night, after Lewis had left, Rose wrote a letter to Jimmy in her notebook, as if he could somehow read her words and find his way back to her.

Dear Jimmy,

One of the cops left a white ring on the table with his coffee cup when he was here. I'm sorry that they have gone through all your things and probably broken some stuff.

She thought about not telling him that, and then decided that she shouldn't protect him, because who knew what information might be necessary for him to know? Who knew what she might forget? She told him all the things that were going on in the neighborhood, how the neighbors always drew their kids closer when they saw Rose walking by, how their mother cried at night when she thought Rose was sleeping, how the Bicardis down the block bought a great big Doberman pinscher for protection, which they walked with everywhere, even though they didn't have any children. She'd put down everything so when he came back, if he couldn't remember anything, she would bring the world back to him.

Rose spent most of her free time wandering around the house or reading. None of the kids were outside anymore. The only time you saw anyone was when their parents were with them, and what fun was that? When she did see them, they asked her about Jimmy. Had she heard anything? Did they have any clues? "Do you want to help me look?" Rose would ask hopefully, but the kids shied away. "My mom won't let me," one boy said. "I have to go right home," said a girl. She saw how the kids wouldn't meet her eyes anymore and their fathers gave her these slow, sad looks that made her look away.

The mothers were worse. One day she was outside by herself, reading on the front porch, when Mrs. Hill strode over. "Go inside," she urged. "I'm on my porch," Rose said. The policemen were still in the house. She was reading *A High Wind in Jamaica*. She was a proper English girl on a pirate ship and here was Mrs. Hill pulling her back to Warwick Avenue.

"You didn't even hear me until I was right on you," Mrs. Hill said. She reached forward and grabbed Rose's arm, her fingers handcuffs. "Anyone could do this. Someone you don't know. Someone you don't want to know. Do you see what I'm saying?"

Rose tried to pull away and Mrs. Hill held on tighter. "Rose, I'm just worried about you. Please. Don't give me a heart attack. You're safer in your house. And where's the whistle you kids are supposed to have? Why aren't you wearing it?" She let Rose go and Rose rubbed her arm. The skin was still red where Mrs. Hill had grabbed her.

Rose opened her front door and went inside. The house smelled stale, and she didn't have to look in her mother's room to know she was sleeping again in her clothes. There was that bottle of pills by the bed. Dot was in bed almost all the time now. The laundry sat piled in chairs. The dishes towered in the sink. Meals, if Rose didn't cook them, were cereal and whatever fruit was around.

Lewis used to tell Rose how he ran his house because his mother was always working. He had shown her how he could cook dinner, and even made her spaghetti one afternoon, which impressed her. But now she ran her house, too, and suddenly it didn't seem that great anymore. It seemed terrifying. Neighbors kept bringing them food—hot-dog casseroles and Tater-Tot hot dish with potato-chip crusts, things she was advised to just heat up and then serve, but Rose's mother often didn't get up for dinner.

Rose didn't want any of the casseroles, which always smelled funny, but today there was nothing in the refrigerator except a few soggy tomatoes and an onion, which she took out and put on the counter. She pulled a box of spaghetti from the cabinet and tried to remember how Lewis had cooked the spaghetti. Oil spattered in a pan. She cut up the tomato and the onion and threw them in the oil, hoping for a kind of sauce, hoping, too, that the smell would rouse her mother. She tasted it when it was a kind of mush, and when it didn't seem too bad, she poured it over the noodles. She brought a plate to her mother's room. "Mom," she said. "You have to eat." Her mother rolled over, covering herself with the blanket.

Rose nudged her mother. "I made you some food," she said and her mother lifted herself up and looked at Rose as if she didn't know her. "Let me sleep," she said.

My beautiful girl, her mother used to call her. *My little dollface.* Her mother used to invite the Avon lady in just so the two of them could get the little gold samples of lipstick without buying a thing. Her mother sometimes took her dress-shopping at Zayre's, both of them giddy over the clothing, dresses so inexpensive you could get three of them at a time. Sometimes, after school, Rose would come home and find outfits from Filene's Basement spread out across her bed. Sharkskin sailor dresses with gold buttons and silk ties. Corduroy skirts with red ricrac trim on the hem. "Look at the labels!" her mother said, pointing out Bergdorf Goodman, I. Magnin. "Look at the price!" She showed Rose how she had gotten a twenty-dollar designer dress for two dollars. "You don't have to have money to look like a million dollars," she said.

Well, Rose didn't dress like a million dollars anymore, or even ten dollars. In fact, Rose had worn the same yellow corduroy jumper all week, just changing the blouse underneath. She barely brushed her hair but kept it braided. People made allowances for her. "What she's been through," she heard a teacher say, but Rose always wanted to blurt, "What about Jimmy? What about what he's going through?"

Rose went into the kitchen and ate the spaghetti by herself. She wasn't really hungry, but told herself she had to be healthy to find her brother. Afterward, she cleaned the dishes and the pots and all the coffee cups the policemen had used. Then she went into the bathroom and stared at herself in the mirror, at her bangs that were so long now they hid her eyes. Her teachers always asked her to pin her hair back, which was as thrilling as it was embarrassing. Her hair was down to her waist now, so long and black that the kids sometimes asked her if she were a witch who could do spells. "In your dreams," she said. If she could cast spells, wouldn't she have done so already? She waved her hands. "Abracadabra," she hissed, but all that happened is she heard the heat clicking on.

She had lost so much weight now, there were hollows in her cheeks and her eyes seemed more luminous against her pale skin. Jimmy's absence made her somehow more mysterious. The other kids watched her, and the older boys began to take new and sudden notice. She was the girl with the missing brother. She had been through something and now, because of it, she knew something that they didn't.

She continued to write Jimmy every night in her notebook, and the more she wrote, the more she felt as if he were standing behind her. *People are saying your body is in the woods, in the water. I don't believe any of it.* Sometimes she read what she wrote out loud, as if it would help make her words a bridge to him. The more pages she filled up, the more hopeful she felt. He would hear her. He would find his way back.

She slumped down on the toilet seat, suddenly panicked. She had done this to him, this awful thing. She was responsible. If she had been there, she could have stopped the car that took him, or bit and kicked the person grabbing him. She could have screamed—everyone listens when a girl screams. She could have saved him.

Jimmy's green toothbrush was still in the holder. She touched the bristles and then ran water over them, as if he had just used it. She stared at herself in the mirror. She had her brother's eyes. Maybe in the right light, she had his chin. She wondered if people looking at her would see her brother. If the man who had taken her brother thought so, maybe he would take her, too, and lead her to Jimmy.

Opening the medicine cabinet, she found her mother's scissors. Taking up a hank of her hair in her hand, she cut it to her ears. The hair drifted to the floor, dusting her with strands. She'd worn it long all her life. She had refused to go to Clip N' Curl, or to wear curlers at night and spray every morning and she hated the styles her mother kept suggesting to her: artichoke or shingles or a poodle or a pixie. It was a shock to see all that hair on the floor, but she kept snipping, even her bangs, making her eyes look cartoon-character large. When she was done, it was short as a boy's. Looking in the mirror, Rose reached up and touched her reflection.

She looked like Jimmy now.

She cleaned the bathroom, stuffing the hair in the wastebasket, swabbing out the sink. Her head felt impossibly light, as if any moment it might float off like a helium balloon. She looked different and that felt good.

Rose went into Jimmy's room. She opened his drawers and got out a pair of his jeans and his favorite T-shirt and put them on. They were too big but her hips held them up and she could grab his Teepee Town belt from the closet. She put on his sneakers with three pairs of his socks until they fit.

Rose settled onto a chair in the living room, reading the pirate book, so lost she didn't realize her mother was in the room until she heard her gasp. Rose looked up and her mother had her body braced along the wall. "What have you done, Rose?" she said. Her mother shuffled over. She smelled like sleep and sweat, and Rose anxiously stood up.

"We can go to Clip N' Curl. They can fix it."

"I don't want anyone touching it. It's my hair."

Her mother's eyes slid along Rose's clothes. "Why did you do this?" she said. Then her mother put her hand on Rose's hair. "I'm sorry," she said. "Baby girl, I'm so sorry." She bent and Rose felt a kiss through her hair, but before she could grab her mother and pull her closer, Dot was gone, ambling back to her bedroom.

DOT SAID NOTHING when Rose came to breakfast in Jimmy's pants, though she handed Rose a hairbrush. "At least brush it back," she said, and Rose gave her hair a few perfunctory licks. The kids stared when she showed up at the bus stop, but no one said a word to her, though some of the girls touched their own hair self-consciously and edged away from her, whispering, their eyes on her. She climbed the bus and found a seat in the back, alone, which was fine by her because she could gaze out the window and look for signs of Jimmy. She strode into the school and immediately she heard murmuring, like a tide following her, the waves tumbling closer and closer, which made her feel even more defiant. The only person who spoke to her was the principal, who called her into his office after third period. "If you need to go home, I won't mark you absent," he told her, but she said she wanted to stay.

As soon as she got home from school, she stood out on her porch, waiting for a car to come by. Waiting for the man who had taken Jimmy to come and find her. A car passed and she stretched up taller, her heart like a fist inside of her. Come on, she thought. I dare you. Come and get me. We'll do a trade. Take me instead. She'd know the kidnapper as soon as she saw him. She'd feel it.

She was sitting on her front steps when she saw Lewis. He was in the center of the road, his eyes glued to her, not moving. Her hands floated to her hair and she stood up. "You thought I was him, didn't you?" she said. "For a moment you thought it was him." She heard the crack in her voice and her body began to shake. She pressed her lips together as if she might swallow them.

He walked up and sat down beside her. She could feel the heat of his body. "I knew it was you," he said, and then he put one arm about her while she cried.

❖ Chapter Nine ❖

A month after Jimmy's disappearance, on a cool May evening, Ava showed up for the neighborhood patrol walk in black stretch stirrup pants and red flats, a gold chiffon kerchief holding back her hair. She was a half hour early, but she had been too anxious to wait. Her hands were so cold she pressed them together, digging her heels into the ground as she walked, as if that might stop them from trembling. No one had called her to come, but she had seen the notices posted on the phone poles. PARENTS ONLY, the sign said. ELLIE ROBERTS OFFERS BABYSITTING, 105 WARWICK. Ava didn't want Lewis leaving the house and reminded him not to answer the phone or the door. She checked the window locks and the doors.

He didn't want her kissing him good-bye anymore, not on the face, not on his milky cheeks or the slope of his neck or even his nose, but he dipped his head so she could press her mouth to the top of his head, his silky hair against her lips, like a barrier.

"I won't be long," she told him.

They were all supposed to meet in front of Bob Gallagher's at six, but the street was empty. She couldn't just stand here—she was too tense, too jittery—so she walked around the block, wishing she had paid more attention to everything in the neighborhood before so that now she'd know if anything was different.

She found a shoelace in the middle of Greer Street, frayed at the ends, but really, it could have been anyone's. She tucked it in her pocket, like a talisman. She noticed something glinting by the sewer, but when she stooped down, it was just a skate key, and she knew Jimmy didn't skate. She left it and kept looking. Everything could mean something, and the harder she looked, the more it all seemed to elude her, and the queasier she felt, as if her heart were drowning.

She walked down to Abbot Road and then turned around, and by the time she came back on Warwick, there was a crowd around Bob Gallagher's. She waved and as she came closer, she felt some of the men's eyes sliding down her. Ava looked down at her stirrup pants. A saleswoman at Filene's had talked her into these, assuring Ava that she could pull them off. "Those really work with your gorgeous figure," the saleswoman had said, and Ava had looked at herself in the mirror, skimming her hands over her hips, loving the feel of the stretchy fabric. Now she felt as if she had made a mistake. Look at the way Ellie walked right over to her husband, who was regarding Ava. Ava wished she had brought a sweater so at least she could tie it around her waist.

Debbie looked at her with surprise. "Oh Ava, you're here," she said.

"Dot is my friend," Ava said.

"Dot's not here tonight," Debbie said.

As they started moving down the street, Ava trailed to the back of the group, so it wasn't as obvious that no one was really talking to her. The group had flashlights to hand out, but she had brought her own, swinging it proudly. "Why do you need such a big flashlight?" Tina Gallagher asked her pointedly.

"It casts a big light," Ava said. She waved her flashlight across the sidewalk and into the bushes.

"Save your batteries for the woods," Bob Gallagher said, but Ava kept pointing her flashlight every which way. She couldn't afford to miss anything. Ribbons of light hit the houses. A cat scurried out from under a car. She followed everyone into the woods behind the school, stepping over the mushy damp ground, the thickets scratching her ankles. "They ought to burn these woods down," someone said, and Ava remembered how when she rented the house, these woods were a selling point. "Do you know what people pay to have nature right in your backyard?" the realtor had told her.

She could catch snippets of conversation. Someone mentioned how little the police seemed to be doing. Why didn't they set up a hotline? Why weren't they at Dot's every day? Why weren't the detectives patrolling with them? Ava had heard the cops say they had been over and over this ground, that there was nothing left to find here. "You aren't doing us any favors trying to help," that detective Maroni had told them. "You could be messing up key evidence without even knowing it." But how could they do nothing? And what evidence? As far as anyone knew, the cops had found nothing. The neighbors kept talking, their voices growing louder and louder.

"This is what I think we should do," Bob Gallagher said. "We need to spread out more, maybe get walkie-talkies. I think my kid has one." Everyone had a suggestion, and to Ava, they all sounded worthless. "We ought to stop everyone who comes into Waltham and if they don't have a good reason for being here, we take down their license plate number," Debbie said.

"We could set up checkpoints," Debbie's husband said.

"What about the Morgan Memorial bin?" someone said and Bob sighed. "We looked there already."

"I heard the detectives say they just want to find someone and fast," Debbie said. "Would they say that if we were Belmont? Or Cambridge?"

They talked about Dot, how horrible it must be for her to have lost her husband so young, and now this, and how lucky it was that at least Dot had Rose, though wasn't she the strangest little girl? She didn't seem to have many friends and what kind of mother would let her run around in her brother's clothes and chop her hair off like that?

"She's not strange," Ava said. She cleared her throat and spoke louder. "Rose is a lovely young woman."

Two of the women in front of her turned and looked at Ava.

"She's good friends with my son," Ava said. A flush of heat rose up along the back of her neck. As soon as she said it, she felt a sting of guilt, as if she had done something wrong.

Debbie moved her mouth as if to speak and Ava braced herself. Then Bob Gallagher shouted, "We've found something!" The women stopped looking at Ava and then everyone was running forward. Ava sprang forward, too, moving to the front, crowding around a patch of land. Her breath came in hard catches. Bob Gallagher was holding up a muddy sandal, the strap hanging like a tongue. His hands were shaking. He held it high up so everyone could see, the lights hitting the silver buckle.

"Oh, for Heaven's sakes," someone said. "That's my Marsha's sandal. She lost it last week."

The sandal was handed over to the woman, who took one look at it and dropped it back on the ground "It's ruined," she announced.

They all went home after that, even though Ava felt they should keep looking. "There's tomorrow," said Bob Gallagher, but was there? What if they had gone a foot deeper into the woods and found something? Ava stared into the woods. She'd go by herself if all that dark didn't make her feel suffocated.

She looked around for support, but no one else seemed interested, no longer eager, as they were when the walk had begun. The group started back. This time, Ava was in the lead, but the only sound was the crunch of the leaves under everyone's feet, and the swish of a branch that caught in someone's clothing. As soon as they left the woods and hit Warwick Avenue, it was as if someone had turned on a light switch. The world seemed so bright, shined up as a spinning coin. "See you tomorrow," Ava said, but no one responded.

She came back to the house, happy to see that Lewis had double-locked the front door like she had asked. His bedroom door was closed, but she heard his music. Her son was here. He was fine. She opened the door to check on him, to see his face. He was asleep on his bed. She shut off his radio, threw a blanket over him, and turned out the lights.

The night stretched out in front of her, cold and lonely. Ava looked out the window. Some of the neighbors were still milling around, talking to each other, and here she was alone.

She heard a motorcycle, and then a knock, and she felt flooded with relief. She opened the door and there was Jake.

They sat in the living room and she quietly told him about her night. He cleared his throat. "I've been thinking," Jake said, and then she noticed how carefully dressed he was, in a clean silky white shirt, his hair combed back. "This isn't going to get better, Ava."

"Don't say that," she said quietly. "You don't know that."

"No one's finding him, and it's just feeling uglier and uglier," he said. He leaned forward. "What if you and Lewis and I hightail it out of here?"

"What?"

"I've already made some phone calls. I have work lined up on the West Coast. We could rent a house on the beach. Lewis would love it. You would love it, Ava."

"You want to move? Jake, I can't move. I have Brian threatening custody. If I take our son out of state—well, he's just looking for a chance to make things difficult."

"So let him try. We can handle it."

Ava tilted her head. "Are you talking marriage?"

Jake's silence made Ava wish she could burrow under the couch. She knew how he felt about marriage. How many times had he pointed out couples sitting at dinner in restaurants, not saying a word to each other. "That's what married looks like," he said.

"Can't we just see how things go for us, first?"

"I can't just move in with you," she said. "Brian would take Lewis from me and the courts would let him."

"Are you sure about that?"

"You don't know him. He already accuses me of being a floozy. Plus, how can I move Lewis from his school and his friends?"

Jake sighed. "Ava, if Brian were going to do something, wouldn't he have done it by now?"

"I can't risk it," she said.

Because of Lewis, Jake didn't stay that night. In the morning, Ava called her lawyer, but when she got to the part about moving, he cleared his throat. "I don't know if this is the best time. You have to prove you have a stable home, and moving with some guy you're not married to isn't going to do it for a judge."

When she told Jake, later that day, he was silent. "What am I sup-posed to do?" he finally said. "You don't want to be with me?"

"Of course I want to be with you! I am with you! But I told you what the lawyer said."

Ava felt him drifting away. After that, she didn't see or hear from him as often, and when he called, it was so late at night that she had a hard time staying awake. He asked her about her day, and she told him, but every time she brought the conversation to Jimmy, to the neighborhood, he always said the same thing, more and more insistently. "We can leave this behind, Ava," he said. "We can move on."

"I told you I can't leave. Not yet," she told him.

"I don't want a long-distance romance," he said. "Whether this re-lationship goes on or off is all up to you." He was quiet for a moment. "Look, I'm tired. I don't want to get into this tonight. Come meet me at the club tomorrow. We'll really talk."

She felt flooded with relief. They would talk. It was just what she needed. It was always better to discuss things in person than to try to do it over the phone, and wasn't so much of communication nonverbal anyway? She thought of the dark woods, and how safe she might feel if he would search through them with her, how much better it would be if he were there at night.

"I'll see you at eight," he told her. "The Hornet."

Now, Ava sat at a small wooden table across from Jake. He was on his break and had just a half-hour pocket of time he could devote to her. Usually, he took her hands and kissed the tips of her fingers. Tonight, he didn't reach for her, and even when he had been playing, she could tell something was wrong. The notes sounded bristling, as if he were forcing them. She noticed, too, how he now kept checking his watch, shifting in his seat. She wanted to touch his hair and smooth it from his face. She wanted to rest her forehead against his, as if his thoughts might race into hers. Instead, she reached out a hand for his, but he pulled back. "Hands all wet from my beer," he apologized, wiping them on a napkin before reaching for his drink again. Conversation buzzed all around her, but her own words stuck in her throat.

Ava felt her hair frizzing in the swampy heat of the club. Another hour and all the pin curl would be gone and her clothes would smell like cigarettes. She moved closer to Jake, scraping her chair on the floor. "I've missed you," she said. Her voice sounded strange to her, like it had rusted. "I've really missed you," she said again. Every cell of her seemed to be snapping awake. She wanted to bite his shoulder, to take his hand and put his fingers to her mouth.

"I've really missed you, too," he told her. "Don't take it personally."

But how could she not take things personally? All the advice in the magazines told her to let the man call the shots. To talk about what he was interested in, to wear your hair for him. Cook his favorite meals. Make his friends your friends. She had done all that and more with Brian and look where that had gotten her. She had learned to fish because it was something Brian loved, even though the rock and sway of the boat made her nauseous. He had urged her to dye her hair blonde and she had, bleaching out her skin tones, making her silky hair feel like straw. "I admit it was a mistake," Brian had told her, giving her money to go and dye it back to its natural brunette.

Jake hadn't asked her for anything. "I like everything about you," he had said, but clearly there was something about her now that bothered him. What was she supposed to do? Who was she supposed to be?

She smoothed her dress, white eyelet cotton with a fitted top and tight waist and little cap sleeves, with a built-in crinoline that made the circle skirt sway. She knew she looked good. Four men had tried to pick her up as she walked to the club, and she had ignored every one of them. "Hey, good-looking," they had called. But now, Jake was staring past her. He drained his beer and then motioned for the waitress, pointing to his empty glass. "You look like you haven't been sleeping," he told her. "Or eating. Look at the shadows under your eyes."

"It's all that's going on in the neighborhood—" she said.

"I want you and Lewis to leave with me. I don't know how many times I have to say it."

The waitress brought a beer and he took a swig of it, wiping his mouth off with the back of his hand. "Look, I know this horrible thing happened, but we have a chance to leave it behind."

"I told you. I can't just leave right now. There's all this with Brian—"

"It's not about Brian." Jake set his beer down, leaving a rim of foam on the table. "What has Brian done exactly, except threaten?"

"I had to hire a lawyer," Ava said tightly.

"Come with me, Ava."

She cupped her glass of wine, trying to keep her hands from shaking. "I want you to stay here," she said, her mouth dry. "With me and Lewis. I need you to help me get through this."

He leaned back in his chair, away from her. He looked at her as if he hadn't slept in her arms or kissed her mouth, or sang Billie Holiday songs to her. Brian had kept the lights off during sex, but Jake always wanted to see her.

"Why can't you stay?" she persisted. "Did the cops come to talk to you again? Is that what this is about? They talk to me all the time. We can form a united front here." She shook her head. "Something's going on with you and I don't even know what it is."

He twirled his beer glass around in his fingers. "You have to make the decision, Ava. Come with me or stay here."

Ava took her glass of wine and drained it. She knew nothing about wines, but this one tasted sharp and vinegary in her mouth. What she had loved most about him was that he had made her feel that she was steering the relationship. "I can't leave," Ava said. "And you won't stand by me. Doesn't what I want matter?"

"You're not listening to me. I want you to come with me."

"And I told you we can't."

"Ava." Jake looked pained, as if he were just seeing her for the first time.

"This is about you, not me," Ava whispered. "This is about something that happened to you and I don't even know what it is." Ava felt as if the world had dislodged. When had he changed and she hadn't noticed it? Was it when she was out walking the neighborhood looking for Jimmy and wishing Jake was with her? She wanted him to tell her he'd stay with her and fight, that he'd support her until this was over and be loyal to her. She yearned to kiss his face and bring him back to her. Tears pricked behind her lids and she willed her eyes to dry. She sat up straighter. "What if I come later, when it's all sorted out with Brian?"

"And when will that be? Six months? A year? Will we get to talk on the phone or are you worried Brian's going to tap your phone, too? Should I send smoke signals so they can't be traced?"

The room folded like origami. She had had too much wine. "Why are you doing this?" Ava asked him. His face turned serious, but she didn't really want to wait to hear what he would say, because she had heard it all before, from other men. She knew what it all really meant. It had to be a smoke screen for something else. *I'm not good enough for you, Ava. You'll find the right person. You'll be happier without me.* It was all just another way of saying good-bye, good-bye, good-bye, I'm moving on. The thing she had loved the most about him was he was easygoing, but now she saw how wrong she had been to think that was a good thing, because here it was, so easy for him to leave her.

She didn't know how she stood up, but she did, balancing her hands against the edge of the chair. "Ava, wait," he said. He was saying something else, but she couldn't hear him anymore. She kept rising. She noticed he didn't get up, too. What a fool she had been, wasting her kisses on him. Shame on her for believing this time might be different. She remembered her mother had told her once that the way to true love was to find someone who would be good to you when things came crashing down around you. Someone who would think you were beautiful even when you had the flu, who would let you weep so hard on his shoulder you might ruin his shirt. "It's easy to love someone when things are good," her mother had told her.

The skirt of Ava's new dress bloomed out around her, the crinoline scratching her thighs. An edge of it caught on a splinter in a chair and made a tiny rip. Twenty-five dollars for this dress, but she'd never wear it again.

"I'm staying," she said. "I have to."

He stared at her. "I asked and you answered," he said flatly, and then she turned before he could say anything more to her, before she could see his expression, and walked toward the door. Like an idiot, she kept expecting him to follow her and grab her arm and tell her, *Wait Ava, I'll help you. We need to be together. I love you.* She got to the door and swung it open. She felt the sharp cool of the evening on her face, like a kiss. She couldn't help it—she turned and the table was empty, and there was Jake, climbing the stage as if he hadn't just broken up with the woman he was supposed to love. Saxophone in hand, he was smiling at the cheering crowd, at the women leaning forward, their bare shoulders gleaming in the light. "How're you doing tonight, Boston!" he shouted. The applause was like pony kicks. Her whole body felt as if it didn't belong to her anymore.

As soon as she got in the car, Ava started to cry. But after a few minutes, she collected herself. She started the car. She would drive home, take off this stupid dress and throw it out, and tell herself that Jake had been a dream, and now she was awake, and if she were lucky, she would stay that way. She would never let herself dream again.

The tears came back and didn't stop until she reached Trapelo Road. She turned onto Abbott Road, swiping at her eyes with her fingers. It was nearly midnight, but a woman was walking along the side of the road, her face hidden in a silk scarf, a thin-looking jacket bundled around her even though it was the beginning of June. No one should be out alone this time of night, especially after everything that had happened.

She slowed and got closer, and the woman tilted her face up, and Ava saw Dot's strong nose, her startled blue eyes, the fiery hair. Ava pulled over and Dot stopped and stared at Ava as if she didn't know her. A curl flew into her face, but Dot didn't bother to brush it away. "Dot," Ava called. "Let me give you a lift."

Dot hesitated.

"Come on, it's late," Ava said. "You shouldn't be out here walking all by yourself." Dot peered at Ava. "Is Rose okay? Are you?"

Dot started to speak and then shook her head.

"Please. Get in the car."

Dot slowly climbed in and then shut the door. "Rose is with a neighbor. I didn't leave her alone," Dot said.

"Of course, you wouldn't have done that," Ava said. She thought of Lewis, asleep in their house, the doors double-locked.

"I've wanted to come see you. I haven't stopped thinking about you since all of this happened," Ava said. "I didn't want to just barge in."

Dot stared out the window. "Dot?" Ava said. She wanted to grasp her hand, to share everything she knew about Jimmy, every memory, as if it might help, but Dot turned to her, and her gaze was stony.

"Please," Dot said finally. "Can we not talk?" She lifted her neck and shut her eyes. "If I get a call from one more reporter I'll scream. Always the same question. *Where did he go that day? Do you know what happened?* If I knew, don't they think I would have said something?"

"Of course you would have."

"Do you know people I haven't seen or heard from in years have been calling me? People telling me that this wouldn't have happened if Benjamin was still alive, if there had been a man in the house. As if a man could have done anything different." Ava looked at Dot's hands, the veins ropey, her nails bitten. "I was a fool to let Jimmy run around loose."

"Do you want to stop somewhere and get coffee?" Ava asked, but Dot shook her head. "The priest keeps telling me it's an act of God, but all that does is make me wonder what kind of God would act that way? He wants to do things like that, then what do I need Him for?"

Ava drove slowly. She felt Dot beside her, Dot's red curls ruffling in the wind. She thought of Jimmy standing on her porch that day, his wide smile. "Dot," she said. "I have to tell you something."

Dot held up her hand. "Don't," she said. "Please, don't tell me anything. I don't have room in my head."

Ava hesitated. "I just wanted to say I was sorry."

"I know my Jimmy hung around your house, even when Lewis wasn't there," Dot said. "Maybe I was glad I had time to myself. Maybe I was glad he had a place to go, another adult to watch him. We were friends. What was I going to say about it?"

"We're still friends."

"You had plenty of boyfriends. What could you possibly want with a boy?"

"It wasn't like that—"

"I found a love note he wrote you in his drawer." Dot stared straight ahead out the window. "I didn't know what to do with it, what to say to him, so I left it there. I didn't say anything to him about it, but the next day I was in his room cleaning, and the note was gone."

"I never got a love note," Ava said. "He was just a kid. He didn't know what love was."

"And now he won't ever know, will he?" Dot folded her hands. "I stuck up for you in this neighborhood," she said. "When people called you 'the Jew,' I told them not to talk that way."

A wire tightened in Ava's spine. "Who called me that?"

"Doesn't matter."

Let her talk, Ava thought. Let her say whatever ugly thing she was going to say. If Ava was in her position, she'd probably be coming apart, too. It didn't have to mean anything, and if it didn't really carry weight, well, then, it didn't have to hurt. Ava pulled onto Warwick Avenue. The neighborhood was dark and quiet. She thought of how Dot used to bring over cakes, thanking her for letting Rose and Jimmy hang out at her house and eat countless meals there. "You're a great neighbor," Dot wrote on a card she had sent Ava. "And a good friend."

"Everyone loved my husband, did you know that?" Dot said abruptly. "He was the nicest guy in the world. He was this big, strapping, handsome guy. When the streets were snowed in, he'd get out the shovel and clear the walk. If I was sick, he'd go get the groceries. He remembered birthdays and anniversaries and he was always smiling. You would have liked him. And I bet he would have liked you, and not the way you think, either, because he was so crazy for me that there just wasn't room for anyone else. You might be beautiful, but even if I was in curlers and Pond's cream, my Benjamin would have gone for me."

Jake was crazy for me, too, Ava thought, and then she thought how stupid that was, the many ways you could fool yourself. She had never met or known Benjamin, and only knew what Dot and the neighbors told her about him, and then, it was all so reverential, she didn't really know what to believe. Maybe Dot's husband really did dote on her and never cheated. Perhaps he came home every evening with a smile and waltzed her in her housedress and pearls and kissed her nose. When he died, the last thought he had might have been about how much he wanted to see her face.

She pulled up in front of Dot's house and let the motor idle.

"Isn't it funny that it's easier to talk about Benjamin than about Jimmy? Maybe it's because I know how Benjamin's story ended." She looked at Ava. "You think you know how your life is going to turn out and then it turns around and kicks you in the teeth. You don't know what's in store for you, and maybe it's better that you don't."

"Do you want to stay at my place?" Ava blurted. "So you won't be alone?"

"Alone? There can be a hundred people near me and I'll still be alone," Dot said.

"You have Rose."

Dot averted her face. "Yes, I have Rose," she said.

"You can call me," Ava said. "It doesn't matter what time."

"I won't call, but thank you."

"I'll check on you tomorrow," Ava offered. "I'll make you and Rose dinner if you like."

Dot shook her head. She got out of the car heavily, as if she were sleepwalking. She made her way up the walk and the last thing she did before she went inside was to flip the switch for the outside light, so it shone brightly, like a beacon.

❖ Chapter Ten ❖

Jake didn't call. Every time the phone rang, Ava jumped to answer, but it was always a wrong number or someone wanting to sell her something. At work, every time she heard the glass door open to the reception area, she looked up expectantly, waiting to see his face, but it was never him. I never promised you anything, he had told her, but hadn't he? Wasn't a kiss a promise? Wasn't wanting to meet Lewis a contract?

Lewis didn't seem to notice Jake was gone from Ava's life. June turned into July, and sometimes at night she heard him crying and she'd go in, but as soon as she opened the door, he had the covers over his head. She once heard him talking to Rose in his room, the two of them mapping out where they'd look next. She didn't interfere.

Ava began to have conversations in her head with Jake, and the more she did, the more furious she became. Why hadn't he been more supportive? How could he expect her to upend her life? Imagine him not calling her or giving her time!

One day, when she didn't have to work until the afternoon, she put on her favorite red dress and earrings and heels and then she took the car and drove to Jake's Cambridgeport house. She was going to confront him, give him one last chance. "Don't chase," the women at work always cautioned each other, as did the glossy magazines, but Ava told herself she needed to make sure, and that was different. And besides, what did she really have to lose?

By the time she reached his neighborhood, she felt dipped in sweat. Her dress was pasted along her back and her curls were fuzzing. She fluffed them with her free hand and then turned onto Jake's block, an enclave of apartment buildings and old houses, and there was a moving truck. When she got out of the car, her body was shaking. All her plans began to fade. The front door slapped open and a young couple sprang out of the house, laughing, holding hands. The woman was wearing a gingham shirt tied above her waist.

"Are you lost?" the man asked Ava.

"I don't know." Ava stared at them and then at the moving truck.

"Can we help you?" The wife's voice was full of bells.

Ava could have made something up, that she was indeed lost and needed directions back to Waltham, but all her energy seemed to have left her. Plus, she hated lying. "My boyfriend used to live here," she said. The man and the woman exchanged glances, and she felt like an idiot. What they must think, Ava thought, and then she turned to go back to the car.

"Wait!" the woman said and Ava stopped and looked back at her. The woman was still holding her husband's hand. "Did you want to come in?" the woman asked.

"I've never been inside," Ava admitted.

"It's just empty rooms now, but go have a look if you want."

Ava hesitated. "Really, it's fine," the woman encouraged. "We don't mind, do we, Bobby?"

"Be our guest," Bobby said.

Ava didn't know what she expected. Maybe that she'd feel Jake in the rooms, that she'd find a photo of herself that he had left behind, but all she felt was empty. He had sold his house so fast, the same way he had left her. She wandered the rooms, the big living room with a bay window, a smaller room that must have been the bedroom, the kitchen and the bath. The rooms smelled faintly of Ajax and floor polish. The windows sparkled and light danced across the wood floors. She sat in the middle of the bedroom, running her fingers on the floor. Lewis, who had believed in magic, told her once that rooms carried the personalities of the people who had lived there, that if you shut your eyes you could hear them whispering to you. She had laughed at that time, but now she shut her eyes and strained to hear what message Jake might have left her. All she heard was the sound of a plane flying overhead.

Ava got up, smoothing her dress, rubbing her ankles. Wherever he was, Jake wasn't here, and she was, and that was a problem.

She walked out. The man and woman were in the back of the truck. They couldn't see her, which was a relief because the last thing Ava wanted was to have to chat right now. She quickly made her way to her car and drove off.

Ava arrived at work just a few minutes late. Her dress was really too fancy for the office, her heels too high, but she couldn't afford to take the time to go home and change. Well, the other girls would think she had a date. They'd be impressed. She had made the mistake of saying the words *my boyfriend* at work a month ago, something the other women never let up on. They both wanted to know who he was, what he did, and how serious it was, and every answer Ava came up with seemed to be the wrong one. "A jazz musician? Really?" Charmaine had said, although she really seemed to mean "Couldn't you do better than that?"

As soon as Ava sat down, Betty came over. "Jeeze Louise, what's with the sad puss?"

"I broke up with my boyfriend," Ava said. She didn't know why she said that. It was and it wasn't true, but she didn't want the women thinking she'd been dumped. Betty peered closer at her, and that made Cathy and Charmaine study her, too. "It wasn't working out so I gave him the boot," Ava said. "You were right. A jazz musician is no boyfriend. I should have listened to you."

"Didn't I tell you?" Cathy said, but her voice was sad when she said it.

"I dated an engineer once," Charmaine said. "The first day he came to get me, my mother told me, 'He's not for you' because he hadn't bought her a little gift. I didn't believe her, but then I saw how stingy he was, and soon after, he just broke it off."

Betty put one hand on Ava's shoulder. "Forget that jerk," she said.

All that day, the women were kind to her. Betty loaned Ava her smock so Ava wouldn't get carbon marks on her dress. At eleven, when the other women went to break, Cathy stopped at Ava's desk. "You want to come?" she said.

Cathy's face was open, but Ava didn't think she could move. "Thank you for asking," she said. "But I think I'll work through this."

Cathy put one hand on Ava's shoulder, a touch so gentle, Ava wanted to grab her hand and hold on to it. "If you change your mind, you know where to find us."

When the women returned, Betty put a small paper plate with a lemon square on it on Ava's desk. "I know you aren't hungry, but eat. Sugar gives you energy."

Ava took a bite of the square because the women were watching her. It was crumbly and overly sweet and the middle didn't taste as if it were quite done, but she ate all of it. "Delicious," she said. "Just what I needed."

"My mom made it," Charmaine said. "Everyone loves her world-famous squares."

Ava couldn't concentrate on sinks and tubs and toilets today. The new claw-footed tubs made her think of Jake soaking after a session. The plaid sink that no one wanted reminded her of the plaid shorts she had worn to picnic with Jake when he had told her he couldn't wait to get her out of them. She thought of Jake, driving somewhere new, a U-Haul loaded with all the things he owned pulled behind him. She didn't even know his new address.

At ten to five, before the closing bell rang, Betty leaned over. "If you want to sneak out, I'll cover for you," Betty said. "I'll tell Richard you're on the rag. That always shuts him up."

Ava quickly got up, keeping her typewriter uncovered, her little lamp switched on. If she ran into Richard now, she'd pretend she was going to the ladies' room. She nodded at the other women and headed for the elevator, not relaxing until she was back out on the street.

As soon as she got home, the phone was ringing and she picked it up. Jake. It was Jake.

"Mrs. Lark," said a voice. "Did you know one of your boyfriends has a record?"

Ava swallowed. "Who is this? What are you talking about?"

"Hank Maroni. One of your boyfriends, Jake Riverton. Actually Jake Richardson. He did time for assault in juvie. Did you know that? Did you know that he had another name?"

She flinched. Assault. It was an ugly word and she couldn't believe it, but suddenly, sickeningly, it explained why Jake wanted to get out of town so fast. What was she supposed to say? "It's got to be a mistake," she said. "Jake would never harm anyone."

"Where is he now, Mrs. Lark?"

"I don't know," she said. "I don't know anything anymore." She began to hear something humming in her ear, like the whine of an insect.

"If you hear from him, if he calls you, you let us know," Hank said. "We're going to be checking further into this." The humming in Ava's ear grew louder. She had never seen Jake even get angry. Could he really be violent and she hadn't seen it? No, it couldn't be true. She wouldn't believe it because then it would mean that she hadn't known him at all. It would show how stupid she really had been to love him. She hung up the phone and then she planted her hands flat on the table, as if that could stop their shaking.

Jake was gone from her life. The next few days, she forced herself not to think about him, not to remember. If she felt like crying, she did it quickly and then drew herself up. No matter how she yearned for him, she knew he wasn't worth it. She wouldn't waste time trying to find him. She'd only try to find Jimmy.

Now, when the phone rang, she didn't immediately wonder if it was Jake. Instead, she thought it could be the boy, and why not? If Jimmy was going to call anyone, he would call her. She was an adult he trusted, but not a parent who might punish him. And she had already kept one secret for him.

About a year ago, she had been home from work with the tag end of a cold, when the bell rang. She had thought it must be the mailman with a package, but there was Jimmy, in a pressed white shirt and dark pants and good leather shoes. "Lewis isn't home," she told him, a blossom of tissue at her nose.

"That's okay. Can I come in?" he asked.

She didn't know why she let him in. Maybe because he looked so pained. She showed him in and he sat carefully on the edge of the couch. "Are you okay?" she asked.

His dark eyes looked everywhere but at her face. "Jimmy," she said his name, and then he looked at her and his face was so full of longing, she felt struck.

"I like you," he said, his voice a rasp. He looked at his feet, at his carefully shined shoes.

"I like you, too. I like all the neighborhood kids."

He sat there, fumbling his hands in his lap.

"Is something wrong?" Ava asked. "Do you want some juice or chocolate milk?"

"I've never kissed a girl," he whispered.

She didn't laugh. "You're twelve. You have lots of time for that," she said. "That's nothing to be ashamed of."

"Would you give me kissing lessons?'

Ava stood up then. Her nose was red and she hadn't combed her hair. She wasn't wearing any makeup and she knew she must have looked a thousand years old. Yet here was this boy.

"Why would you ask me that?" she said quietly.

"I told you. I like you. I think you're beautiful."

"Jimmy—" She sat back down. "I want to tell you something," she said. "I am flattered more than I can tell you, but I'm far too old for you, plus I'm your best friend's mother, plus I want you to save your kisses for someone your age who deserves them."

His mouth wobbled. "James," she said. She had never heard anyone call him that, but she knew it sounded more adult.

He lowered his head. "Everyone acts like I have cooties. I have no one to do things with except Lewis and Rose. No girl will sit next to me. Not the way they do with Lewis, even though he doesn't notice."

She knew that. She had seen the way Lewis missed all the signals Rose was throwing toward him. She sighed. "You wait," she said. "Girls are dumb about these things when they're young, but when they get older they smarten up. They see that your best feature isn't your eyes or your thick hair, but your good heart."

"So you won't give me kissing lessons?"

"No. But I want you to promise me something. That your first kiss will be from someone near your age who loves you, who really sees you for who you are."

He stood up. "You won't tell anyone I asked, will you?" he said and she lifted up her hand and made a motion as if she were locking her lips shut.

"You probably shouldn't come around here anymore when Lewis isn't home, either," she said quietly.

"Why not? I can't even talk to you?"

"Of course you can. But when Lewis is here."

He still came by. He brought over a Wooly Willy toy, a big, bald cartoon face under a bubble of plastic, with tiny metal particles settled on the bottom, and he showed her how all you had to do was touch the screen with the special magnetic wand and you could guide the particles to make whiskers or eyebrows or a big mop of hair. She made him grilled-cheese sandwiches and TV dinners with apple brown betty for dessert, and when he didn't touch the peas, she didn't say a word. Still, she became more careful when he was around. She didn't hug him the way she used to. When Jimmy came over to see Lewis, the two of them would head to Lewis's room and shut the door. Ava wondered if Jimmy had told Lewis that he sometimes came over here by himself. She wondered what her son might think, but as far as she could tell, Lewis never treated her differently or even looked at her with suspicion.

One evening, when she was in her room reading and the kids were playing cards in the dining room, she heard Jimmy ask Lewis, "Do you have a father who's still alive?"

"Of course I do," Lewis said hotly.

"Where is he, then? Why doesn't he come to see you?"

"My father is crazy about me." Ava heard the stutter in Lewis's voice. "He writes me letters all the time. He's tall and strong and he used to win prizes for being the best salesman and stuff."

"Really? Can I see the letters?"

There was a silence. "They're private," Lewis said.

"Do you have pictures of him? What did he look like?"

Ava walked into the room. "Who wants to go to Brigham's for ice cream?" she said, and the boys jumped up.

The whole drive to Brigham's, she worried. She saw how wistful her son was when he talked about his dad. Lewis didn't hear the anger in Brian's voice when he called to talk to Ava. He didn't know that his father could have easily come and visited him but simply chose not to. To him, his father was a hero and Ava was somehow the reason why Brian left.

She pulled into the parking lot. "Come on," she said. "Let's go get something sweet."

SEVEN MONTHS AFTER Jimmy had vanished, no one went on the neighborhood patrol anymore, though people did keep their eyes and ears open. Even the kids were walking to the elementary school again without an adult. The detectives finally stopped asking anyone anything. They stopped coming to the neighborhood. The case was cold, they said. They had done their best. No clear suspects had emerged. Jake must be off the hook, Ava thought, but it didn't change anything.

It was October and Ava sat watching the rain from her window, the world growing gray, and listened to the news. Red Army troops had invaded Hungary. Gas prices were going up. But there were no longer reports about the Jimmy Rearson case.

She still missed him. Dot had grown thinner and almost never changed out of her bathrobe. Rose and Lewis were at the same school now, both secretive and sullen, always scribbling away in a notebook or whispering together. Ava was so lonely she thought sometimes she might go mad.

Some nights, Ava stared out the picture window and looked across the street at Dot's house. She almost always saw Dot, standing on her porch staring out at the night sky. Ava would wave, but Dot never responded. If ever Ava walked over there, Dot didn't want to talk. "We don't have to talk," Ava said. Instead, she sat there with Dot. Occasionally, Ava looked across at her own house. The inexpensive paint she had bought for the shutters was peeling already. The porch steps were lopsided. No matter what she did, her home still looked shabby, as if it had been stuck into the neighborhood like a mistake. She felt heavy with fatigue, but stifled her yawns until Dot inevitably pushed herself up from her chair. "Well, "Dot said, "Time to go." And then she let herself into her house, leaving Ava alone to walk back to her own.

❖ *Chapter Eleven* ❖

Lewis woke up to the first December snowfall sifting against his window. He and Jimmy would have immediately run outside. Jimmy always threw snowballs, but Lewis liked to collect snow to look at under the microscope. He had tried to get Jimmy to look through the eyepiece at all the different shapes, but Jimmy tended to dawdle. By the time he took a gander, the flakes had usually melted.

He grabbed his notebook and wrote: *Jimmy liked snow. He may have gone someplace cold.* Alaska had been one of the places they had pricked on the map. If Jimmy didn't go himself, maybe someone took him there. He wondered how he could get ahold of the Alaska papers to see if there might be a photo of Jimmy. He could call the cops and be a hero.

He picked up a book, *The Time Machine,* and went into the kitchen to read. His mother was sitting at the table, staring at the phone.

Lewis knew whose call she was waiting for. The one good thing to come out of everything was that the jerk Jake was gone. He didn't know if his mother had broken it off, or if Jake had just decided it all on his own, but things felt different around the house. Lewis didn't want to ask his mother what had happened with Jake. Who knows, maybe she'd say, "Oh, yes, that reminds me," and call Jake up and then everything would just start up all over again.

"Want something to eat, honey?" Ava said. She got up and sliced him a piece of supermarket yellow cake she had on the counter. She poured milk in a jelly glass and set it in front of him.

"We should call Dad," he said.

Ava started. She wiped her hands along the skirt of her apron. "Why on earth would we want to do that?"

"We're alone. Everyone else here has a father."

"Not everyone," she said, and he knew she meant Rose. "Now drink your milk," she said shortly and went to the sink to wash the dishes, noisily splashing water. He toyed with the cake, cutting it with the edge of his fork. He didn't like it very much because it had no frosting and it was one of those day-old cakes she got on sale that always tasted like all the ingredients had gone bad. She left the room and he heard her rattling around in the living room as he chewed the dry cake. Maybe she was thinking about calling his father, he thought. You never knew. Rose had told him that her mother said that there was nothing worse for a woman than to be alone, that it was unnatural and unhealthy. She told Rose it had been the luck of the draw that her husband had died and she would get married again in a heartbeat, but the problem was nobody wanted a woman who had already been married, and especially one with children. It was even worse if you were divorced because that meant you had done something wrong, you hadn't been able to keep your man. "No one wants leftovers," Dot had said.

"That leaves both our moms out," Rose said to Lewis.

Lewis began mashing up the remaining cake on his plate so it would look like he had eaten most of it and his mother wouldn't start in about wasting food. He thought about his dad. His mother didn't have to be a leftover. His father wasn't dead like Rose's. Maybe Lewis hadn't seen him for years, but his father was still alive and all his mom had to do was get to him, show him what he was missing, and surely he'd come around. The last time Lewis had spoken to him was a year ago, on Lewis's birthday, when his father promised him a present that must have gotten lost in the mail. But he heard his mother on the phone some nights talking to him, and even though she sounded angry, he never heard her hang up on him. If his father knew how dangerous things were, wouldn't he at least call, if not come for a visit?

His mother came back in from the other room and he felt her watching him. He kept his fork in midair, not moving, waiting to see what she would do.

"This is cake," she said. "You can't even finish cake."

She pulled out a chair and sat down beside him. "You have your whole life ahead of you," she said quietly. "You have so many people around you who care about you." She tried to smooth his hair, but he pulled back. He picked up *The Time Machine,* which he didn't even like that much. He had thought it would tell him something practical about time travel, how you might go back in time and change what had happened, like with Jimmy or his dad, but it was clearly all made up. If Lewis had the chance to go back in time, he knew what he would do, and it wouldn't be going to that stupid library after the dentist. He would go straight to Jimmy's house. He would find his dad and beg him not to leave and his father would listen.

He felt his mother's gaze. He dipped back into the book, the only way he could think of to get her to leave him alone, and as soon as she did, he shut the book and put it aside and started thinking about Jimmy all over again.

She wouldn't be so friendly if she had known what he had done, that he could have saved Jimmy if he had met him on time. His mom might think he had a lot of people around him who cared about him, but who were those people, and why didn't he see them?

His teachers told him they cared about him, but only if he would stop interrupting their lessons with questions and try to be more like everyone else. His teachers liked him best when he didn't bother them at all, when he sat at his desk and had no more presence than a ghost.

Who did he really have to talk to, except for Rose? He was so glad they were in the same school now, that they took the bus together, and sometimes just seeing her walk by him in the halls made him feel better. His world was narrowing, closing in like two walls pressed together. Everything was split up between before and after. Before, he used to spend every day with Jimmy and Rose, roaming the neighborhood, sitting in the woods behind Northeast Elementary with a bag of jelly sandwiches, but those woods were off-limits now, and Jimmy was gone. The only future Rose and he discussed now was about finding Jimmy. Even then, he felt as if he was falling behind, as if he needed her more than she needed him. She was always scribbling in her notebook, filling the pages, whipping them ahead so furiously they sometimes tore, but his notebook had only three pages filled. Every place Lewis had listed as a place to visit for clues was now crossed out. Jimmy wasn't at the library. There were no clues at the Wal-Lex roller rink. No one he had talked to had seen him. He often stared at the blank pages, trying to think what he could write down. He sank into gloom and worry every time he saw Rose, because he was afraid she'd ask to see his notebook and her face would flood with disappointment when she saw how little he had written. He wanted to take a peek at what she was writing, but she always had her notebook clutched to her chest, and besides, if he asked, he would have to share his. "We can find him," she insisted, "you have to think positive," but Lewis wasn't so sure. How long before she would tire of his doubt and leave him, too?

That night, he couldn't sleep. Lewis felt as if his skin were moving separately from him, crawling like a live thing. He touched his arms, his legs, as if that would keep the skin in place.

He opened the door and could see there was no light under his mother's door across the hall. The radio she listened to at night, the endless loop of talk shows, the voices tangling into one another like strings of yarn, was quiet, which meant she was sleeping. He went back in his room, grabbed up a flashlight, and shone it into all the corners of his room. There were his books, most of them loaners from Rose, the pages turned back, the covers torn from rereading, plus a few books from the library that he needed to return. He saw his magic tricks, all the old kits he had cobbled together, pushed next to his books on Houdini. He thought of Houdini's wife, all those years waiting and waiting for him to give her a sign that he was still alive, holding séances for ten years, and finally giving up. Everyone thought that was proof that the dead stayed dead, that there was no such thing as ghosts or an afterlife or, if there was, the living couldn't reach them. But maybe she gave up too soon, Lewis thought. Maybe Houdini had appeared in a way she hadn't noticed, like a cool breeze blowing on her on a hot summer day, or her favorite flower suddenly strewn in her path. Who knew how people who were dead could communicate with you?

From where he was standing, he could just make out Rose's window across the street. He moved closer and pointed the flashlight at her window and clicked it on and off, like Morse code. S-O-S. Over and over. Rose, he thought, as if he were calling her on the phone. Pick up, pick up, pick up. He clicked the flashlight off. He was just about to put it down, to turn and go back to bed, when he saw something blinking, cutting through the darkness.

S-O-S. S-O-S. Rose was sending him a message.

HE DIDN'T SEE Rose the next morning or on the bus, but later that day, after school, he headed outside the building and there she was, waiting for him on the sidewalk. "What are you doing here?" he asked.

"I felt you wanted to see me and here I am," she said. She crunched her boots in the snow. "I don't want to take the school bus home. Come on, we'll walk home together," she said.

"How'd you know that?" he asked. They walked all the way to the Northeast schoolyard, dusted off the snow from the swings, and sat down. She leaned back on her swing, twisting it so it would wind her in circles.

"You can do it, too, you know," she said. "Know where and when I might appear." She told him when he was at school and feeling lost, to look for signs that she was around. "It can be as simple as a light suddenly going on," Rose told him. "It can be someone humming a song that you know I like." She tilted her chin to the air. "Sometimes when I think Jimmy's near, it's like everything has a charge. Like something is about to happen."

"I don't know," Lewis said doubtfully. He turned his swing around, scraping his boots along the snow. "Shut your eyes," she ordered. He did. The world went white. He felt the frosty air on his face. "Stay still," she said. "Concentrate. I'm going to walk away and you tell me which direction I went. Keep your eyes closed. When you know, you tell me."

He heard the thump of her feet hitting the ground when she jumped off the swing, but then he couldn't hear anything. He sniffed experimentally at the air. His knee itched and he yearned to scratch it. He felt hopeless. He pointed in back of him. "You're there," he guessed and Rose laughed, and he turned around and opened his eyes and there she was, smiling triumphantly at him while he blinked at her in amazement. "It was no guess," she told him. "You knew."

He felt dizzy. He wanted Rose to stop moving around so quickly, to stay in one place so he could really see her, but she was a blur. She walked over to him and pressed her forehead against his. "Read my thoughts," she said. She closed her eyes. He shut his and he felt a pulse of heat. "What color am I thinking of?" she said. "Don't think. Just let it happen."

"Blue," he guessed, and he opened his eyes to see her smiling at him. "What did I tell you?" she said. "You knew. You just knew."

"Come on, let's get out of here," he said.

They tore around the block to Greer Street and there was Mr. Corcoran, his head covered by a blue watch cap. He was shoveling snow along his walk, but when he saw them, he paused. "Why are you kids on your own?" he said.

"We're with each other," Rose said. "We aren't alone."

Mr. Corcoran dusted his hands off against his pants. "Your mothers know where you are?" he asked. "You're sure about that?"

"My mother's at work," Lewis said.

"Well, maybe she ought to be home with you."

Lewis scowled. He already hated that his mother worked, but it bothered him even more when people commented on it.

Mr. Corcoran studied Rose and Lewis, his gaze falling on the notebook Rose clutched to her chest, which had a photograph of Jimmy Stewart on the cover. "Jimmy Stewart, huh," he said. "He's more than a little *pink,* if you know what I mean."

"He is?" Lewis asked.

"Look at that movie, *Mr. Smith Goes to Washington*," he said. "You think a real American would interrupt a Senate proceeding the way he did? And smile while he was doing it?" He tapped his forehead. "Use your noggin."

"I liked that movie," Lewis said. He had watched it with his mother, a bowl of popcorn between them, and when his mother had cried, he had pretended not to notice.

"That's just the point. You're meant to like it. You're meant to be sucked in and think one thing, while another is going on. You can't trust these Communists," he said. "And do you want to know why?"

"No, why?" Rose said, so politely that Lewis shot her a look.

"Because they lie. They couldn't tell the truth if they wanted to. My Stanley knows that. You kids should know it, too."

Lewis bit down on his lip so he wouldn't laugh. Mr. Corcoran pointed at the sky. "You kids think it's funny, but any second a missile could come down at us," he insisted. "And we wouldn't even see it or be prepared. One minute we're here talking in this nice neighborhood, and two seconds later, *boom,* we're ash. You think it can't happen?" He lifted his two hands in the air and then kamikazied them down. "The Russians hide explosives, did you know that? And there are lots of Reds right here in America. They could be in this neighborhood and we wouldn't even know it."

"Who?" Rose asked. "Who in this neighborhood?"

He tapped Lewis's notebook, the photo of Tony Curtis.

"Him for one."

"He's an actor. He played Houdini," Lewis said. "And he doesn't live here."

"A Jew. Both of them. Houdini was a Commie, though I don't know about Curtis."

"I'm Jewish." A flare of pain rose in his belly. He didn't like the way Mr. Corcoran folded his arms and rocked on his heels. If his Jesus was so great, why hadn't He helped them find Jimmy? He wanted to say it out loud to Mr. Corcoran to see what happened, but he chickened out.

"You kids better get home now," Mr. Corcoran said, dismissing them.

As soon as they were out of sight, Rose made "he's crazy" circles, spinning her hands about her temple, but her mood seemed to have darkened. Lewis didn't feel like roaming the neighborhood anymore. A plane zoomed across the sky. Lewis looked up. He imagined Mr. Corcoran's missile flying down from the sky, aimed right at them, lean and silver as a needle. Would he see it before it struck or would it happen so fast that everything would be obliterated? Would he know a Communist if he saw one? "Rose, do you know any Communists?" he asked, worried.

"Yeah, me. I'm a big, dirty Red and I'm going to eat you. And you're a big, dirty Jew and you drink the blood of babies." She bared her teeth, tickling him until he laughed, too.

Lewis's stomach growled, but Rose seemed in no hurry to go home to dinner. "You hungry?" he asked. She shrugged. "Because I am," he said.

"Then go home and eat."

He studied her, the way she was kicking at the snow in front of her, not going anywhere. "Come with me," he said.

As soon as Lewis brought Rose into his kitchen, where Ava was stirring something in a pot, Rose dipped her head shyly.

"Hi, honey," Ava said. "Did you want to eat with us? Would it be all right with your mother?"

"My mother ate already," Rose said quietly.

"Call her and tell her you're having dinner here," Ava said. "You don't want her to worry."

Rose curled around the phone, speaking in a low voice. "Yes. Okay, I will," she said. She hung up the phone, and for a minute, it almost looked as if she were disappointed. "She said it's fine," Rose said.

"Your company is just what we need," Ava said, setting a plate for Rose. Lewis had eaten enough meals at Dot's to know that his mother wasn't nearly as good a cook as Dot was, but he noticed how Rose was looking longingly at Ava's potatoes boiling on the stove. "Make yourself at home, honey," Ava said.

Every night after that, Ava simply set a plate for Rose and stretched whatever she had planned for dinner. There was never a lot, but all through the winter Ava boiled up spaghetti as a side dish so it would be enough, adding water to the sauce or more milk to the potatoes to increase the servings. Rose showed up and ate every bite of whatever it was, and afterward, Ava always gave her a Tupperware container of food to take home for Dot. "She has to eat," Ava said. "And if not, then you have yourself a nice snack for later." Ava and Lewis always walked Rose home. "I'd love to talk to Dot," Ava said one evening, but the windows were dark, and when Ava knocked, no one came to the door. "You go inside then, honey," Ava said gently. They waited until Rose unlocked the door herself, got inside safely, and closed the door again. Only then did they turn and head back.

One night, though, when Rose didn't show up for dinner, Lewis went to find her. "I'll keep everything on warm," Ava said. He ran to her house, and there she was, standing on the front porch as if she were waiting for him. "Aren't you eating with us tonight?" Lewis said. Then he noticed how red her eyes were, how her hands were trembling. "What aren't you telling me?" he asked.

"You're nuts. I tell you everything," she said. She looked past him, at the blinking street light. Her breath looked like puffs of smoke in the air.

"You can't tell me to sense things about you and then, when I do, tell me it doesn't exist."

"In this case, it doesn't." She shook her head. "I'm just not hungry tonight."

"Fine. I'll see you tomorrow," he said. Lewis got up and bounded back to his own house.

Ava was in the living room, curled up with a book, in dungarees and a sweater, her hair tied back with a kerchief. She looked like a mother, not like a working woman, not like the divorcée the neighbors all talked about.

"What do you think happens when we die?" he asked. Ava started. She turned to him, her face serious. "Why do you want to know that?"

"I just do."

"I'm smart enough to know I don't know," she said finally. "What do you believe?"

He bit on his lip, the place where it was chapped. "I don't know. Maybe there's another parallel world."

"That sounds as good as anything," she told him. Lewis thought of Jimmy, lost in a parallel world, with a whole new set of friends and family, but instead of making him feel better, he felt as if he were trapped inside a maze.

"Rose can't make dinner tonight," he said.

"We'll see her next time," his mother reassured him.

That night, Lewis woke up in the darkness. He blinked at the clock. Four o'clock in the morning. His mother called it the hour of the wolf, the time when nightmares were at their most fierce. He put his hand over his heart, feeling the pulse thump against his fingers. He thought of Rose. After their dinner tonight, his mother had brought a container of chicken and noodles over to Rose and Dot. When she came back, it seemed as if she had been gone for a long time. "What took so long?" Lewis said and Ava shrugged. "We were talking."

"About what?" Lewis said.

"Just things."

"What was Rose doing?" he asked, but Ava walked past him into the kitchen.

Now Lewis went to the window with the flashlight and blinked it, S-O-S, over and over. He waited, but the night stayed dark. She didn't answer, and he felt something loose and unsettling inside of him, like a lightbulb that wasn't screwed in tightly enough.

❖ Chapter Twelve ❖

Rose stood in the kitchen, foraging for breakfast, trying to find something that wasn't stale or with an expiration date of two weeks ago. She found an unopened package of cheese crackers and an apple that was only brown on one side.

She chewed on one of the crackers, which turned powdery on her tongue. Her mother used to wake up at six and have breakfast ready: eggs and toast with bacon or sausage. There used to be clean clothes laid out on her bed, lunch bags for her and Jimmy to take to school. Dot had always kept busy cooking and cleaning, playing cards with neighbors, but now she didn't seem to do anything.

Everything familiar was vanishing, and it scared her. Rose had to wet the chips in the soap dish so she could mash them together into a semblance of a bar. When she came home from school, her mother looked relieved when she saw her, but she never asked her any questions about school or homework, and when Rose brought home a D on a math test for her mother to sign, sure her mother would yell, Dot just scribbled her name without comment. Her mother didn't even suggest Rose go to the teacher and ask for a makeup.

By spring, her mother was someone she didn't know. Rose couldn't even have Lewis over the house anymore because she didn't know how her mother was going to act, if she'd be dressed and speaking in monosyllables or if she'd just be lying on the couch in her ratty night-gown. "I want you home," her mother said, "not traipsing around." But when Rose stayed around, her mother ignored her.

One afternoon, when the only thing in the fridge was an old casserole someone had brought over from the previous week, Rose made a decision. She leafed out a ten from her mother's wallet and went out, even though she wasn't supposed to. If she didn't go and buy groceries, there would be nothing to eat.

The whole walk down Trapelo Road to the Star Market, Rose was nervous. Walk fast, like you know where you are going, the teacher had told the kids. Swing your arms purposefully. Be prepared to run.

She bought two bagfuls of groceries, green peppers and tomatoes and apples, detergent and soap, and when she got home, she put the groceries away and read the back of all the cleaning products to see what to do.

By the end of the night, she had scrubbed the kitchen floor and washed the wood floors in the living room, dining room, and her own bedroom. She had dusted the venetian blinds and folded the laundry, and all she had left to do was straighten up the den. But as soon as she walked in and saw the pile of newspapers, she couldn't help scouring the pages for photographs. Secrets, she knew, could hide in all sorts of places. She looked for the articles that had crowd shots, and then poured over the faces, just in case one might be his. She rummaged in the drawers and found a magnifying glass, then studied each and every face, sure that one might belong to her brother. She stopped at a blurry head of a boy, in the back of the crowd. She circled his face with a pen, so she wouldn't lose sight of him.

"What are you doing?"

Rose looked up. Dot was standing in the doorway in her nightgown, her hair awry. "Doesn't this look like Jimmy?" Rose showed Dot the shot, the place where she had circled a face. Dot took the page to the wastebasket and buried it, and then walked out of room.

Rose fished it out again, smoothing it down. She squinted at the photo. The eyes were wrong. She saw it now.

Rose heard her mother in the kitchen and she went in to find her staring at the cupboards filled with food. "Where did this come from?" Dot demanded. "Did neighbors bring this by?"

"I bought it," Rose said. Dot stared at her. "Do you want to take a walk?" Rose asked her mother.

"What for?" Dot said.

"To be with me, to do something," Rose told her mother. "At least get dressed. Let me wash your bathrobe." She reached out, but Rose's mother flinched and drew the robe more tightly around her. Dot looked around. "Did someone clean in here?" she said. For a moment, Rose thought her mother was going to roll up her robe sleeves and dig into the cleaning that was left, but instead, she shook her head. "I'm just going to lie down," she said.

"We have overdue bills," Rose blurted, waiting for her mother to get mad, to tell her to mind her own beeswax, but Dot just waved her hand. "I'll take care of that," she said, but Rose didn't believe her, and she was terrified.

Rose had just turned fourteen. She couldn't handle all this herself, the cooking, the cleaning, the worrying about her mother and money. She needed to tell someone, but who could she tell? Lewis couldn't really help with something like this. A grown-up could call Social Services and they might take Rose away because she was still a minor. She had heard of things like that happening. It would kill her mother, and it would probably kill Rose, too, having to live with a strange family, with new rules, people who might say they loved her, but you knew deep down that they really didn't.

Her mother was in the other room, probably asleep by now. Rose flew out of the house. She gulped at the air. Come with me, she wanted to scream at her mother. Come with me.

❖ ❖ ❖

ROSE WAS IN her home economics class, trying to figure out how to thread the needle in her sewing machine, when there was a knock on the classroom door. All the girls looked up. A hall monitor, one of the kids, came in and whispered something to the teacher, who looked sternly at Rose and beckoned her over. "Go to the principal's office," she whispered.

The whole way to the principal, Rose knew it was about Jimmy. Jimmy would be standing there. She bit down her lip to keep from crying, stilled her legs to keep from running.

But as soon as she got to the office, the only person standing there was stern-faced Mr. Morang (the kids all called him Lemon, snickering at the joke). "Your mother called," he said. "She wants you to go right home."

"Did something happen?"

Mr. Morang shrugged. "I think she just wants you home," he said gently, and then he went to call her a cab. He told her the secretary would wait outside with her and make sure she got in the car safely.

WHEN ROSE GOT home, there was an envelope attached to the door that said CABBIE on it, a fistful of money inside. She gave it to the driver and came inside, calling, "Mom?"

Rose found her mother in the kitchen, sprawled on the floor in her nightgown and her dirty robe, her feet bare, her hair uncombed. "Mom!" Rose shouted. She crouched down, her heart pounding and reached for her mother's hand. There was a pulse. Her mother jerked her hand away and turned her face to Rose. "I can't do this anymore," Dot said, and hearing her voice, Rose felt so relieved she could have cried.

Rose struggled to get her up. Her mother was heavy and perspiring. She dragged her into the bathroom and ran a bath. She didn't want to see her mother naked, but she pulled the dirty clothes off. "Get in," she ordered, and her mother silently did, sinking into the hot water. "Oh, that feels good," Dot said. Rose was afraid to leave her, so she sat on the toilet, waiting, watching, until her mother's eyes fluttered and then focused on Rose. Dot grabbed the shower curtain and pulled it closed around her, shutting Rose out. "Go," she said, her voice muffled. "I'll be fine."

Rose waited outside the door, leaning forward, listening. She heard the water draining from the tub. She heard her mother's long sigh, and then the door opened and Dot walked down the hall to her room, not looking at Rose, but padding into her room and firmly shutting the door.

THE NEXT DAY, when Rose came home from school, Dot was dressed, and she had even made a snack for Rose: four Ritz crackers and a piece of American cheese. Rose was about to head over to Lewis's for dinner when she heard something crackling in the pan, a snap of grease, the smell of bacon. She wandered into the kitchen and there was Dot making bacon in a pan, slices of bread set out in front of her. "BLTs okay?" Dot asked, and Rose sat down on the chair in wonder. "They're great," she said.

Every night after that, there was some sort of dinner. It was never anything special, but there were eggs and toast ("breakfast for dinner," Dot called it), spaghetti and butter, and even fried chicken and a baked potato. Dot ate, too, and afterward, she did the dishes, humming to herself, staring out the window as if she were the only one there. "Want to watch TV?" Rose asked and Dot shrugged, but she came and sat beside her on the couch. It didn't matter what Rose put on, Dot always seemed to be somewhere else.

It was the beginning of June, the week before school ended, when Rose came home, and right there, in the living room, there were two suitcases, their tops wide open like jaws. Her mother was packing, her face flushed. "I've made a decision," she said. She told Rose they were going to stay with her sister Hope in Pittsburgh, a woman Rose barely knew, and when they were on their feet, they'd get their own place. Maybe in Pittsburgh or in some place else altogether. "She suggested it out of the blue and as soon as I heard it, it felt right," Dot said.

"We're leaving?" Rose said. "You didn't even talk to me about this."

"You're a child. You don't get a decision in this." Dot folded more clothing.

"I'm not a child. And I don't want to go."

"I already called a realtor. He says the market is good, the house should sell quickly."

"What about Jimmy? How can we leave Jimmy?"

Her mother stopped packing and turned to Rose.

"You're going to let him come home to a strange house?" Rose said. "You're going to let him think we didn't care enough about him to stay here? How can you leave?"

"Rose—" Dot warned, but Rose felt a bubble of grief rising in her throat. "Do you think we'll just leave and everything will be all right?" Rose cried.

"We need a change. I want to be someplace where everything doesn't remind me and every morning I don't wake up and wish I hadn't. If the police need to find us, they can." Dot looked around the house. "This is the first day I've felt alive," she said quietly.

Rose fled the house. The streets were empty and the air felt thick and heavy as a coat around her. She was crying when Lewis opened his front door. He grabbed her hand and took her to his room, shutting the door, sitting her down. She couldn't stop crying, so he moved closer and put his forehead against hers, and then she began to tell him what had happened. "I'll write you as soon as I have a real address. I'll call. Pittsburgh's not so far away," she said. She could feel his breath on her face, his mouth so close all she had to do was move a bit closer and his lips would be touching hers. She draped her arms on his shoulders and he let her. She held him so close she felt his heart beating against her. Then she pulled back. "We need to have another pact," she said. She put her hand up and he placed his against hers. "We'll find Jimmy. We'll never give up looking."

"We'll never give up," Lewis assured her.

There was a knock on the door and their hands flew back into their laps. "What's going on?" Ava said, opening the door. Rose looked at Lewis, who had a blank look on his face. "Rose is moving," he said.

Ava walked into the room, knelt down, and cupped Rose's face. "Oh, honey," she said.

ROSE AND DOT were leaving as soon as the house was sold. Already, there was a thick white FOR SALE sign planted in their yard like a dandelion. Rose spent every minute she could with Lewis. "I'll write you every single day," she promised. "As soon as we have a real address, I'll give it to you. Maybe I can figure out a way to visit, or you can visit us." As soon as she said it, she knew how stupid it sounded. She didn't even know what Pittsburgh was like. How would she get from there to here again, if her mother wouldn't drive her or put her on a train, two things she could tell you right now her mother would never do? How would Lewis get to her? She kept asking her mother for her aunt's address in Pittsburgh, to write it down so she could give it to Lewis. "I'll get it," Dot said, but then she never did.

The neighbors were murmuring about their move. Even though they lowered their voices when Rose walked by, she heard the comments. How could a mother move when her son was still missing? What if he came back? What if there was only an empty house to greet him? There was something wrong with the whole picture and what did you expect when it was a woman alone? But Dot kept talking about how this was going to be a whole new life, how they'd be settled in a new neighborhood before school even started up again.

One night, Rose lay sprawled across her bed, ignoring the empty boxes Dot had pushed into her room, and wrote in her journal to Jimmy, *We are moving but I will never stop looking for you.* And then, to make herself feel better, she added, *Maybe you are in Pittsburgh, too.* And then, like a postscript, she wrote, *I promise I will find you.*

Her mother wanted her to take only what was important, but Rose knew her mother's idea of what to take was different from hers. She packed only one box, filling it with the clues she had collected about Jimmy, with all the objects that meant something to her: Jimmy's favorite shirt, the map. Then Rose looked out the window, taking the flashlight and flashing S-O-S at Lewis's house, but his shades stayed drawn, and after a while, she gave up. It was past one, really late, and she knew he must be asleep. She picked up her journal again and leafed through it. It was filled with letters to Jimmy and feelings she had about people or places that might be clues, and an occasional story she had written, always about a girl like herself looking for and always finding her lost brother. Taking up the pen, she began writing again, but this time, before she even realized what she was doing, she was writing about a girl about to move away from her best friend, a boy. At the very end, the girl tells the boy she loves him, but as she scribbled that part, Rose's hands trembled. She couldn't write the next sentence because she didn't know what the boy would say back, and the not knowing made it seem as though her room was reeling.

She got up and made her way to her closet, looking at the walls. If Jimmy came back, he might look for a message from her. A sign. *Find me in Pittsburgh,* she wrote, and then she scribbled her name.

AT THE END of July, the house was sold. When Lewis saw the sign, he wanted to kick it out from the grass. He waited for Rose, who tumbled out of the house, her face stormy. She made her way to Lewis.

"A dentist," she said. "That's who bought our house. Ron and Rhonda Brown. Isn't that so cute you want to throw up?" Rose said. "My mother's given them free range. As far as she's concerned, it's their house now."

"It's not their house. It will never be their house."

"She thinks this is going to fix things, but it won't," Rose said. "How can we leave?" Rose scratched at the dirt along the curb with her toe. "You have to keep watch for him," she told Lewis. "Hair might be dyed and cut. People can get fatter, too." She put up one hand like a visor, scanning the neighborhood. "He could walk right back up here tomorrow."

"I'll never stop looking," Lewis told her.

"Neither will I." She pressed her forehead against his, her lids lowering.

THEY WERE MOVING August 15. Lewis had the day marked on his calendar with a small red *x*. Rose told him they were leaving early in the morning, that they were renting a U-Haul and driving. The neighbors had all chipped in, including Ava, to buy Dot a red suitcase, a white bow tied around it. When they had brought it over, Dot had looked at it like she didn't know what to do with it. "Thank you," she said, but she didn't open it.

Every day when Lewis woke up, he was sure something would happen to prevent their departure. The Browns might decide they didn't want to live in such a nosy neighborhood. Dot might realize she couldn't leave while her son was still missing. Maybe a Communist missile would blow up Pittsburgh. Sometimes he imagined that Rose would get sick—not sick to her death, but sick enough so that they had to stay. And there was the other, amazing miracle: they would be all out on the street, watching the U-Haul being loaded, when Jimmy would appear, his jeans ragged, his hair longer, looking at them in astonishment. "Where've you been?" he'd say, as if it were everyone in the neighborhood that had been missing and not him.

The night before Rose's departure, Lewis and Rose hung out at the schoolyard, sitting on the swings, scraping their sneakers in the dirt. Neither one of them said anything about this being the last time they might see each other. "I have to get going," she said finally.

"I'll see you tomorrow," he said. Rose turned from him and he grabbed her hand. "I'll see you tomorrow," he repeated.

She was still for a moment. "Yeah. Tomorrow," she said, but she didn't look at him when she said it.

IN THE MORNING, the clock blinked at Lewis and he grabbed it in his fist like a baseball, panicked. Seven. How could it be seven? He fiddled with the dials. His alarm hadn't gone off. He swung his legs over the bed and shoved his feet into his sneakers. Rose had told him that they were leaving at six, before anyone was up, but maybe they had gotten a late start. Maybe he could still make it. He ran to the living room, grabbing a coat to throw over his pajamas, then dashed out the front door. The frosty morning air made him shiver. He could hear the thwack of his shoes on the pavement. He ran and even before he got to the house, he could feel it for the first time, the connection Rose was always trying to get him to feel with her, only now it was raw and empty, and he knew they were gone.

He stopped, bracing his hands on his knees, panting. The U-Haul wasn't there. The house looked empty. He thought of Rose, waking up, waiting for him. He wondered if she was mad or sad or if she'd ever forgive him. He knew he'd never forgive himself.

You could look right through the front windows and see how bare the house was. He tried the front door, but it was locked, so he went around to the back and pried open one of the back windows. He and Jimmy used to climb up from here to sit on the roof and survey the street. He got inside and saw that everything was ready for the Browns. The wood floors were glossy, the carpets clean. He walked into Jimmy's room and was struck by the emptiness. There was a faint block on the wall where their travel map had been. The bed, the curtains, every trace of Jimmy was gone. It was just any old room now.

He explored the rest of the house, his skin hot. The kitchen was empty. So was the living room. He went into Rose's room. The walls were still pale pink. He went to her closet, sliding down into a crouch and then sitting. "Rose," he said out loud, and his voice echoed. He saw something in the corner and peered at it. *Find me in Pittsburgh* was etched on the wall, and under it her name.

Lewis touched it. Her handwriting. When had she written this? Did she mean it for Jimmy or for him, or for both? How did she even know he'd go into her closet? He pressed his hand over her words. The new people would hire someone to paint over this and then it would be gone, too.

Lewis got up. Already the morning light was sifting into the house. Soon, the fathers would be coming out of their houses, their lunches under their arms, and getting into their cars. Lewis went outside, crossed the street, and sat on his porch, his head in his hands. Rose had never gotten her aunt's address in Pittsburgh from Dot. The world was wide and terrifying and there was no place for him in it alone.

ALL THAT WEEK, Lewis stayed in his room, staring at the ceiling. School was starting in a few weeks, eighth grade. Rose was gone. He kicked the book he had been reading about Houdini to the ground. Houdini, with all his tricks, now irritated him. He was tired of tricks and feelings and things you couldn't touch. At one point, his mother came by and opened the door to his room. "Hey," she said. "Aren't there any kids around today?"

Didn't she know he had no friends? He waited, but Ava didn't leave.

"I have an idea," Ava said. "What about the Penny Pool?"

The Penny Pool was a big community pool that cost a penny. It was always jam-packed and all the little kids peed in the pool. "No?" Ava said. "Well, how about you and I go to the movies? *Johnny Tremain*'s at the Embassy."

"I don't want to see a movie." He willed her to leave, but she sat down on his bed, studying him. "Don't you think I feel bad, too? Dot was a friend of mine, but this street is only a tiny part of the world. People leave all the time. That's what life is," she said quietly.

"Do you know where they went in Pittsburgh?" he said. "Did Dot give you an address or the aunt's last name?"

"I asked, but she didn't tell me. I think Dot just wanted to leave everything behind," Ava said.

Lewis turned his back to her, facing the wall.

"If you change your mind, we could make the four o'clock show," she said, as she got up and walked out of the room.

THE DAY THE Browns moved in, it seemed that all of the neighborhood was outside, watching the big van unload, commenting on the furniture, which was white and ornate. "Oh, do I love French Colonial," Debbie Hill said. She commented on the brass lamps and the wooden rocker. "What taste!" Tina Gallagher said. When Mrs. Brown spotted Lewis, she waved, but he pretended not to see her, and soon she was talking to someone else. He watched them going in and out and he suddenly wished he had scratched away Rose's message. He didn't want them finding it. It belonged to him. But when he tried to sneak into the house, Mrs. Brown stopped him. "Whoah now," she said. "We're not open for business just yet."

Every night he wrote Rose letters. He told her how sorry he was that he had missed her leaving, that he would do anything to make it up to her if she would only let him. He told her how strange and lonely the neighborhood was now without her. He sealed the letters in envelopes, but because he didn't have an address, he put the letters in a drawer, hiding them under his underwear.

Then it was fall and suddenly all the teachers were telling them what a big deal it was, how before they knew it, they would be in high school. "You aren't children, anymore," Lewis's teacher said.

Lewis read books about different places: San Francisco, Chicago,

Rome. He went to a gas station and asked for a free United States map and he taped it up in his bedroom, trying to remember all the routes he had planned out with Jimmy. He stuck a red thumbtack in San Francisco. He could go on the road. When he turned eighteen, he could leave home and live anywhere he wanted. He could do anything. When he lay back on his bed, the tack seemed to twinkle at him, like a star he could wish upon. Yeah, soon he'd be gone.

Part Two

1963

✧ *Chapter Thirteen* ✧

Halfway through his night shift, Lewis walked the hospital floors at St. Merciful's in Madison, quietly opening doors and checking in on the patients. He looked at the top of each door to see if the yellow call light was blinking. His step was clean and precise as a cat's, his white sneakers gliding along the red line the hospital put down for visitors to find their way. Visitors got lost anyway, standing in the center of the busy hall, their arms full of flowers or stuffed bears, turning around searching for a sign, and finding Lewis instead. He would take people wherever they needed to go, never minding that he wasn't usually thanked or even remembered. Well. People had things on their minds in a place like this. Lewis knew he was the least of their problems.

Lewis had just turned nineteen, and he was on the surgical ward this month. He had been on the job almost a year, and it suited him just fine. He was one of two nurse's aides for ten or so patients, the youngest one and the only male, too, which was either a conversation starter or stopper, depending on whom you talked to. Elaine, his supervising nurse on surgical, certainly wasn't happy to take him on at first. Nothing about him seemed to please her, not his too-long hair or the fact that he was a man, which seemed like the greatest affront of all.

He had gotten this job as a fluke, going through the paper the week he had arrived in town, eighteen years old with only a little money in his pocket. He told himself he would be lucky. He had responded to all the job ads that didn't require college, and when he saw one for a nurse's aide, it seemed like a destination. They offered training. He wouldn't be ashamed to tell people that was what he did. He didn't need much sleep and he liked the idea of taking care of people, of making them feel better, even if all he was doing was filling a glass with water. He loved the idea of being needed. And though it was nursing, nowhere did he see the word *female*.

He went in for an interview and talked his way into the job. He nodded when Elaine told him what he'd have to do, all the unglamorous business of cleaning bedpans, putting ointment on bedsores, trailing the nurses around and hopping to do whatever anyone told him. He needed a uniform, but he could hardly wear a blue dress like the other aides. "Get yourself some blue dress shirts," Elaine told him. "Wear black pants. With a name tag, you'll be fine."

For the first few days, all he did was follow Elaine around. He made mental notes about where things were so he could find them again quickly. The supply closet was by the elevator, the nurse's station was at the end of the hall. He tried to pick up the lingo. "Feeders" were the people he had to feed, the ones who couldn't hold a spoon or fork. "Slow feeders," he soon learned, were the worst. "Code brown" was when someone defecated in the bed and guess who had to clean it up? He mopped up pee and vomit. He changed lightbulbs and helped people walk the corridors to get back their muscle strength.

The protocol was the hardest to learn and Lewis began to carry a small notebook and pencil with him to take notes. There were nurses who wore black shoes and no cap because they didn't have their license yet, but he still had to listen to them and do what they said. Lewis made a point of looking at everyone's name badge because Ava had always told him that people liked it when you called them by name. But the nurses didn't like it. "Morning, Laura," he said and Laura frowned at

him. "Miss Miller," she said pointedly, and then she told him to go collect the bedpan from room 209. He had questions, but every time he
asked one—why did they thump the chest of someone with bronchitis?
why did you need to flush an IV line?—a nurse would look at him as
if he had interrupted her thinking. "Why do you want to know?" she
would respond, as if he couldn't possibly understand.

The doctors, of course, totally ignored him. They were all men, who
swept through the rooms in their white lab coats, and when Lewis was
in their path, they glanced at him as if he were something unpleasant in
their way, and then refused to make eye contact or to return his hello,
which made Lewis want to thunk his own chest, just to make sure he
was still there. "Don't speak to the doctors, they're busy," Elaine said.

"Like we're not?" Lewis said, and Elaine laughed. "You're learning,"
she said.

His first week at work, he watched Elaine change the dressings of
an older patient named Mr. Walker, whose wife had shot him in the
stomach. Elaine sat on one of the yellow plastic chairs and bent over
Mr. Walker and motioned for Lewis to sit and watch. "There you go,"
she said, finishing up, looking at Lewis. Mr. Walker grunted and turned
his face to the wall. "Where's my wife?" he said.

Lewis was about to say something when a doctor strode into the
room. He was young, with a Band-Aid on his neck, and he cleared his
throat, looking meaningfully at both of them. Elaine leaped to her feet.
She nudged Lewis. "Stand," she hissed, and Lewis did.

"Good morning, Dr. Ryan," she said. She glared at Lewis.

"Morning, Dr. Ryan," he said.

The doctor didn't respond. Instead, he glanced at the chart and then
at the patient. "He was coughing earlier," Elaine said, and the doctor
nodded, not taking his eyes off the chart, not writing anything down.
He leaned over and looked at the dressing.

"We'll do a CBC," the doctor said. "What?" Mr. Walker said. "What are you going to do? A CB-what?" The doctor ignored him, gliding out and as soon as he did, Elaine sat back down again. "What's happening?" Mr. Walker said. "What did the doctor just say?"

"He's going to do a complete blood count," Lewis said. "Here, I'll write it down so you can remember. Don't worry, it's routine." Lewis scribbled into the notebook, tore off the page, and handed it to Mr. Walker.

He took the piece of paper and looked at it. "Now I know," he said.

Lewis followed Elaine out of the room. "That was good, what you did," Elaine said quietly. "Best medicine in the world is acting like a human being to someone else."

At the end of his shift, he was always so tired, he felt as if he were sleepwalking. When he got back to his small rented room, he would smell the hospital—antiseptic, feces, urine—and it took him a minute to realize the smell was on him. He washed out his blue shirt, one of four he had bought at the Thrift-T-Mart, so it would be ready when he needed it, smoothed his pants across his tiny table because he didn't own an iron, and got in the shower, turning the water as hot as he could stand it. He carefully set his alarm, flopped on the bed, and fell asleep. When he awoke the next morning, he was always startled it was a new day.

He had a whole hour before he had to be at work. Lewis spent the time tearing apart the sheets from his bed and practicing making hospital corners. He threw his laundry in the center of the mattress, bunching it up like a patient, and pretended to make the bed with a body in it. He went through all the procedures, wanting to perfect them all.

It didn't take him long to show Elaine how responsible he was, what a quick learner, and soon he was on his own. "You're ready," she said.

She gave him a pager for when she needed him and told him to walk the floors, to pay attention to the call lights over the rooms. He had a list of patients he was supposed to check up on, to feed them meals, to make their beds, to get whatever it was that they wanted, and his job included cleaning. "I'll check up on you when I can, okay?" she asked and he couldn't help but feel a skip of joy.

All day, Lewis was in and out of patients' rooms. Sometimes it was terrible, pain radiating from the beds, patients curled up. Once he came upon a woman sleeping, a smile on her face, and though he was trying to be quiet, he woke her. She jolted up, bursting into tears. "I was dreaming!" she cried. "And now I'm in the goddamned hospital!" She rubbed at her eyes. "Get out!" she shouted at him. "Get out!"

Patients wanted to know why he had become a nursing assistant, where was he from because his accent was so funny, and how old was he anyway? The women mothered him and fussed. They wanted to know if he had a girlfriend, but Lewis noticed they didn't ask him if he wanted to meet their daughters or nieces. The men, though, stiffened at his touch and said little. Well, they didn't have to love him. Most of them stayed only a week at the most, and then they were replaced by someone else. All he had to do was care for them while they were there, and that was easy enough.

Lewis had been alone for so long that he found he liked talking to the patients. Every illness seemed to have a narrative to it. A patient wasn't just a heart attack, but a man who had been overeating because his wife had left him and now food was the only thing that gave him solace, other than his Beach Boys records. A young girl with diabetes was madly in love with her boyfriend, who came every visiting hour and held her hand, and she confided in Lewis that she was terrified about his going to war. "He wants to fight Communists," she said bitterly, and Lewis thought of Mr. Corcoran from the old neighborhood, how he threw around words like Red Scare and Yellow Menace in even the most casual conversations.

All these lives and he got to glimpse them. He was disappointed when he came into a room and someone was sleeping, faced turned into the pillow, or worse, when someone was hooked up to tubes and machines, their eyes shut. Still, he sat by them. He spoke to patients by name, took their hands, some of them mottled and bruised from the IVs. "You're going to be fine," he reassured, even if he didn't know if it was true. He loved how patients perked up when they recognized him, how they needed him. A patient wanted something—a cup of water, an explanation of a procedure—and Lewis could take care of it. It made Lewis feel as if he had a place in the world.

Every floor had its own feeling—and its own nurses. The only floor he hadn't been on was the maternity ward, where he wasn't allowed because he was male. "It's inappropriate," Elaine told him.

"There's men on that floor," Lewis said. "I see them get off there all the time."

"Dads and doctors," Elaine said. "And the fathers stay in the waiting room with the TV, right where they belong. No one wants men messing around in the delivery room. I sure as hell didn't."

Sometimes, depending on the nurse on duty, he wasn't allowed to do certain things for female patients, no matter what floor they were on. He couldn't give a sponge bath to an elderly woman, even though she was so heavily sedated, she'd have never known he was there. He wasn't supposed to help the teenager in room 404 to change out of her clothes into a johnny, though she had been waiting for a nurse to help her for over an hour.

He asked how it was different for male doctors, but the head nurse gave Lewis a glassy stare. "Since when did you go to medical school?" she said. "Don't compare yourself."

The nurses all knew about him, the only male nurse's aide, and sometimes Lewis would see a group walking by, as if they had come deliberately to gawk. Elaine told him they had had a man three years ago working as a nurse. "But he was different," Elaine said. "He came from the marines. Really strong, really gentle. Anytime we needed help carting a patient somewhere, he was our guy. He didn't stay long, though. After he saw a few patients die, that was it for him. He ended up going back to school to be an engineer." She looked pointedly at Lewis's hands, at his bitten nails. "He was married, too," she said.

"I'm only nineteen," Lewis said and she shrugged.

"I was married at eighteen," Elaine said. She held up her hand so he could see the ring, large and sparkling on her finger.

ALL THAT HAD been almost a year ago, and now being at the hospital had a sort of routine to it. Lewis loved his days, but when the workday was over, he didn't looked forward to going home alone to his tiny room. Once he was there, there was really nowhere to go. His loneliness pounded like a headache. All around him were young couples from the university, holding hands, kissing, flirting. He was surrounded by opportunity, so why couldn't he make something happen for himself? He tried. He went to double features at the Bijoux, his feet up on the chair above him. During the second, older movie, *Hud,* a young woman slid into his row and sat beside him. She had long, dark hair and a small, serious face, and he couldn't concentrate on Paul Newman anymore because he wanted to talk to her. He imagined what he might say to her after the film, how they might go grab a coffee. When the lights came on, he leaned toward her, smiling. "Wasn't that movie amazing?" he said, and she blinked at him, as if she hadn't realized he was sitting beside her. She turned and moved out of the row, not saying a word to him, and when he left, he tripped over her popcorn box. He sat in on evening classes, but when he tried to talk to a woman, she held her finger up across her mouth for silence, her gaze turning to the lecture. He kept hoping he'd see the same people around town, so he could say hello without anyone thinking he was nuts, but he never did.

At work, the nurses and aides might not have wanted to have much to do with him, but there were other people on the hospital staff. Every morning, he and Mick, an orderly, would toss a "Hey, how you doing?"

at each other when they passed on the floor. "Can't complain," Mick would say, swabbing the floor, and then Mick would concentrate on the spots he had missed and go silent. Lewis figured this would go on forever if he didn't press for more. He was leaving work when he saw Mick with John, who worked in the cafeteria dishing out the food, and both of them were carrying bowling bags. "Where do you bowl?" he asked and Mick turned to him. "Pins Palace. You know it?"

Lewis had no idea where it was, but he nodded his head enthusiastically. "Great place to bowl," he said.

Mick considered him. "A few of us get together every Friday. Bowl a few games, have a few beers, some laughs," he said. "You want to come?"

The last time Lewis had bowled was with Jimmy and Rose, back when they were kids, candlepins at the Wal-Lex, all of them so bad that no one bothered keeping score.

"I'd love it," Lewis said.

NONE OF THE guys were older than thirty-five, but to Lewis, they looked weathered by life. Mick already had a slight paunch he covered with a yellow bowling shirt, and John was balding, and Tom, who was new to him, had faded tattoos on both forearms. All of them were married with families, and as soon as they all got settled on their lane, John pulled out his wallet to show off his kid. "Get a load of this little one," John said, showing Lewis a photograph of a little girl with a gap-toothed grin. "That's my Gracie." Mick had an eight-year-old girl who loved horses, and Tom had twin freckle-faced boys who were in kindergarten. "Bedlam at my house," Tom said, but he was smiling when he said it.

The men talked about their wives, too. Tom rolled up his sleeve to show Lewis a big gauze pad. "That's from making fried chicken," he said. "And I was just an innocent bystander, watching my gal doing the frying." They all laughed and Mick told about how his wife put all their extra change in wish jars, one for a trip to Niagara Falls, another for a new washer, as if a few extra quarters could make their dreams come true. "You have someone?" John asked Lewis.

"Not yet," Lewis said. "But I'm open to suggestions."

Mick laughed. "You wouldn't like anyone my wife would fix you up with."

"I might," Lewis said hopefully, but Mick waved his hand. "Trust me on this one," Mick said.

"It'll happen when it happens," John said.

The other guys were decent bowlers, but Lewis barely broke ninety, and he had more than a few gutter balls. None of the men seemed to care. "Straighten your arm," Tom told him. "Keep your feet farther apart." They cheered when Lewis did better, clapping when he got a spare. They bought him a beer and slapped him on the back. By the end of the night, Lewis's arm was sore, he was drunk, and he couldn't wait for the next outing.

One Friday night, Tom didn't show up. "Where's Tom?" Lewis said, and Mick and John exchanged glances. "What?" Lewis said. John took him aside. "His wife left him," he said, his voice low. "He moved to Detroit."

"What?" Lewis remembered the way Tom talked about how beautiful his wife was, how lucky he was. Tom had never shown up at bowling looking morose; his game had never changed. "When? Why?"

"It's been going on a long time," John said.

"I don't get it," Lewis said. "How did I not know this?"

John picked up a bowling bowl and put it in Lewis's hands. "C'mon, we're here to bowl, not jaw like dames," he said.

All that weekend, Lewis thought about Tom. Lewis had thought he had known him, or at least was getting to know him, but look how wrong you could be. It made him wonder how well he really knew John or Mick, or when you thought about it, how well they knew him. When he talked, he shot the breeze about the hospital or Madison. It was all casual, loose as pocket change that never added up to anything.

He didn't want to stay in his apartment so he grabbed his map of Madison and struck out on a walk, looking for new pockets of the city.

IT WAS SATURDAY night, at work, and Lewis rounded the corner, nearly bumping into an old woman. She had on a pink floral bathrobe and she was hanging on to an IV, but when she saw him, she stopped short, staring at him. Her white hair flew about her face like dust motes. "Do you need help?" Lewis always asked, because sometimes people didn't want to feel like they did, and if you asked, at least they felt that they had some control over the situation. Her hands began to tremble and she walked toward him, dragging her IV. She touched the pads of her fingertips to his chest. Her fingers were so cold, Lewis immediately began piecing together a diagnosis from what he had read in the nursing manuals. Circulation disorder. Thyroid. "Are you okay?" Lewis asked.

"You're real," she said, in amazement. Her finger sped across his forehead. They felt like mice feet to him. Then her fingers flew through his hair. "It's you," she whispered.

"Who?"

"You're Jesus," the woman said. "I've waited all my life to see you and here you are. Have you come for me? Is it finally my time?" Lewis let her take his hands. He folded his fingers around hers, while her eyes searched his face. "I'm not Jesus," he said. "I'm a nurse's aide. And I'm Jewish," he added with a smile.

"Jesus started as a Jew." Her mouth wavered, and for a moment, he wondered if he should have let her think what she wanted. She coughed and then she suddenly laughed. "Don't you think I know that the Lord works in mysterious ways?" she said.

"Let's get you back to bed." He took her arm, like an escort to the prom, guiding her back toward her room. The whole time they were walking, she kept looking around at all the other people, holding her head up like a show pony. "I'm walking with Jesus!" she crowed.

"What's your name?" he asked.

"Don't you know it? Don't you know everything?" She winked at him.

He smoothed her around the corner and into her room. Her bed had the covers thrown back as if she had been in a hurry. There was a glossy magazine on the bed, the pages spread open.

"Doris," Lewis guessed. "Mary." He glanced at the cover of the magazine. *Top Ten Tips to Keep Your Man.* He pressed his lips together so he wouldn't laugh. "Adele."

"Wrong, wrong, wrong." She shook her head.

"Lisa," he said. "Mary Ellen. Betsy."

"Sheila," she said triumphantly.

Lewis held her as if she might break. "Careful now," he said, as he lowered her onto her bed. She sunk against the pillows, and she took his hand. "Talk to me," she said. "Nobody ever talks to me."

He sat down next to her bed. "I grew up right here in Madison," she said, yawning. "What about you?"

He told her about growing up in Waltham, about Rose and Jimmy and his mother, but he left out what had really happened. Sheila was supposed to be talking, too, but every time he slowed down or grew silent, she would wave her hands. "Tell me more," she urged, and she was so interested, so focused on him, that he spilled out more of his story. The more he talked, the more he felt as if he were unbottling himself. His hands relaxed on his knees. He breathed more deeply.

Her eyelids fluttered shut. She sighed and burrowed into the sheets. "It's so nice to hear conversation," she said, and then she yawned again. He put one hand gently on her head, like a blessing, and she sighed and shut her eyes. "Sleep," he gently ordered.

"Will you come back? To talk to me?"

"Of course I will."

"Promise me."

He promised and Sheila's breath slowed and evened, and then he walked outside, back into the corridor, and leaned against the wall to steady himself.

There it was. The missing feeling.

For so many years, he had wished he could see or talk to Rose. All he wanted was an explanation for why she had vanished from his life. He wanted to know if she was still looking for Jimmy, though he had given up, knowing that if there was any news, his mother would tell him. He tried to imagine Rose now. Most women got married, had kids, but he could no more imagine her staying at home and being a housewife than he could his mother.

What did it matter anyway? How many people did he know who were still friends with their childhood buddies? He had heard a story recently from one of the nurses who said she had been contacted by her boyfriend from sixth grade, shortly after Kennedy was elected. "I've been thinking about you," he had said and she had gone to meet him. She had gotten all dressed up in a sparkly marigold-colored dress, her hair bouffant like Jackie Kennedy's. She had walked into the restaurant and the only person sitting at a table alone was an overweight man with pasty skin who was wearing a terrible brown toupee. "So much for memory lane," she said.

Lewis walked by the windows, where he could hear the wind howling outside. A blizzard was expected, with temperatures so cold that the aged and those with respiratory problems were urged to stay inside. That was Madison for you. The summers so hot and muggy you didn't feel like moving, the winters icing your bones until they seemed as if they might shatter. The first time he had walked outside in the winter, damp from a shower, his hair had frozen. A lock of hair actually broke off in his fingers. He hadn't known what to do with his broken hair and had ended up leaving the pieces in the snow for the birds, thinking maybe they would want it for their nests when it thawed.

LEWIS HADN'T EXPECTED that he'd wind up in Madison, but he had wanted to move out of Waltham since the day that Rose had. He had begged Ava to leave, but she kept refusing, especially after she was finally put on staff full-time. "We're lucky to have a house to rent here.

And where would I work? I'm lucky to have the position I have now. It isn't so easy for a divorced woman with a kid to start over," she said.

"There are tons of jobs."

"Oh, there are?" She grabbed the newspaper and flipped to the Help Wanted, scanning the ads. "Ah, here we go. The Women's Section. A quarter of the size of the men's, which is a problem right there. Let's look at this," she said. "Perky young woman with good personality." She tapped another ad. "Pretty young woman with pleasing speaking voice." She put the paper down. "Perky. Pleasing. Pretty. Young." She punctuated each word with a snap. "You see me anywhere in there?"

"You're young," he said, though he had no idea if she really was anymore, and then, he instantly felt guilty that he hadn't also called her perky and pleasing. She brushed him away. "What we need to do is get on with our lives here," she told him.

It wasn't even their house, yet she was spending all this time fixing it up, painting the rooms herself. She watched pennies and kept a ledger and every month she said, "We're almost there for a down payment." All Lewis could think was, why would anyone ever want to buy this house, least of all her, after all that had happened? How could she have so much pride in the run-down kitchen, the scratched-up wood floors?

"It's important to have something that's yours," she said. She was grouting new adobe tiles around the sink, her hair pulled back in a kerchief. She made a sweeping gesture. "I'll buy this house and then I can borrow against it so you can go to college."

"I don't need college."

"What are you talking about? Of course you do." She sat up, the putty knife in one hand, making parabolas with it in the air. "And eventually, I can give the house to you."

"I won't want to live in it," he said.

"You might change your mind when you get out in the world and see how expensive things are," Ava had told him. "A house is equity. It's peace of mind, owning it. And if you really don't want it, then you can sell it, with my blessing. Then you can get enough money to live wherever it is you want to live."

"Why do you want us to stay here?"

She had spread grout along a green tile. "Why do you want us to leave?"

He had always wanted to leave. Every minute he had been in the neighborhood and in his house, without Jimmy, without Rose, he had felt as if his real life were somewhere else and he just needed to find his way to it.

The worst time of every year was the anniversary of Jimmy's disappearance. There was always something in the local papers, though there was less coverage as time passed: *Local Boy Still Missing. No New Clues in Disappearance Case.* There was a grainy photograph of Jimmy, his sixth-grade school picture. How would anyone ever recognize Jimmy in that? Patsy Baker, the newscaster known for her freckles, always did a segment on the show, talking about the lack of clues, giving sad updates, as if she were taking it personally. There was usually one neighbor or another willing to go on camera, but it was inevitably the person who knew the least about Jimmy, or who had the weirdest theories, like Mr. Corcoran blaming it on a Communist infiltration on Warwick Avenue, or even hinting it might have something to do with a Negro family who had moved in six blocks away, a statement that made Patsy Baker quickly wind up the story.

Lewis had waited and waited for Rose to write, but no letters ever arrived. He had even gone out and bought special stationery to write to her, and a new felt-tip pen in deep blue. "What have you heard from your friend?" the neighbors would ask him at first, which always made him feel worse, as if it were his fault somehow that yet another person in the neighborhood had vanished. He had called Pittsburgh information but there were no Rearsons listed and he had no idea what Rose's aunt's last name would be. He even tried writing to Rose's address in Waltham, in case the mail would be forwarded, but it came back, and when it did, he tore it up in his hands. One night, he shut his eyes and tried to send her a message telepathically, the way she had shown him. *Write me. Find me, Rose.* All that happened was he began to hear the dog barking outside, louder than ever before.

But it wasn't just Jimmy and Rose who haunted Lewis. There hadn't been news of his father for years, but still, every time the phone rang, or the mail came, Lewis couldn't help but hope. No matter what his mother had said, he knew there was some explanation. There had to be.

Lewis, though, kept changing. His voice bumped to a lower register. When he caught his face in the bathroom mirror, it seemed to have new hollows, and downy hairs sprouted along his upper lip and on his body. He tapped the length of his nose with a finger. It looked longer to him, more pointed. Even his eyes looked different, as if he had grown more lashes. He pulled on his dungarees only to find they didn't reach past his calves. His shirts exposed his wrists and forearms. How strange it was that he was now taller than the Jimmy he remembered. How would Jimmy recognize him if he looked this different, and how would he recognize Jimmy? He swiveled, studying himself. From this angle, he almost looked like the old photographs of his father.

Shortly after Lewis turned fifteen, he was eating dinner with his mother when she turned to him and said, "Why don't you ever talk to me anymore? You used to."

"I talk," Lewis insisted, though the last conversation he could remember having with his mother was over whether or not he wanted baloney for lunch, and he chose American cheese instead.

"Where are your friends?" Ava asked. "It's not good to be a loner. You need kids your own age to do things with, to talk to. I worry about you."

"Excuse me? You're asking *me* about friends?" He shook his head and she waved her hand.

"We're not talking about me," Ava said. "And I'm with people all day at work."

It wasn't true anyway. Lewis wasn't such a loner. He had friends he palled around with. He played chess with a guy Greg from his science class sometimes. He often biked with Scott from gym. He was fine while he was with them, but something always felt as if it were missing. Sometimes he noticed girls looking at him, their mouths opening as if to speak, but he never knew what to say back to them. He had heard the girls, too, talking. "My parents would never let me date a Jew," someone said, and Lewis withdrew. There was no one he could really talk to, and even if he could, how could he be sure they would stay?

When he turned seventeen, he got a job as a stock boy at the Star Market on Lexington Street, saving half the money for himself, giving the other half to his mother. Every week, he counted his earnings, spreading the bills out on his bed. Inside, this feeling that he was bound for something new, something better, kicked against him like a can. His old life could be erased, just as easily as an Etch A Sketch drawing. He just needed to find the way.

One afternoon, he was at work, putting canned corn in a display, when the assistant manager, a guy named Robert, only five years older than Lewis and with an angry cluster of pimples on his chin, came by. "Do a good job," he barked. Lewis knew better than to respond, but he watched Robert leaving and he suddenly thought about how awful it would be if this were your life. Assistant manager of canned goods at the Waltham Star Market.

He didn't know what he wanted to do, but he did know that he wanted to do something. He didn't want to wind up pumping gas or joining the army like half the guys did, especially with Vietnam heating up. He also didn't want to grow old here, watching his life receding in the same place, like he was vanishing. Panic clenched his throat. Robert turned around. "Are you working or not?" he sniped. "Have some pride in what you're doing." Lewis picked up another can of corn and wedged it into the display.

Ava was always pushing Lewis about his future, nagging him about his grades. She left brochures around about scholarship applications and local colleges where he could save money by commuting, but he brushed them away because the schools were always right within the area, and what kind of a change was that, living at home? But maybe college wasn't a bad idea. The more he worked as a stock boy, the more suffocated he felt. If he went to college, he'd have professors instead of the dopey teachers at school. Kids paid to go there so they would be smarter, more serious. It would be different from regular school, wouldn't it? He felt a bright ray of hope.

He decided to talk to Mrs. Geary, the guidance counselor. Mrs. Geary, heavyset with a frosted blond fall anchored to her head with a bow, stared at him impassively. "What's on your mind?" she said.

"I want to go to college. How do I get a scholarship?"

Mrs. Geary sighed. She got up and went to the big gray file cabinet and pulled out his file, sitting back down, riffling pages until she got to his report cards. "Oh you do, do you? Look at this, D, C, F, C, D. Those are not college grades. Your Scholastic Aptitude Test scores were rock bottom."

Lewis had not taken the test very seriously. He had barely read the questions, let alone tried to do well. "I can turn things around," he insisted.

"A little late for that now, isn't it?" she said. "It's nearly January."

"I know I messed up."

She adjusted her glasses, peering at him. "Who do you think will even give you a recommendation?"

He felt a pulse in his neck. He tried to think. Miss Koledo, his English teacher who spent most of every class talking about her skier boyfriend, wouldn't. Mr. Rowan, his science teacher, was still angry with Lewis for insisting that it was scientifically possible that man could one day land on the moon. "It isn't my fault," Lewis said. "It's just me and my mom at home." He saw the way she was studying him, her eyes almost floating shut. She shuffled papers on her desk and then handed him a brochure for Mass Bay Community College, a joke school. A last resort. "Everyone gets in here," she told him. "Even you might."

He came home, panicked, not knowing what to do with himself. Maybe Mrs. Geary was wrong. He could still apply to schools. He didn't need stupid Mrs. Geary.

He began to pay attention in class, to turn in papers, but his teachers didn't believe it was his work, and his French teacher even accused him of cheating. He signed up to take the SATs again, studying a practice book over the weekends and at night, and he earned nearly perfect scores. When he showed his mom, he saw the tears pooling in her eyes. "I knew you could do it," she said, throwing her arms about him. "This is who you are."

He began to get excited, to imagine his new life. Elementary and high school had been a waste, but college was something different. And he could be different, too. He could be one of those boys on the cover of the college brochures, lolling on the grass with other kids, striding to a lab to do an experiment. Some schools even had independent study where he could learn whatever he wanted, and the professors would even help him.

One night, when he was trying to fill out a financial aid application, he went into his mother's room to forage in her drawers for a good pen. He pulled open her desk drawer, where she kept rubber bands, thumb-tacks, pennies, all manner of odd things she said it was important not to waste. His hands felt a fold of cardboard, and he pulled out a small folder, fastened with a rubber band. He opened it up and pulled out a letter. He didn't think his mother had many friends and she certainly didn't write to anyone that he knew. He opened the letter up, unfolding it like a fan, scanning the type, the official-looking page, the letter-head: *J. T. Smith, Attorney-at-Law.* The date was three years ago. He scanned the page, and then he saw the word custody and his hands began to shake. He turned a page.

It does indeed appear that Mr. Lark has given up all claims for Lewis.
Lewis reread the letter, over and over.

The print swam. He wanted to kick the chair in front of him, to break dishes in the kitchen. What did any of this mean? His mother had told him his father had left, that he didn't want a family anymore, and that it wasn't anyone's fault. "If it's anybody's loss, it's your father's," she had told him. Lewis hadn't believed her. He had thought maybe his dad had developed amnesia and forgotten them. Or sometimes he blamed Ava for keeping his father away. But this letter seemed to mean that his father had fought for him.

When Ava came home from work an hour later, her veiled hat perched on her head, a bag of groceries in her arms, Lewis was still so angry he could barely think. He walked toward her, with the letter in his hand. "What's that paper?" Ava said. "Is that from school? Something I need to sign? What's the matter, honey?"

He handed her the letter. As soon as she saw it, her shoulders tightened. "Oh," she said slowly.

"Were you ever going to tell me?" he said. He was taller than she was now, so she had to look up at him to meet his eyes. He felt like he might burst into flames. "What else didn't you tell me?"

"Where did you find this?"

"How come I didn't know there was a custody battle?"

She shook her head. "There wasn't."

"It says right here—"

"I'm telling you there wasn't a battle. He threatened and I got a lawyer."

"Threatened means a fight."

Ava shook her head. "No baby, it doesn't."

"Why do you always lie when it comes to him? I'm not a kid anymore. Why can't you just tell me the truth?" His voice scraped in his throat.

"Because the truth is complicated," she said. "He did threaten, but that was all it was. Threats. No one even knows where he is now."

"But he wanted custody. It says right here that he wanted custody. I'm not making that up! You're lying to me." Lewis insisted.

Ava drew herself up. "How many times has he called you?" she snapped. "Has he ever remembered a birthday or come to visit? Where has he been all these years? Are we that hard to find, Lewis?"

"Maybe he couldn't come visit. Or maybe you wouldn't let him."

"You know that's not true."

"He hired a lawyer!"

"People hire lawyers for all kinds of reasons, and sometimes it's just to make trouble."

"I don't believe you! Was he here? Did you get to see him? Where is he? You knew where he was and you didn't tell me!"

"What good would it have done to know where he was when he was making no effort to come and see us? And I don't know where he is anymore. He moved a few times and he hasn't called for years."

"Why couldn't you have told me? It concerned me and I had a right to know. Who knows what you did to make him give up? Maybe he thought I didn't want to be with him. What did you tell him?"

She took the paper, snatching it from his fingers and stuffed it in her pocket. "Whatever I tell you, you're not going to believe," she said quietly. "But you should know that I thought I was protecting you." Then she took the groceries and went into the kitchen, where he could hear her banging things into the cabinets, and he knew enough to leave her alone. Lewis got his jacket and slammed out of the house, not coming back until long after the dinner she made was cold on his plate.

THE NEXT DAY, as soon as he got home from school, hours before Ava got home from work, Lewis was on the phone. It had been a long time since he had tried to find his father, but now everything was different. There had been a custody battle. The operator in Houston had no Brian Lark listed. It was the same with Phoenix and San Francisco and every city Lewis remembered his father mentioning. His father could be anywhere. He could be a truck driver in Canada or a teacher in Santa Fe. He could be remarried with a whole new family, a whole new life, or God, he hoped not, his father could be dead. Lewis knew it was futile, but he still couldn't keep himself from picking up the phone and trying again, and each time he did, he felt more defeated. He took his allowance money and put an ad in the *Boston Globe*, imagining his father might still read it. BRIAN LARK, CONTACT LEWIS. It was all he could afford.

No one answered the ad.

After that, he stopped imagining what it would be like to find his father, how the two of them, both now grown men, might sit and talk about their lives. He went into his drawer and dug out everything he had saved from his father. A peso his father had brought back from a business trip to Mexico that he told Lewis was enough to buy a stack of delicious tortillas. A tiny gold star his father had won for selling the most cars one year, with Brian's name etched across it. It didn't seem like very much to Lewis. He thought of all the things about him that his father had missed seeing. That Lewis had grown a foot taller. That he still couldn't shoot a basket, but he could run really, really fast. That Lewis now shared his father's strong, straight nose. That his dad might look at Lewis and actually see something of himself there.

Lewis never discussed his father with his mother again, but he could tell that she was trying to make amends. "Do you want to go bowling?" she asked one night.

He thought about being trapped with her, having to listen to her talk about her job, having to hear her talk about his life as if it still belonged to her.

"I have to study," he said, which was his all-purpose response. "I want to do more college applications." All he wanted to do now was get away from her.

She was quiet for a moment. "That's what I like to hear," she said.

He was a senior and it was March when the college letters began to come back and he was always the first to see them because Ava was at work. He didn't get into Stanford or UCLA. The University of Michigan also said no thanks. He tore the letters up. It got so he could feel defeat just by the thinness of the envelopes. The only acceptance letter that came was for Mass Bay. The joke school. That was his road out of this, his only road. He thought of commuting from home, going to classes with all the kids who never read, who paid him to write their papers because they were too dumb to do it on their own. He crumpled the letter in his hand.

When he finally told Ava, she was quiet. "You can take a few classes at the community college," she suggested. "You wouldn't have to go there full-time. And you can apply to colleges again. People do that." He knew she was trying to make him feel better, but instead, he felt worse.

"Maybe," he said, and then left the room.

ONE AFTERNOON, AT the end of May, when he came home, Ava was primping. "I have a date," she said. She carefully pursed her lips at herself in the mirror. "I want you to meet him, his name is Frank," she said. "He sells bathtubs, but he seems awfully nice."

When the doorbell rang, she flew to the door. She opened it and her voice chimed, "Oh Frank, come meet my Lewis."

Frank's hair was so shiny with oil, Lewis swore he could see his reflection in it, and he was wearing a dark suit like an undertaker. Frank looked at Lewis as if he were an affront. "He's so big!" he said to Ava. "What is he, sixteen?"

"Eighteen," Lewis said.

"What are you doing here home on a Saturday night?" Frank asked Lewis. "You should be stepping out yourself." Ava adjusted the veil on her hat so that her eyes were hidden. "Don't wait up," Frank said, and winked at Lewis.

"I'll see you later, darling," his mother said to him. He saw the way her eyes darted to Frank and then back to her skirt, which she was smoothing, and Lewis walked over and hugged her. "Oh, this is nice," she said, and Frank pulled her toward him, peeling her from Lewis.

Lewis watched Frank guiding his mother to the car, one arm about her waist, as if he owned her. He saw the careful way his mother was walking in her heels, as if she thought she might trip, how she dipped down into the car. She looked up and gave him a wave and he waved back.

He had the evening to himself, so he watched an old movie on TV. Then he made himself dinner, and went to bed to read because he didn't want to wait up for his mother and hear her talk about the nice restaurant Frank took her to, or how Frank wanted to get to know him better. Plus, she kept asking him if he had made a decision about taking college classes, and he kept lying, saying, not yet. He knew she thought Mass Bay was his chance, just like she thought Frank was hers.

At midnight, he heard the key in the lock. Was that a good sign or bad? His door was closed, and he turned out his light, listening, hoping she hadn't brought Frank back home with her. He didn't want to have to feel trapped in his room.

He didn't hear another voice. Instead, there was a bang, as if she had bumped into a table or dropped something heavily down. He heard her sigh and he didn't move. He heard the radio click on and then he heard her crying, soft muffled sounds, her voice catching like a skip on his records. Stop, he wanted to tell her. Don't do this. Don't be this person anymore. He might have been saying that to himself. He had cried for his father and for Rose and Jimmy, but look where that got him. He had thought his father had loved him. He had thought Rose had, too. Sometimes, to live your life, you had to protect yourself against what other people might take from you.

Lewis heard his mother walking to her room, shutting her door. He heard her crying grow quiet, and then silence. In the morning, she'd act as if nothing were wrong. She might not even bring it up and if he did, she'd tilt her head as if she were remembering something. "He's not for me," she'd say, as if it had been her decision all along.

The night crowded around him. He didn't want to spend any more nights listening to his mother's crying. He didn't want to see her hopefully putting on her face, introducing him to men who looked at Lewis as if he were a burr they couldn't wait to remove. He didn't want to go to the Star Market and make displays of canned beets that housewives would dismantle. He couldn't stand to be here. There was a whole huge world spinning out there, a roulette wheel, and he could bet on it.

Lewis got up out of bed. There were two more weeks of school, but even if he didn't go, he'd still graduate. He took the money he had been saving from his job for college—three hundred dollars—and tucked it into his knapsack. He took out a piece of paper and carefully wrote his mother a note, because he knew if he tried to tell her in person, she'd try to talk him out of it. She might be so upset that he would falter and stay home, and if he didn't leave now, he might be stuck in Waltham forever.

After all that had happened, he couldn't just vanish. "I promise I'll let you know where I land. Love, Lewis," he wrote. He thought a minute and then wrote, "This is not your fault." She would wake up with her alarm at seven, rushing to work. She would knock on his door to wake him, and then she'd be frying eggs, making herself coffee to get through the day. She might go into his room and see he wasn't there, but even then, she would think he was just out for an early walk. Maybe she wouldn't see the note until the moment she was leaving. He didn't think he could bear to see her standing there, like a pull of gravity on him, pinning him in place.

When he left, the house was dark and quiet. He put the note in an envelope and propped it up on the kitchen table, where she'd see it. He thought of her waking up, changing from the person who had had a bad date to the person who held a job. Soon she'd be the person who didn't have a son at home, and maybe that would be better for everyone.

When he stepped outside, the neighborhood was empty. The whole walk to the bus, he thought about his mother. She would see his note. He knew her. She'd get in the car and try to find him, going to the places where she thought he might be. The bowling alley. The movie theater. The school. Just like she had when Jimmy was missing. She might call the police and they might tell her that Lewis was eighteen now, that there was nothing she could do. They might remember her. Oh yes, you're the one who knew that boy who disappeared.

You're the one.

She might just sit on the couch with his note in her hand.

He stood at the ticket line and he remembered all the cities on the map that he and Jimmy were going to go to. San Francisco because it was by the ocean. Kansas City because of the song. Madison because Jimmy thought they had good cheese and rodeos. By the time it was Lewis's turn at the window, he had decided. He'd go where Jimmy would have gone. He'd live some of the life they had planned. He bought a ticket to Madison and climbed on the bus. The seats were only half-filled and people were looking out the windows or rustling paper bags and no one noticed him or paid him any attention. There was an empty seat at the back of the bus, and he slid into it.

By the time he was out of Massachusetts, Lewis began to make up a new story for himself. He had been born in Florida, and his parents were happily married. His father was an accountant, his mother a housewife, and they lived right off the beach. Oh, but they were an absurdly close family, so much so that he missed them greatly, especially his father. He had gone to a private school where he had lots of friends, and yes, they all kept in touch, and no, he was just putting off college for a few years until he found himself.

He'd never look back. And someday he might even believe his own story.

❖ ❖ ❖

ANOTHER YEAR PASSED and he turned twenty and Madison now felt like home. Jimmy had been wrong about the cheese being so great here (it was mostly plain old cheddar) and there were no rodeos, but he liked the city nevertheless. He had called his mother as soon as he was settled. He told her how he didn't want to take classes at Mass Bay, that he needed to be somewhere different, and though she cried, she didn't try to make him come home. "I understand," she said, though she didn't sound like it. He could sense her biting back words she wanted to say. She asked when she could visit, or when he'd visit her. "We could always meet halfway," she said.

When he told her he was a nurse's aide, she didn't laugh. "You're my son, all right," she said. "I'm proud of you," and there was that confusion, that feeling where he didn't know whether to be ashamed or pleased about being anything like her. "I just want you to be happy," she said.

❖ Chapter Fourteen ❖

It was Saturday, and Lewis was at Suds over on State Street, finishing up his laundry. He had called Mick earlier to see if he wanted to grab a pizza afterward, but Mick had to take his daughter to get a Halloween costume, and when Lewis called John, John told him that his wife wanted him to go look at carpet for the den. "We'll catch you at Pins Palace Friday," John said, and Lewis pretended it was okay. Lewis didn't even really like bowling all that much. He just liked hanging out with them, having something to do and someone to do it with.

Suds was crowded with housewives lugging plastic baskets and kids hanging on to their slacks, and the only other guys there were students, which wasn't such a bad thing, because they usually stuffed all their bright colors and whites together in one load, making things move a little more quickly. The Beatles boomed into the place, though you couldn't really hear much over the noise. Plastic seats lined the walls and if you weren't folding or washing, you were waiting for the next available machine, which Lewis knew from experience could take awhile. In the corner, the matron who gave you change was smoking, tapping the ashes on the floor. Lewis had positioned himself to be next in line for the washer over in the corner, sitting at a chair catty-corner to it, but he hadn't realized that the woman commandeering it was going to do two separate loads plus a hand-wash. When he sighed audibly, she glared at him. "Hey, I was here first," she told him.

By the time he was done with his wash, the dryer situation didn't look much better. Already, a fight had broken out because a girl had taken out someone else's dry clothes, piling them on the folding table, so she could stuff in her wet ones. At the far end, a dryer stopped with a whoosh, and a woman in a blue hat swarmed toward it. Lewis sat, resigned to a long wait, telling himself he had no plans anyway, and wishing he had brought a book, when a woman ran into Suds, all pineapple-blond corkscrews and dark eyes. She was out of breath, but Lewis couldn't take his eyes off her. Every woman he knew now had hair as long and straight as Joan Baez's or big teased bouffants, but here she was with all those ringlets. She opened the door to the dryer and even from where he was sitting, he could see the clothes inside were still damp.

"I just have to run it another cycle," she apologized to the waiting woman. She dug in her jeans. "I know I have some change," she said, shifting her hips.

"You don't have change, then this dryer's available, wet stuff or not," the other woman snapped.

"Just wait. Please," the blonde said. She patted down her back pockets. "I don't know where my wallet is. Maybe it's in the car."

"I've been waiting here an hour," the other woman said. "I'm not waiting for you to go to your car," and she put one hand on the dryer, claiming it.

Lewis got up and walked over to the dryer. He dug out the change he was going to use for his own wash and quietly put it in the dryer, sliding the change slot closed. The dryer sputtered and whirred.

"Hey, you can't do that!" the other woman said, but the blonde was looking at him, her mouth curling into a smile.

"You're so kind," she said.

They sat together on the plastic chairs while her clothes spun around. He ran out and got more change, and when he came back, not only had she held his seat for him, but she had claimed a dryer for him. He threw his clothes in, and when he came back to his seat, she pointed to the map that was sticking out of his pocket. "Are you new here?"

"Not really."

She gave him a funny look.

"No sense of direction," he admitted.

They both got coffee out of the machine by the door and she kept blowing across the top of her cup. "What can I say?" she said, smiling. "I wish they would sell iced tea."

It was hard to hear over the din of the machines, but she leaned forward so she could talk to him. Her name was Rita and she said she had grown up in Manhattan and come here for school and unlike all the other East Coasters who fled back home as soon as school was over, she had stayed and opened up a little dress shop, Fine Frocks. "I know it probably sounds ridiculous," she said. "But I think I change lives. I know what people should be wearing, the colors they need to perk them up, give them confidence. I have some clients who tell me to just pick things out for them and have them ready. They trust me that much." She gazed at him. "You could use more green," she said and he suddenly wanted to go out and buy a green shirt just to please her. She told him she had a lot of friends, but she didn't see people as often as she'd like outside of the shop. "They all have kids now," she said. "Families. Work. You know how it is."

Lewis thought of the guys he bowled with. "I know what you mean," he said.

She began to talk about her parents, how her mother had been an opera singer who gave it up when she got married because it would have meant traveling all over and she wanted to be at her husband's side. "Every day at four, she'd peel me away from her so she could shower and put on a dress and perfume," Rita said. "And every time my father walked through the door, her face changed. She just lit up, even after all those years of being together. Isn't that something?"

Lewis thought about how hopeful his mother used to be whenever she had a date, and how most of those evenings ended with her crying quietly behind her bedroom door. "It's something," he said.

She told him how she and her brother would fling themselves at their father when he walked through the door and he'd always have something for them, a red rubber ball or a brown paper bag of rock candy. "Then my parents would talk together for ten minutes and we weren't allowed to interrupt," Rita said. "It was nice, though, hearing them talking." Lewis thought about all the days he had sat on his front porch, waiting for his father to show up, aching at every car that passed.

Rita didn't finish talking until she was done with her coffee, then she looked at him as if it was his turn, and he felt like someone had shined too bright a light on him. What story was he going to tell her? It was hard with people you wanted to keep seeing, people you wanted to know better.

"So," she said. "Are you going to tell me that you're wanted by the FBI?"

That smile was making him want to tell her the true story of how he ended up in Madison, but then she'd feel sorry for him, and he didn't want that. So instead, he told her what he had told Elaine. He told her as much of the truth as he could, listening to himself carefully because he didn't want to lose track and forget what he had said.

He told her he was a nurse's aide, that he sometimes talked to this old woman Sheila, who was always in and out of the hospital, but most of the time he just sat and listened to her talk. "That's lovely," Rita said. He told her about all the movies he went to, the bookstores he frequented, even the bowling on Friday nights, and she showed him her long fingernails, laughing. "Can you imagine me bowling with these?"

He could imagine it. He could see himself having dinner with her and walking with her and kissing her mouth. But maybe she was just passing time in the laundromat, being nice to him because he had rescued her dryer for her. Maybe she always told her life story to strangers.

They sat at the laundromat until it it grew dark outside, the air nippy with fall. Almost everyone else had cleared out by now. He kept buying more cups of coffee, although he was now so wired, his hands were shaking, but he didn't want to leave because what if he didn't see her again? He noticed Rita glance at her watch, but he saw, too, how she took her time folding her wash, lingering over each piece the same way he was. When she finished balling the last pair of socks, she turned to him. "Well, it was nice meeting you, Lewis," she said. "I hope I see you the next time your clothes are dirty."

She pulled on her jacket, wrapping a kerchief around her hair. She bent to pick up her basket of clothes and he knew that he had to do something.

"Can I get your number? Would you like to go out to dinner some time?"

She looked at him, considering, and for a moment, he thought she was going to say no. "Yes," she said finally. "Yes, I think I'd like that."

HE MADE A reservation at Prunella's, which Mick had told him was his wife's favorite restaurant because the waiters kept refilling the bread basket without being asked. It was one of those new fondue places that were springing up, and though Lewis wasn't sure how he felt about dipping bread in melted cheese, he thought it might impress Rita. They were supposed to meet there, and he got there first, his heart hammering. The restaurant was dark, and every table was lit with candles, and all along the walls were green, leafy fern plants.

As soon as he saw Rita come in, in a fancy dress, her ringlets piled on top of her head, he wanted to kiss her, to touch her hair, but instead he waved. They were led to a table, and he held the chair for her, before the host could. "A gentleman," she said, pleased.

He didn't want to blow this. He could tell that she was nervous, too, by the way she kept twisting one of her hoop earrings round and round. Maybe he couldn't calm himself down, but he knew, from his work at

the hospital, how he could make her relax. It was all in how you spoke
to people, lowering your voice, tilting your head to show you were really
listening. It was how you looked at someone, and she was so pretty that
he could have looked at her forever.

They were halfway through the fondue, Lewis already sick of the
cheese, when she started telling a story of how she had been so traumatized seeing *White Heat* that she refused to go to high school because
her science teacher looked just like Jimmy Cagney. "*White Heat,*" he
said, amused. "That's an old movie."

"I saw it the week it came out."

"You must have been five, then," he said, and her fork hovered in
the air.

"Seventeen," she said.

He looked at her in wonder, doing the math in his head. "I'm thirty-
two," she said quietly.

"Twenty," he said, and she put her fork down.

"Seriously?" She tilted her head. He reached across the table and
took her hand, feeling a jolt of heat. "Who cares how old we are," he
told her. "What matters is we're having a good time."

He saw her relax, her features softening. "Maybe," she said.

All through dinner, he didn't worry about the age difference. He saw
only how the light seemed to shimmy through her curls, how delicate
her hands were. Plus, he liked listening to her. She was smart, and she
made him laugh. But that night, after walking her home, he began to
worry about it. She was in her thirties. She must have had other boyfriends, and how could he compare with someone who probably knew
how to tip a maitre d', or who even had a passport. He had kissed
women before, but he had never slept with one. He had always thought
he'd fumble his way through with someone as new to all of this as he
was, but he hadn't counted on someone like Rita. How long would it
be before she learned he was too green for her? He told himself he'd just
have to show her that their age difference didn't matter.

He didn't want to go bowling Friday nights anymore, because he wanted to be with her, but he didn't know how to tell the guys, so finally, he just told them the truth. Mick grinned, waving his hand. "Go, go," he said. "When your feet hit the ground again, we'll be here to bowl with you."

THE FIRST TIME they made love, he was careful because he didn't want Rita to know she was his first. He knew the mechanics of sex, but he wasn't a hundred percent sure how you went about it. She had opened all the windows in her apartment, so the air felt like a drug. She shone in the moonlight and then he kissed her, and it didn't matter that he didn't know what to do because he stopped thinking altogether.

Afterward, they sprawled on her bed, the sheet over the two of them. He couldn't get over the shape of her shoulders, the way her neck sloped. Every time he looked at her ears, he felt a pull of desire. He wanted to kiss them. "Tell me everything," she said, and he told her how Sheila had told him that her husband had died when he was about to take his first subway in New York, getting dizzy and falling off the platform right onto the tracks. He told her how John was taking up golf, and how Mick was going to night school to get his GED because he didn't want to be an orderly all his life. Rita sat up. "Tell me something about you now," she said.

He angled his body over hers. "This is what I want to tell you," he said. He kissed her neck, the hollow below her throat, and then he kissed her mouth until he felt her kissing him back.

ON MONDAY, WHEN Lewis walked into the break room to get a packet of sugar for his coffee, one of the aides actually smiled at him. "I saw you the other night with your girlfriend. I waved but you didn't see me." She pulled a chair out at her table and Lewis sat down. There it was, the coffee pot, bubbling as always. The donuts layered onto a tray, even though all the women always complained they were too fat and they really shouldn't.

Just like that, things changed. The nurses began to talk to him and even confide their secrets. They told him that, unlike their boyfriends, he really listened, and how could they get their guys to do the same? They began to rely on him more at work, too, to appreciate that he might just be an aide, but he had a reputation for calming patients down. "Mr. Tranquilizer," one of the aides called him. They began to give him useful tips, like showing how to rely on a drawsheet instead of lifting patients up under their armpits ("Your back will give out in two years," one nurse said).

He found himself gravitating back to the nurses, wanting to hang out with them in the break room. "Call me Angie," one nurse said, even though he had always called her Miss Roget.

He was walking down the halls when he saw that Sheila was back, sitting in a hospital bed surrounded by magazines. "Hey stranger," he said, coming into her room, and she smiled, waved, and then tapped her chest. "Always my heart," she said. "Come talk to me." He pulled up a chair, listening to her talk about how the doctors were treating her, why she especially loved the lime Jell-O. He couldn't resist telling her about Rita, as if the old woman's approval would cement things. "She's beautiful," he said and Sheila nodded, settling into her sheets. "My Bill was beautiful," Sheila told him. "His being pretty got us through a lot of rough patches."

They had been going out a year when Rita came down with a flu, the first time she had been sick since he had met her. She called him, her voice froggy and miserable. "I'll see you as soon as I'm better," she said, but Lewis came over with soup and orange juice, knocking on her door. He heard her fumbling with the lock, and then there she was, in her robe, her hair matted in damp coils, her eyes bleary with fever. "I can't believe you're here," she said. She kept trying to fix her hair, and he pulled her hands down. "I like it mussy," he said. She half smiled.

"Come on, let's get you to bed," he said. Lewis changed her sweaty sheets and heated up the soup, helping her eat it, cupping his hand under the spoon with each bite. When she finished it, he put a cool cloth on her forehead.

"You're so kind," she said.

All that week, he took care of her, coming over in the morning and then after work, even taking her laundry to Suds and doing it for her. And then, as soon as she was well, he came down with it.

"My turn," she said, showing up at his door with soup and crackers, but he wouldn't let her in. "I don't want you to get sick again," he insisted, and she looked at him, perplexed. "I was already sick," she said. "I've got immunity. You work in a hospital so you should know things like that." She held up the bag. "I have chicken soup and those crackers you like." She peered past his door. "Plus, your place is a mess. I can clean it up for you."

"Rita, please, I just need to sleep," he said. He thanked her, but kept the door half-closed. He sent her away that day, and the next day, too, and when she called to say she wanted to stop by, he said, "I'll call you soon as I'm better." By the end of the week, he had bounced back. He couldn't wait to see her, but when she came over, she looked smaller somehow, and her face was pinched with hurt.

"I'm sorry. I shouldn't have sent you away," Lewis said. "But honestly, I wasn't doing anything but sleeping."

"I missed you," she said. She sat on the couch next to him, leaning her head against his shoulder. "When I was sick, one of my older customers actually left me a box of Miss Lydia's Powders for Female Troubles outside the door. The landlady sent up cough medicine because she said she needed to get some sleep and I was hacking too loudly. And I had you to care for me. It made me feel so good. I wish you had let me take care of you."

"I said I was sorry."

Like an engine running down, she was suddenly quiet. She took her head off his shoulder and looked at him. "I'm bound to say something wrong, since I'm the one who has to do all the talking."

"Okay by me. I like hearing what you have to say."

"But what about what you have to say? Don't you ever want to talk with me, share things?"

"Isn't that what we're doing now?"

She got up from the couch. "Why didn't you let me help you when you had the flu?"

"Come on, it's my job to take care of sick people, not yours."

She shook her head. "But I wanted to take care of you, to feel needed, to get closer to you."

"You're making a big deal out of something that's not a big deal at all."

"Lewis, I feel lonely with you. You never talk about anything important with me. I never know what you're thinking. I don't even know that much about your past. I thought maybe things would change when you got to know me better, but now I think that maybe they won't."

He felt as if every cell of his body was exposed. She was inches away from him, but she looked so far away. "I'll tell you what I'm thinking," he said. "I'm thinking how lucky I am that I met you. I'm thinking that you make this town feel like home to me."

"What did home feel like?" she asked. "Tell me about your parents, about what you were like as a kid. Anything."

He felt as if a hood had been dropped over him. He couldn't say a word, couldn't look at her.

She stepped back, and looked at him sadly. "I don't think we should see each other anymore," she said. She grabbed her jacket, heading for the door. "It's just not going to work out."

"You're leaving because of this?"

"This isn't what I want for myself. I need someone who lets me in." She was watching him, as if this was a test she knew he'd fail.

"Maybe I want someone who doesn't leave the first time things get difficult," he countered.

"The first time?" she said, astonished. "Are we in the same relationship?" She took her hand off the doorknob and studied him. "Okay," she said quietly. "Let's try this. Do you have anything to tell me?"

His mind fished for things to say. "My mother worked for a plumbing company that made plaid sinks and toilets. She was almost never home." His words hung in the air.

He thought she'd be happy, but Rita frowned. "You told me she didn't work," she said curtly. "You told me she was always home."

She put one hand on her hip, shaking her head, and he felt an itch of anger that she was blaming him, because this time, he had really tried. "Rita, what does it matter? Who cares what my mother did or how I grew up? What does it have to do with us today?"

"I'm thinking about tomorrow," she told him. "About us down the line. I'm thinking about giving more and more of myself, but you've never even let me stay over the whole weekend," she said. She leaned along the wall, waiting, and he knew that he was supposed to invite her, tell her how much he wanted to be with her. But he thought of a whole weekend of her questions, her wanting to know everything about him. And besides, she kept telling him how much she wanted to be with him, but look at how easily she was ready to leave. How would it be if he got used to having her around and then she left again? He thought of the way he had waited and waited for his father and all there had been were broken promises and then silence. His own mother had lied to him about his dad. Jimmy had vanished and Rose's letters never came. "I have a really physical job," he said quietly. "I get up early. I come home late. And right now, I just got over the flu."

He saw how her face hardened, how she drew herself up. He wanted to grab her hands, but instead, he stayed planted to the floor, folding his arms across his chest.

"I had really fallen for you," she said, and then, before he could open his mouth to stop her, she was gone.

THAT NIGHT, HE roamed Madison, stunned at how much he missed Rita already. He walked to her apartment and rang her buzzer, but either she wasn't home or she wasn't answering. He stopped at a pay phone and called her, and then he began thinking about what she wanted from him, how he'd have to revisit his past and spread it out in front of her like a poisoned banquet. He had come here to reinvent himself, to start anew, and she wanted to take him back to what he had been.

Pained, he hung up the phone before she could answer.

HE DIDN'T TELL anyone he had broken up until the next week, after he had given up hope that she might call. Missing Rita was like an ache he couldn't soothe. Lewis thought he saw her everywhere. Even the smell of the soup in the cafeteria, the watery canned tomato stuff, made him remember the way he had fed her when she was ill, how grateful she had been and how good it had all felt.

After two weeks, he admitted to the nurses and his friends that he and Rita were through. "You're a young guy, you should be playing the field, anyway," Mick told him, but it didn't make him feel any better.

The nurses took him on as their pet project, inviting him to dinner, telling him there were more fish in the sea. It was as if going out with Rita had left a shine on him that other women were drawn to. He ended up dating one nurse for two weeks. He dated an aide's best friend for over ten months. What Rita had said thrummed inside of him, and he tried his best to be different, to talk more, to open up, but no matter what he did, sooner or later, every relationship fell apart. His latest relationship, with a nurse named Dolly, didn't last through August. "You have so many beautiful qualities," Dolly said. "The way you look after me, the way you open doors. You never once forget to say God bless you when I sneeze. But I feel like I'm the only one in this relationship."

"What do you mean?" he asked, and she shrugged. "I feel like I don't really know you."

"You know me."

"Fine. Let's try this then. Tell me one thing personal you've never told anyone else."

Lewis felt the world clamp shut. He could talk about Jimmy, about Rose, about how his mother had so many boyfriends, but that old world seemed too large for him, as if it might swallow him whole and he'd never emerge again. "I have a rotten sense of direction," he said, and Dolly sighed. "I rest my case," she said, "and I knew that already." After that she refused to go out with him anymore.

He still dated, but he began to read the signs that a relationship was going to end. The look in a woman's face when he leaned in to kiss her, how her body angled away from his. A woman would tell him she wanted time to think their relationship over, and then a week later, Lewis would see her holding another man's hand. They always said the same thing. I can't get to know you.

ANOTHER YEAR PASSED and it was winter again, New Year's Eve, and Lewis was working, walking the halls, ignoring the HAPPY 1966 signs that were posted on the doorways. Already, he'd seen a patient with a broken leg who'd skidded on a patch of black ice. Two seventeen-year-old kids had been treated with Thorazine because they had taken too much LSD at a party, and their parents, mistaking Lewis for a doctor, had grabbed his arm. "We didn't even know he smoked marijuana," the mother cried. "That's how it starts, isn't it?" Lewis just nodded because they wouldn't believe him if he said no. One of the aides had actually brought in hash brownies for the break room tonight, and the only reason Lewis hadn't grabbed one was because he still had to work.

Maybe when he was done, if everything wasn't all gone, he'd drop over there later and have one, along with some champagne. He looked in a room and saw that Sheila was here again. She never seemed to stay out the hospital for long, always back with heart or stomach pains, needing tests. She was sleeping, but he came in and sat beside her, just for a moment. He had looked up her chart after he had first met her and had asked the other nurses about her. She didn't have any family. She was back in the hospital now because neighbors had noticed a smell coming from her apartment. They had knocked on the door repeatedly and then someone commented that he hadn't seen Sheila in days, even though she usually went out every single day for a walk to the local church, her hair veiled, her hands clutching a white leather Bible. They knew she lived alone, without even a pet to keep her company. But this silence scared them. The landlord had broken in and found her on the floor, lying in a pool of urine.

The nurses all thought Sheila was a lot of trouble. She would get up and wander off by herself. She wanted to know what every pill and every procedure was for. She would listen to the news on a little transistor radio and then, five minutes after she had heard it, she'd want to talk to the nurses about it. In November, when there had been a march on Washington to protest the war, she insisted she wanted to go. When there were race riots in Los Angeles, she clucked her tongue, and when Bob Dylan came on, her favorite, she sang along to "Blowin' in the Wind." "She's just lonely," Lewis would say, but the other nurses sniffed. No one came to visit her in the hospital and she received no cards.

Lewis sat looking at her now in her bed. He had learned that sometimes sleep was like a kind of hypnosis, that sometimes even comatose patients would know there was a presence beside them. "I'm here," he told her and took her hand. St. Merciful was a good hospital. He knew that. But he knew, too, that good doctors and good medicine weren't always enough. He had seen it himself in the hospital. It was something all the nurses knew. Patients with family, with people who loved and needed them, just got better faster.

❖ Chapter Fifteen ❖

Ava, bundled in her winter coat, came home thinking about the new year—imagine, 1966!—and Lewis again. He came to see her every six months, and a month ago, she had taken the train and visited him, letting him show her around Madison. She hadn't been able to take her eyes off him, her big, tall son. He was a man now, twenty-two, and orbiting away from her even more. Their visits never seemed long enough, and when she went to hug him good-bye, she could feel his body pulling away, which made her want to tug him closer.

Most of the other boys in the neighborhood Lewis's age had joined the armed forces, which terrified Ava, but at least more and more people were protesting Vietnam. Even Ava had gone to Boston Common to march. She had come home exhilarated, with a little flag she had been waving and an END THE WAR button pinned to her lapel. Spotting her, Ted Corcoran, whose son Stanley had just joined the marines, came over to scold. "You're making a big mistake, Ava," he told her. But she didn't think so. Lewis was against the war, which made her proud and happy, and she had heard through the grapevine that Bob Gallagher's son Eddy, now living in Canada, his brush cut now grown down to his shoulders, had actually burned his draft card, something Bob refused to discuss. It could be just wishful thinking on her part, but even

Lyndon Johnson's Texas-twanged speeches seemed a little less gung-ho these days, and he looked increasingly lined and tired. Ava saw a few of Lewis's former classmates when they were pumping her gas at the local station. Some, when they spotted her, would blush furiously as if embarrassed, while others would preen, as if now that they had a job, everyone had to take them seriously.

The girls were changing, too. The younger ones looked like beautiful English sheepdogs, with all that long pin-straight hair and bangs that hid their eyes, dressed in short little miniskirts or long flowy dresses. Of course, not everyone was like that. She still saw many a girl with teased-up hair and spit curls, hanging on to a boy with a wiffle cut. Even worse, she saw girls with wedding dresses over their arms, or with bellies swollen like little beach balls.

The neighborhood, too, was changing. The Hula-Hoops, the trikes on the lawn, the occasional Beatles bubble-gum card, all belonged to a whole new sea of kids Ava only vaguely knew. The Browns, who had bought Dot's house, had sturdy twin boys now. How had that happened so fast?

It hadn't taken long for word about Lewis being gone to spread. After he had left home, Ava got the feeling that everyone in the neighborhood expected her to leave, too. When the Bokma family two blocks away moved because Cindy, the wife, wanted to live in California, Cindy made a point of coming over so she could give Ava the name of her realtor. "Why would I want that?" Ava asked her.

"You never know," Cindy said. "And even a small house is a lot for just one person, isn't it?"

"Not really," Ava said.

"Maybe you'd like to rent something smaller," Cindy said. "This guy knows all the good places. Or maybe you could move closer to your son." Ava turned away so Cindy wouldn't see Ava's confused pain. "Thank you, but I'm staying here," Ava said.

She kept thinking about the day Lewis had left. She had found the white envelope on the kitchen table, and she had known what it was before she opened it. She had read his letter three times, standing in the middle of the living room, but she hadn't cried. She always had known he'd leave eventually. You didn't raise your kids to keep them. You wanted them to be independent and strong and the last thing she wanted was to have a relationship like the one Charmaine had with her mother, the two of them more like equals than mother and daughter. She had expected that when Lewis left she'd feel lonely, but she had also thought that maybe she'd feel good, too. She'd know that she had raised him right, that she was sending him off happy. Maybe, too, she had thought that as an adult he'd still be in her life.

She had taken his letter and gone to his room. He must have slunk out early in the morning, before she had even thought to struggle out of bed. Had he planned this or was it spur of the moment? She had looked around as if she might find clues, trailing her hands along his desk, his dresser. She felt relieved that almost nothing there was gone, that there was so much he had left behind. His bed was made. She opened his closet, his drawers, and some of his clothes were still there. His books.

She sat on his bed. He had the right to do this. He was eighteen. You couldn't stop anyone who really wanted to leave, and he was so angry at her. His rage was like a hot little heart and all she could do was listen to it beat.

AVA BEGAN STAYING later and later at the office, marking off the days on her calendar. She didn't really have that much work to do. Now that Richard had bought them all brand-new Selectrics with a little typeball and roller, work was faster and easier, but that meant she had even more time when she had to pretend to be busy. She barely looked up when the other women left, their arms linked, hats bobbing on their heads as they gossiped. When Richard strode out, he nodded at her, that tight, pleased grin on his face because he thought she was still working, and she waved and kept typing the same words over and over again, killing time: *Ava. Ava Lark.*

She liked the way the office felt when it was empty. None of the men were asking her to make coffee or copies when they were steps away from both the coffee machine and the copier. She wasn't summoned over to deliver papers to yet another associate in another office, whose gaze would linger on her body as he made some lame joke that she was expected to laugh at. *Hey Ava, you could be a train conductor because you're sure stopping me in my tracks!* The phones were silent so she didn't have to deal with customers wanting to talk to Richard because they were angry that the pink Satin Glide vanity case looked wrong in their bathroom, that the antique-looking faucets on their new sink didn't really look all that antique. If, every day, she could have done her job without anyone else around her, she would have been done by noon.

She wandered the empty rooms, passing the other women's desks, looking at their decorations. Charmaine had a sad little picture of her and her mother, two grown women both dressed up like witches for Halloween and a WAR IS NOT HEALTHY FOR CHILDREN AND OTHER LIVING THINGS button, which Betty, who supported the war, kept pointedly taking down. "Vietnam falls and it's dominoes, all the way to us," Betty insisted, flipping her hands. "You want to live under Communism? I don't." Only Cathy was gone, two months now. Tired of pining after Richard, she had grown out and straightened her hair with Curl Free, coming into the office flashing fishnet tights and miniskirts, and in six months, she had snagged a husband from accounting. When Cathy left, triumphant, Richard threw her a party and immediately replaced her with an older woman in her fifties, a widow who wasn't likely to marry again and leave the company.

Ava walked into Richard's office. It was decorated with all sorts of knickknacks that he thought were funny. A fake brass statue of a grinning man in a suit holding a trophy that said WORLD'S BEST BOSS. Two windup toys, a walking tub and a clacking toilet. He had his diploma

from the University of Massachusetts framed so it was the first thing
you saw, and there was a photo of his wife perched on his desk. She
was a little blonde with a toothy smile and big round sunglasses and
her arm was thrown carelessly around his shoulders. The two of them
were beaming over their little girl, who thankfully didn't have their
mother's grin.

The typing pool had straight-back wood chairs that they sometimes
padded with a cushion to support their backs. You had to get up to
stretch every few hours or you'd really regret it. But Richard's chair was
deep brown leather and so plush it looked as if you could sink down
into it and never want to get up. Ava sat, half shutting her eyes. The
leather cushioned her whole body and there was an extra ridge of support right where she needed it at her back. The chair was tall enough
so she could rest her head and neck, too. So this is what it felt like to be
king of the castle. If she had a chair like this, she could type for hours
and never feel the aches. For a moment she saw what he saw, the grand
sweep of his office, the line of desks in the other room, the elevator at
the end of the room so he could note who had arrived and who had
snuck out early. He had a fine view of the typing pool, with Ava's desk
right in front, framed by his doorway.

She had felt his stares before, but only for a moment, because she had
ten invoices to get out before noon, because she had calls she had to
field, and because she didn't like looking at him. Now, though, sitting
in his chair, she felt how exposed she was. Anytime he wanted to take a
gander at her, he could. Her desk was open in front so he could watch
her legs. If she bent over, he could look right down her blouse.

She flushed, anger rising up her throat. Tomorrow she'd start wearing
scarves tucked around her neck. She'd make sure her legs were covered
in dark nylons. If she caught him staring, she'd stare right back.

She leaned back in his chair, resting her head. God, but this chair
was comfortable. She could fall asleep right here, right now. She had no
idea what he did all day, no real clues what his family life might really

be like. Look how happy he was in this photo, but didn't she know how photographs could lie? For all she knew, his wife could be a harridan, his daughter a tantrum machine. "I have everything," she had heard Richard say to one of the other salesmen, but did he? You could look at the last picture she had taken with Brian, at the beach, the two of them posed awkwardly in the sand, her hair in a white puckered bathing cap, the strap fastened under her chin. Everyone had thought they were a golden couple and maybe Ava had thought that, too.

Suddenly, a woman from the cleaning staff appeared in the doorway. She was middle-aged, with a frowsy mop of fake black hair, dressed in a blue uniform and a kerchief, a white name tag perched on her chest. Jane. The other women in the office always complained about Jane. She broke knickknacks and then just put the pieces in the trash. She ate any remaining candy on a desk. The other typists looked down their noses at her, and once Charmaine had even put a big sign on her typewriter that said: CLEANING PERSON, DO NOT TOUCH THIS AREA!

Ava knew what a thin line there was between one job and another and Ava never complained, not even when her ashtrays weren't emptied and she had to clean them herself. She knew it was just her speedy typing that kept her from a job like Jane's.

Jane cleared her throat, regarding Ava.

"Jane," Ava said, because unlike her boss, she believed you should be kind to everyone, you should recognize them, no matter their job. "Don't worry," Jane said. "I do it, too. Sometimes I even catnap in that chair." She winked at Ava. "Sleep," she said. "I can work around you. And I won't tell. I'll wake you up before I go, if you like."

Ava grinned at Jane. She didn't stay in the chair very long after that. Instead, she got up and went to the break room and made herself and Jane some coffee, pouring it into Richard's fancy cup and then her own. She brought both cups over to Jane, who was polishing the desk of an account executive. Jane blinked when Ava handed one cup to her. "Go ahead," Ava said.

"Why, aren't you nice," Jane said, taking Richard's cup. Jane breathed in the coffee, sighing. "This will get me through the next floor," Jane said. "You should see what pigs the accountants are. Condoms in their wastebaskets. Once vomit on a desk. I think they do it deliberately."

"I know what we need," Ava said. "Come on with me." She walked Jane back to Richard's office, to the row of liquor bottles, the special gold-rimmed glasses he kept on the ledge. She had seen him pouring alcohol for clients, the toilet-and-tub guys who sauntered into his office in their fancy suits, wanting him to buy the novelty items, the toilets made out of fake gold. Richard's voice would grow more boisterous, the other men would guffaw, and then Richard would carefully close his door. She tried to find the bottle that was the most expensive, scanning the labels. There it was, Chivas Regal Royal Salute. Brian had ordered it for their honeymoon and when she had made a face at the taste, how strong it was, he had laughed. "You're drinking money," he had told her.

She picked up the bottle. "Scotch okay?" she said.

Jane hesitated.

"Come on, let's drink some money," Ava said. She liked the way that sounded.

"We won't get in trouble?"

"I take full responsibility," Ava said. "If we get caught or anyone notices, you can blame it all on me." She poured a little of the scotch, warm and golden into their coffee mugs. "Really, it's fine," she said. "He doesn't notice anything but himself." She lifted her cup, waiting for Jane to do the same. "To us," she said, clinking cups with Jane, and she drank it down, and she didn't know if she felt giddy from the alcohol or from the fact that they had dared to drink it.

When they were finished, Ava took the cups and washed them and put them back. She hoped that Richard wasn't the type to notice the level of his scotch.

Ava hung around until Jane headed to the next floor. "Maybe I'll see you tomorrow," Jane said, and Ava waved and thought what that would be like, staying here every night just so she could have the cleaning woman for company. It made her think of all those days with Jimmy, when she was so lost and lonely that she was grateful to see him showing up at her door, a little boy who made her feel better. How she had depended on his company!

She got up and put on her coat and then walked down the five flights instead of taking the elevator because it spooked her being the only person in it late at night. She had heard that last year the elevator had gotten stuck, and one of the cleaning staff had been cooped up by herself for six hours before someone came to rescue her.

When she got home, the neighborhood streets were dark, but the houses were lit up from within. There were all these signs of life still and though it should have made her feel better, instead, she felt her skin tensing, like it was stretched too tightly over her bones. A small headache was already forming, as the fizzy lift of the drink plummeted. She went into her house and flicked on the living room lights. She turned on the radio, and there was that song, "Strangers in the Night." Sinatra's voice grated against her so much, she felt like hitting him. When was the last time someone brought her roses? And his tone was so sweet. That godawful word *sweet.* Wasn't that just another word men used to turn women into children? They might as well call you *docile.* Like sheep. She thought of how Jake used to call her *kitty,* which she didn't mind, and then, out of the blue, it was *jungle cat,* and when she raised her eyebrows at him, he said, "You're no house kitty. You're a wild thing. You don't like it?"

"I love it," she said. And she had. The whole image of herself as a sleek, powerful jungle creature, of something undomesticated, made her want to kiss the spot where his neck joined his shoulder. *Jungle Cat.*

Suddenly sleepy, she turned off the lights and headed for her room. Lewis used to believe in ghosts when he was a little boy. He'd insist on sleeping with the lights on, and sometimes he would grow so frightened, he'd ask for Ava to sit in the rocker and wait until he was sleep. Lewis would pull the covers up to his chin. She would see him trembling. "Be a man," Brian would urge him.

"He's not a man, he's a little boy," Ava said, one night.

Brian shined a light under the bed. He poked in Lewis's closet, pushing the clothes aside. "No zombies. No devils. No nothing," Brian said.

"Zombies?" Lewis quavered and Brian sighed again. "Don't you start," he said.

"Leave the door open as wide as it goes," Lewis pleaded.

"Fine, but don't complain if you hear the TV," Brian said.

Ava bent and kissed her boy goodnight, breathing him in. "I'm right here," she whispered. When Ava checked on Lewis later, she saw him sleeping with the blanket all around him like a shroud, with only his tiny nose poking out. God, but it broke her heart. She carefully bent over and loosened up the folds so he'd get more air.

Now she went into his room. She opened a drawer and there was an old rugby shirt of his. She pulled it out and held it against her face, breathing in his scent, and when she started to cry, she told herself she was being stupid. She had lied when she had told him there were no ghosts. There most certainly were, and they were right here in this room, haunting her.

IN THE MORNING, the phone rang and she ran to the kitchen to get it and as soon as she said hello, she somehow knew it was Lewis. She was still his mother, no matter what had happened between them. His voice sounded tinny, like the scratch of metal on a can. Her knees buckled and she reached for the kitchen stool, sloping her body down onto it. "Lewis," she said because she didn't know what else to say, and because she didn't want to say anything that would make him hang up. He told her about his job, a little about his life. He wished her a Happy New Year.

She wanted to ask if he had a girlfriend, if he had friends or if he was lonely, but instead, she pressed the phone against her temple. It was like talking to a stranger sometimes.

"I'm tired from work," he said. He told her how he had sat with a cancer patient all night, holding her hand, listening to stories about her grandkids until she felt better. He was glad it was Saturday and as soon as he got off the phone, he said he was going to sleep all day. "I read medical books at night," he told her.

"You were always smart," she said. She could hear something humming through the wires.

"I'd better go," he said. "I just wanted to say hello."

She started to say something else, to tell him how much she missed him, but then she heard the click of his phone hanging up. She sat there, holding on to the receiver, unable to let go.

The hours spread before her. Maybe she should make herself something to eat. Ava had always been a lousy cook. When she was growing up, her mother used to joke that Ava couldn't even boil water and kept prodding her to make a meal, telling her it was a talent she needed to cultivate if she was ever going to get married. "Men love my meat loaf," she had assured Ava. "It has the surprise of a whole hard-boiled egg right in the center." But every time Ava tried to make it, her mother standing by, coaxing her, Ava's heart just wasn't in it. The meat came out rubbery. The potatoes were starchy. "I followed the directions," she insisted and her mother held up her hands in defeat. "Get a mix," her mother urged. "Use cans. Everything's so easy now."

When she had married Brian, he assured her that he hadn't fallen in love with her for her cooking. In fact, she had only made him spaghetti once, with sauce from a jar. He wanted to show her off, so they went out to eat almost every night. "Isn't she a beaut?" he asked everyone and Ava felt as if she had been dipped in silver so she gleamed.

Marriage, though, changed everything. He began to look at her in a new and distressing way, lowering his eyes, as if he were taking her measure. He called her "the Mrs." which sounded so much less sexy than "honey" or "doll." He began noticing things around the house, stooping to pick up a tumbleweed of dust on the floor. He frowned when his shirts weren't pressed. "Didn't you know I'd need them?" he asked. "What do you do all day?"

"You didn't tell me—"

"But sweetheart, isn't it your job to know?"

"I'm not a mind reader," she said.

"You're my wife," he said, and it sounded like an accusation.

Wanting to please him, she went to the bookstore and bought a cookbook called *Meals Men Love.* The glossy cover had a picture of a smiling man, his elbows on the table, a fork in one hand, a knife in the other, and coming toward him was his wife in a frilly apron, carrying a huge platter with a roast and potatoes on it. Ava riffled the pages, glancing at the Jell-O molds and the list of what ingredients would float in the gelatin and which wouldn't (who knew to put cucumbers in lime Jell-O?), the sweet-and-sour spinach with a potato-chip crust that made Ava tired. Carrots had to be curled and celery had to form a spray like a living green plant. You were supposed to have salads and desserts and even a theme, like the Polynesian luau meal complete with leis by each place mat. There was only one recipe in the whole book that urged wives to "let the men do it!" and that was for a salad, and how hard was it to tear lettuce, pour on some bottled dressing, and toss it around? Why was the man in the picture beaming like he had discovered how to send a rocket to the moon? It all irritated her. She wanted to shake his wife and ask her, was she a fool? Didn't she, like Ava, want to go out to dinner and have it served to her? Did she really want to make a meat-loaf train with carrot wheels and spend hours cutting hard peas in half for the heads of the passengers? She put down the book and called Brian on the phone. "I hate cooking," she said, and he laughed, which made her feel better.

That night, she tried to make Beer-Battered Chicken. She dredged the chicken in the batter and fried it, but her timing was off, and by the time Brian came in through the door, the chicken had burnt on the outside, but was still pink and raw when she tore at it with a fork. The peas, she saw, were overcooked, all the color drained from them and the pearl onions looked like tiny eyeballs rolling in grease.

Brian might have been sweet and funny on the phone, but she noticed the way a tic pulsed near his mouth when he saw the plate she set before him. She heard the scrape of his fork on the plate, reluctantly teasing a piece of raw chicken.

It wasn't long before Brian began telling her he had eaten before he came home. She felt a flash of relief. She began to eat by herself before he came home, too, or later, with Lewis, the two of them happy with peanut butter and jelly.

She hadn't cooked for Jake. When he came into the picture, neither one of them couldn't have cared less if they lived on TV dinners.

Well, she was alone now and could eat whatever she wanted. A meal didn't have to include meat or vegetables. She could have pie for dinner if she wanted. In fact, blueberry pie sounded just delicious. There was ice cream in the fridge and no one to tell her not to have it on top.

She put on the radio. Ray Charles was singing that he couldn't stop loving you. "A lot of good that will do you," Ava told him. She went to the bookcase and took out her mother's old cookbook and leafed through it until she found a recipe for blueberry pie. She got out the butter, shortening, cornstarch, and flour, and some frozen blueberries she had bought. "Stop acting like an idiot," she told herself. "You can do this." And if she couldn't, she'd throw it out and no one would know. She got out a mixing bowl, tied an apron around her waist, and took a deep breath.

An hour and a half later, Ava stared in amazement at her pie. The crust was golden and when she tapped it with the edge of a fork, it flaked.

She took a bite. The crust melted along her tongue. The fruit was tangy. It wasn't perfect, but it was pretty good. She sat there, in her tiny kitchen, and slowly, carefully, devoured the pie.

AFTER THAT, AVA began to bake pies whenever she could. She found she looked forward to it on the long nights when there was nothing to do, when everyone else was home with their families. She began to experiment, buying apples one week, and pears the next. Sometimes nothing worked right. The crusts came out hard or tasted like cardboard. More than a few times, the fillings were gelatinous or runny. Ava leaned against the counter, surveying the damage. So what if a few pies were disasters? She didn't feel like giving up. There was no one judging her, no one telling her not to waste the flour and the butter. Plus, with a whole night ahead, she could throw out the bad pies, clean her work area, and then start again from scratch. Humming with pleasure, she made pie after pie until they began to look better, to smell better, and when she put the fork in her mouth, she shut her eyes and swooned.

She began to realize that she didn't have to follow the recipes exactly, that she could use maple syrup instead of sugar and it would still taste delicious, that she could add less corn starch or more fruit for a brighter-tasting pie. She worked to perfect her crimp, studying the photos in her cookbooks, laying one finger along the dough, taking her time. She remembered her mother telling her that so much of cooking was your mood. You could have the best ingredients in the world, but if you were feeling ornery, nothing would taste right.

What got Ava, though, was there was no one to share her giddy joy when a pie came out right. "Oh, smell that!" she said to herself as a waft of cinnamon rose in the kitchen and the apples began to bubble. "How pretty!" she said, but the only other sound was the music from the radio. She wished she had a camera so she could photograph this pie and send a print to Lewis, with the words, *look what I can do!*

Ava brought one of her blueberry pies into work. She didn't know what she expected, but she felt jumpy. Every once in a while people brought in food. There were always Charmaine's mother's famous lemon squares or Richard's wife's chocolate cake, which was always too sweet for Ava's taste, and sometimes, someone would splurge and bring something in from Bell's Café down the street. Well, this blueberry pie was Ava's simplest, the filling just blueberries and real maple syrup, vanilla, and cinnamon, but it was so perfect looking, so beautiful, she wanted to show it off. As soon as she stepped into work, she felt nervous. Charmaine was sipping a can of cherry Metrecal, making a face even as she smoothed the fabric of her skirt around her hips with her free hand. Betty looked at the pie. "Where'd you get that? Is that from the Teacup Café?"

"I made it," Ava said.

"You?" said Betty. "You told us you were a lousy cook."

"I am. But I can make pies," Ava said.

Charmaine gave the pie another, more serious glance. "It looks good," she decided. She put the can down. "I can diet tomorrow," she said.

Ava placed the pie out by the coffee. By noon, when she returned to the kitchenette, the whole thing was gone. Richard was standing there, scraping his fork on the plate. "Did you have some of this?" he asked. "It's fabulous."

"I baked it," Ava said.

He lifted his brows. Ava felt a flush of pleasure creep up along her neck. He had never said anything particularly kind about her work. Every few months, he had evaluations of the staff, and when it was Ava's turn, he always told her "Keep up the good work," and then refused to give her a raise. Last time, she asked him to tell her what she was doing that was good. She wanted to hear it. "Just keep on doing what you're doing," he had said. Now, he set the plate down. "Really?" he said. "Best pie I've ever had." He winked at her, something she usually didn't like. "Ava, you've got something," he told her. For the first time that she could remember, he was looking at her face and not her bosom.

All that day, while typing up invoices for tubs, she thought about pie, about a new kind she might try. Bourbon chocolate. Pear spice. Apple pecan. She thought about how, when the weather got warmer, more fruit would be in season. She could drive right down to the DeVincent Farm Stand and get it.

At lunch, instead of staying in and eating at her desk, she began to frequent different cafés, just to taste test their pies, to examine the crusts at close range. She went to Juniper Tree and ordered the apple pie and when she couldn't tell what the spice was, she asked. "Cloves," the waitress said and Ava made a mental note to buy some. She went to Bell's Café and had the Dutch apple, wanting to compare, but when she asked the waitress for the ingredients, the waitress laughed. "Bell won't tell you any trade secrets," she said. "Don't even think of asking. She'd probably tell you the wrong thing anyway, just to throw you off the track." The waitress nodded at an older woman with a long gray braid, who was angrily fussing with a blue-checked tablecloth.

"Is she always that intense?" Ava asked and the waitress laughed.

"That's just Bell," the waitress said.

"Well, please tell her this pie's delicious," Ava said. She watched as the waitress went over to Bell and spoke to her quietly. Bell stood up, her hands braced on her waist. She nodded when the waitress was talking and then glanced over at Ava, narrowing her eyes, as if she were sizing her up. It made Ava so uncomfortable that she quickly wolfed down the pie and left a big tip.

Every night, Ava couldn't wait to get home. She no longer minded coming home to an empty house because she would soon be moving around her kitchen, baking, experimenting, listening to music. She made three small pies, each one different, and cut tiny slices for herself.

She tried to cook other things. She made a beef stew, which had no flavor. She roasted a chicken, which was dry. Never mind, she told herself. It didn't matter if those things were not part of your gift. You just had to have one thing that was your own.

She brought more pies into work and suddenly people were not only friendlier to her, they seemed to be waiting for her. "I know it's only nine, but this key lime pie is screaming my name," Betty told her. "I'll just have a sliver," Charmaine said and cut a thick slab. "Now, this pie is something you want in your hope chest." The men in accounting and sales had their secretaries cut them big slices and bring them into their offices. By ten, the pie was gone. "Great, now I can never fire you," Richard said.

"Maybe you could give me a raise," Ava said. "Then I could make more pies."

Richard laughed. "You're such a card," he said.

That night, when Ava got home, she was planning on making three new pies: orange cream, lemon cream, and raspberry, made with frozen berries. She had never tried cream pies and she was a little anxious, but when she opened the door, she nearly skidded on the mail. She picked up the envelopes: bills, more bills, a postcard from Lewis of a snow-storm, and on the back he had written, "Doing fine, love Lewis." She traced his words with her finger. "Love." It got her every time.

She was spending more money now on groceries, which made her worry a little about her bills. She always paid them on time, and she was careful about money, but how she wished she had a cushion in the bank. How many more times could she ask Richard for a raise and hear him say no? She knew how lucky she was that he had put her on full-time, but his face closed up every time she mentioned salary.

She went into the kitchen, knowing she'd feel better as soon as she could get her hands in dough. She poured out the flour and it spilled on the floor. She put too much water in and, almost instantly, the dough turned sticky. Her mother had been right, emotions did get into the food. She looked at her messy kitchen. If she kept on, she knew the crust would be hard and the filling too sweet.

Ava sat heavily at the kitchen table. She looked at all the rows of spices on the shelf and wanted to clean and alphabetize them. She wanted to scrub the walls and the floor and then make herself a bath so hot, the tension would float away, but she knew the way she felt, that as soon as she started to touch the spices, they'd spill. As soon as she got in the bath, she'd scald herself.

She had to get out. She needed to do something. She got her coat, then went back to the kitchen and took one of the pies she had forgotten to bring to work, a chocolate mint pie. She put it on a plate and wrapped wax paper over it. Maybe it was time to try to sell her pies. The worst that could happen is she'd get some advice on how to make her pies better.

She drove to Bell's because it was closest. As soon as Ava walked in, she felt suddenly bold. The café was filled with people, couples holed up in the back, a family arguing over spaghetti. It was freezing outside, but the café was warm and welcoming. There were only two waitresses, both in black aprons, gliding among the ferns and the rustic wood walls. And there, in the back, was Bell, who looked up at Ava and then glanced suspiciously at the plate. She strode over. "Excuse me? You're bringing pies into my café?" Bell said.

"I guess I am." Ava pulled back the waxed paper. The sugar on the crust glistened.

Bell studied her. "And?"

"I thought maybe you might want to buy my pies," Ava said.

"We make our own pastries here."

"Try a bite." Ava knew she was begging.

"Let me see your hands," Bell said.

"My hands?"

Bell gestured. "Hands," she said. She took the plate from Ava and then she waited until Ava held out her hands, and then she took them. "Cold hands," she said.

"I have a circulation problem," Ava told Bell. She ran one hand against the other.

"Don't do that." Bell said. "Don't rub your hands that way." Ava stopped, confused.

"You don't want to warm them up," Bell said. "Every time I hire a pastry chef, I check if their hands are cold or warm. If they're warm, too much dough is going to stick to their fingers, but cold, you get perfect crust every time. The art is in the crust." She glanced at Ava's pie and pulled off the wax paper. "Don't get your hopes up, though. Still doesn't mean the pie will taste good," Bell said.

Ava scrutinized her crust. She had spent nearly an hour crimping the edges, making sure it was perfect.

"Crimping's not bad. That's a nice signature." Bell touched the crust. "Different people crimp differently. It gets so I can see a pie, look at the crust, and I know who baked it." She touched the edge of the crust and then reached behind the counter and took a fork. She took a bite while Ava waited and then she put the fork down.

"If it's not good enough, why isn't it good enough?" Ava said.

"I didn't say that," Bell said. "I'll buy this pie, slice it up. If it does well, I'll order more."

Ava felt like throwing her arms around Bell, but the other woman stepped back from her. "This isn't charity," she said. "I just think you might have a white thumb."

The only thing anyone had ever told Ava she was good at was in bed. She couldn't help smiling.

"What?" said Bell.

"My ex-husband thought I was a lousy cook." As soon as she said ex-husband, she wondered if she had made a tactical mistake, but Bell nodded thoughtfully.

"Well, what did he know?" she said. "There's a reason he's your ex." She leaned on the counter. "Men expect you to cook up a storm at home, but if you dare to go in a professional kitchen and there's money involved, forget it. Do you think it's in their genes to be such stinkers?"

Ava laughed, and then Bell did. "My husband was different, but he's gone now," she told Ava. "Anyway, right now, we'll see how this goes."

The next day, when Ava got home from work, she was too anxious to bake anything. Instead, she was watching Jimmy Cagney on *Million Dollar Movie,* when the phone rang. She backed toward the phone, watching Cagney smash a grapefruit into his girlfriend's face.

"The pie is gone," Bell said. "People want more. And so do I."

INSTANTLY, AVA HAD a new schedule. She got up two hours early on workdays to bake, so the pies would be fresh when she brought them to Bell. Money changed everything, Bell had told her, and she had to admit it did. The whole process of baking became different, more exciting somehow. It wasn't very much money, just three dollars a pie, but it was twice what it cost her to make each pie. She set up a little savings account at the local bank, and by February, she was seeing it grow. She began to dream about all the fresh fruit she could buy when they came in season, expensive things like raspberries. Every time she made a deposit, she couldn't help smiling. Plus, it made her bolder. She knew her chocolate pies sold out, but what if she grated a dash of ginger in there? What if she put in orange peel? What if she let the dough sit even longer than usual?

Being up so early made her see and hear things she had missed before in the neighborhood. She spotted the milkman now, in his dapper white uniform and cap, and she waved him over, because now that she had a little more money, she could afford delivery. Early one morning, when she was retrieving the bottles and cartons out of the metal milk box, she heard a door slam across the street. She looked up and saw Dick Hill stride of the house with a suitcase, his face set. Debbie was flying out after him, in her robe and fluffy slippers, her hair in pink sponge curlers, and it wasn't hard to tell Debbie was crying. Debbie reached for Dick, but he peeled her hands off his shoulders as if he were removing sticky tape. He strode to the car and drove off. Debbie looked up and saw Ava and immediately turned and went back into the house, which was a shame because Ava could have told her something about how to heal heartbreak.

Ava had to be at work by nine, but she left the house at seven, carefully balancing the pies in boxes, stacking them carefully in the passenger seat.

"People say the lemon makes them think of their childhood," Bell told her when she arrived. "Couples in love order the chocolate mint, and lonely people go for your Boston cream. How do you do that? How do you make pies that speak to people?"

"I don't know," Ava said.

"How about four more for tomorrow?" Bell said. "I admit the chocolate made me feel my Henry close by."

Ava stopped baking for work. She didn't have time, and besides no one was paying her. She saw the women from the typing pool milling about the coffee area, looking at her expectantly when she came in and then turning, disappointed, when they saw her empty hands. "What, no goodies?" Richard asked and Ava shrugged.

"I've been busy," she said.

"Doing what?"

"I'm selling my pies now," she told him.

He tilted his head, blinking as if he didn't understand her. "You're selling them?"

"To Bell's Café."

Richard frowned. "For money?"

Ava nodded. "That's what selling means," she said.

"Well," he said, suddenly brisk. "Don't forget your real job. And don't forget us here."

It you want pies, then you'll have to buy them, Ava thought, but she was smart enough not to say that aloud. Instead, she smiled and went back to typing letters about faucets. Charmaine leaned over and tapped Ava. "I don't know if I'd sell pies," she said.

"Why not?"

"I used to be a really good swimmer," Charmaine said. "Once, this boy challenged me to a race. I did everything right. I hyperventilated so I was really oxygenated. I let out only a few bubbles as I swam, and when I got to the surface I turned around and there was the boy, standing up to his knees in water, way behind me, and he wouldn't look at me. Wouldn't talk to me. When I got to shore, my mother was shaking her head. 'Don't ever do that again,' she said. 'Showing a man up. Taking over his terrain. Men don't like that sort of thing.'"

"That's crazy," Ava said, and Charmaine shrugged. "Think what you like," she said.

Ava went out and bought two starchy white aprons and some hairnets. It became more important to her that her kitchen be spotless, and she willingly got on her hands and knees now to scrub. She went out and bought a new smooth wood rolling pin and six new pie pans. Now when she looked at her kitchen, she had a whole different feeling about it. She could make things happen. She was in charge.

One Friday night, after she finished testing out a new pie (raisin apple custard), she felt antsy. She showered and changed, and even though it was starting to snow, she went out to the Club 47 in Cambridge to hear music. She didn't care who was playing, and it ended up being a young woman with long fuzzy hair and a voice like a bell, singing with her guitar about how her lover stabbed her by a raging river. The club was blue with smoke so you couldn't really see clearly, but even so, Ava felt a man watching her. She felt him sitting beside her before she looked over and saw that he was younger than she was, with longer hair than she had on her own head, and before the first set was over, she knew two things: that his name was Damien and that she was taking him home.

When he automatically slid into the driver's seat, his hands primed on the wheel, Ava said, "No, I'm driving." He shrugged and let her, but he kept one hand on her thigh. As soon as they got in her house, he put his mouth on her neck and drew her so close she could feel the heat of his skin, but she gave him a gentle shove away from her. "Playing hard to get?" he said, amused.

"Come with me," she said. She took him to her kitchen, sitting him down at her red Formica table. She went to the refrigerator and took out the raisin apple custard pie. He looked at her curiously. "Really? You want me to eat right now?" he said.

She cut him a thin slice and put it on a plate, got him a fork and a napkin and set them both in front of him. "Yes," she said.

He took a bite and then looked up at her, as if he were taking her measure. She saw the surprise in his face, the pleasure. "Cloves," she whispered into his ear. "Nutmeg." He took another bite and another and soon finished off the whole piece. "Is there more?" he said and she laughed.

"Yeah, there's more," she said. She kissed him and tasted the cinnamon. She took his hand and lifted him up so he was standing, facing her, and she put his hand on her breast. "Maybe I'll stay the night," he whispered. He told her she looked like Joan Baez, which made her laugh, because she looked as much like Joan Baez as she did Marilyn Monroe. Ava rested her head against his chest so she could feel his breathing, so she could remember this moment, so she wouldn't forget, because she knew after this night, she wouldn't see him again.

He wasn't a bad lover, but he was quicker than she would have liked, and when he started to fall asleep, his head on her breast, Ava pushed him awake. "Did I do something wrong?" Damien asked. He reached for her, but she slid out of his arms. "You have to go," she told him. She got up, pulling on her clothes, glancing at the clock.

"You want me to go?"

"Yes," she told him. "Please." She kissed his nose, handed his clothes to him, and watched him tug them on. He called a cab, and the two of them waited by her front window. When the cab arrived, he turned to her. "Wait," he said. He spotted a pen and paper and wrote his number down for her. "See you soon," he said, and then went out the door.

Ava felt ridiculously free. She dropped his number in the wastebasket and then she headed for the kitchen.

It was still night, but she began to bake, and by early Saturday morning, she had six new pies for the café. She was used to just walking into the kitchen and setting them there, leaving her list for Bell to tally up and pay her later. The café was always busy, and Bell barely had time to even say hello to her, which was fine by Ava. Ava liked walking by, like a voyeur, seeing who was eating her pies, whisking by the circular display Bell had at the front of the café to see which pies were going the fastest. She was pleased to see the circles of them growing smaller and smaller. Her arms were lighter without the pies, and she started walking out when Bell stopped her at the door. "You know, you can't be selling pies here without knowing my menu," Bell told her.

"I've eaten here," Ava said, though all she could remember was a muffin and coffee.

"Really? When? Name the last thing you ate here, and no looking at the blackboard menu for ideas. I'll know if you lie."

Ava shrugged, embarrassed.

"You're not the only one who takes pride in her cooking," Bell said. She motioned to a table. "Have a seat," she said.

Ava complied, but when she reached for a menu, Bell shook her head. "Let me surprise you," she said. "It's soul food night." Bell brought her a stew, silky with wide flat noodles and chunks of chicken, some turnip greens on the side, and then she sat down opposite Ava. "You ever had turnip greens?" She waited for Ava to take her first bite. "Good, right?" Bell said.

"I could never cook like this," Ava said and Bell snorted.

"Bull," she said. "Maybe you just don't want to, and there's nothing wrong with that." Bell rested her head in her hands.

"I think you might be right about that."

"My husband Henry started this café," Bell said. "He worked here doing everything, the cooking, the cleaning, the buying, right up until he got cancer, and then I took over. Everyone thought I was crazy, that it was just grief talking, and that soon the place would run into the ground with a woman at the helm. I had all these buyers for it and then I decided I liked running the place. It gave me something to do. Plus, it made me feel close to Henry still."

"You miss him?" As soon as Ava said it, she felt ridiculous, but Bell took a breath. "Everyone misses someone," Bell said, and Ava thought of Lewis. "Yes," Ava said. "They do."

Ava was finishing the stew when she recognized a voice spinning across the restaurant. She looked up and Debbie Hill had come into the café. She had a wrinkled raincoat thrown over what looked like her flannel pajamas, and her hair was tied back in a chiffon kerchief. Shivering, Debbie looked right at Ava and then pretended she didn't know her, turning quickly away. She slid into a booth in the back and popped up a menu so it hid her face.

Bell followed Ava's eyes and then leaned forward. "See that woman?" Bell said, lowering her voice. "She comes here every night and has your lemon pie and cries."

Ava looked at Debbie again. She remembered how Debbie's husband had walked out with a suitcase, leaving Debbie standing on her front porch in a robe and fuzzy slippers, her face pale. Ava hadn't spotted Dick since, and she didn't see Debbie so much anymore, either, or even Barbara, their girl. Ava looked over at Debbie, who was clutching the top of her raincoat, avoiding looking over at them. "Do me a favor," Ava said. "Don't tell her I make the pies, but next time, give her a really big piece and I'll pay for it. Tell her it's on the house."

TWO WEEKS LATER, Ava was shoveling snow off her front walk when she saw Dick's car drive up to his house. He got out and Debbie came out of the front door, wavering for a moment before she walked toward him, her hand raised as if she were going to strike him, but instead, she rested her head along his shoulder. He stroked Debbie's hair and said something quietly to her. Then Barbara ran out and wrapped her arms ecstatically around her father.

It made Ava feel better, even though Dick was no prize, and she wondered if Debbie would come back to the café anymore.

The cold air bit her cheeks, energizing her, and when she was finished shoveling, Ava decided to take a walk around the neighborhood. The people down the street were building an addition, making their tiny ranch house look more like a colonial. Someone else had painted their house this funny bright pink, with deep plum shutters. She was coming back around the block, her boots caked with snow, when she bumped into Bob Gallagher, planting a big FOR SALE sign on his lawn, hammering it down.

She was surprised. She had been so busy she hadn't really seen much of him or his family. For ages, it seemed. "You're moving!" she called to him. He strode over to her.

"Company's moving me to Florida. Much more opportunity," he told her. "Though I don't like being so close to Cuba and that Fidel Castro." He told her he was being paid for the move, that they had a nice brand-new split level right by the beach, something Tina had always wanted, and that realtors would sell this house. "I'll miss it here," he told Ava. "I'll miss you."

"Me?" She saw the way his mouth curved and then he leaned forward and hugged her. "Yeah, you," he said.

IN MARCH, BOB and Tina left. The house was sold to a doctor and his wife who wanted it as a teardown. As soon as the snow melted, there were bulldozers razing the property. Ava saw the new owners prowling about the grounds, the man tall and thin as a swizzle stick, in a fancy dark suit, his wife in a pink maternity dress with a big satin bow on the empire waist, her hands laced across her belly. "Hello!" Ava waved, walking over.

The woman glanced over at Ava and her husband thrust out his hand. "Stan Morton," he said.

"Doris," the woman said.

"It's such a nice neighborhood," Doris said. She waved her hand. "And the school so close."

"We're building everything brand-new," Stan said. He told her they wanted a split-level, something imposing and different. They wanted a big fenced-in pool in the backyard. "You'll see, we'll have everyone over for a housewarming party when we're done," Doris said graciously.

The construction went on for weeks. The workers had to put up a fence around the property because two kids had written their names in a patch of wet cement. The sound of the trucks woke her every morning when the contractors arrived, six of them in old dungarees and T-shirts. For the first time in a while, Debbie Hill came outside and this time, her eyes were clear. "That house is going to make everyone else's look plain old shabby," Debbie said.

The family dug up everything, including the beautiful old willow tree in the backyard. They pulled up the sod lawn, and then, one sunny day in April, Ava came home from work to find, like the reopening of a wound, a police car in front of Bob Gallagher's old house, the lights on. There was a line of sawhorses and yellow rope leading to the backyard, and cops standing around. But what was most disconcerting to Ava were the photographers, coming around the front of the house, snapping everything they saw, including the people. Ava blinked at the flash. Debbie, her hand resting on her mouth, looked at Ava, and that was when Ava began to get really scared.

Ava grabbed at Debbie. "What happened?" she asked. "What's going on?"

Debbie stared at Ava. "They found an old bomb shelter," she said. "And they found bones."

❖ Chapter Sixteen ❖

Ava felt as if she couldn't move. She stared at the lot, all those beautiful trees gone, the flowers, everything, really, just gone, like someone had punched a piece of the landscape away and filled it up with this dirty wash of sky.

She could see the new owners, standing helplessly, staring at their property—and it was theirs now, no matter what had been discovered.

She cautiously walked closer. She didn't recognize any of these cops. Their faces were all new, but the feeling of dread was not. One of the officers stopped her. "Step away from the crime scene, please," he said.

"Whose bones are they?" Ava's could barely speak. One of the onlookers told her it was a boy, that they knew from the size of the femur. Someone else had said they heard there was a disintegrated pair of plaid shorts, a pair of sneakers with scribbles on them. Debbie put her hand to her mouth and then lowered it. "They called all the local dentists. They got a match already. It's Jimmy."

"How do you know? How do you know for sure?" Ava cried.

"I'm not going to ask you again, ma'am," the cop said. "You need to step away."

Ava thought of the day that Jimmy had vanished. The whole neighborhood, the cops, everyone had looked everywhere. Cars had been stopped. Strangers questioned. She tried to remember all that had gone on. The neighbors had been looking for someone in a car, for a stranger, for things outside the neighborhood. She hadn't even known there was a bomb shelter. When had Bob even built it? And why hadn't the cops found it in their investigation? They had checked every house on the block, every backyard, every basement. Hadn't she heard someone say that? How could any of this be true?

"A bomb shelter! Who knew there was one in this neighborhood? What was he thinking?" Dick asked. "Why didn't he tell anyone?" Dick shook his head. "I never trusted the guy." All Ava could think of was all the times she had seen Dick and Bob playing badminton in Dick's backyard, the net strung across the lawn, the two of them sweaty and puffing, not stopping until Debbie came out with cold drinks.

"Can you imagine? Bob a murderer?" Debbie shook her head.

"Don't say that," Ava said. She hadn't liked Bob very much, but she had seen the tender way he kissed his wife in the mornings, the playful way he hugged his son.

"Are you sure? Are they sure it's Jimmy?" Ava asked and Debbie looked at her with pity.

"Ava," she said. "What do you think?"

The press had been here that morning while Ava was at work, a TV truck, a newsman in a suit. A neighbor had told Ava that Bob Gallagher was coming back from Florida for questioning.

A few neighborhood kids—kids Ava didn't know so well anymore—in Keds and dungarees, roamed on their bikes, veering close to the house and then swooping away again.

AVA WENT HOME. She sat in her living room and stared at her walls. She thought of all the times Lewis ran wild over the neighborhood, how everyone's house had an open-door policy. She remembered how Bob had once leaned in close to her when he was fixing one of her lights, as if he wanted to kiss her, how every time she needed her gutters cleaned or a drain unclogged, he was always there and as soon as he was done, he'd linger until she'd say, "Want coffee?" and of course, he always did.

Jimmy had been right here all this time and no one had known. What if Bob hadn't gotten that new job? What if he had stayed? Would anyone ever have known? Or would there be more bones?

She picked up the phone and dialed Lewis. She wanted to hear his voice, as if she could touch him through the wires. This was something he would want to know. This was something they had shared. It rang and rang, but he didn't answer.

The next morning, Ava stood in the middle of the street, when Stan walked over to her, his hat almost apologetically in his hand.

"We're staying with my mother," Stan said. "I don't even know if we'll come back here. Doris is just too spooked."

Ava nodded.

"You knew this kid," he said.

"I did." Ava thought of Jimmy waving good-bye to her. The crooked smile. She thought how long the neighborhood patrols had gone on, how how much time the cops had spent on the case, and now they had found bones, and in less than a day, they knew they were Jimmy's.

"I heard that there was no sign of struggle," Stan said. "No evidence of anyone being around the shelter at all except for that kid. I heard the cops say that he must have known that place was there." Stan looked past Ava. "Crazy kids," he said. "They always think they're invincible." Stan folded his hat between his fingers. It was a cool day but his face was dappled with sweat. "Who's going to buy this house now?" he said.

IN THE FOLLOWING days, Ava tried repeatedly to reach Lewis, but to no avail. She watched the news constantly, wondering if any national channels would pick up the story. Every local channel aired photographs of Dot, Rose, and Jimmy, and every time she saw them, she flinched, but the news told her nothing new. All those nights, everyone had searched for Jimmy. They had all wondered and panicked, passing stories around like party nuts, about what they thought might have happened, and none of them had been true. He hadn't been pulled into a car. He wasn't kidnapped and living as someone else's son. She turned the channel. Patsy Baker, the freckle-faced newscaster she liked, was staring out at her, talking about Jimmy. Ava hadn't seen Patsy at the crime scene, but she was talking as if she knew all the facts. She talked to a cop Ava didn't recognize, either, who looked uneasy and defensive, and when she asked him about the bomb shelter, when she asked why no one had looked for it back when Jimmy had first disappeared, he sighed. "No one told us about any bomb shelter," he said. "Don't you think we would have checked it out if we had known?" He pointed out that when a kid vanishes, the first twenty-four hours are the most important. "You have to do everything you can do fast," the cop said. Patsy nodded gravely at him and then she mentioned that some people felt the detective in charge, Hank Maroni, had botched the case, hurrying it along, cutting corners because it was a working-class neighborhood rather than a wealthy one. He had been fired a few years ago for tampering with evidence on another case, and had died of a heart attack shortly after, believing he had been made a scapegoat.

Ava sighed and then Patsy began talking about how they were calling in some of the old suspects. Ava felt relieved they hadn't called her, but she wondered if they had found and called Jake or her other boyfriends, if once again, she'd be getting those angry phone calls. Then Patsy switched to talking about Bob Gallagher, how he had come back for questioning. He had insisted on a lie detector test, and the cops had had to call in to Boston to borrow a polygraph machine, and he had passed. "We have an interview tape," Patsy said, and there was Bob, his face drawn, his forehead pinched in worry. Bob insisted that he had forgotten the shelter, that he had started building it when his son was a baby, but he had never even totally finished it. He'd given it up years ago, letting it rust shut, and he was sure that no one ever knew about it but him.

The whole time Bob was talking Ava leaned forward, as if the real truth might be floating on top of his words and all she would have to do would be to be quick enough to skim it free. He kept talking and talking, revealing much more than the interviewer asked for.

"I was afraid of Communists," Bob said. He said he had read this pamphlet, *Is This Tomorrow: America Under Communism!* that spooked him every time he looked at the cover, where people were screaming in horror and running from a nuclear attack. What struck him most was the panic, the way neighbor clawed over neighbor to escape the bombs.

He bought plans to build a fallout shelter, but he told no one what he was doing, because he couldn't risk his neighbors wanting to storm the small space if there was an attack and jeopardize his family's safety. There just wasn't room. He hadn't even told his wife, because he knew she was more soft-hearted than he was and she wouldn't dream of shutting anyone out. He'd never tell his little boy who would consider it a playhouse, plus who could keep kids quiet about a thing like that? Instead, he crept outside at three in the morning, when his wife and son were sleeping. His yard was ringed by big trees and a fence. No one could see what he was doing. The building materials were all in the garage, mixed in with his workshop supplies, and he would carefully take them outside to the area he had specifically cleared, concealed by overgrown hemlock bushes. Surprisingly, no one seemed to wake at the noise, or if they did, not enough to come over and see what was going on. He worked by flashlight, hidden by the hedges and the trees and the dark night. When he was finished, he covered the opening with sod and then brought everything back inside or hid it in the yard. During the daytime, he yelled whenever he saw anyone even attempt to cross his lawn, and gradually people learned not to do it. Sometimes, walking in his backyard, he felt a surge of comfort just knowing it was there, that he could protect his wife and his son.

He had it just about finished, stocked with canned goods and water, even a little cot. And then, one day at the dentist, he had picked up a magazine and read a piece by a scientist that said that a bomb shelter wouldn't be enough in an attack. It wouldn't protect anyone, and people who thought so were objects of ridicule. Bob had felt hot with shame. The more he read, the more he began to agree with the writer, and the more embarrassed he became. He felt duped, and the only thing to do was to try to seal it up and forget about it. No one had to know he had made a fool of himself. Not his wife, or his kid, or any of the neighbors. He'd find another way to protect his family.

Patsy Baker looked out at the audience, her face grave. "On a sunny day, when most of the neighborhood was away celebrating at a local church carnival, one young boy's tomb was a bomb shelter hidden under hemlock bushes. His mother died without peace, never knowing what had happened to her only son." Ava stood up, sweating. She hadn't known Dot was dead. She wanted to shake Patsy, to tell her to shut up. Tears tripped down her cheeks, but she couldn't stop watching. She wished Bob had come back to the neighborhood so she could have spoken to him.

"Let's go inside," Patsy said meaningfully. Film flashed on the screen and Ava thought, when had the TV crew filmed this? Why had the cops even allowed it? The film showed the bomb shelter. It was a metal well with a circular hole, a rusted ladder torn from the wall. "He must have fallen because his ankle was broken," Patsy said. The camera panned across the two empty glass bottles, which had held water. It pointed out the flashlight, with batteries that had worn out, the two cans of tuna and one can of corn niblets, punctured with the rusty can opener. There was the rusted cot propped up against the wall, almost like a ladder, almost as if Jimmy had tried to escape. "Sources say he could have lived a week," Patsy said. There were no books, no phone, no window. Just those thick walls that kept anyone from hearing Jimmy. Just the sealed over ventilation system that would have suffocated him. "If more people had known, if the police investigation had been more thorough," she said, "perhaps this tragedy could have been averted."

Ava swiped at her tears. She turned off the television. She thought of Jimmy showing up on her front step, standing there as if he knew he was somehow expected. She didn't know what she had thought, but sometimes she had imagined that she would hear from Jimmy again, that he'd just appear. When she saw him in her mind, he was in his twenties, like her Lewis, tall and handsome and so very adult. "I remember you," he'd tell her, and she could say, "I remember you, too," right back at him. She could take him out for coffee, show him off, a big, strapping, handsome boy now, and ask him about the girls he was dating, the ones who were in love with him. All that promise.

Poor Dot, she thought. And oh dear God, that sweet little Rose. She hadn't heard from either of them in years. No one had. The police must have contacted Rose and maybe it was a blessing Dot was dead, because what mother could bear hearing such news? At least Ava knew Lewis was alive, that he had a job, that he seemed happy, or at least he made a show of it on the phone to her when she called.

It could have been Lewis in that shelter.

Ava picked up the phone and called Lewis again. The phone rang three times, and then there he was. "Lewis," she said, breathing into the phone. "I have to tell you something." The whole time she was spilling out the story, he was quiet. She couldn't even hear his breathing, which unnerved her. "Lewis, are you there?" she said.

"I don't understand," he said. "This can't be right."

"It is," Ava said. "The cops said there were dental records. The sneakers."

"Jimmy wouldn't go near that bomb shelter."

Ava started. "You knew there was a shelter? How did you know?"

"We came across it once and went inside. But none of us would go down there ever again. It was too scary."

"What? You were inside? Why didn't I know this?"

"Mom, I don't know—I was a kid, I didn't tell you everything."

"But when the cops were here, why didn't you kids mention it?"

"We'd never, ever, think of it as a place he'd be. It never entered our minds."

She hesitated. "Do you want to come home?" She heard Lewis rustling in the background. "I have a job, Mom. I can't just leave it." His voice was so sad she wanted to burrow into it. He hung up the phone. For a while, Ava sat there, listening to the dial tone.

❖ Chapter Seventeen ❖

Two weeks before Rose heard about her brother, she was standing in the middle of a playground, watching her third-grade class swarming around with the fourth graders. Though it was the beginning of April, it was still cold, and her breath was pluming out in front of her. Her hands were buried in her coat, her collar turned up against the freezing wind. She tried to concentrate on the kids, to make sure no one was getting pummeled or teased, but the wind kept whipping her hair into her face and making her blink. She was twenty-three and she had been teaching less than a year, and she hated being in charge of two grades. No one was listening to her today. She kept shivering, clutching her coat tighter around her, wishing she had brought a sweater to layer under it. The kids were running wild, screaming like banshees, and every time she thought she knew where one kid was, he or she would run someplace else and vanish, and Rose would feel a clip in her heart. Just like that. They'd be gone.

Usually, there'd be another teacher out here, someone who would huddle near Rose and gossip with her. She liked the other teachers, for the most part. When Rose was hired, the other third-grade teacher, Emily, had put her arm around Rose and said, "I'm taking you under my wing," and she had. Emily not only helped Rose with lesson plans, she made her join the teachers' Friday night pizza parties.

Rose wished Emily was outside with her now. Sometimes there'd be a Thermos of milky hot coffee they could share, something to warm their hands, but it was flu season and half the teachers were out, including Emily, and the substitute had to watch another class. They couldn't spare two adults for recess today. But they shouldn't have left her alone out here.

As her hair flew against her face, Rose grabbed a hank of it and tried to braid it as best she could. Through her bangs, she watched the kids prowling around the edges of the playground, by the woods, something they weren't supposed to do. A boy in a too-big camel hair jacket, headed for the big maple tree the kids liked to climb. "Bobby!" she shouted, but the wind swallowed her voice. She waved her arms and he saw her. He dragged his feet coming back toward the other kids.

She hated the woods. She didn't understand why a school would want to be so close to a forest, without even a fence to separate all that wildness from the pavement. The woods were so vast, filled with lush and inviting plants, with bushes and trees that could hide so much. The principal wouldn't listen when she suggested at least putting a fence up. "Fences cost money," he had told her. "What are you so worried about?" he had asked.

She told herself that she was in Ann Arbor now, far away from Waltham. There was no apparent danger here in this schoolyard. No one seemed afraid. She lived on East William Street, in a small apartment in a big white house, surrounded by university students and families. Crimes, when they happened, were usually petty robberies or someone crashing a car because they had drunk too much. Last month, a group of college kids had been busted for breaking into houses, but they never stole a thing. They had rearranged the furniture in funny ways, putting an armchair in the kitchen, a kitchen table upside down. They made and ate cheese sandwiches, leaving the crusts and the crumbs behind, using up all the fancy mustard. When they were caught and asked why they had done it, one of the kids had said, "Because we could," and it had unnerved Rose. It made her think anything could happen.

Rose stared into the woods. There it was, that feeling. Like she was thirteen years old again and she had swallowed ice. Like she knew something would happen. All she had to do was shut her eyes and she could remember how the woods smelled that day Jimmy had disappeared. She remembered the crunch of the leaves under her feet, the scratch of Lewis's breathing next to hers. She could still feel the neighbors looking at her, as if they either blamed her or thought she knew something that she wasn't telling.

She wrapped her coat around her thin rayon dress, another vintage find from the thrift shops she loved. The kids thought the way she dressed was weird. "When are you going to get some style?" one of her students, a little girl in white go-go boots and a velvet headband had asked, and Rose had just laughed. She knew they thought she was mysterious, that she harbored some dark secret. Every time she taught them current events, they applied it to her in the most personal and strange way. A boy asked her if she had Negro blood. A shy little girl wanted to know if she was Vietnamese. Flabbergasted, Rose promptly taught a lesson on tolerance. But if Rose knew anything, she knew that you couldn't stop people from believing whatever it was they wanted to believe.

Rose glanced at her watch. They had five more minutes out here, but she had had enough. She took the whistle around her neck and blew it and the kids all turned toward her. They were all arms and legs, and it still astonished her that she was in charge of them, that they trusted her and did what she said for the most part. It always astounded her when their parents called her to ask for advice. Mostly, though, they listened intently, as if she held the key to their children. She knew what to say: that one child needed more attention at home; that another sometimes came in half-asleep, which made her wonder why he wasn't sleeping at night. The parents nodded and leaned forward as if they had to catch every word she said, writing down her advice and singing her praises to her principal, who gave her a raise and clapped her on the back, telling her how valued she was. "You work harder than any of the other teachers," he said. But how could Rose tell him that she worked so hard because what else was there?

Rose got the kids into a semblance of a line and watched them go in the building. They socked one another, they chattered and hooted, but they did get inside, every last one of them. She made sure of it. And then, before she followed them inside, as she always did, she took one last walk around the playground, just to make sure no one had gone astray.

WHEN ROSE AND her mother first moved to Pittsburgh, Rose had hated it. Pittsburgh was dirty and gray and the air always smelled like it had been dunked in iron. She asked her mother to buy her a big wicker box, lying, saying it was for school papers, and she kept all her clues about Jimmy in there: an old T-shirt of his, a wallet, her notebooks. She was the family historian, keeping it all alive. Every night, after her mother and Aunt Hope were asleep, she'd pull the box out from under the bed and touch the objects as if they were talismans.

Living with Aunt Hope was worse than she had imagined. Hope had a horse face and wore clunky orthopedic shoes that sounded like drumbeats on the floor, and she was always yelling at Rose to set the table, to help fold the wash, to stop being so fresh even though Rose hadn't said anything. Rose had her own room, but it was small, and it had a window that was painted shut. Every night Rose wished to be back home, to see Lewis's window from her own, to feel soft carpet beneath her feet instead of this hard wood.

Rose's mother took off her wedding band and put it in a drawer. She stopped talking about her husband. She never talked about Jimmy. "How many kids do you have?" a new neighbor asked and Rose heard her mother say, "One."

A few days later, Dot put on a brand-new red dress and took the bus into town. When she came back, flushed, she held up a bakery box, tied with red and white string. "Guess who's the newest cashier at the Giant Eagle supermarket?" she said.

It wasn't much, but it was enough for them to rent their own place, a small one-bedroom on Howe Street with a fake gold lion at the front door. The Lion's Head, the building was called, even though it was just a crummy block of apartments with green shag carpeting and fake wood beams stretching across the lobby ceiling.

As soon as they moved, Rose couldn't wait to write Lewis. She opened her Jimmy Stewart journal, half-filled with letters to him already. She turned to a clean page, sitting at the small white desk in her room.

Dear Lewis.

She didn't know what to say. It was one thing to be right there with him, but here she was in a strange place, and without seeing his face, she had no idea what he might be thinking. *I miss you,* she wrote, but it didn't seem like enough. She pushed the paper aside, figuring she would do it later. Lying in bed late at night, she began telling herself stories. Maybe he had new friends now. Maybe he even had a girlfriend. Was Lewis even still looking for Jimmy? She picked at the chenille spread. Jimmy was Lewis's best friend, but he wasn't his brother, no matter how close they were. Did Lewis still care?

Out of sight, out of mind. That was something her mother always said. Every time she looked in a mirror, she saw Jimmy in her own face. Every time she watched her mother staring into space, she knew what her mother was thinking about and she knew she was somehow responsible for her mother's sadness. But Lewis was on his own. Did that make him more vulnerable or less? She got up and went back to her letter. *Dear Lewis,* she started again.

She had loved the dark sweep of his hair, the flecks of green in one eye, like bottle glass. Other girls must notice how handsome he was. Lewis would have girls who weren't damaged, who didn't have a piece missing. Every time he looked at them, he wouldn't be reminded of a terrible thing that had happened.

She sat up and suddenly felt too stupid to write to him. How could she tell him how unhappy her mother was? How could she tell him what her life was really like? She was fourteen and in ninth grade in a new school and all the girls clumped together and ignored her. When she walked into class with her hair still rough-cut like her brother's, the girls, their hair teased into smooth bubbles, snickered. "Nice hair," they laughed. When she asked a boy about the math homework in the hall, two kids walked by bumping her, so she dropped her notebook and pen. She had to dip to retrieve them and when she stood, the boy was gone.

Loser, she heard. *Freak.* What had her mother done, moving them here? The first time she was invited to sit at a table with other girls in the cafeteria, she felt so glad and grateful she could have cried. She eased into a seat, half listening to the girls talking about mascara and whom they wanted to go steady with.

"You always look sad," one girl announced, looking at Rose, and then all the other girls stared at her, too. "You do," said one of the girls.

"My brother vanished," Rose said.

There was silence. Rose could hear the girl next to her chewing her gum. And then one of the other girls dug in her pocketbook and pulled out a gold tube of lip gloss, swiveled it open and handed it to Rose. "You'd look good in this," she said. "Purse your lips like you're kissing someone. Try it on." And then Rose did.

Rose kept trying to write to Lewis, but every time she did, she felt tongue-tied. She felt the same shame crowding in her life, making it so she couldn't move from the table. She began to forget things about him. The sound of his voice. The exact color of his hair. Maybe it was a sign, she told herself. Maybe it meant that it wasn't to be. She thought of him with another girl and imagined him leaning forward for his first kiss, only the girl wasn't her, and she crumpled up the paper into a fist. She wished he could somehow just come find her. She smoothed the paper out again. She wrote to him about the day they were together in the woods, how she was afraid of the woods now, how she wanted him to write her, and then she sealed it.

"Can you mail this for me?" she asked her mother. Her mother looked at the address and then frowned. "Girls don't chase boys. If he wanted to write you, he'd write you."

Rose felt her mouth trembling. "He's my friend."

"Was. Was your friend."

"He told me to write." Rose could hear the desperation creeping up in her throat.

"Fine," Dot said finally. "You make your own decisions. You don't listen to me. You never did." She watched Rose put the letter on the table, on top of the outgoing mail.

AFTER THAT, ROSE wrote Lewis every week. She told him about how gray and sooty Pittsburgh was, how the only part she liked was Schenley Park. She told him how she still had Jimmy's map, that it made her feel better to still have it, because it was the one thing he'd want her to have for safekeeping. Was anything new going on in the neighborhood? Were people still looking for her brother? Was he? "Write me back," she urged, printing her address in clear block letters with a big inky arrow pointing to it. She waited. She kept writing. Lewis never answered.

ROSE GOT THROUGH high school. She stopped writing Lewis, telling herself that he was part of a childhood she had outgrown. She forced herself not to look at the mail when it flopped in through the slot, not to get excited when the phone or the doorbell rang. When she was a senior and applying to colleges, she couldn't figure out what she wanted to do. What would Jimmy have majored in, she wondered? He had liked so many things, maps and rocks and insects. They used to play school when they were little, Jimmy at the front of a portable chalkboard, being the teacher even though Rose was older. In the end, she decided to go into teaching, not just because it seemed like it might have been his path, but she liked the idea of watching over kids, seeing them grow. She got a scholarship to the University of Pittsburgh for a special four-year program where she could get her teaching certificate the same year she got her diploma. She lived at home, telling her mother it was so she could save money, but really, it was because she worried about her. Her mother's jaw line had grown thick and slack, and she moved in a slow, careful way. At dinner, she often just picked at her food.

"Are you all right?" Rose asked her one night, and her mother waved her hand.

"I just want to lie down," Dot said.

Dot spread out on the couch and slept so deeply that it alarmed Rose. Her mother would have slept through the night, but Rose shook her, wanting to make sure she was still alive. Her mother sat up, squinting, and then she took Rose's face between her two hands. "I'm fine, honey," her mother said, "just tired."

When Rose graduated, she looked for local teaching jobs, but the market was flooded and the only jobs were out of state. "I can do something else," she said, but her mother was adamant. "You'll do no such thing," she told her. "I'm fine here, and you'll be fine away." So Rose got a job teaching third grade in Ann Arbor, Michigan, at the Whittemore School.

She returned to Pittsburgh to visit her mother every chance she could, which was usually during school breaks and the summer. One visit, during Christmas, Rose brought her mother some newspaper clippings she had found. One detective had found a missing child after six years! "There's always hope," Rose said, but her mother waved the clipping away and changed the subject. "Are you seeing anyone nice?" Dot interrupted, and when Rose sighed, Dot announced she had a headache and went into the bedroom with a cool cloth and shut the door. Rose sat in the living room, her head in her hands, waiting for her mother to fall asleep. When she left two days later, she made her mother promise to see a doctor.

But instead of getting medical attention, Dot began to do all the things she was always after Rose to do. She began to take classes in yoga and painting. She sent Rose photographs of her in full lotus. *"Ten pounds thinner!"* she scribbled across the picture. She sent Rose framed watercolors of the tree in her backyard. She joined a book club and mailed Rose all the books after she had read them, well-thumbed paperbacks with the pages turned back, which Rose read not because she enjoyed the books (she often didn't) but because she liked the idea of reading the same book her mother had read. Dot got three raises in three months. She kept sending Rose photos about her new life as if it were a strange new country where she was vacationing—*"Having a blast! Wish you were here."*

But other times, Dot would swing in another direction. On the anniversary of Jimmy's disappearance, she had called Rose at two in the morning, her voice thick with grief. "I have to get away," Dot said.

"Come here then for a visit," Rose said, but her mother brushed her off. "You'll be working. What will I do?" Dot asked.

"You can read. You can hang out at my apartment or you can come to my class and read to the kids. You'd be a special guest. And I'm not working all the time. By three in the afternoon, I'm done. Please, I want to see you."

"I just needed to hear your voice," Dot said, wearily.

Rose went on trying to cheer her mother, talking about the third-grade boy who had kept a live mouse in his desk for two days before she had found out, regaling her with a story about how a student had brought her a gift, which turned out to be his mother's best pearls. She heard her mother sigh. "I'm fine now, you go off to work," Dot said.

Rose's mother was only forty-seven when she died. She had called Rose that morning, excited because she had a date, which astonished

Rose because when was the last time her mother had even noticed men? "Why now?" Rose had asked and her mother had laughed.

"Who knows?" Dot said. "Maybe it was just the right timing. He's smart, he reads, and he's single." She told Rose that she had actually gone to a wine-tasting class, even though she didn't usually drink wine or any alcohol, for that matter. She said all of the vintages tasted the same to her, no matter how hard she struggled to taste the cherry or the oranges or whatever else was supposedly lurking. Eventually, she became tipsy and she stumbled on her way out, and that's when a man caught her arm. "His name is Tim," she told Rose. He was a locksmith, and he helped her into a cab. He got her phone number, and later that night when he called and she said she didn't feel well, he got worried and he came to her house. When she didn't open the door, he jimmied it open, finding her fainted on the floor. "Wait, you fainted?" Rose said. "Wait! Are you okay?"

"You're missing the point of the story," Dot said mildly. "It isn't that I fainted—it's that he came to check on me. It's that he actually broke in to make sure I was all right."

"Are you all right? Do you need to see a doctor?" Rose swallowed. "I should come out there."

"Rose," Dot said. "We're going out to dinner tomorrow. He's taking me to Nino's and I'm going to Kaufmann's to buy a new dress."

"But what about the fainting?"

"What about the dress?" Dot said. "You remember how you used to love Kaufmann's."

Dot was trying on dresses at Kaufmann's when she crumpled in the dressing room. It took half an hour for a salesperson to find her— casually slumped over, as if she were asleep, a silky green floral designer dress, more expensive than she had ever even considered buying, spilled over her lap—and then another half hour for a doctor to come and pronounce her dead of a heart attack. A policeman phoned Rose with all the details, his voice deep with sympathy. She pressed the receiver to her forehead and cried, feeling just how alone she was going to be in the world from now on. She didn't even know the last name of her mother's boyfriend to tell him.

It hurt her at different times of day, missing her mother. It came in waves. Sometimes when she was explaining fractions on the board, she thought of how her mother used to try to help her and Jimmy with their homework, once using her pop beads to illustrate subtraction, snapping off beads to make her points. Once, when Rose was crossing the Diag on a beautiful spring day and she saw a mother walking with her daughter, stopping to smooth her girl's hair, to lean in for a hug, it was like a punch to the heart. Rose went into Angell Hall, into one of the stalls, to cry in peace, and when she closed the door, she saw the whole stall was covered with writing, in red and even green ink, question after question that people had posed as if this stall were Dear Abby. *What does an orgasm feel like? Why doesn't my boyfriend love me anymore? Help! I cheated on my exam and I need to find out if the professor knows it!* The answers spilled over the door, around the side of the stall. Rose traced her hand along the wall. She got out her pen and looked for a spare space. She wrote: *My mother died, my brother is missing, the boy I loved is gone, and I feel lost.* Then she left the stall.

She went back a week later, sure the joke was on her. The bathroom was empty and she walked into the stall where she had written her piece, shutting the door, and there, filling all the space, were six or seven responses. *I know how you feel. Give yourself time.* Someone left her the phone number of a detective and the admonition, *Call! He's great—he found my dog.* Someone else wrote, *Let me know how you are doing. We've all been in tough places.* Rose rested her head along the wall of the stall. The messages seemed like the whispers of friends.

SHE MISSED HER mother, and Jimmy, and Lewis, almost always at odd times, when the memories would bite like a mosquito. She sometimes went to the question-and-answer stall, which she had discovered everyone somehow knew about. "Oh yeah, the oracle," a woman she sometimes had coffee with told her, laughing. "We all use it at one time or another." The woman leaned toward Rose. "I won't ask you what your question is, if you don't ask about mine," she said conspiratorially.

Rose kept coming back to the stall, reading the questions and answers avidly. It made her feel better that she wasn't the only one who felt as if she were foundering, that there were answers, and hope. Every few weeks, all the messages were scrubbed clean by the janitor, which always made Rose feel bereft until she saw them start up again.

Rose tried to get close to people. She had friends, of course, and every Thursday, they all went out to dinner at the local diner and then to a movie. She had dated a guy named Ted, an accountant. She had made the mistake of telling him about Jimmy and he said, "Well, that happened a long time ago."

It was funny how every man she dated she compared to Lewis, though really, she had no idea what he would be like as a man, as a real lover. She had wanted to kiss him that day in the woods, imagining his lips soft against hers, but she hadn't dared. She had been so young! Back then, she had thought he was the whole world.

NOW HERE SHE was in her class, at the end of the day. She had been teaching a unit about the space race, and the kids were all excited. She had posted pictures from *Life* and *Look* magazines all over her bulletin boards and brought in Tang to make because it had been taken up into space with the astronauts, even though no one really liked the taste, including her. Today she had had the kids write letters to Neil Armstrong, which Rose promised to mail for them. She had thought the day had gone well until one boy told her that his father thought it was a big hoax because no one could go into space. "It's not a hoax," Rose had said calmly. Josephine, who was the smartest girl in her class, and the most sensitive, suddenly burst into tears.

"What if the Russians get to the moon first?" Josephine sobbed. "Will we still get to look at it every night?"

"No one can take the moon out of the sky," Rose assured her. "Not even the Russians."

She clapped her hands for the kids to put their things away, and then she rounded up the kids to go home, counting their heads to make sure they were all accounted for. "See you tomorrow!" she called.

She came home to her little apartment and got ready to go meet her latest boyfriend, Brady, at We All Scream, their favorite ice cream place. They had been dating for six months now, and to her relief, it was only slightly awkward. He was the new sixth-grade teacher at the school, and as soon as she saw him, she liked him for his dark hair as thick as a beaver pelt, and mostly for his mischievous grin. He was a botany nut who was always taking the kids on nature walks, helping them find lady's slippers and identify maple trees just by the shape of the leaves. Her friend Emily had brought him around to Rose's classroom to introduce him, and when he left, Emily nudged Rose. "Bet you two would like each other," Emily said. Teachers weren't really supposed to date, but when they did, they all kept it under the radar, sometimes not even saying casual hellos to one another when they passed in the hall.

Brady was the same age as Rose. All the kids liked Brady, and the other female teachers crowded around him at the tables in the teacher's lounge. Rose watched how easily they flirted, how they managed to swing over to Brady's classroom and offer an extra stapler or home-baked brownies and cookies. Rose would see Brady out of the corner of her eye eating the treats, laughing, one arm thrown over the back of his chair. Before he began to date her, Rose could always tell when he was dating another teacher, because there would be a kind of intimacy just in the way he would pluck a grape from a stem and hand it to the other woman. Rose could tell, too, when a relationship soured, because the woman would start to eat lunch in her classroom rather than in the teacher's break room. Nancy Lovell was so traumatized by the breakup that she stopped covering her short raggedy black hair with her fall. Flora cried and then began telling one joke after another, but she was never really laughing when she told them. All that fake pretense hid a smashed heart.

Still, Rose couldn't take her eyes off him. She loved when she and Brady shared a recess because she could watch him teaching his class how to bounce a soccer ball off their heads. None of the kids really knew what soccer was, but they were game to try. "Use your noggins!" he shouted at them, demonstrating, thunking the ball with his forehead while the kids watched, openmouthed. He jumped up, his face shining. When he threw back his head and laughed, she felt her own mouth curving. He was such a big kid.

When he had first asked her out, she was rolling out butcher-block paper and tracing her kids' bodies on it. They were making life-sized as-exact-as-they-could-get-them replicas of themselves, cutting them out and coloring them, matching their hair, their eye color, the clothes they had on that day. Then they'd all tape the replicas to their chairs at their desks for the parent-teacher conference that evening. "You'll be attending your first parent-teacher conference!" she joked with the kids. "These will be the first things your parents see when they walk in our room!" The kids squirmed on the paper while she carefully traced their outlines. Rose made a plump little boy a couple of pounds leaner. She gave a girl with thin wispy hair an outline of a more glorious mane. "Looks just like you!" she proclaimed. The kids took their time cutting out their figures, and then one kid, a girl named Janey Adams, tugged on Rose's sleeve. "You should do it, too, Miss Rearson," she said.

"I'll be there for real," Rose said, but Janey shook her head. "Oh, come on," Janey said. So Rose lay down on the paper and allowed her class to trace her. It felt funny being prone on the floor, the kids crouched around her, the smell of the heavy paper rising up like yeast, the sound of the tracing crayon skittering. From this angle, she could see a purple crayon ground into the floor in the corner, a drinking-straw wrapper deep under her desk. There was a tiny spider crawling along one of the open windows. One of her kids was tracing along her arm and she laughed. "That tickles!" she said and then she looked up and there, leaning along the door, looking down at her and grinning, was Brady. She got up, suddenly embarrassed, brushing down her skirt, smoothing her hair with her fingers. "We're going to paste the pictures on our seats," Rose said to him. She held out her hands, as if she were demonstrating holding onto the top of the desk. "It'll look like the kids are here in the class, even though they aren't."

"I like that idea," Brady said. He looked at Rose again. "I'd be able to see you even when you aren't there." Rose felt the color rising in her face.

That evening, to meet the parents, she put on her favorite striped T-shirt dress and her lace-up sandals. She brushed her hair and held it back with a leather clip Ava had given her when she was a young girl. She didn't look anything like the paper figure of herself, in her buttoned-up dress, her sensible black flats, her hair in a ponytail. She got to the school early and as soon as she walked into her room, she felt a kind of giddy shock. Her paper image was taped into her seat, looking out at the sea of paper students, sitting up straighter in their seats, paying more attention than the real ones ever would. It was eerie, and yet comforting, to have all her kids frozen in time like this. You'll be with me, she had told them.

She checked her watch. Ten more minutes and parents would start arriving and she would need to talk to each of them about their children. She wanted to make them feel their kids were the most important thing in the world to her, and the truth was, they were. Already, she felt her first year of teaching ending, and it made her feel bereft, because she knew her kids would leave her, and when they came back, it would be to another grade.

She heard footsteps and turned and there was Brady, in a tie and a suit jacket.

"Did you come to see the paper me or the real one?" she tried to joke

"Both," he said. "There's a new store that opened called Wind Me Up. Two floors with nothing but windup toys in it," he said. She thought he must be thinking about the kids, but his grin spread across his face. "Want to go check it out some time?"

She hesitated, wondering if she was just the next girl in line. But part of her was curious about the toy shop, and too, she wanted to see what the fuss was all about him. She didn't expect anything other than a nice time out. But she was surprised when he came to get her a few nights later. He showed up wearing a suit jacket, tie, and good pants again, instead of his usual chinos and casual shirts. He even had a handful of irises for her. The whole walk to the store, while they made small talk about school, he looked at her as if what she was saying were the most important thing in the world.

Wind Me Up had half a dozen clacking teeth walking in front of the open door. "Allow me," Brady said, giving her his arm for support so she could step over them. Inside there were shelves and shelves of windup toys. She picked up a walking nose, a teapot that opened and shut its own lid, and a kitten that mopped at the floor. "Pick the one you want," Brady urged her. He held up a blue little robot and wound the key in its belly, until it moved its legs and spit sparks. "Oh, that one," she said. "Definitely that one."

She was surprised what a good time she was having. He walked her back to her apartment, slowing at her door. She didn't want to give him the wrong idea, but she didn't want the evening to end. "Come have some tea," she said.

As soon as she let him in, she was glad she had thought to clean her apartment that morning before school. On the way to the kitchen, his eyes went to the wall and the photo of Jimmy, standing in their back-yard with his hands on his hips, squinting at the sun. "Who's this cute kid?" Brady said.

"Jimmy," she said quietly. "My brother." She moved closer to the photo. She had looked at it every day since she had hung it up, but every time she did, she saw something she hadn't noticed before, a wrinkle in his shirt, an untied shoelace.

"I hope I get to meet him," Brady said.

Rose's eyes filled with tears. Brady looked at her, concerned. "Hey," he said.

"He vanished when he was twelve," she said. "I don't know where he is. No one does." She swiped at her eyes with her fingers. "I'm sorry," she said, but he shook his head.

"Sorry for what? For being human?" He drew her to the couch and held her close. "It's okay," he said. He dug in his pocket and handed her a clean white handkerchief. He was so sweet and sympathetic that she slid against him, fitting her body to his.

"I just have this feeling that he's out there somewhere in the world," she told him.

He shrugged and held her closer. "Who knows," he said. "Maybe he is."

THE MORE SHE was with Brady, the more she liked him. One month turned into two and then three. He popped into her classroom several times a day to tell her a knock-knock joke. He sang Beatles songs into her ear. "You're just a big, crazy kid," she told him and they both laughed. He was a sweet and tender lover, spooning against her when they were finished, and getting up to make her breakfast. She had to admit that she really liked his family, too, even though they all lived in California. One night, when she was at Brady's, his mother called and insisted on saying hello and her voice was soft and rich as pudding. "I can't wait to have another woman around," she told Rose. "You come visit and you'll fall in love with California and maybe you can convince that one to move back." In the background, she heard Brady's father's voice booming. "You let me talk to that girl!" and when he got on the phone, he wanted to know, "Is my boy treating you right?"

By the time Rose hung up the phone, she was still laughing at Brady's father's elephant jokes. ("How can you tell if an elephant has been in your fridge? Footprints in the cheese!") "Your parents are great," she said.

She had no family anymore, but Brady's seemed ready to let her into the fold and all she had to do was ask. Already, one of his brothers said he would teach her to golf. "I'll give you a slew of new elephant jokes to spring on my dad," he promised.

She felt so comfortable with Brady. She knew the other teachers were looking at her when she was with him, wondering what she had that they didn't, but all she knew was it felt like a good fit.

One Saturday morning, she couldn't get out of her bathrobe because she was missing Jimmy so hard she could barely breathe, but when Brady came over, he wrapped his arms around her and swayed her against him. "I know it's hard, baby," he told her.

She never really got leads anymore about Jimmy, and because the case was cold, she couldn't call the detective, but every once in a while, someone tracked her down to tell her they thought they had seen someone who could be Jimmy. Brady never told her she was crazy to talk to these people. He never said, "I told you so" when she tracked down a lead who was supposed to be Jimmy, and it turned out to be a man who had been born and raised in Texas, who had living parents, and who didn't appreciate Rose's call. One time a lead was actually in Ann Arbor. A woman called Rose and said she worked with a man who fit Jimmy's description and who refused to talk about his past, except to say he grew up in Waltham. "I think it's him," she said. She told Rose to meet her at Troubles, a local diner, and she would show her a photograph. Brady insisted on driving her there himself. The diner was empty except for a family with a baby, and a woman with scraggly dark hair sitting there waiting for them. The top button of her coat was missing. "Please, can I see the photo right away?" Rose asked.

The woman smiled. "Give me fifty dollars and then I'll show you," she said. She patted the seat beside her. "Sit," she ordered. "Or I won't tell you nothing."

Rose stared at her, incredulous. "There's no photo, is there? There's no man."

The woman held out her hand. "You won't know that until you pay me now, will you?" Rose turned away. "Wait!" the woman called, but Rose kept walking, and she heard Brady's footsteps behind her, like an echo. She got in the car, watching the diner window, where the woman was still sitting. "Take me home," she said, but he didn't.

He kept driving, and she lay her head back against the headrest, watching the car swallow up the white lines of the highway. She fell asleep, waking with a jolt to find the car parked. She blinked, looking around, and Brady was half smiling at her. "Where are we?" she asked, and he beckoned her outside.

He had parked in a field somewhere, but he pointed up at the sky. "Look," he commanded.

She raised her head and saw thousands of spangling stars. He put his arm around her. "Did you know that every element that's in these stars now was here when the world began? We're all made of stardust. Doesn't it make you feel great, to know we're all part of something so much bigger than we are?"

"What if he's looking at the same stars that we are?" she said.

Brady sighed. He tilted her face so she was looking at him, closing her mouth with a kiss.

Now, ROSE PUSHED open the door to We All Scream, waving at Brady, who was already there. After all these months of dating, he had never left her waiting, at least not after the first few times he saw how anxious she got when he was late, how she craned her neck to search for him. We All Scream was crowded with parents and kids and she wound her way to Brady and kissed him, loving the feel of his cheek against hers. She had finally talked him into growing his hair longer, and though he complained that he wasn't the type to be a Beatle, she saw how he sometimes preened in the mirror. She bet if she tried she could even get him into some floral shirts and wide ties. "We did the space race today," she told him, and he nodded, leaning over the case to study the flavors.

"Chocolate mint, right?" he said to her, moving toward the counter girl.

Rose was looking around when a mother and two kids wandered in, a boy and a girl. Rose gauged the kids to be about six or maybe seven. They were fooling around, not paying attention, but neither was their mother. Distracted, she was studying the flavors. The woman didn't notice when her kids sprang outside the shop like jumping beans, but Rose did.

"Those kids aren't with their mom," she said to Brady and he shrugged. "Let her take care of it," he said.

But Rose couldn't. If she turned to the right, she could see the kids on the street. All a car had to do was move closer, a door swing open, and they would be gone. Rose cleared her throat. "What's wrong with her?" she said to Brady in a low voice. "Doesn't she know they're outside by themselves?"

"They're fine. She can see them through the window." For the first time, she heard an edge in his voice. "You don't have to be so overprotective, especially about someone else's kids," he said.

She looked outside, and one of the kids, the girl, was wandering around the sidewalk, looking up at people passing by her, chatting to a couple, who then walked away. Rose strode over to the mother. "Do you realize your kids are alone outside?" she asked. "And your daughter is talking to strangers?"

The woman glanced outside. The kids were sitting on a bench, lazily swinging their legs and intently talking to each other. "Why don't you mind your own business?" the woman said.

"Why don't you watch your kids?" Rose snapped, and that was when she felt Brady's arm on hers. She was so angry she was trembling. She glared at the woman, but she let Brady guide her away. She heard the woman muttering something to another customer. "The nerve of her. She probably doesn't have kids of her own, and if she did, she'd drive them crazy." Rose twisted around to respond, but Brady's grip tightened and he tugged her out the door. They passed the kids and Rose crouched down and sharply said, "Go inside. Your mother wants you to go inside." The kids stared at her. "Now!" Rose said, her voice louder, and the children scrambled up, striding back into the store.

She could tell something was wrong by the look on Brady's face, but she kept walking. "She should watch her kids," Rose said to fill the silence, and then Brady stopped walking and she could see how angry he was.

"Why did you do that?" Brady said. The corner of his mouth twitched.

"She wasn't watching her own kids! This is a city, not Sunnybrook Farm!"

"You overreacted, Rose."

"What? I get mad at a mother who's irresponsible and suddenly I'm in the wrong?"

"This isn't even about that woman."

"Of course it is. What are you talking about?"

"It's about Jimmy. Like everything else in your life." His face was so grave, it made her uncomfortable. She couldn't help but think he was looking at her like a scientist, trying to figure out how to fix her.

"He's my brother," she said, and he looked at her impatiently.

"He's gone, Rose," he said.

"Don't say that," she said stiffly.

They walked to her apartment without speaking, and when they got to the door, Brady hung back. "I'm tired," he said shortly. "I'll see you tomorrow."

"I did the right thing at the ice-cream place," she said, but he was already halfway down the walk, retreating from her.

He didn't call the next day, but she was still sort of mad at him, so it didn't matter. Sunday, she felt like she was coming down with a cold. She tried to sleep and couldn't, and she was about to call Brady just to see what he was doing, to smooth things over, when her bell rang. She came to the door in a ratty bathrobe, exhausted, and there was Brady, but before she could feel relieved, he gave her a look of deep concern. "It's nearly six and you're not dressed," he said quietly. "What's going on here?"

"I couldn't sleep last night," she said. She tapped her nose. "I think a cold's coming on." She wandered into the kitchen to make tea. He followed her, and the first thing he noticed were the dishes piled in the sink, the basket of laundry by the door that she hadn't had time to put away yet. He looked at them and then at her. "What?" she said. "I'm busy. I can't afford a maid."

"Is everything okay?"

She moved some newspapers off the table, stacking them on a chair. "Because I didn't wash a few cups?"

The kettle bleated and she poured two cups, dunking a mint tea bag into each, sitting down at her table with him. "You're still mad at me about the ice-cream incident, aren't you?" she said.

"That was bad, but that's not what I'm upset about," he said. "It really bothers me how you can't let go of this, how it's front and center in your whole life."

She gripped her cup, the warmth of the mug moving through her hand.

"It's all you talk about," Brady said.

"Maybe I don't want to let it go," she said. She didn't like feeling that he wanted to change her. She thought of the psychic her mother had dragged her to, the way the neighbors kept watching her as if they wanted to take an eraser to her and redraw her from scratch. She was overtired and Brady was making her cranky. Her nose felt clogged with cotton, and all she wanted to do was crawl back into bed and watch television until she could sleep. She took a sip of the tea, scalding her tongue because it was so hot, wincing. Her eyes flooded with tears.

"But look at you. Maybe talking to someone impartial would help. I'd even go with you."

"And do what, sit in the waiting room?" She thought of Brady waiting, how she'd sense him outside expecting her to come out and slough all this off, like an extra skin. She didn't have the energy to explain any more of this or herself to him tonight and it made her tired just to think about any of it.

"I'm beginning to feel like there's three people in our relationship," Brady said. "You, me, and Jimmy."

"He's my brother."

"He's dead."

"Shut up."

"Rose, he's dead. You've got to face that and move on with your life."

"Don't tell me what I have to do," she said. "I thought you understood—"

"I understand that you're stuck, that you need a little help."

She tried to breathe. She got up, bracing her hands on the counter. She thought suddenly of the way his other relationships at school had soured and she had never understood why. She saw a flash of Flora, one of the teachers, crying into her sandwich and she thought maybe Flora hadn't been whom he had expected, either, and maybe he had tried to fix her, too.

"Can you please leave now," she said. She looked at him and she couldn't understand anymore what she had ever seen in him. The slow, methodical way he was standing made her want to scream.

"Well, if that's the way you want to be," he said, and there was something new in his tone, like he was talking to a stranger. He was changing right there in front of her. Even his face looked different, as if his features were rearranging themselves. His eyes didn't look as green. His hair wasn't as thick. You tried to hold on to a person, and they floated away. No matter what you did. She stood up, her legs buckling. She felt as if she were swimming through sludge, sinking with every step.

"When you feel ready to deal with this, you can call me," he said. "But I don't want to do this anymore."

"Don't slam the door when you leave," she said, her voice with an edge.

He blew out a breath of air. "You don't even realize I'm trying to help you," he said and then he was at the door, jerking it open, letting it bang closed.

As soon as he left, she began to clean her apartment, as if she were scrubbing Brady right out of her life. Who did he think he was, telling her what to do about her brother? When the phone rang half an hour later, she was sure it was him. She was still angry and she'd tell him not to call her again. "Brady," she said into the receiver.

"Miss Rearson?"

She swallowed. "This is Rose."

"This is Detective Roy Shuler. Waltham Police." He hesitated. "We found your brother's remains."

❖ *Chapter Eighteen* ❖

Lewis sat on his couch, hands gripping a coffee cup, still reeling from his conversation with his mother. He didn't believe it. If Ava had called to tell him that Jimmy's body had been found at the side of a road, or in a ditch, or washing up on some shore, he would feel it was true. If she had called to say they had found him living with another family, brainwashed, he might have bought that, too. But he couldn't believe the bomb shelter. His mother kept asking questions like, "Why didn't we know that you knew?" until he finally told her he had to get off the phone. He couldn't catch his breath.

The bomb shelter. All those years ago, he had taken an oath to forget they'd ever found it, to erase everything from that day, and now bits were resurfacing, like flotsam in a pond.

It had been hot, he remembered that. The shiny yellow heat, the way they all had to squint their eyes. He was in fourth grade, and he and Jimmy and Rose were running around the neighborhood, crossing lawns, hoping to hear the tinkle of the Good Humor truck, money jingling in Jimmy's pocket, enough for all of them. "It's there! I hear it!" Rose shouted, and Lewis swore he heard the snappy little tune, too. He wanted a blue banana Popsicle so badly, his mouth was watering. They cut across Mr. Gallagher's lawn, something they rarely did because either Eddy would be outside and want to tag along with them, and who wanted a baby trailing them, or Mr. Gallagher would yell at them for stamping on his precious grass. "It's not your yard, it's God's yard!" Jimmy had always shouted, but Jimmy was always the first to run away from Mr. Gallagher, as if he were scared of him. "Quick! Hurry up, let's get out of here!" Jimmy cried, racing after Lewis. That day, Lewis tripped over something and tumbled into the hemlock bushes, and it was then that he saw the loose sod, the ventilation pipe dotted with rust, and then the latch. "Hey, what the heck?" Lewis said. He pushed away more sod, clawing with his fingers, and there was a circular metal lid with some sort of handle. He crouched down, pulling the door open, peering into the dark. "There's a room down here!" he said. "And a ladder!" Because they were curious, because they didn't like Mr. Gallagher very much, they had gone down inside, climbing down one by one on the rickety ladder. There were twelve steps down, and by the time they hit the bottom, it was almost completely dark and twice as cool as it was outside, but it was also small and cramped, and as soon as Lewis was down there, he wanted to get out. He knocked elbows with Jimmy and bumped up against Rose, and when Jimmy grabbed him, he jumped. "Quit it!" he cried.

"It's too dark in here!" Jimmy said. "This place gives me the creeps."

"We've got a little light from the entrance," Lewis said. He touched the wall, which was wet and sticky.

"I found a flashlight!" Rose said, rolling the beam around the room, illuminating a narrow shelf with cans of niblet corn, string beans, and tuna, some deviled ham and chicken, and two big bottles of water. "Yuck, who wants to eat that?" Jimmy said. "Don't they believe in potato chips?"

"When did they even build this?" Rose said. "Who even knows it's here?"

"Creepy," Lewis said.

"Yeah," Rose agreed.

Lewis sneezed from the dust and Rose pasted her body next to his. "What is it, though?" she said. "Some sort of hideout? A bomb shelter?"

Jimmy edged back toward the ladder, one hand on the rung. "I can't breathe down here," Jimmy said. His voice was like a skip on a record. "Can we go now, please?"

He grabbed the ladder then, scrambling up the rungs until he was back onto the lawn, and then Rose and Lewis quickly followed. Once they were all outside, Jimmy broke into a run. "Jimmy, wait!" Rose shouted. "Where are you going?" Colors seemed suddenly dazzling and Lewis felt dizzy and sticky in the heat.

"Come on!" Rose called to him and then she was running, too, and there was nothing to do but follow, springing across the lawn, following Jimmy into Lewis's backyard, where Jimmy had stopped, scooped over, his hands on his knees, his head down. Rose shot Lewis a look, but he didn't understand what she was trying to tell him, not until he saw the dark circle of pee spread on the back of Jimmy's shorts. "Jimmy," Rose said, and Jimmy sank to the ground, so he was sitting, so you couldn't see. "You couldn't get me to go in there again if you paid me a zillion dollars," Jimmy said. His mouth trembled. He put his head in his hands.

You couldn't get me to go in there again.

"It's okay," Rose said. She crouched beside him, sliding her arm about him, but he kept his head tucked down.

Lewis sat down, too, so close to Jimmy, he could smell the pee. He nudged Jimmy. "Hey," he said, but Jimmy shook his head, refusing to meet Lewis's eyes.

"Look," Lewis said quietly. "We need to take a blood oath." Jimmy looked up. "We need to all agree to never go back there again. No matter what," Lewis said.

"Never. Never. Ever," Rose said.

Jimmy pleated the edges of his shorts with his fingers. "And we can never talk about this," Jimmy said. His voice sounded small and shaky. "Nothing about what happened today."

"Right," said Lewis.

"You promise?" Jimmy said. "No one can know?"

"We can't ever even mention it," Rose said. "Not to each other, not to anyone. We shouldn't even think about it."

"All in?" Lewis said.

"In," Rose said.

"Me, too," Jimmy said.

Rose fumbled with a sparkly circle pin she had on her collar, springing the clasp and taking it off. She pricked her finger until a bead of blood showed and then she passed the pin to Lewis and then to Jimmy. "I'm going first," Jimmy said, pressing his index finger to Lewis's and then to Rose's.

"This never happened," Lewis said.

"It never happened," Rose said.

"This never happened," Jimmy said.

They wiped their fingers on the grass, and then the three of them got up and Lewis led them into his house. "My mom's not home yet," he said. He gave Jimmy a pair of his shorts, and when Jimmy changed in the bathroom, he took Jimmy's old shorts and threw them in the garbage, covering them with trash so his mom wouldn't see them.

After that, they stopped walking across Mr. Gallagher's yard. They never again talked about anything that happened that day. Lewis never even thought of it.

Until now. Until his mother had told him where Jimmy had been found.

If he or Rose had remembered that day, they might have found Jimmy. He might have been alive. They would have pulled him out, and Mrs. Rearson would have wept and hugged them, and he and Rose would have been heroes. And Jimmy would still be alive.

Lewis rested his head in his hands. Jimmy hated it down there. Why would he even think to go in the shelter? It just didn't make sense.

Lewis got up from the table and went to work. He couldn't shake the feeling that somehow he was to blame. Jimmy should have been with them. Lewis shouldn't have dawdled at the library that day. But more than that, he should have known where Jimmy might be.

All that day at work, he tried to pay attention to his patients, to concentrate on his job and do the things that made him feel good about himself. But when he brought the gallbladder patient in room 304 some magazines, she sniffed at him. "Who asked you for those?" she said. "Plus, you woke me up." When he gave an asthmatic man a sponge bath, he turned around too quickly, spilling the water on the bed. "Oh, for crying out loud," the man said, annoyed.

Lewis wasn't sleeping anymore. He couldn't eat, and when he tried to force himself, the food tasted spoiled. He was desperate to talk to someone, to dislodge the ache in his throat, but he couldn't talk to Ava because she was his mother. She'd want to protect him and he'd hear it in her voice, the way she wouldn't be totally honest with him for fear of hurting him or making him feel worse about everything. He couldn't talk to the guys he bowled with because they never talked about anything deeper than whether they should get chips or fries with their Cokes. Rita, too, was gone. He had even seen her walking in town the other night, holding some tall blond guy's hand, and though he had felt happy for her, he had felt bereft, too.

That was his fault, her leaving him.

He scanned the roster of patients for the night, and when he saw Sheila's name again, he went to see her. As soon as he walked in the room, he felt better. "Can't stay away from this place, can you?" he teased.

She winked at him. "Hello, handsome," she said. She patted her chest. "My ticker doesn't tock right again," she said. Then she pointed to the chair by the bed. "Talk to me," she said, and he sank down into the chair.

He started to tell her the basics, how he and Jimmy and Rose had been so tight as kids, like a knot you couldn't untie. He told her how much he had loved them, how he considered them family. She didn't say anything, didn't ask questions or judge, but she kept her eyes on him, occasionally nodding her head sympathetically, and every time she did he felt like telling her more. He was about to launch into his feelings about Jake when she reached across and squeezed his hand, and he suddenly noticed how frail she was, how tired she looked. "You'd better get to sleep," he told her, rising.

"You come back, though," she told him. "You have to always come and talk to me. You promise?"

"I do," he said.

He did come back, the next day, and the next. He made sure she had fresh water, enough blankets, and company. "Sit and talk," she ordered. Each time, he told her a little bit more about his past.

He came home but couldn't sleep. Talking about Jimmy with Sheila had just brought back so much. He picked up one of his library books, about a scientist who journeys to the North Pole with a team of sled dogs, but he couldn't stop thinking about Jimmy.

Jimmy had missed so much, the world had gone on without him. Jimmy had never heard the Beatles. He didn't know how to do the twist and he'd never seen *Star Trek*. He had never heard about Vietnam or had a first kiss or slept with a woman. He had never grown older than twelve.

Lewis let the book drop. Because he had to do something, he took apart his kitchen and cleaned it. Finally, at five in the morning, he was exhausted enough to fall asleep. But the next day, he was a mess at work. He forgot to bring a patient a bedpan and she wet the bed, and even though he apologized and gave her clean linens and a fresh johnny to wear, she wouldn't look at him, and he heard later that she had requested he not come to her room again. "You look like hell," Elaine snapped at him. "Pull yourself together and don't make more work for people here."

He felt it building inside of him all day, this voracious need to talk. He wanted to tell Sheila about the last part of the story, the part about the bomb shelter, but the more he thought about it, the more anxious he felt. Was she even really understanding him or was it just the wash of words that she liked? She never really asked him questions or said much, so was it really a conversation or was he fooling himself? Still, he couldn't wait to get to her room, to unburden himself and talk, and in the end, what did it matter what was going on as long as they both felt better?

By the time he got to Sheila's room, it was past midnight and his shift was over. When he walked in, her bed was empty, the sheets pulled off. All the personal items on her end table were gone. A nurse walked by and he called to her. "Sheila went home?" he asked, and the nurse shook her head, continuing to walk. "She died," she called to Lewis. "Peacefully in her sleep."

Lewis couldn't move. He sat by Sheila's empty bed, his hands over his face. She had been old and sick and frail and he knew patients died in the hospital all the time, that you had to steel yourself against it, but this time, he couldn't. He wished that Sheila had had family, because then there might be someone he could tell how much he had liked her, how she had helped him, probably without even knowing it, and how he hoped that he had helped her. He stayed, not moving, until he heard footsteps, and he turned, but it was only another aide, her arms filled with linens. "Got to make up the bed," she said, and Lewis got up and left the room.

That night, he walked all over Madison. He passed the shops and the lakes, but he couldn't stop moving. He ended up at the library and combed through four sets of Boston newspapers until he found all the articles on Jimmy. They all said the same thing, mentioning the bones, the old bomb shelter, the surprise that Jimmy was there in the neighborhood the whole time, under their noses, just waiting to be discovered. It didn't make sense, not any of it. There was no sign of a struggle. Lewis was about to leave, when he saw the line, buried at the end of one of the articles and his mouth went dry: *James Rearson is survived by his sister, Rose, a school teacher in Ann Arbor.*

Rose. He could always talk to Rose.

SHE WAS NO longer hard to find. All he had do was get an Ann Arbor white pages in the library and trail his hand down the line of *R* names, and there she was. She had fallen out of his life when they were kids, but they were adults now, and they had shared this past. He didn't know what to expect, or even what she'd be like. He only knew that he had to try. He copied the number down, put it in his pocket, and went home to call her.

When she answered, her voice was so close, she seemed to be standing next to him. He heard papers rustling in the background. He swallowed, unable to speak. She sounded the same, and different, too, as if her voice had gone down a register. "Is someone there?" she asked, and then he straightened. "Rose," he managed to get out. "It's Lewis."

He heard her sip in her breath. "Lewis," she said. "My God. Lewis."

"I heard about Jimmy," he said.

"I just—" she said, and then she stopped.

"Are you okay?" he asked. "Oh Jesus, that's a stupid question."

"I don't know if I am," she said. "Are you?"

"No."

"I was so sure he was alive."

"I know," he said.

"I never gave up," she said. "Never. I talked to everyone about him. I followed leads—"

He rested his head against the receiver. "I never forgot him, either."

Her voice came at him like a rush. "People keep telling me now you can move on, now it's over. But Lewis, it's still not over, you know? If anything, there's even more to figure out. I keep going through all the newspapers, even the old ones I kept. I keep calling the cops, but they don't want to take my calls anymore."

There was a funny silence. "He wouldn't go in that shelter willingly," Lewis said finally.

"That's what I thought," she said, her voice rising. "That's exactly what I thought."

"It wasn't an accident."

"No, no, I don't think so, either. He'd never go even near there if he could help it," she said. "There's got to be more to this, more reason why he was there. People think I'm wallowing in this, that I'm crazy, that I need help, but something isn't right. I just feel it. And I need to know what happened."

He heard the papers in the background stop rustling. When they were kids, she was always telling him to look at her face, that her expression or her eyes would tell him what he needed to know, but all he could see now was his shabby apartment, the phone in his hands. He wished that she were right there in front of him. "Can I come to see you?" he asked.

She was quiet, and for a moment he was afraid she was going to say no.

"You want to come here?" she asked.

"Please, Rose."

"I don't know," she said. "I'm not good company these days. I don't sleep. I don't eat. I burst into tears at the cookie aisle at the supermarket yesterday because I saw a whole rack of Sno Balls."

"Who else but me would know Jimmy only liked the white ones? And fuck being good company. I just want to see you. Rose, I'm a mess, too. But maybe we can talk about this. We can figure it out together."

She was quiet again.

"Rose, please. Isn't it worth a try?" He tried to think about what he would do if she said no, how he'd get through the endless long days ahead. "I'll come just for a few days."

"I'm a teacher," she said finally. "Spring break is coming up in a week." I'll have nearly ten days off. He heard the hum of the wires. "I have two weeks vacation coming to me," he said. "You could come here, if you want, I suppose," she said slowly. "You could even come a little early and see my class. You could camp on my couch if you wanted to."

THE WHOLE TIME Lewis was in Madison, he had only taken a few brief vacations, and those were to visit his mother. He stayed only three days in Waltham each time because it was too strange being back in the neighborhood. The truth was that he liked working, being busy, being on his own. He liked the buzz of the hospital, the feeling of community. Now, though, he called in his vacation days. "You deserve it," Elaine said, "Go somewhere fun and don't think of us slaving here."

Before he knew it, there he was, on a Friday evening in Ann Arbor, three days earlier than he said he'd come because he couldn't wait, and maybe, too, because he was afraid to give her too much time to change her mind. He was sitting in a small café. He had never thought he'd see her again, and he wasn't even sure what he would say to her.

"Lewis?"

There was that shock of time, the way he felt when he once saw a photo of himself as a kid that he never remembered had even been taken. She was and wasn't familiar. She still had that long hair, shiny as glass. Those bangs that hid her eyes. She was wearing cowboy boots and some sort of minidress. As soon as he saw her he realized he didn't know anything about her. Did she have a husband? A child? He hadn't even thought to ask her about her life when he called, but she hadn't asked him about his, either. He glanced at her hands. There were no rings.

She sat down. A waitress ambled over and set down two red plastic menus. "I can't believe I'm seeing you," Rose said.

"Me, too," he said. He didn't know what he expected, that like in the movies, it might seem that no time at all had passed. That he'd feel instantly close to her and connected, but instead, he felt as if he were floating

She studied him and then reached across and brushed her fingers against his hair. "I just wanted to see if you were real," she said.

"Sometimes I have my doubts," Lewis said. She had dark circles under her eyes, like stains and he wanted to touch them.

Neither one of them talked about Jimmy at first. Instead, she told him about her third-grade class, about her apartment. "I never guessed you would have been a teacher," he said. "You were such an adventurer. I thought you'd backpack around the world or live in Costa Rica."

She laughed and he saw suddenly how beautiful she was, which made him feel uneasy and strange, as if something were off. "What about, you?" she asked. "Let me guess. A scientist. Or a shrink." She looked at him expectantly. "Am I right?"

"I didn't go to college," he said.

"You didn't? But you were so smart. You used to borrow all my books, remember?"

He didn't want to talk about why he hadn't gone, so instead he shrugged. "I thought I could get myself an education on my own. I'm a nurse's aide," he told Rose. "I like what I do."

She nodded. "Okay then. That's good."

"No kids, no husband?" he blurted and she smiled ruefully.

"I just broke up with someone," she said.

"I'm on my own, too."

He told her about his job, how he was the one the patients called for by name, how they dubbed him "that nice young man who doesn't hurt," and Rose laughed again. The waitress came by and they both ordered spaghetti. "Back in a jiff," the waitress said. Rose leaned forward on her elbows. She told him how Dot had died, how she had stopped talking about Jimmy, how she kept all the photos boxed away where you had to get a step stool to reach them. "I think maybe it's good that she died when she did, that she didn't know how it ended," Rose said.

The waitress set down their plates, drowning in sauce. Lewis took a bite and then put it down. It was like hospital food. It had the same smell, that texture, like socks boiled on a stove.

"You never wrote," Lewis said.

She picked at her spaghetti, winding the noodles around her fork. "What are you talking about? I did write you. Every week. You never wrote back and I couldn't understand why."

"I never got any letters from you," Lewis said. "I would have written you whole novels if I had."

Rose put her fork down. "None?" she said. He shook his head.

"I wrote so many," she said. "Every week. My mother kept telling me that if you had wanted to write me, you would have, that I was wasting my time."

"I don't understand," Lewis said. "You remembered your return address? The stamp? You mailed them?"

"My mother did," she said.

Lewis frowned. He thought of how Dot used to send back the casseroles people brought her, how his mother would go over to talk to her and Dot would sometimes refuse to even open the door.

"Did she want you to write me?" Lewis asked.

"God, no. She said girls don't chase boys." Rose put her fork down and frowned. "Oh no," she said abruptly. "I never once thought that she'd—"

"Me, either," Lewis said. He looked at her and thought how different his life might have been if he had gotten her letters, if he had had her friendship to get him through high school. She wouldn't have been like a phantom limb all those years, there but not there. Maybe he would have even tried to go to college where she went or at least near her. But he couldn't say any of that to Rose, not now.

"I'm so sorry," she said. "For both of us."

"Me, too." He pushed his plate away, no longer hungry.

"What about your mom? How's she doing?"

"I don't see her all that often."

"You're kidding. Why not?"

"I'm in Madison. She's in Boston. You know."

"Want to know something? I always wanted her to be my mother. She used to talk to me like I was important and smart and special. She listened to whatever I had to say, even if it was just about clothes, and she'd look at me like it was crucial information she just had to know. I ate dinner at your house every night, remember? She gave me her lipsticks." Rose paused. "She was amazing. You know, in the mornings I used to hear her collecting bottles out of the trash for the refund money. I knew she didn't want anyone to know."

"My mom did that?" He felt hot with shame.

"One time, I saw Mr. Hill come out and he watched her collecting the bottles, not helping or anything, which made it sort of creepy, and she looked up at him and he said, 'You don't have to do that.' He walked over to her and he put his arm on her shoulder in a funny way. He leaned in closer to her, and she froze and then he said something to her that I couldn't hear and I don't know why, I ran out in my nightgown and bare feet, and as soon as he saw me, he took his arm away, and then suddenly the conversation was about me being barefoot." Rose dipped her head. "I wanted to stay outside and help her, but she wouldn't let me. I told her she had to walk me home even though I could have gotten there by myself. Mr. Hill gave me this look, and then he finally turned and went back inside his house."

Something knocked in his head. "I never knew about that"

"You would have hated it if you had known, so I never told you. But me—I lay in bed and every night I knew she was outside and near me, collecting bottles, and I liked that. She seemed powerful to me. There were all these bad stories about your house, but it was the only place I ever felt safe."

She tapped his hand. "You should go see her more often," Rose said. "You can't wait on these things because one moment people are here, and then they're not." She motioned to the waitress, making a check mark in the air.

They went to her place, a square little apartment in a squat building on East William Street. By the fifth flight up, Lewis could see how this would get old fast, but Rose didn't seem to mind it. He trailed behind her, watching her legs flash on the stairs, and he suddenly wanted to take her hand. He dug his hands deeper into his pockets.

Her apartment was all wood and green plants, with a well-worn Oriental rug in the center of the floor, which had plant patterns in it, too, as if she were outdoors even while she was inside. He stopped as soon as he passed the photo of Jimmy she had hanging on her wall, staring at it because Jimmy seemed too real, so immediate. She touched his arm. "Sit," she said, motioning to the red velvet couch and he did, running his hand along the nap, thinking of her mother's orange and brown plaid couch back in Waltham. Rose sat on the couch, too, facing him.

"Do you think we would have stayed friends if we had kept in touch?" she asked.

"I wanted to," he said.

She swept a curtain of hair to one side of her neck, leaving the other side exposed, and he suddenly couldn't swallow. He looked away, embarrassed, and then back at her again. He had come to her apartment to talk more about Jimmy, but neither one of them had said a word.

"What's wrong?" she asked. "You look worried."

"I thought I was hiding it."

"You still can't hide anything from me," she said, half smiling.

"I think I'm just tired," he said, because he didn't know what else to say, and as soon as he said it, he hated himself because she got up and started taking blankets from a side closet, ending the conversation.

AFTER ROSE SET Lewis up on the couch, she closed her door and though he heard her rustling in the other room, he couldn't imagine what she was doing or how she was feeling, or if she'd be able to sleep. As soon as he shut his eyes, he saw Jimmy, crouched down in the bomb shelter, his arms around his knees, the way he had when he had peed his pants. Lewis turned over on the couch, so he was facing the window. There was no window in the bomb shelter. No air. He bolted upright, and then Rose's door opened and she came out, a blue robe tied around her. "You, too?" she said and she came and sat opposite him.

"I keep thinking about Jimmy," Lewis said.

"I never stop." She rubbed her eyes and then leaned toward him. "Why did he go in there?"

"We never would have thought to look there for him. Never," Lewis said.

They talked about it, how the cops had searched everyone's house, closet, basements. How it had been so chaotic and urgent. "Remember that one cop Maroni?" Rose asked. She shook her head. "Moron-i," she said. "That's what he was. A big Moron-i."

Lewis remembered the cop, big and beefy with slicked-back hair. He was always clapping his hands at the kids, scattering them. He warned people not to mess things up. "Just let me do my job," he snapped.

"It doesn't make sense. Everyone was looking everywhere," Lewis said.

"But we didn't look there. We didn't even think of it."

"Neither did Mr. Gallagher."

He thought of how the neighbors had made lists of all the areas that had been checked out so they wouldn't waste time searching the same places. He remembered the checklist of places in one of the neighbor's rec rooms. "It feels so awful. That we'll never know."

Rose adjusted and readjusted the pillow on her chair, settling one on top of another. There was a silence like taut wires. She went over to her bookcase. "I'm the family historian," Rose said, crouching to the bottom shelf. "I keep looking at these things over and over." She hesitated. "Do you want to see them? Some people don't—"

"Of course I do."

The creases on her forehead smoothed. She tugged out a big wicker box, dragging it over to the couch, opening its lid like a mouth.

She pulled out an old photograph album, the black paper pages filled with clumsily pasted pictures. There Jimmy was at ten, grinning, flashing silver toy pistols into the air. There was a photo of Jimmy with Rose, the two of them dressed up for church, Rose in a fussy plaid coat buttoned to her throat, Jimmy in a tie and a dark suit. She traced one finger over it. "God, but I hated that coat," she said. She pointed to another picture. The three of them, Rose, Lewis and Jimmy, standing in Lewis's backyard, their arms around each other, in shorts.

Now his hands were trembling. "I don't think I ever saw these photos."

"Sure you did," she said.

She dug deeper into the box and then brought out a folded, tattered piece of paper and handed it slowly to him, like it was something important. Her face was grave and he opened it. The map. She had saved the map. He touched the soft surface as if it were ancient parchment. The map was riddled with pinpricks and he followed their path marks as if they were Braille. If he shut his eyes, he could see the colored pushpins he and Jimmy had placed in each point, the blue pins for the places they had to go to, the red ones for side trips. Every place and every pushpin had meant something to both of them, like prophecies they were determined to fulfill.

"My mother threw out almost everything of Jimmy's, but I held on to this."

He could just barely make out the notes Jimmy and he had written under each state, the writing so faded now, he had to squint. *Our First stop. Uncle Bob lived here.* Lewis looked up at Rose helplessly. "Let me show you some more things," she said, and he reluctantly gave her the map and watched her fold it back up.

She pulled out birthday cards from Jimmy, one with a cartoon dog wearing a birthday hat, another with a duck perched on top of a cake. There was one from Rose's mother, with garlands all over it, and then one expensive-looking big one that was all purple with white lettering made out of lace that said simply "Happy Birthday," and when he opened it, Ava's name, like a shock, jolted him. *With lots of love,* Ava had written. "My mother sent you cards?" he said, and Rose nodded. "She was really good to me," she said.

Lewis fingered the card. Why did his mother's secrets always ambush him? He felt a flare of jealousy that Rose had known this soft, loving side of his mother. He looked back down in the box, rummaging a bit, and then as he was about to lift up a plastic slider puzzle, he spotted half of Jimmy Stewart's face on Rose's old notebook, the same one she had used to collect clues about Jimmy's disappearance, and his hand stopped in midair.

Rose glanced at the notebook. "I saved everything. I thought I'd be able to give it to Jimmy when I found him."

Lewis's own notebook was long gone. He had stuffed it in a drawer the week Rose had left, and when he took off for Madison, he didn't even think to take it with him.

He had never even seen what was inside her notebook before. They had always planned to compare notes, but they never had somehow. He leafed through the pages. His notebook had been full of facts: the times neighbors came and went, the license plate numbers of cars he didn't recognize, and lists of all the places Jimmy might have gone: the Star Market, Harvard Square, the zoo. But Rose's notebook was full of poems, drawings, letters to Jimmy, and even what looked like stories. "I thought we were putting clues in here," he said, turning the pages, and she shrugged, embarrassed. "They were my kind of clues," she said.

He turned a few more pages and caught sight of his name scribbled in a girlish looping slant. *No one knows how much I love Lewis.*

He looked at it, shocked, reading a few more lines. *Even Jimmy never knew, though he sometimes wondered why I wanted to hang around with someone younger all the time. I don't know what to do, who to talk to about this. I can't talk to my other friends because a) I don't have any and b) they're all too busy having crushes on older boys in high school, and c) they think I'm immature, that I don't feel as much as they do, but I know I feel more. I can't talk to my mother because she's busy blaming me, and forget Ava because she's Lewis's mother. Worst of all, I can't talk to Lewis because he doesn't know I love him, either.*

"Oh, no," Rose said, her voice lowering, "No, no, no," and she put her hand over the page. She tugged the journal back to her, but not before he saw another line: *How can I love Lewis like this when my own brother is missing?* She quickly began stacking things back in the wicker box, closing the lid and latching it tight.

"Rose," he said.

"I was such a kid," she said quickly. "So dramatic." She smoothed the cover of the basket, and he saw how flustered she suddenly was, and it made him feel unmoored, as if everything he had thought he had known about his past wasn't quite true anymore.

"Why didn't you ever tell me?" he said quietly.

She hesitated, fanning her fingers over her mouth for a moment, before letting her hand drift back into her lap. "I was afraid."

"But we were always together and you never said anything. And when you left, when I didn't hear from you, I assumed I didn't matter."

"You mattered," she said. He heard her swallow. "Remember how we used to touch foreheads? How I'd think the color red and you'd just know what it was?" she said.

"I didn't always know." He remembered thinking he was always guessing, trying to please her. She'd smile and clap him on the back no matter what he said.

"Every time we did it, I knew how I felt about you," she said.

"Rose, I'm so sorry—" he started to say, but her smile had turned funny. He didn't know what else to say to her. She got up and slid the closed box back into the bookcase, shrugging. "It's in the past," she said, but she wouldn't look at him.

"It's late. We should get some sleep," she said shortly, and then retreated to her room.

THE NEXT DAY was Saturday and they were awkward around each other in the morning. Lewis didn't know what to say or do. "My apartment is your apartment," she said, opening the cupboard and showing him the collection of cereal boxes. He chose the Sugar Frosted Flakes and poured them each a bowl. Neither one of them was talking much, and the click of their spoons was driving Lewis crazy.

"I have an idea," Rose said, her whole body brightening. "Let's go swimming. I know the perfect place, Pickerel Lake. It's only a twenty-minute drive from here."

"Swimming?" He remembered when they were kids and Rose would take them to the pool at Green Acres Day Camp when no one was there. Lewis couldn't swim, but he didn't want anyone to know. He knew Jimmy would tease him, so he stayed in the shallow end, pretending that he wanted to be just lazily walking around the pool on his tiptoes, occasionally dunking his head. But one day, when Jimmy was at the doctor, Rose took him swimming, just the two of them. Rose dove into the water and then swam over to him in the shallows. "Hey," she said. "I learned this cool new stroke." She paddled her hands in the water, her eyes on his, and then he mimicked her. "Come on, let's have a dog-paddle race," she said, and he had lowered himself in the water, scooping at it, and to his surprise, he was moving, swimming, actually covering ground. When he finally stopped, grabbing on to the edge of the pool, he turned and saw her treading water, acting as if this were no big deal at all, but her eyes were shining. "You won," she had said casually.

He had loved swimming after that, but he hadn't gone since he had been living in Madison.

"We can stop on State Street and grab you a swimsuit," Rose said.

As soon as they got to the lake, Rose wondered if she had made a mistake. She remembered when Lewis was little, the one way she could get him to relax was to get him out of his head, to make him run races with her, or go for a bike ride or anything physical. She'd suggest crazy things to do back then, and he would just do them with her. This morning, when he was so silent and strange about the cereal, she hadn't known what to do or what to say, and swimming seemed like a good idea. But now, here she was, in her little black bathing suit, the one Brady always said made him want to carry her off to her bedroom, and she suddenly felt naked and embarrassed. It was a small lake with a beautiful sandy beach, and no motors were allowed, so it was quiet and private. She had thought it would be pretty, and it was. You could see bluegills, sunfish, and she had spotted a catfish already. She looked up at the sky and a hawk was lazily swooping in the air. And there Lewis was, in the swimsuit he had bought, and she could see his strong chest, the muscles in his arms and legs, the warm olive tone to his skin. She felt her face heat up. She ran into the water and began swimming, the shock of the cold water making her shiver. She could hear him, and then she turned and watched him in the water. She didn't know why she expected to see him sloppily swimming, still doing a dog paddle. Instead, his strokes were graceful. He looked as if he had been born in the water.

Rose turned over so she was floating on her back, looking at the sky. This was a bust. They drove all this way and she didn't feel any better. Lewis was swimming so far away from her, they might as well have come separately. She shut her eyes, and then suddenly, she felt him near her and she blinked and righted herself. Lewis was treading water next to her. He looked relaxed and even happy and she didn't know what to say, but then he drew her forehead to his. "This was a great idea," he told her. She felt his breath against her ear. "You were the one who always kept my head above water," he said, and for a moment, she felt the warmth of his skin before he let her go and began swimming again.

ON SUNDAY, ROSE gave him the guided tour of Ann Arbor. She made him spin *The Cube,* the big black metal box in the center of the Diag. She took him dancing at a local club, not suggesting they go home until they both were sleek with sweat. That night, they went through another box of Rose's old photographs and papers, but there was nothing there that gave them any clues as to what might have really happened.

She pulled out an old pipe of her father's and studied it. "My mother saved this," she said. "And now I have it."

"I used to have a fishing lure of my dad's. I never really enjoyed the fishing, but I liked going with him."

"You did? Do you still have it?"

He took the pipe from her, stroked his finger along the bowl, and then gently put it back in the box. "Nope. Gone. Along with him."

"You ever think about him?"

He stood up, stretching. "I'm really tired," he told her, and she knew enough not to press.

Tomorrow she was taking him to her class, to be a special guest. She didn't know what was going to happen after that. He had told her he was only coming for a few days and then he'd go home. All she knew was that she was glad he was there.

MONDAY MORNING, LEWIS stood in the center of Rose's classroom, astonished. The kids were noisy, racing around, but as soon as they saw Rose with Lewis, they stopped. "Who's this?" they clamored, their eyes round as planets.

"This is my friend Lewis and he's going to talk to you about being a nurse's aide."

The low hum of the class quieted. The kids sat at their desks and wove their fingers together. Lewis stood in front of the class. The kids stared at him, frowning, as if he didn't belong there. He took a deep breath. He knew the secret with kids was to surprise them. How many times had he pretended to take quarters from the ears of sick kids to relax them enough so he could move them? He glanced at Rose, in her dress, her hair held back by a leather clip. She gave him an expectant look, like he was about to audition and she wasn't sure he knew his lines.

"Burping," Lewis said, and instantly the kids perked up. A girl in the back dropped her mouth open. A boy in the front row grinned. "Burping is caused by swallowed air. It comes up through this tube called the esophagus." He drew an esophagus on the blackboard. The white chalk dust sifted in the air like flour. "It's nothing to worry about, and in fact, you can even make yourself burp by drinking soda or swallowing air," Lewis said. He gulped in air, hoped for the best, and burped. There was a stunned silence. One of the kids, a little girl in the front, giggled, and then the boy in back of her sucked at the air and burped.

"It's okay, you can do it!" he told the class.

The kids began burping. "I can burp the alphabet!" one boy cried and began to burp loudly, and there it was under the belch, an *A*, a *B*. There was a jungle of burps, and all the kids were laughing. "Listen!" one little girl yelped and she stood up on a chair and threw her head back and gave a tight little burp. Rose was still and quiet, and for a moment he felt a curtain of gloom. He was disrupting her class. She'd never get them back in line.

He looked over at Rose. She lifted her hands as if she were raising a curtain. "Class," she said, her voice commanding, and all the kids turned to look at her. For a moment there was a shamed quiet. He was going to apologize, but then she thunked her chest and burped so loudly the kids stared at her in wonder. The kids clapped and Rose took a delicate bow.

ALL THE REST of the week, he came with her to her class. "Mr. Lewis is going to be our extra helper," Rose told the children. Lewis coaxed kids struggling to read. He set out supplies and collected papers, and in the evenings, he helped Rose grade their homework. While he liked being at her school, he couldn't help but feel happy when it was finally Friday and spring break, and he had Rose all to himself.

"Happy vacation!" Rose called to her class. It was pouring outside and neither one of them had an umbrella. The kids were shouting, stamping their feet in the puddles and soaking their shoes, refusing to open their umbrellas. "See ya, Mr. Lewis!" a voice called, and Lewis looked around. "Oh, my shoes," Rose said. She leaned on Lewis to slip them off.

"It's only a few blocks. It's not too bad," Rose said, fanning her hands out into the rain, but in minutes her dress and her hair turned dark with rain, his soaked shirt and pants clung to his body. "Whoops," she said. "I lied. Her arm bumped against his and he took it, as if to steady her. They were rounding her corner, when she suddenly winced and then made a small cry and they both looked down and there was a bright star of blood around her foot, a sparkling of broken glass like diamonds at her feet. Bending, she struggled to pick out the big pieces in her foot, but Lewis shook his head. "There could be all sorts of tiny pieces," he told her.

"Lean on me," he said, and he helped her to her place, up the five flights, leaving a trail of blood she kept looking back at. "I'll get it later," he told her. He sat her on the couch. "I can do this," she said, but he went into her bathroom. As soon as he opened her medicine cabinet, he sighed. She had a bottle of Arpège perfume, a Tangee lipstick, and some lotions. He couldn't find even the simplest first-aid items like Bactine or bandages. He pushed aside the Pond's face cream, grabbed a washcloth and big towel, and found some tweezers that he wiped with rubbing alcohol to sterilize.

When he came out, Rose had peeled off her stocking and there was a long pale leg, a flash of creamy skin, and he saw that she had painted every nail a different, bright color, and he wanted to touch every one. "You're going to get bloody," she warned.

"Occupational hazard," he said. He gave her the big towel to drape around her wet body. He lifted up her foot in his hands, the warmth of it, and gently turned it on its side. He could feel her pulse along her ankle. He took the tweezers and gently pulled the first piece of glass out. When he looked up at her, she didn't wince. Instead, her face was grave and lovely, watching him. He took his time, carefully setting each piece of glass on the washcloth. "It looks worse than it is," he told her. "It's all for show, this blood." When he was done, he ran his fingers along the bottom of her skin, checking for rough, tiny pieces of glass, and when he finished, he did it again. "Your patients must love you," she said. He glanced up at her. She was still watching him. "Does it hurt?" he said.

Her eyes were deep as pools and he couldn't stop looking at them. "Everything hurts," she said.

His mouth went dry. "Your eyes? Do your eyes need medical attention?" he said, and when she nodded, he couldn't help it. He leaned up and kissed them. She didn't move away. "What about your nose?" he said.

"It kills." He kissed the tilt of it. He was so close he could see the shadows her lashes made on her cheeks.

"And my lips. Awful," she said quietly, and then he cupped her chin, his eyes on hers. He placed his forehead against hers and she moved closer against him. He kissed her mouth, and then she was kissing him back, unbuttoning his shirt, and he was pulling her to the floor.

IN THE MORNING, Lewis got up first and dressed and went into the kitchen, opening the refrigerator. It was as bad as his. A half a loaf of bread, some cheese, a few pieces of fruit, and a stalk of limp broccoli freckled with mold. "Hey." He turned to see Rose, sleepy and beautiful, her hair a storm about her shoulders. She rubbed her eyes. "Sleepy?" he said and she shook her head and sat down. He couldn't stop sneaking peeks at her. He had known her since they were kids, but everything about her seemed new, the way her neck curved into her shoulders, the graceful way she walked. She drank her juice as if she were considering each sip.

"Are you okay about this?" she finally said. He didn't know what to say. He was used to women changing suddenly after sleeping together, wanting to make him breakfast and then lunch and then dinner, wanting things he wasn't sure he had in him. But with Rose it was different. He didn't want to be anywhere else in the world, but this kitchen. "I'm good," he said.

She drew a circle in a damp spot on the table. "What do we do now?"

They went out to eat breakfast at a little café Rose knew and then walked around the campus until they found a sunny spot to sit on the grass. "I spend so much time thinking about my past and here you are, a real part of it," she said. She tugged up a dandelion and blew on it, scattering the gray seeds. She brushed her hand against the soft grass. "Maybe you should try to find your father," she said.

He looked at her, surprised. "What? Why would I want to do that? Why would you even think about that?"

"It keeps hitting me how I don't have any family left," she said. "What that means, how it feels. But you do, and maybe you shouldn't throw that away like it doesn't mean anything. Don't you want to know what happened to him? I know he wasn't there for you as a kid, but maybe he's changed. Maybe he deserves a second chance. Don't you ever wonder about him?"

He couldn't lie. He had thought about his father. Sometimes when his relationships soured, he wondered if it was because he'd never really had a man in the house to model himself after. When he was dealing with children at the hospital, he went by instinct, by what he thought he'd want if he were a kid in a bed. Sometimes, too, he wondered if his father ever thought about him, if he ever regretted leaving them.

"I think you need to find him," Rose said.

"And then what?" Lewis said.

"Whatever happens happens. But at least you'll know him."

"I'm just not sure it's a good idea."

"He's your father," she said. "A father is a father. You can't just throw that away like it's nothing." She took his hand. "Besides, I want to know everything about you, and that includes him. I want to know if you got your eyes from him or if you have the same sense of humor."

"I can tell you we don't."

"You don't know that," Rose said. "You were so little when he left. You're a man now. It's all different. You should find him, Lewis."

"He could have found me if he wanted."

"You can't leave things up to other people. Sometimes you have to just go and make things happen. Come on. It's something we can do something about." She tugged on his sleeve. "I'll go with you," she said. She tugged his sleeve harder.

"You would?"

He saw that her eyes were full of light. He still didn't know how he felt about finding his father. It was all dark and confused inside of him, but he knew how he felt about going on a road trip with Rose, maybe taking the whole rest of his vacation to do it. She moved closer to him.

"How are we going to find him, though?" Lewis asked.

"You could ask Ava."

"My mom? She doesn't know where he is. And if she did, she wouldn't tell me."

"She might know." Rose touched Lewis's arm. "Call her. Ask."

HE CALLED FROM Rose's apartment and his mother answered on the second ring, and as soon as she heard his voice, her own voice changed, growing warmer. "Honey," she said. "How are you?"

"I'm with Rose," he said. "I took vacation days to come see her."

"Rose." She sighed her name. "But that's wonderful. I'm so glad. How is she?"

He told her a little about Rose and then his mother insisted on speaking to her. As soon as Rose took the receiver, she brightened. "Me, too," Rose said, and then she gave the phone back to Lewis. "She said she missed me," Rose whispered. "She said she's glad we're together."

"So, Mom," Lewis said, hesitating. "I think I want to find Dad."

There was silence, but he didn't know whether she was buying time or whether she was trying to think of a new reason why he shouldn't do this. "Do you know where he is?" Lewis pressed.

He heard his mother sigh. "I don't know," she said.

"Mom, please."

"I'd have to track down the lawyer, see if he had an old address. I don't even know if he'd give it to me, or if he even has it after all this time."

"But you'll try?"

"Why do you want to do this, Lewis? How are you going to feel if you don't find him, or if you do and he's just the same?"

He wanted to tell her that he wasn't twelve anymore. She didn't have to protect him like this or lie about his father. "Rose is coming with me," he said. "We're going to find him together."

"You and Rose?" He heard the change in her voice. She was his mother, after all, and he could sense her weighing how much she wanted him to have a nice girlfriend, one that she approved of, against the fact that she didn't want him to find his dad.

"Mom. I'm an adult now. I'm not going to fall apart over this. I just want to meet him."

"Okay," she said finally. "Give me the number there and I'll call you back, but I'm not promising anything."

Lewis hung up the phone. He didn't know how he felt about finding his father, not really, but when he looked at Rose, he felt as if something were lighting up inside of him. She was leaning against the counter. "What?" she asked, and he swallowed.

"She's going to help us."

Two DAYS LATER, they had an address in Cleveland, courtesy of Ava's old lawyer who remembered Ava and called in a few favors from friends. Lewis was surprised that Ava didn't give him advice about how to act with his father. He thought she would have told him not to talk about her, what to be wary of and what to say, but all she did was recite the address and tell him to call if he needed her. "Mom, thanks," he said, and he meant it.

They took Lewis's car and the old map because it was symbolic, but they stopped at a gas station and got a new map for Ohio, spreading it out in the car. "Okay, so what's the best way to go?" Rose asked.

Lewis was driving and Rose held the map, but every time he looked at it, he couldn't quite get where the route was. After he turned off at a wrong exist, Rose proclaimed herself the navigator. She put her feet up on the dash and sang heartily to the radio. It was all he could do not to pull over and kiss her.

By the time they pulled into a diner to grab a bite to eat, they were famished. They ordered burgers and fries before the waitress could even set down the menu.

"She reminds me of your mom," Rose said when the waitress sped away, and Lewis wasn't sure if that was a compliment or not. He hoped his mother wasn't wearing black toreador pants or blouses that shiny and tight to the café where she sold her pies.

At night, to save money, they parked and tried to sleep in the car. Rose took the back, her knees curled up. In the front seat, Lewis could hear her tossing and turning. Rose finally sat up, sighing, a strand of hair pasted along her cheek. "How much could a motel cost?" Rose said, rubbing her shoulder.

They drove to the nearest motel, but at the door, there was a small sign that read: PLEASE LEAVE YOUR GUNS AT HOME! "Are we sure we want to go here?" Rose asked, and Lewis looked around. The area was desolate. There were no cars around, no people, and he thought, well maybe that meant there would be no guns, too. He didn't know where there were any other motels, how far away they might be.

"Come on, we'll be fine," he promised. They reached the counter and rang the little bell, and a bored-looking man came out. When it was time to sign the register, Lewis wrote Mr. and Mrs. Lark with a flourish, and Rose put her hands in her pockets so the clerk wouldn't see she didn't have a wedding band on. Fighting back yawns, they made their way into the elevator, which had a rug in the middle of the floor and as soon as Rose stepped on it, she stumbled. She jumped back surprised and lifted the edge of the rug. There was a hole in the linoleum as if someone had punched it in. Lewis pulled Rose over to the side of the elevator. "Maybe the room is better," he said hopefully.

The first thing Lewis noticed about the room were the two tiny twin beds. There was a huge painting of migrating geese on the wall, and someone had drawn a handlebar mustache on one of the birds. The bathroom had a line of fungus along the shower and there was a spider-webbing of cracks moving across one ceiling. Rose silently went and got a chair and wedged it under the door. She came back and flopped on the bed, motioning Lewis to lie beside her. "I guess we can call this an adventure," she said weakly.

"Thank you for coming with me," Lewis said.

"That's what friends do." She looked at him seriously. "You don't know the half of how Jimmy used to stick up for you."

"He didn't that day. That's why I was so mad at him."

Rose shook her head. "I remember some kids were talking about how they could get you to do anything if they gave you money or offered ice cream, and he stood up for you."

Lewis felt a flash of shame. As a kid, he had felt the lure of cookies, of presents, of privileges he didn't have. He had been helpless against his own yearning. It pulled at him like a tide. Once he had taken off his pants when he was five for an Oreo cookie, standing helplessly on Danny Zaroni's porch, his face hot with fear, but all he could think about was the cookie, the sugar melting on his tongue, the taste of the chocolate. Danny's mother suddenly appeared and she took one look at Lewis standing there with his pants hanging at his ankles and accused him of peeing on her front porch. "You wait right there," she warned him, and he had tugged up his pants, terrified, and Danny wouldn't look at him. She came back with a bucket of soapy water and Lysol and she made him scrub the porch while she watched, not caring how the cement scraped his knees. "All those germs!" she scolded.

Lewis put one hand along Rose's face, where the skin was cool.

"He loved you," she said. "He would have done anything for you." She got up and stretched. "Tomorrow, we'll see your father," she said.

❖ Chapter Nineteen ❖

Ava was at home on Saturday morning, lost in a novel about a widowed pioneer woman who was fighting off wolves and despair on a Kansas homestead, half wondering how Lewis and Rose's road trip was going. She hadn't wanted to help him find Brian, but maybe it was time to let that go. Brian wasn't holding anything over her anymore. There was nothing he could do to Lewis now. Lewis was a grown man and able to make his own decisions about people. Plus, she couldn't stop thinking of Lewis with Rose. She had always loved that girl, and who knew, maybe her son would, too. When the bell rang, the sound startled Ava.

She tossed off the blanket she was curled under, wondering who it could be. She wrapped her robe tighter about her, catching her reflection in the hall mirror as she went to the door. She hadn't set her hair last night, but she found to her surprise that she liked the way it looked today, wild and curly and doing as it pleased.

She opened the door and there, like a shock, was Jake, in a suit and tie, his hair so long it touched his shoulders. "Ava," he said, and for a moment, she was drowning just looking at him. "What are you doing here?" she asked, her voice tight.

"Please. Let me come in and talk to you."

"No." She tried to push the door shut. She didn't want to have to look at his face. He had left her behind when everything around her was falling apart. It had been years and there had been no letters, not a single phone call. No matter what she did to forget, he bounced back inside of her, reminding her of all she was missing. Every time she kissed a man, she thought of Jake's mouth. When a man took off her blouse and lowered her to a bed, she felt Jake's arms about her. He was like an imprint on her skin, a stain she couldn't wash out.

"Do you know what I went through?" she said. She thought of what Charmaine always said about bum boyfriends: You can't chase someone who doesn't want to be caught. He's gum on the bottom of your shoe. Scrape him off and forget him. Move on.

"What do you want?"

"You."

"You had your chance."

"Ava, the neighbors. Please let me come in."

"Screw the neighbors," Ava said, but it pained her to see the hopeful way he was standing there. She opened the door wider and stood aside so he could come in, his shoulder brushing hers.

Jake hadn't been in this house for years. Since then, she had rearranged the room and painted the walls, but he didn't even register a flicker of surprise. He acted as if he had as much right to be here as the furniture. But just his being in the room changed things. The air felt warmer and smelled like he did, all pine and wood shavings and smoke. He stood, shifting his weight from foot to foot. She nodded at a chair and took the couch. "Sit," she said and he did, leaning toward her as if he were swimming through air.

"You look good, Ava. Different."

"You look the same."

"No. I'm different."

"Why are you here?" she said.

He was quiet for a moment. "I missed you."

"Just like that? You missed me?" Ava snorted.

"You think I wanted to leave?"

"You did leave," she said bitterly.

"Ava, I begged you to come with me. You refused."

"You had a criminal record," Ava blurted. "You changed your name."

He was so quiet, she was frightened.

"Oh God, it's true, isn't it?" she said. "I didn't know if they were making it up to get me to say something about you."

"I was sixteen," he said quietly. "You know how young that is?"

She thought of Lewis, how silent he had become by the time he was sixteen, how he had this whole secret world about him. "I do," she said. She looked at Jake and his mouth was one tight line, his face darkened, but she couldn't tell whether it was in shame or anger.

"You want the story like everybody else? Fine, I'll give it to you," he said shortly. "This kid at school kept stealing my money, roughing me up. Every fucking day and there was nothing I could do about it. When I told the principal, he didn't believe me because the kid was from a rich family, and why'd he need to steal anything? But it kept going on, and finally, one day, when it was snowing, this kid surrounded me outside with his Neanderthal buddies and demanded my jacket. He was standing there laughing, like there was nothing I could do about it. Like I was nothing. The other kids were waiting, like it was a show and I was the main attraction and I popped. I boiled over and I started to beat him up."

Ava stared at him.

"I could have stopped after I bloodied him, but I kept going until his eyes closed and he was like jelly under me. I broke his nose and his jaw. I couldn't stop myself even when his buddies were pulling me off him. When they looked at me, Ava, they were afraid. But that was it for me. They sent me to juvenile detention, and if I thought high school was horrible, it was a cakewalk compared to juvie." He couldn't look at her. "I did it on purpose, Ava," he said. "That's who I was."

"You were a kid," she said, but the words jammed in her throat.

"I was old enough to know better than pounding on someone who was already knocked out. I was wrong and ashamed and scared and I paid for all of it." She watched the anger drain from him, and he slumped onto her couch. "I haven't been that person for a long time."

"I'm sorry," she said.

He shrugged. "Don't be. When I got to juvie, I had to fight for everything, every day. When I got out, I was through with fighting for the rest of my life. All I did at home was hang back and play my sax like my life depended on it. When I played, it was like I was talking to it, and it talked back in the only language I wanted to know. The better I got, the better I felt about myself, the more the rage melted away. The day I got good enough, I changed my name and hitched to Boston."

"Why didn't you tell me this before?"

"I wanted to start over. All that was dead."

"You could have explained this to the police. One thing didn't have to do with the other."

"Oh no? Ever hear of once guilty, always guilty? I thought the records might have been sealed, because I was so young, but they could have gotten a court order to look at them."

"But the case went cold. They must have dropped you as a suspect the way they did everyone else."

"If I had been there, they might not have. Think of the field day the papers could have had. They were so desperate for a lead. The police called me again, you know, after they found the bones, to see if I had any more information, but after a few questions, they left me alone."

"And you left me to handle the whole mess by myself," she said quietly.

"Ava, all that time, in that little room, with those cops hunched over me, I kept thinking how they put innocent people in jail all the time," he said. "If you can't afford a good lawyer, you're screwed, and I certainly couldn't. I've seen it, Ava. Half the musicians I work with have stories. Nabbed on everything from drugs to robbery and they're suspect just because they don't have regular jobs. And I had a record. I'd have been stuck in jail for months until the truth came out, if it came out at all. What good could I do you if they put me away? How could I have helped you and Lewis? Can you imagine how your neighbors would have treated you then?"

"Please don't tell me you did this for me." Ava folded her arms. "You gave me a choice to come with you or not, like it was cut-and-dried. Like there really was a choice. I never got the sense that you were leaving to protect me."

"I wanted to be there for you. But I was the perfect scapegoat. Single, a musician, a guy who rides a motorcycle and has a record. And there's such a thing as guilt by association."

"There was no note. No calls. You never even helped look for him."

"I couldn't."

"Don't give me that. I just can't believe you were thinking of me and not you."

"All I do is think about you," he said.

"You didn't even write me after you left."

"There hasn't been a day or night that's gone by that I haven't thought of you and wondered what you were doing, how you were. I told myself it was over, that I needed to move on. And then, later, I began to beat myself up for being a coward. I knew that I was. There's nothing you're saying to me now that I haven't said to myself. The more time went on, the worse I felt. I figured you'd never take me back so I didn't even try. Then I saw the story about finding Jimmy, how everybody knew it was an accident, and everything changed."

"Just stop," Ava said, but when he got up and sat beside her, she didn't move. Now he was so close, he made her nervous. "Where were you?" she said. "What were you doing?"

She thought he was going to tell her that he had been recording in California, playing the beach clubs, but he got that pained look again. "Teaching music in Des Moines."

"Iowa?" She looked at him askance. She tried to imagine him in all that flat prairie, but it made her think of the games Lewis used to love when he was a kid, the "What's wrong in this picture?" drawings. "You've spent all these years in Iowa?"

"A friend got me the job. It's steady income, plus I had money from the sale of my house in Cambridgeport, so any gig I get is just extra gravy." He shrugged. "It's not the way it sounds. I like it there. I'm used to it."

"Is 'used to it' the same as being happy? How could you end up in Iowa?"

"Ava, look at me. I'm here now."

"What's the matter, no single women where you are? You're getting older and you just thought I'd be here waiting for you?"

"I love you, Ava," he said.

She stood up from the couch, looking at the door. "I can't do this right now," she told him. She wondered if she was being a fool. "Please go," she said.

"Can I call you later? Can I come back?"

"I don't know." She felt a flush of relief when he got up and walked out the door. Ava watched him from the window, his car driving off. She saw him wave wistfully at her, almost as if he were beckoning her to him, but she kept her hands at her sides.

FOR THE REST of the day, she couldn't do anything right. She picked up her book again and then realized she was reading the same page over and over. She tried to color her hair, a new shade called Kicky

Redhead, in the bathroom and got a streak of auburn in the grout she couldn't scrub out. When the phone rang, she didn't move until it stopped. When it rang again the next morning, she grabbed for it. "Can I see you today?" he said.

"I don't know."

"I rented a place," he said. "A little efficiency on Moody Street. I even got a gig in Cambridge."

"Why?"

"I'm just showing you how serious I can be."

"What about your job in Iowa?"

"Leave of absence," he said.

"You didn't quit."

"Ava, I'm a romantic, but I'm also a realist. Let's have dinner. Please."

"All right. Dinner. But that's all."

AVA ASKED HIM to take her to Bell's, because Bell had once told her she was an excellent judge of men and because she wanted to show off for Jake.

"Every pie here is mine," Ava told him, pointing to the displays. She sat opposite Jake and when Bell came over, Ava felt the way Bell was studying Jake. "You good to this girl?" Bell asked him pointedly.

"Absolutely," said Jake.

"You better be, because I'm cooking tonight and you wouldn't want to cross me." She winked at him and he laughed, and then she laughed, too. "Good. I like a man with a sense of humor," Bell said. She tapped Ava on the shoulder as she left.

Jake insisted they order the most expensive things on the menu. All through dinner, her concentration was hazy. She couldn't taste the steak because of the stones in her throat. "I'll take that if you don't want it," Jake said, spearing a slice of meat on his fork. When the waiter came by, Jake said, "Isn't she beautiful?" nodding at Ava, who blushed. When it came time for the pie—coconut this evening—one of her better pies, she watched his face. He shut his eyes when he took a bite. He sighed. She felt her whole body warming.

After dinner, he drove her home. She felt buzzed on the wine Jake had ordered, and starving from all the food she hadn't eaten. It felt as if her senses had all been shuffled. "You can come inside," she said.

She stood wavering in the middle of the living room, grasping the edge of the couch, looking for steady ground. "What do you think, Ava?" he said. She was used to men teasing her, testing her by the way they might stroke her wrist, or sigh into her hair, but Jake was just standing there. He was leaving it up to her, the way he always had, but she wasn't thinking about the future right now. She was thinking about the feel of his skin against hers, the deep thrumming of desire. You didn't always want the right thing for you, but sometimes you just had to make the same mistake to find out for sure. So she crossed the room and pulled his shirt out of his pants and then slid her hand under his shirt, along his back, in the hollows. She heard his deep intake of breath. She stopped thinking then. She let herself fall against him, hearing his breath in her ears, kissing his mouth as if she wanted to swallow him whole.

AVA AWOKE IN her bed to the sound of a lawn mower. She had a headache, thumping like a rabbit paw in her head. Jake was sleeping, beautiful and still, the daylight splashed across him. He had one arm hooped about her possessively. They had never slept this way, and it made her feel strange, uneasy. His mouth moved as if he were saying something. "*Shfll*," he said, as if it were a secret language. She traced a finger on his mouth, but he didn't stir.

She touched his shoulder and his eyes flew open. He gave her a lazy smile. "Well, hi," he said and rose up and kissed her mouth. She pulled away. "I'll be late for work," she said.

"Don't go today."

"I have to."

"I'll drive you," he told her.

"No, I'll drive myself."

She ran the shower so hot, her skin blossomed red. She felt self-conscious and dressed in the bathroom. By the time she got out, Jake was already fully clothed and making coffee for both of them in the kitchen. "One for me, one for my baby," he said.

He wanted to come to the office with her to meet the people she worked with. "Come on, show me off," he joked.

"Not yet," she said.

THEY BEGAN SEEING each other again. Ava found herself watching the calendar, marking the days with the red ink of her pen. Jake stayed for two days and then three, but instead of feeling a thrill or growing calmer, content, she couldn't shake her unease.

One night, Jake was playing his sax for her in the living room. His eyes were shut, his body swaying, and occasionally he'd turn and look at her before he was lost in the music again. She used to be able to sit for hours, just listening, or she'd get up and lean against the length of his back, so the vibrations of the music would flow through her. But tonight, watching him made her want to get her hands in flour. Hearing the way he slid the notes made her think about adding coconut to a pear pie, or dusting the rim of fluted crust with brown sugar. As soon as he was finished, she got up and went into the kitchen to bake. "Hey, where you going?" he called, and she laughed. She let him sit on a stool and watch her, but she wouldn't let him help, and she got so lost in concentration that she actually forgot he was there. Later that night, when they were eating the pie, she talked to him about how she made it, the same way he spoke to her about music. He scraped the last bit of filling from his plate and then pointed his fork at her. "I don't know which one is more delicious."

Later, in bed with Jake, his head was on her breast, his arm wrapped about her waist. The two of them were so slick with sweat, he got up and came back with a bowl full of ice. He tilted a piece out and traced it down her body until she shivered and then he lay back against her. She heard the ice fall back into the bowl. The chill of the ice, the heat of his body. She shut her eyes.

She took a chip of ice from the bowl and put it in her mouth, letting it melt, cool against her tongue. It was going to be summer soon. Before she knew it, the neighborhood would be awash with kids home from school, fathers watering their lawns, the wives bringing out frosty pitchers of lemonade. The neighbors knew Jake was back, but to her surprise, they waved when they saw him. Bell seemed to like him, too, and every time they came to the café, Bell would tease him and give him extra-big portions.

"You and me, we're like music," Jake told her. "It's just all in the timing. There's no neighbors breathing down our throats. Your son is grown and on his own. There are no exes. It's just us." He kissed her mouth. "What do you say, you want to get married?"

She stared at him. "Is this a real question?"

"Will you give me a real answer?"

"I don't know. I have to think about it."

He cupped her face. "Whenever you're ready," he told her.

AT WORK THE next day, Ava felt as if she were in a cloud. She barely heard Richard when he yelled at her about a typing mistake she made. "The client's name is Bohart, not Bohert," he sniped. "If you need to take time off to go to the eye doctor, go and do it." He watched her put a carbon between two sheets of paper and slide it in the machine. Charmaine looked at Ava with concern. "Are you all right?" Charmaine asked.

"I'm not sure," Ava said. She started to type again. Her eyes hurt, as if she had seeds in them. She wished she could go out now and find Jake and talk to him. By four that day, Ava realized she had only typed up six invoices and she had at least twenty shuffled into her in-box.

She walked to the candy machine, but instead of putting the money in the slot, she turned to the pay phone and dialed Jake. There was that strange swimmy feeling again. When he answered, his voice sleepy, she cleared her throat.

"You love me," she said.

"I always have."

"Then yes," she told him.

"Yes what?" he said.

"What do you think?" Ava said, and then Jake laughed and she heard this rattling sound. It took her a moment to realize it was her hand shaking, banging the receiver against the wall. A week later, she flashed the small ring Jake had bought for her, a tiny chip of light on her finger, and Betty and Charmaine swooned. "Imagine that. First Cathy gets hitched and now you," Charmaine said wistfully. Ava knew how lucky she was. Most women didn't get remarried, let alone when they were in their forties. Jake was going to move into her house—their house—soon. With his extra income, she could probably buy it by next year.

She called Lewis on a night when Jake was out playing a gig at the Blue Owl. He had never liked Jake. What if he wouldn't come to the wedding? She couldn't get married without her son being there. His phone kept ringing. He was probably still on his road trip with Rose. Maybe the two of them had given up finding Brian and had had gone on an adventure instead. She couldn't help but hope that the pull of love was stronger than his wanting to find his father.

She hung up the phone. She had had her share of uneasy nights, the times when just the sound of the phone would make her start because she never knew who it was and what they might want from her. The nights when she'd sit up, the bills fanning around her on the dining room table. Those nights, she'd walk into Lewis's room and watch him sleep, all tangled boy, the heat of his skin rising up, his hair mashed against the pillow. I made this, she thought. He was her reason. She would stand there watching him until she felt better.

Ava went into Lewis's old room. She knew he probably wouldn't ever live there again, but she had kept his bed in there, his books, some of his things, and sometimes during the day she came in here and read. Boys. Way back when she had been pregnant, she knew Brian wanted a boy. He kept bringing home miniature-sized baseball bats and gloves and balls. Still, the whole time she was giving birth, she kept thinking, *Annabelle, Christine, Joella,* and then the doctor had boomed, "It's a fine boy!" and for one second, Ava had thought there had to be a mistake.

But she had fallen hard for Lewis. He had been a cautious little boy who preferred to keep his feet on the ground. He could be happy right now. He could be in bed with Rose, the woman he loved, that Ava loved, too, and she wouldn't know, and that was the way it was supposed to be.

She heard a key in the lock and glanced at the time. Just after midnight. Almost the hour of the wolf. She walked out into the hall and there was Jake, and even from there, she could smell the smoky club on him, she could feel the cold of the night air on his skin. "Hey babe," she said, and he looked at her, surprised.

"You're up," he said. "I was going to surprise you in your sleep." He gave her a grin. She walked to him, her bare feet padding on the cold floor and she rested her head against his shoulder. "I missed you," she said. "I've missed you for so long."

LATER, IN BED, she curled around him, warming her feet between his. He looked down at her, laughing. He grabbed her hand and kissed her fingers.

"I wish I had known you before," he said. "I wish I had been your first boyfriend, your first husband, that you hadn't had to go through all that stuff. I wish you had never had to live here."

"I like it here," she said.

He took a strand of her hair and wrapped it around his finger, tugging her closer to him. "I know this is horrible to say, but I can't help thinking that we've been made possible because of a horrible tragedy," he said.

Ava drew the sheets around her. "What do you mean?" she said.

Jake turned so he was facing her. He took her hands in his, blowing on them, as if they were cold. "Well, we have this great thing, don't we? I just remember how it was, with all the neighbors watching us, with Lewis not really liking me."

"Lewis was a child then. And the neighbors are different now."

"I know that, but Jesus, back then. And those cops. And then when Jimmy vanished, it all fell apart. But now, it's like we met at a better time. Do you know what I mean?"

Ava stared at him. "No," she said. "I don't." Jake leaned closer to her, as if he were about to tell her a secret. "Something happened the day Jimmy disappeared," he said.

JAKE TOLD AVA that the first time he came into Ava's neighborhood, he had been spooked before he even knocked on her door. He knew people said that the suburbs were the life, that they fled from their city apartments in droves just for a patchy plot of grass and a squashed little ranch house with a backyard. Kids were safe here, people could have real lives, family lives. He'd heard it a million times. But he was a city guy. He wanted to be in the center of things, and he was lucky he had found a house in Cambridgeport. It had been a dump when he had bought it dirt cheap, but he took his time fixing it up until it was worth twice what he had paid for it. He had loved the buzz of Cambridgeport, how you could ramble out of bed at three in the morning and find the streets hopping, where you could find coffee or eggs or spaghetti at all hours. He had loved the sea of people washing along the sidewalks, the way any moment he might catch someone's eye. The city had a rhythm, its own melody, propelling him.

Ava's street had made him want to turn right around and get out of there. All Jake could see was the line of houses, like an endless row of shoeboxes, neatly perched on lawns all carefully trimmed like an expensive haircut. There weren't enough trees, at least not yet, just these spindly seedlings aching to grow. All of the houses, except for Ava's bright blue one, were the same washed-out pastel shade with identical patio-stone walkways—you'd never be able to tell them apart. Suburbia. You could take it, as far as he was concerned, and throw it into the ocean. "It's convenient," she said, telling him about the Drake's Cakes truck that came by every week, the Fuller Brush men and Avon ladies, the scissor and knife sharpener, the milkman. "I step outside my door and I can find those things anytime I want. We have these things called stores," he told her, and she laughed.

There were other things that had unsettled him. He knew Ava came with a child, that Lewis was part of the package, and though Jake wasn't really a kid person, he did his best to position himself right, to know what to expect. He asked Ava about Lewis a lot. What kind of kid was he? Did he play baseball? Was he smart? Did he have friends? He got her to show him pictures and he exclaimed over the kid's freckles and big eyes. Ava was always happy to talk to him about her son, her voice sounding like it had been dipped in honey. God, but she loved that boy. She told him how smart Lewis was even though he didn't get good grades in school. She mentioned how Lewis ached for his father, a man who didn't deserve such adoration, and she told him about Rose and Jimmy, how they were practically like her other set of kids. Especially Jimmy, Lewis's best friend. Good, Jake thought. Lewis had a best friend, which meant he'd be kept busy and wouldn't interfere too much with Jake's alone time with Ava, but when Ava told him how often Jimmy came around and how she got the impression Jimmy was a little in love with her, Jake felt uneasy. "Don't encourage him," Jake said.

On the day Jimmy had disappeared, he had hoped to come over early, but she had told him she was leaving to go to work around four. He thought that while she was gone, maybe he'd surprise her by fixing her broken porch step. It only took him a few minutes to fix and he was about to leave for home to shower and get dressed for their date that night. Of course, he was a little nervous, since it would be his first time meeting Lewis. But then he felt someone watching, and he turned to see a kid skulking in the bushes, watching him through a bright turquoise toy periscope.

"What, you think I'm spying for the Reds?" Jake said. He made his own hands into binocular circles and put them to his eyes, as if he were lining up the boy in his sights. "Who are you?" Jake asked.

"Jimmy."

Jimmy lowered the periscope and stood up and Jake's hands fell back along his sides.

"Aren't you supposed to be in school?" Jake asked him.

"School's over for today," Jimmy said, tucking the periscope into one of his pants pockets.

"Where are your friends?"

"At a dopey church carnival. And Lewis is my best friend and he had to go to the dentist." He shrugged. "I can't wait for my sister Rose forever. I don't even know where she is." Jimmy looked around the neighborhood. "Anyway, nothing's happening."

"Why don't you wait for them at your house?"

"I can be here. It's a free country." Jimmy just stood there, his feet planted in Ava's scrubby grass. "So are you and Ava getting married or something?" Jimmy said.

"I would say that's none of your business," Jake said. The kid stood his ground for a minute until Jake said, "You should go home," making his voice an edge and then Jimmy moved to Jake's motorcycle, casually stuck out a sneaker, and kicked the motorcycle. "Hey!" Jake called, and Jimmy jumped back, but the look he gave Jake was defiant.

"What's the matter with you? Why would you do something like that?" Jake said. "This is not a toy."

Jimmy's mouth trembled and for a moment Jake thought he was going to cry, which was all he would need. He cleared his throat. "The problem with us is, we're both in love with Ava," he said quietly. "Am I right?" The kid didn't deny it. He just continued to stare at Jake.

"Be a man and talk to me," Jake said. He knew kids liked it when you treated them like equals, like adults, but Jimmy's mouth was pressed shut. Time to try another tact.

"Then I'll talk to you. You know what the big difference between us is? I'm an adult and you're a kid, and you need to be with other kids your own age," Jake said. He said it louder than he had expected. "Go," Jake said. "You need to get lost."

"I live here," Jimmy said. "This is my neighborhood and Ava's my friend. Maybe you're the one who needs to get lost." Jimmy turned and kicked the motorcycle again, harder this time, sending it crashing to the ground. Zigzag lines cracked in the rear view mirror, and Jimmy's face paled. The mirror was expensive. The bike was Jake's pride, and here was this kid pushing it over like it was nothing. Without thinking, he grabbed Jimmy's shirt, gathering it in his fingers. He tugged him up hard, so the boy rocked off his heels and was lifted into the air. Jimmy gasped, and as soon as he did, Jake's hands flew open, his fingers trembled. Jimmy tumbled to the sidewalk. Jake bent to offer his hand, but Jimmy refused it. What was the matter with him, grabbing a kid like that? What was he thinking?

"Are you okay?" Jake asked, forcing himself to soften his tone.

"I'm telling," Jimmy said hotly.

"There's nothing to tell," Jake said, but he felt something snaking up his spine.

"You grabbed me," Jimmy accused.

The sun was too hot. A thin line of sweat prickled along his back. In the distance, he heard a dog barking hysterically. "I didn't mean to," Jake said. Jimmy put his hands on his hips and Jake suddenly felt how ridiculous the whole situation was. The kid's face was dirty. His shirt was untucked from his shorts, his sneakers all scribbled over. What was the matter with him, feeling jealous of a little boy? Better to befriend this kid, have him be on his side, and Jake knew just the way to do it, too. "Hey," he said. "How'd you like a ride on my motorcycle?"

A light flickered in Jimmy's eyes. "Really? It's not broke?"

"Just the mirror and that can be fixed."

"You're not kidding?"

"We'll go really, really slow."

"Honest? For real?" Jimmy stretched up toward him, his body tense with excitement.

He gave Jimmy his helmet. "Sit in back and grab me as if you're glued to me."

The helmet was too big and was rolling off Jimmy's head, but the kid was beaming, holding it on. Jake waited for Jimmy to get on the bike. Jimmy grabbed him tightly. "Easy now," Jake said. He started the bike, moving it so slowly, he might as well have been walking it, but Jimmy didn't seem to mind. *"Vroom!"* Jimmy shouted. Jake kept it nice and slow, once around the block, past this huge tree that had fallen, past two of the neighborhood women standing on the sidewalk, deep in conversation. He pulled back around to the house and helped Jimmy off. The kid's face was shining with glee. Jake stuck out his hand like he would to another man, to an equal, and Jimmy solemnly shook it. "Thanks," Jimmy said. "I mean it. Thanks a billion times. That was so, so cool."

"We're friends now, right?" Jake said.

Jimmy nodded. "I'm going home now," he said.

Jake watched him run across the street. He could probably get to like this kid, his spunk. Maybe he would like Lewis, too. He glanced at his watch. Not even four thirty. He'd be back here by seven.

A few hours later, he had dressed up in a suit, the present he had carefully picked out for Lewis (a magic kit, because she said he liked magic) tucked under his arm. It was a big night, his meeting Lewis, and he wanted everything to go right.

But when he got to her neighborhood, Ava was distracted because

Lewis wasn't even there, not even after hours had passed. He did his best to support her. "It's going to be all right," he told her. He put his arm around her. He wasn't worried. Not then. He figured those kids were just being kids, that they'd show up sometime, and maybe even this was Lewis's way of telling Jake to screw off. But Jake could handle that, too. He'd give Lewis the gift, make sure he got whatever flavor ice cream he wanted. He'd show Ava how he had fixed the step, and later, when they were alone, he'd tell her how he had made friends with Jimmy, leaving out the part where he got so angry.

But then Ava had begun to really worry, especially when that kid Jimmy's mother called to say Jimmy and his sister were missing, too, and that she had called the cops. Jake stood out on the street with Ava, the neighbors, and then the cops, and then Lewis and Rose had stumbled into view. Jake saw that Jimmy was missing, and that was when he suddenly felt as if he were drowning under water. *Get lost*, he had told Jimmy. *Vamoose*. And the kid had and nobody knew where he was now. Everyone was asking questions, like the rat-a-tat of machine guns. He thought of how he had driven around the neighborhood with the kid. He wondered who might have seen him? His neck prickled with sweat.

It kept getting worse and worse. The police were questioning Ava, and then they called him, pulling him out of a gig, always asking the same things. "A jazz musician, huh," a cop said, as if that itself was a crime. They kept asking him what had he done that day, where had he gone? "How much time did you say you spent with Jimmy?" the cops asked.

"None," Jake lied. "None. I never met the kid."

"We'll talk to the neighbors, see what they say," the officer said.

JAKE STARTED TO hate to come to Ava's neighborhood. The neighbors were outside, and if the kids were outside, they seemed glued to their parents. He was afraid someone would point to him and say,

Hey, you were the one with Jimmy on your motorcycle that day. Or
what if someone came forward and said, You're the one who grabbed
that kid. Everything felt different. The last time he came over, he had
watched Ava talking to a group of neighbors. People kept remembering
things they had seen, and even Jake could hear how they changed their
stories, how a strange black car on the street was suddenly brown, and
then it was speeding, and then it wasn't. He saw how they turned their
backs on Ava, leaving her standing helplessly in the middle of the street.

"Let's get out of here," he had told her. He had it planned out. There
were always people asking about his house. He could sell it in a minute.
They could move to California. He could almost imagine it, coming
home every day and finding her, getting to know Lewis. But then she
started hedging, coming up with excuses about Brian and the investigation, and he felt caught. Why couldn't she just trust him and come with
him? If he stayed, the cops would keep asking him questions. But if he
left, he'd be leaving Ava.

Then he and Ava had that final argument at the club. He kept
urging her to come with him and she kept saying no until it turned
into something final. Fine, let her break up with him. Let it be on
her head, he thought. But then one night, he missed her so much, he
got on his bike to go over there and apologize and try to work it out.
It was eight at night, and dusky. There were neighbors standing in
groups, slowly walking, their ribbons of lights making a path, and
he thought of that old Frankenstein movie, with the villagers angrily
waving torches on their way to finding the monster. He heard the
neighbors' voices, growing louder. "We'll get that guy!" someone
said, almost making it a chant. It didn't matter whether you had
done something or not. All that mattered was if people thought you
had. And from where he stood, he seemed like the perfect target.
They didn't even know who this person was and they wanted to kill
him. How long before Ava would turn on him, too? He had made a

mistake with Jimmy. He knew it was wrong, but he also knew that in this world, that distinction didn't matter.

He turned his motorcycle around and headed back to his house and as soon as he got there, he started making phone calls. He had friends in California who owned a club. He knew people in San Diego where he could crash until he got himself settled. He even had friends in Des Moines. He thought of the beach and the ocean and the weather so warm, he could ditch his leather jacket entirely.

In all, it took him only an hour and about half a dozen calls and then he had a new life spread before him in Iowa, of all places. The realtor was coming the next morning to put the house on the market. He didn't even have to be there for it.

He told himself it wasn't just his fear of being blamed that was making him leave, his refusal to ever go back inside any sort of prison. It was that it would never work, the two of them, not with Jimmy hanging over them. He told himself it would be better for her, too, with him gone, that she'd be less of a target for the cops and the neighbors. It was what she wanted, to stay here, anyway. He had asked and she had answered.

He just didn't bank on his never being able to forget her.

AVA STARED AT Jake. He put one hand over his mouth and then took it away. "That's the whole story," he said. He reached for Ava but she pulled away.

"All this time and you left out the biggest part of the story," she said.

"I was wrong to have left you," he said. "I can admit it."

He looked weathered, as if someone had rubbed at his outlines. It was the first time she noticed the downward pull to his mouth. His handsomeness had faded. He touched a curl of her hair, swinging it like a jump rope. "Aren't you my girl?" he said.

She was silent. The words bunched in her throat. "The criminal record," she said carefully. "You were a kid and you paid for it. But, this, with Jimmy. You were an adult. You had choices."

"I didn't hurt him, Ava. He was just scared. I lost my temper but then I stopped. And I made it up to him. I did the right thing afterward. The whole thing took five minutes and when I left, he was fine. He was happy."

"But you never told me."

"I grabbed Jimmy. I knew what that would look like, how easy it would be to pin something on me."

"You let me think your leaving was about something entirely different. You put yourself in a better light, like you hadn't done anything wrong. It was really yourself you cared about. Not Jimmy. And certainly not me."

"What would you have thought if you knew I had grabbed Jimmy? It didn't have a damn thing to do with his vanishing, but what would you have thought?"

"Do you hear what you're saying?"

"You're looking at this all wrong."

"It's easy to be here, now that you're safe." She tried to think of all the times she had felt secure with him, the way she had felt riding behind him on the bike, like he had unpeeled the world for her, showing her the stars from Cambridge Common, hiring a boat so they could go out on the Charles, the wind whipping her hair like an eggbeater. "No," she said.

He frowned. "Ava," he said.

Ava got out of bed. She pulled her robe around her, watching him.

"Ava, you love me. You know you do."

"I've stayed here all this time, but you didn't even think to come back until they found the remains. And it wasn't because you missed me, because if you had, nothing would have stopped you. It was because you figured you were off the hook and it was safe. You are still lying to me, don't you see that? What other pieces of the truth are missing?"

"Don't do this," he said. He stood up, and he tried to touch her, but she stepped away. "How can you deny what we have? I want to take care of you now."

"I've been taking care of myself for a long time. And I think you should leave," she told him. When he didn't move, she bent and got his clothes, throwing them on the bed. "Now," she said.

He looked at her, incredulous, and then reluctantly starting pulling on his shirt, his pants. He shoved his feet into his shoes. "We'll work this out," he said.

She walked out to the front of her house and opened the door, waiting, and when he left, she locked the door, leaning against it, and wept. She was so very tired.

JAKE KEPT CALLING. The only reason Ava picked up the phone was because she was afraid it might be Lewis, reporting on his father. "We can put all this behind us," Jake said.

"Don't call me," she told him.

She thought of how happy she had been. Well, she had seen what she wanted to see. He treated her like an equal. He had a steady job and a house. He actually gave her choices. Did she want to eat at a steak house or a fish place? Did she like when he touched her thigh or did she prefer he nibble the back of her neck? And there were those nights when he played his music, swaying with the notes, as if he had tapped into a whole other magical world she could only watch and envy. She couldn't take her eyes off him, and yet, how badly had she been blinded? How had she missed the truth? Maybe subconsciously, she just hadn't wanted to know.

That Friday, he showed up at her office. Ava was in the back making Xerox copies. "A guy's here for you," Charmaine said. "And he looks like hell." She put one hand on Ava's shoulder. "Should I tell him to scram?"

"I'll go talk to him," she said. She walked out and there he was, slumped by the elevator. She could feel the other women watching her.

"Here we are again," Jake said. He looked rumpled, like he had slept in his clothes, and there were bags under his eyes. "I have to go back to Iowa, but I want you to come with me."

Ava heard the ring of the other elevator. How was this different from the last time they broke up? In a way, it was worse because now she was the bigger fool. She saw Richard striding by, taking her in. She couldn't get past this, couldn't forgive or trust Jake again, but if she spoke, she was afraid she'd burst into tears. Instead, she just shook her head. She saw his face crumple, but she steeled herself. She walked away from him, past Charmaine and Betty, into the break room. She didn't hear Jake's footsteps or his voice. He wasn't following her. Again.

She fell into one of the chairs, shutting her eyes. She heard the door open and shut. She opened her eyes and there was Charmaine, who sat down beside her. She took Ava's hand and held on to it. "Let him go, the jerk," Charmaine told her and that's when Ava began to cry.

Charmaine took Ava to the ladies' room and made Ava wash her face. She gave Ava some foundation to put under her eyes so no one would know she had cried, using a little triangle sponge she kept in her makeup bag. "My mom showed me this trick," Charmaine told her, blotting a tissue with cold water on Ava's skin. And when the two of them walked out of the bathroom, Charmaine tried to shield Ava from Richard. "Someone's got his panties in a knot today," Charmaine whispered.

Ava sat back at her typewriter. She could feel the makeup caked on her face but she left it where it was. In front of her were more invoices than she could possibly handle in a week, let alone a day. She looked up and saw him at his desk, his feet up as usual, not working, just watching her, like he was the lord of the jungle. She felt herself closing, like a door slamming. She picked up a sheet and started to type.

THAT NIGHT, AVA came back home, and all around her, families were carrying on their lives, and she was in her little house alone. She sifted through the mail, half hoping there might be a postcard from Lewis and Rose, though it was probably too soon for any mail to get here. Why was she always the one waiting? Why was her life full of maybes?

Jake didn't call that night or the next morning. She finally phoned him and a voice told her that the line was disconnected and there was no forwarding number. He had left. She had told him to and he had done it. So why was she surprised?

She walked into Bell's that evening with her pies, and as soon as Bell tasted one, she frowned and Ava knew she had ruined the bunch. "Come in the back with me," Bell said, and then, when Ava started to cry and tell her about Jake, Bell took both her hands. "He doesn't deserve someone like you," Bell said. "I should have known he was a rotter, but he had me, just like he had you."

Ava wiped a hand over her eyes. "I'm such a fool," she said. Her life used to be so full. She was busy with being a wife, being a mother, even a girlfriend. Now, look at her. She was alone. Brian, Jake, and Lewis—even Jimmy—all the guys who had meant something to her, were now gone.

Bell sat up straighter. "Actually, you're not a fool," Bell said. "But I am. I should have done this a while ago. I'm tired. This place is a lot of responsibility. It's a headache and a half."

Ava stared at her. "Please don't tell me you're closing the café," she said.

Bell smiled. "I'm not," she said. "I'm giving it to you to run. If I pay you to learn the ropes, will you manage my café?"

❧ *Chapter Twenty* ❧

Brian Lark pulled the car into the drive and bounded into the house to find his wife Glory sitting on the couch with a young man and woman he had never seen before. He had had a long day at the car lot and was tired, but he knew how to flip on the switch to be welcoming and pleasant. Brian thrust his hand out, nodding enthusiastically. The young man stood, but looked at Brian's outstretched hand and frowned. "I'm Lewis," he said.

Brian cocked his head, disoriented. "Lewis?" He took a step closer. He saw the glasses of cold drinks already out on the coffee table. Glory was watching him carefully.

Brian couldn't stop looking at his grown son. He kept trying to find the things that were familiar about him: the shape of his nose, the deep muddy color of his hair, the way Lewis had gestured with his right hand, the same way he did when he was seven. This young man didn't look anything like Brian and very little like the boy he remembered. He touched Lewis's shoulder, almost as if he expected to get a shock. "Are you okay? Did something happen? Is your mother okay?" Brian asked.

"We're both fine," Lewis said, but he wasn't meeting Brian's eyes. "I just wanted to see you after all this time."

"Well, I'm glad," Brian said. He felt his voice go boisterous, the way it did when he was trying to close a deal at the lot. He saw the girl exchange a look with Lewis. "I'm Rose," she said, standing up and offering her hand.

He was used to picking up hesitation, the clip of fear people felt before purchasing a car that might be too expensive for them. He knew a smile could work wonders and he brightened his. "Sit, sit," Brian said. "Take a load off. We have so much to talk about." But when Lewis and Rose sat down, Brian felt suddenly tongue-tied. There was so much he wanted to know. "Tell me where you live," he finally said. "What you're doing now." He leaned forward, listening as Lewis told him about living in Madison and being a nurse's aide.

"You work in a hospital?" Brian thought of his father, a surgeon, who had wanted Brian to go into medicine and had told him working at a car lot was low-class. When his father had died, he had left Brian only bad memories and a gold watch that Brian promptly pawned.

"He has your eyes," Glory said encouragingly.

"So you're doing well," Brian said. He knew he had been a crappy father, but looking at Lewis now, he felt relieved. His son had what sounded like a good job and a pretty girl at his side. He had turned out okay, and maybe that had nothing to do with Brian, but what did that matter now that they were here together?

"I've heard so much about you," Glory said and Brian looked at her, surprised, because outside of one conversation he had with Glory when they had first met, when they were spilling their lives out to each other, he had never wanted to discuss his past.

He saw the girl gently jostle Lewis.

"All right," Lewis said to her. Then he turned to Brian.

"Can I ask you something? Will you tell me the truth?" Lewis asked.

Brian looked at the drinks on the table. "No alcohol in there," Glory said quietly, and Brian picked one up and sipped. Ginger ale sparkled in his throat, but he still felt parched. He swallowed. "Ask anything."

"Tell me why you left us," Lewis said.

There it was. Right in front of him.

Brian put his drink down. He saw the watery ring it made on the mahogany table, and he bet Glory did, too, but she didn't move to get a napkin or one of their World's Fair coasters to put under the glass. She just sat there, the way Lewis and Rose were, waiting. "Does it matter now?" Brian asked finally. "You're here now, I'm here. We're both adults."

All the sounds in the room boomed in his head. The ticking of the clock, the steady breathing of Glory beside him. Lewis was looking at him as if he understood nothing. "You never called or visited. And then you stopped trying to get custody of me. I found the letter in Mom's stuff. Why did you disappear from my life?" Lewis asked. "What happened? Was it because of me, because of something I did? I just want—I need—to know."

"Lewis, no—" Brian said. "You were my son. I loved you."

"Then why didn't you ever come back for me?"

"What are you talking about?" Brian said. "I did come back."

BRIAN HAD COME back to Waltham a week after his own father died, about ten years ago. He was drunk that day, the way he was most days then, but he could still drive. Grieving for his father, for all that might have been, had made him suddenly want to see his own son, and the more he thought of Ava and her men, the more he felt his blood boiling. He had to see for himself what was going on.

And he missed her, too. He hadn't met Glory yet and he was tired of being alone. He was beginning to wonder if he had made a big mistake leaving his family.

As soon as he got out of Cleveland, he had another beer and felt better. God, but he hated Cleveland. He had left Waltham and his family to be with this new woman, Becky, but it didn't take long for that to sour and for her to start looking at him like he was something she'd stepped in. He didn't know which he hated more, her or his job at her father's paper company, but both of them made him drink.

When he had arrived in Ava's neighborhood, he had wanted to leave. He had promised Ava the suburbs, but he'd never been able to deliver, and here she was, getting it for herself without him. He parked and looked at the house numbers, looking for Ava's. He looked longingly at the six-pack of beer in the backseat. If he drained one, he'd feel better, but then she'd smell it on his breath. She might not even let him in the house. He suddenly felt sick with nerves. Would Ava even be at home? He glanced at his watch. Quarter to five. Didn't she tell him she worked part-time? But then again, there was a lot she hadn't been telling him these days. Maybe there was some man. Maybe he had already taken Brian's place with Lewis.

Don't think like that, he told himself. The thing to do was look ahead. Number 120. There was her house. A small bright blue ranch on the corner, with dried-out looking grass, but she had planted yellow flowers by the walkway, like small, bobbing suns. He parked the car and walked around to the side of the house, peering in the windows. He saw the wood table in the dining room, covered with a rose-colored cloth. He could see a bit of her kitchen, all yellow and sunny. When he walked to the back, he saw the laundry on the clothesline. A red dress. A blue skirt. A pair of boy's dungarees. He walked over and took Ava's skirt in his hands. He pressed it to his face, shutting his eyes. Lemon detergent and fresh air. For a moment, he wavered on his feet. There had been times that he had loved her so much he had thought that he was going mad. He walked back around to the front of the house, practicing what he would say. *Hi, this is a surprise. Hi, I missed you. Hi, I'm sorry. Hi, please forgive me.*

He reached the front porch just as the front door opened. There, shining in front of him, was his son.

"Hi," he said and Lewis faltered.

Lewis stood on the top porch step, looking down at Brian so that Brian had to crane his neck to see him. "You know who I am, don't you, son?" Brian said. He hadn't seen Lewis since he was seven or so, but the kid still should still remember his own father.

Lewis didn't move. "Is your mom around?" His throat was so dry he could hardly speak. "What time does she get home? She must be working, right?"

Lewis kept watching him. "Come on, then," Brian said. "We'll figure it out later. My car's right over there," he said. "Let's go for a drive." He thought maybe he and Lewis could get an ice cream or something and be back before Ava got home. "Maybe I'll even let you drive." He was kidding, but he kept thinking how much easier it would be to charm Ava if he had already won Lewis over. Brian was beginning to feel dizzy from the sun and from the drink. He could feel himself sweating and he didn't like the way Lewis was looking at him. He walked up the porch steps and reached for his son, opening his arms for a hug.

"Don't touch me!" Lewis said, stepping back.

"I understand you're mad," he said. "I'd be mad, too—"

"Get away from me!"

"You don't talk that way to me," Brian said, his patience thinning. "I come all the way here to see you and this is the way you treat me?" It was too hot for this. He wanted iced coffee, a cigarette, a nice cold beer. "Get in the car," he snapped, and he reached for Lewis's arm, but Lewis jerked away. "What's the matter with you?" Brian said. "Get in the car!" he scolded, grabbing Lewis again, this time getting a hand on his son's arm, tightening his grip. "Let me go!" Lewis said, and when Brian ignored him and started dragging him down the porch steps, Lewis twisted around and bit Brian's hand. The shock of the pain made Brian release his son. "What the hell!" Brian said, rubbing his palm. A line of red teeth marks braceleted his skin. "You little devil!" he said, but Lewis was running wide around him into the street. "Hey!' Brian shouted. "Hey! Don't you run away from me! Get back here!"

Brian ran, too. He hadn't run like this since he was a boy himself. Already he felt how his extra pounds slowed him, and his legs weren't the pistons they used to be. The wind sang in his ears. His son! He was running after his own son! He was a quarter of the way down the block when his knees buckled and his breath stitched up. He was too drunk to run anymore. He shut his eyes and the world swam and when he opened them, Lewis was gone. Brian bent over, bracing both hands on his knees, his shoulders shaking. "You come back here!" he cried, panting, but the street was empty, and all he heard was the endless whine of mosquitoes.

He walked around the neighborhood three times, trying to find Lewis. The streets were all quiet and when he called Lewis's name, it felt like it was echoing back to him. Where the hell was everyone? Weren't the suburbs supposed to be filled with people? When he got back to Ava's house, he rang the bell, just in case Lewis had come back or Ava was there. No one answered. His head throbbed. He wanted another beer. He searched his pockets for a scrap of paper, for a pen, so he could write a note. But what would he say? Sorry? Call me? He didn't have any paper. He had no pen. And the only place anyone could call him was in Cleveland, and by then it would be too late. He looked down the street one last time, but it was empty. He couldn't go to a house and ring the bell and ask for a pen, could he? He tried to remember where Ava had said she worked, but had she ever told him? His mind stretched out, blank as a sheet.

He put his hand against the wood of the door. Then he turned and went back to his car and got in it. He rested his head on the steering wheel, trying to think what to do.

His son had bitten him and run. When Ava found out, she'd be furious with him. Any possibility of tender feelings would be ground into glass. He thought of all the things he should have done. He should have called first, set up a time to see them. What did he think, a surprise was a good idea? Who was he kidding? He had fucked it up all over again.

It took him hours to drive home and the whole time he couldn't stop thinking about Lewis running away from him. He reached back around and grabbed up a bottle of beer and slugged it down, and then, because he still felt like crap, he had another. He had to keep stopping himself from turning around and going back, from finding a pay phone and calling until he got someone so he could explain. He kept replaying it all in his mind. The way Lewis had bolted and struggled against him. That wasn't forgiveness. That was not wanting to have anything to do with you. He ran one hand over his eyes.

What did it matter? What would have happened anyway if Lewis had gone with him? He would have taken his son out for a treat and maybe they would have had a good time. But then what? He'd return him to Ava, where he belonged. Ava would make small talk with him, but he knew suddenly how much of a fool he had been. Ava never called him to talk. She hadn't asked him to come back, not once. Not ever. She didn't miss him. And even if she and Lewis were willing to pack up and move with him, did he even want that? Would he return to Massachusetts, where he had been a failure? How long could he keep beating himself up for mistakes he had made? "When you keep hitting something and nothing changes, then maybe it's time to get rid of the whip," he had read once. Brian hadn't known what it meant until now.

He reached for another beer, and then a car zoomed into his line of vision, the horn blaring, driving him off the road. He wrenched the wheel, pumping the brakes frantically. The car slammed up on the shoulder and onto the grass, banging into a tree so hard, his neck whip-lashed. But the car had stopped and he was unhurt.

Brian knew people sometimes could pinpoint the moment when their lives changed for the better, and that day, when he was drunk, by the side of the road, surprised to find himself alive, was Brian's. He managed to get the car back on the road and stopped at the first diner he saw. His hands were shaking so badly, he spilled black coffee all over the counter. "Never mind, honey," the waitress said, mopping it up for him, and she was so kind, so concerned, that he wanted to cry. He got a hotel room and slept it off. When he returned to Cleveland, he found an AA meeting. To his surprise, he actually liked AA. He had never really been religious, but he found he liked when everyone talked about surrendering to a higher power outside of yourself. You could find support, acceptance, and help. Even though he had been a drunk and a cheater who had left his wife and son, even though he'd had a father who had dismissed him, God understood and offered second chances and all he had to do was ask for them. It was a remarkable comfort.

Gradually, Brian stopped drinking. He had chips for three weeks of sobriety and then two months and then six. He displayed them on his dresser so it was the first thing he saw every morning. AA told him to surround himself only with people who supported him and when Becky made a crack about all his sobriety chips junking up the decor, he broke up with her. "Fine," she said. "Who cares? I was about to do it myself." When he stopped seeing Becky, things got a little less friendly at the paper company, but it didn't matter because he had decided he was getting out, going back to what he loved to do. He got a lead through one of the guys at AA and began managing a new car lot, and the first week he was on the job, Glory walked in, a tall gorgeous blonde, and his life changed again.

It wasn't that he didn't miss drinking—he did, sometimes so much he could taste it at the back of his throat. But he liked being able to master that need and walk away from the one thing he wanted the most, the same way he'd had to do with his family. And every time he turned away from drinking, there was someone to cheer him on. When it was his turn to stand up at AA meetings, he talked about everything except his ex-wife and son. You were supposed to make amends to the people you had hurt, to ask forgiveness, and Brian did, every night, in his mind. The only reason he didn't call or go back to Waltham again was because he needed to keep feeling that he had turned his life around, that he was a good man. Ava and Lewis were reminders that that hadn't always been true.

When Brian finished speaking, Lewis felt as if the world had unraveled. He stared at his father. "Lewis," Brian said. He unlinked his hands, opening them as if he were praying. "I'm so sorry. For everything, son. Can you forgive me?"

"You came to see me?" Lewis said. He tried to swallow, but his throat felt as if it were made of fabric. He thought of all the times he had jumped when the phone rang, sure it was his dad. He remembered the many weekends he had sat out on his front porch, watching the cars, imagining that one of them might be driven by his father coming to see him. "You wanted us to be a family again?"

"I did. Don't you remember?"

"When was this? When did it happen? Why didn't you call first?"

"I told you, I didn't think your mother would allow it—"

"Don't blame her."

"Well, she must have told you all sorts of horrible things about me, considering how you ran away from me. Maybe I deserved that, the way you ran. I wasn't such a great father, I know that. And then I didn't call. I didn't visit. I screwed everything up so royally and I don't know why, but can't people change? Didn't I deserve a chance from you?"

"I don't remember any of this."

"Well, it was a long time ago."

"I wouldn't have forgotten. How old was I?"

"I don't know. I've been living here ten years. It was probably ten years ago. Spring. It was a nice day."

"Oh, my God," said Rose quietly, sitting up straighter. "It was spring?" she asked.

"Sure, it was spring, but really hot out."

"Was it April?" Rose said.

"Yeah, probably. That sounds about right."

Lewis looked at Rose, but she was leaning toward Brian now, staring at him.

Brian went on. "You still haven't answered my question. Why'd you run away? Why'd you *bite* me? Did you really hate me that much?"

Lewis's head was spinning. "I never would have bitten you. I really don't remember any of this."

"Don't give me that. You came out of the house. I remember you had on this red shirt, these plaid shorts. These sneakers that looked like you wrote all over them. Bet your mother loved that."

Rose started to cry, little chuffing noises. She dipped her head toward her lap, but her hands stayed tightly folded. Brian reached for her gently. "What? Are you okay?" He tried to put one hand on her shoulder, but she moved away from him. "You need a tissue? Glory—" Glory got up and came back with a box and handed it to Rose. She patted Rose on the shoulder.

There was a metallic taste in Lewis's mouth, like he had bitten down on tin. The sneakers. He remembered the sneakers. He could smell the Magic Marker.

"It wasn't me," Lewis said.

"What are you talking about?" Brian said. "What wasn't you?"

"You ran after Jimmy," Lewis said. "My best friend. He was always at our house."

"Who?"

"Jimmy. Jimmy Rearson, my brother," Rose said. She brushed at her tears and then took another tissue from the box. "He vanished that day."

"What are you kids saying to me? You think I wouldn't know my own son? Don't give me that." He moved closer to Glory on the couch.

"My brother had those sneakers," Rose said. "With words he wrote all over them. My mother kept throwing them out, but he would dig them out of the trash and write on them some more."

"Anyone could have those—"

"I didn't," Lewis said. "No one else did, either."

Rose took another tissue, balling it in her hands.

"They found him?" Brian said.

Tears began sliding across Rose's cheeks, but she didn't move to stop them.

"His remains. They found them recently in a neighbor's abandoned bomb shelter," Lewis said quietly.

"A what? Jesus," Brian said. "But how can you think this has something to do with me?"

"You chased him."

"Because I thought he was you! Why didn't he tell me who he was, then? Why didn't he say his name or tell me he didn't know who I was?"

"Because he was scared! Because a strange man was yelling at him and running after him!"

Brian sat back. He took Glory's hand and Lewis saw how tightly he clutched her fingers. "Who knows who else was out there that day," Brian said sharply. "One moment I saw him and then I didn't. I'm telling you I didn't do a thing. There's no proof of anything. Don't make me feel wrong when I was trying to do something right, and I was trying to do it for you." He leaned forward and downed the rest of his drink. "I was being a good father. I was coming for you."

I was coming for you.

Lewis thought of Jimmy running, how scared he must have felt. Lewis remembered talking to Jimmy about Brian. Lewis made up stories about what kind of person his father was, what he looked like. He had been too ashamed to tell the truth, that he didn't know anything anymore about his father, that no matter how many letters he wrote, how many stars he wished upon, his father was gone, and his memories of his dad had grown fuzzy and thin.

Lewis knew how hard he had tried to find his father. He remembered how he had found the letter from the lawyer saying his dad would no longer seek custody, how he had been so furious with his mother. "Did you want custody of me?" he asked, and his father lifted up his hands.

"But did you? Did you really want custody? It wasn't just a threat? Why did you give up?"

"I drove all the way out to see you, didn't I?" he said.

"Who can remember anything exactly?" Glory said. She looked from Brian to Lewis and Rose and then back to Brian again. "This is a terrible tragedy."

His father didn't need to answer. Lewis understood now. Brian said he had come by that day to make amends, but he hadn't stuck around. There had just been that one moment and then things had gone wrong for him, and he had gotten into the car again and never looked back.

His father hadn't changed. He had never taken responsibility for Lewis. And he'd never take responsibility for anything that had to do with Jimmy, either. He just wanted to look good.

Brian looked up at Lewis and held out one hand. "Hey, come on, now," he said. He glanced at Rose. "I'm so sorry about your brother, but why don't we just talk about something else now?"

Lewis stood, helping Rose up. "We have to go," Lewis said.

"What, you're kidding? It's not that late. You really have to go?" Brian stood up, along with Glory, who put one hand on his shoulder. "What kind of a visit is this? You're here and then you go? Please. I don't get to see my son every day."

"It's late," Lewis said.

"You're welcome to stay over," Brian said. "We have a guest room." As soon as his father said that, Lewis wondered what guests Brian ever had. Did Brian ever expect that that room might be for Lewis?

Rose was looking at him, waiting. "No, it's okay," Lewis said. "But thank you."

Glory insisted on giving them a red plaid thermos of coffee for the road. At the door, Brian stared at Lewis, as if he were memorizing him. "What?" Lewis said, and Brian shook his head. "We finally see each other," Brian said. "Imagine that. After all this time." He turned to the table and scraped open a drawer, taking out a small white card and handing it to Lewis. LARK MOTORS, the card said. WE SATISFY YOUR DRIVING AMBITIONS!

"My address and phone are on the back. Call me, please, or write. Next time you're in town, you'll stay longer," he said. "We'll plan it out and I'll show you the town. We can sit and really talk, finally get to know one another." Then he waited, and Lewis knew he was supposed to write down his own phone number, his own address for the tiny little efficiency he kept in Madison, but he couldn't imagine making his fingers work. The world seemed to have shifted upside down and here he was hanging on to its edges. His father was looking at him, so he scribbled down a made-up address and phone number and handed it to him. Then he folded the paper his father gave him and tucked it into his pocket. "Thanks," he said.

"Everything's all right then, isn't it?" his father said. He looked at Rose. "I'm so sorry about your brother," Brian said, again. Rose stepped silently back from him. Brian reached to hug Lewis, and Lewis instinctively stiffened. His father held him so close, Lewis could see the pomade in his hair, something no one really used anymore, and when Lewis looked up, Glory was standing there, beaming as if something wonderful had just happened.

"Don't forget your old dad," Brian said, a catch in his voice. "No matter what, we're still family here."

His father and Glory stood in the middle of the driveway when Lewis and Rose pulled away in the car. His father waved, his mouth half-open, as if, any moment, he would say something important to Lewis. Lewis watched him from the rearview mirror, his father growing smaller and smaller, and then he saw Glory rest her head on Brian's shoulder. He saw Glory trying to pull Brian back inside the house, but Brian wouldn't move. It was as if Brian couldn't believe that this time Lewis was the one leaving.

❖ Chapter Twenty-one ❖

Lewis pulled the car onto the main road, his head swimming. He thought of his mother, arguing with him about his father, and how he had refused to listen. He hadn't wanted to believe her. He rolled down his window and tossed his father's card out, watching the wind whip it out onto the road. Then he reached over for the thermos and he flung it out of the car as hard as he could, so it smashed. He felt Rose flinch in the seat beside him. He rolled the windows up again, breathing hard.

"Well," Rose said quietly. "Now you know your father."

He and Rose didn't speak the whole way back to the motel. They rode the elevator up to their room with the two twin beds and the green-printed bedspreads, the photo of the geese staring at them. Lewis sank down on one of the beds.

"I never want to see him again," Lewis said.

Rose sat on the bed opposite him, her hands in her lap. She couldn't meet his eyes and she was silent. "Rose," he said. He moved to sit beside her, but she leaned forward and then she kissed him hard on the mouth, moving closer to him, as if she wanted to put her whole self inside of him. He knew what this was, and it wasn't love or need or desire. It was panic sex, when you needed something—anything—to take you away. You didn't even have to like the person you were fucking, but that person was alive, there was a pulse beating up against yours and making you remember you were alive, too. Rose unbuttoned his shirt and he felt his own breathing quicken, and he shut his eyes, and when she kissed his neck, he began to tug away her clothing. He kissed her hair. He kissed the base of her throat, the creamy pearl of her shoulders, and then they were on the hotel bed, naked. "Open your eyes," he whispered, but she kept them closed.

It felt different making love to her now. His body felt on alert, with all his senses so switched on, he wouldn't have been surprised if her eyes or her hair changed color, if he suddenly noticed her skin was blue. His mouth was breathing against hers, and when he finally entered her, he felt a shock of recognition, as if he had been waiting for this all along and just now realized it. "Rose," he said, and then she opened her eyes and looked at him, but her eyes were wet, and all he could think was, *Come back. Please, come back.*

"Are we all right?" he said. "Rose, are we all right?" He tried to keep awake, to keep watching her, but she was curled into a comma. He wrapped himself like a blanket around her. He took her hand in his, her fingers limp with sleep, and he held on fast.

Shortly before morning, Rose dreamed Jimmy was a kid and she was an adult. She was in their old house, watching him through her bedroom window, as if he were on a TV screen. He was walking lazily outside in the neighborhood, which was empty and silent, until Brian Lark appeared. She tried to open the windows, but they were bolted shut. She banged her hands on the glass, shrieking his name, but Jimmy couldn't see or hear her. She ran to her front door and sped out into the street and Jimmy flashed past her, running and terrified. She heard footsteps thundering in the distance and saw Brian. Then Jimmy ran across the street into Mr. Gallagher's yard. She heard his sneakers stamping on the ground, his heart beating so loudly she wanted to clap her hands to her ears. She saw him crouch and tug open the door. "That's no place to hide!" she screamed. "Keep going, run!" she shrieked. "Keep running!"

Shaking, he lowered himself into the shelter, clinging to the rickety ladder, closing the top, and suddenly Rose was right there beside him. Once inside the shelter, she felt his fear. She heard his thoughts, like dictation in her mind. As soon as the coast was clear, he could run back home. He would stay here just as long as it took to be safe and then he would go. And so he waited, clinging to the ladder, listening for footsteps, for Brian's shout, but the ladder, freckled with rust, pulled away from the wall, opening like a zipper, and Jimmy hit the ground. She heard the crack of his ankle, the bright bolt of pain like an exploding star, and she moved down beside him but she couldn't help him. He gulped in the dank, heavy air. She watched helplessly while Jimmy hobbled to the shelf and tried a flashlight he found, but the batteries were no good anymore, and the light made a dull flicker before it vanished. The hunger began hours later. He had to use his hands to feel around for the cans of food he knew were there, for the rusty opener. He went through tuna first, and then corn niblets and he cut his fingers on the jagged edges, but he kept going because he was so hungry. He found the water and finished it. He screamed, but nobody heard him. And then everything she saw became a circle, with her brother at the center, and the circle grew smaller and smaller, and he curled himself up as tightly as he could, his scribbled sneakers tucked under him, his plaid shorts damp and dirty from mud. He gulped at the air until he was panting. She was right there with him when he felt like there was no air left for him to breathe, when he knew no one would ever find him.

She woke up, leaping from the bed, her whole body shaking. She focused on the hotel dresser, the TV, the minibar. Her fingers brushed the bedspread. She was alive in this room. These things around her were real. All these years, she had been desperate for Jimmy to visit her in dreams, frantic to see him, and finally he came and it was more terrible than she could imagine. When she felt a hand on her, she whipped around to see Lewis, and she began to cry. But she couldn't tell him about the dream. "Can we just get out of here?" she asked.

ROSE AND LEWIS went to a restaurant near the motel for breakfast, and then they took a walk, but neither one of them was talking very much.

Rose felt Brian everywhere, like a ghost, haunting her. At the restaurant, Brian was sitting at a table with a child on his lap. When they went to the bookstore, a man with thick hair like Brian's was browsing the shelves. Rose put one hand over her face. "Are you all right?" Lewis asked.

"I don't know," she said.

Everything seemed wrong. She used to think that if she knew what had happened to Jimmy, if she had all the pieces, she'd be able to move on, and instead, she felt even more broken. She had thought all she wanted was to be with Lewis, but being with him reminded her of so much she wanted to forget. She had never understood why her mother had left the neighborhood, but now all she could think was, Of course that's what you did, fleeing from the pain as if it were a wild animal about to tear you in two. How could she not have seen it? When the pain reached a certain point, how could you do anything else?

THEY DROVE BACK to Ann Arbor, as if distance would make things better, but the dreams kept coming. Every night, as she slept beside Lewis, there was Jimmy running and her chasing him. Every night, she felt Jimmy's loss of hope, heard his desperate pleas. *Come and find me.*

She went to the Thrift-T-Mart and bought Sominex, but the pills just made her groggy and cranky and didn't stop the dreams at all. She couldn't speak to Lewis about any of it because she didn't want him sharing her guilt. She was afraid to go to sleep. She wanted to stay up all night. "You have to sleep," Lewis told her. He rubbed her hands and stroked her hair. He stayed up with her as long as he could, and then he was sleeping fitfully and she was staring at the walls, waiting for the dreams to come and haunt her.

She got up and went into the living room and turned the TV on and then off again. She lay down on the couch, waiting, and then, despite herself, she fell asleep, not waking until Lewis shook her. "Come back to bed," he whispered.

She sat up. "I didn't dream," she said in wonder. "I didn't dream." As soon as she went back to bed with Lewis, his arm around her, there she was again, running on the street, trying to grab her brother, following him down into the hole. But this time, Jimmy saw her and when she reached for him, she actually touched his skin, and she was able to hold him, to feel him against her, alive. He pulled away and then looked at her as if it was the most unsurprising thing in the world for them to be there together. "It's over," he said, his shoulders hunching. "It's the end." She bolted awake.

"It's okay, it's okay," Lewis wrapped himself about her, but she felt as if she were suffocating. She broke the band of his arms.

"You just had a bad dream," he said, and she shook her head, crying.

"It's not just a bad dream. And I can't do this anymore," she blurted. "I can't keep being this sad. I can't keep dreaming about me and Jimmy and your father."

Lewis looked at her, shocked. "You've been dreaming about my dad?"

"Yes." She lowered her head.

"All this time?"

"I wish I didn't know what happened," she said finally.

He was quiet for a moment. "I wish that, too," he said. "I never thought I'd say that."

"I can say that," she said abruptly. "But you can't. He's your father.

He's in our life." As soon as she got the words out, she felt as if she were sinking.

"What are you talking about? Who says I want to see him again?"

"You're upset about him now, but you loved him so much as a kid. He was so important to you. How do you know that you're not going to miss him?"

"Are you kidding? I never will. I'm done. Why are you even bringing this up?"

"You don't know that. You can't know that. A father's a father. My mother told me you're with a man, you're with his family, whether you like them or not. That's just the way it is. I have to move on from this. I have to find some way to deal with it. I want to be with you, but how can I be the kind of person who tells you not to see your father?"

"You won't have to, I told you."

"What if he's sick, Lewis? What if he's dying? What if he gets thrown out of his house and Glory is gone and he has no place else to stay, no one else but you to turn to? You wouldn't give him another chance? I know you well enough to know that you would."

"Rose, come on—how long have you been thinking about this? Why didn't you talk to me about this?"

"I know how you feel about me. I know. We haven't talked about it, but what if we stay together and we have a child some day? You know as well as I do what it's like to grow up without family—are you going to deny your kid grandparents? My mother's parents are dead, but my father's family just made themselves dead to us. After my father died, my mother said they froze us all out cold. That's not right. It's family. It's got to mean something."

"How do you know what's going to happen? Can't you just focus on now?"

Her shoulders rose and fell. "I don't want to be sad anymore. I feel like I can't ever escape this."

"You're so upset, you're not thinking straight. It won't always feel that way."

"How do you know that? So we'll be together and every time we see each other, we'll have that day in our minds."

"I love you." It was the first time he had ever said it to her, and she stepped back, blinking her eyes hard. He stood there looking at her, and she thought how easy it would be to say yes to him, and then she thought of everything she'd be saying yes to.

"I think you need to go home," she said, her voice small.

"No," Lewis said, and she looked at him with pity.

"This isn't the real world," she said. "It's just you and me in my apartment."

"We can make it the real world," Lewis said. His voice sped up. "My job's portable. I can live anywhere, hospitals always need help. I can move to Ann Arbor. Or you could come live near me—there are so many schools there—you could find another teaching job. You said yourself, what if we were together, really together—"

"Aren't you listening to me?" she said. "I can't do any of those things. This horrible thing happened and I need to get over it, or at least around it. I can't feel like this anymore."

"I don't understand," he said. "Is this it? We've gone through all this and now we don't see or talk to each other again? How does that make sense? Who else knows you the way I do? How can you do this?"

"Because I have to." She started getting dressed. "When I slept by myself, without you beside me, I didn't dream and it was like a little breath, like a respite. I'm not blaming you. I know it's all in me, but I need to be able to get up in the morning and not feel like I want to die."

"Rose—" he pleaded, but she got up and began straightening the room, and when she came to Jimmy's map, she carefully folded it, hesitating before she gently put it into the wastebasket. "You really have to go," she said.

LEWIS WAS SURE that any moment she'd change her mind. She was just upset. She wasn't thinking clearly. He didn't press her because in the hospital that usually made patients do the opposite of what you wanted them to do. But then she brought out his little suitcase and handed it to him, and he looked at it, dismayed. "Will you call me?" he asked. "Can I call you?"

"Just give me some time."

"How much?" he asked.

"I don't know. I won't know until I feel better." Tears streaked her face and he stepped forward to hold her, but she moved back away from him, drying her face with her hands. "I can't watch you leave. I'm going to take a walk, so when I come back, you'll be gone."

"Rose, come on," he said, but she grabbed her jacket. "You have to let me be by myself," she said, and then she left, the door slapping behind her.

For a moment he didn't know what to do, where to go. He wanted to stay and wait for her, but he didn't want to get her more upset. Maybe he could drive home to Madison and call her later, but he didn't have to be back at work yet, and he didn't want to be in Madison by himself. He found a piece of paper on Rose's table and started to write, *Rose*—just that, that one word seemed to be enough, so he put the pen down, and that's when he noticed Jimmy's map in Rose's wastebasket. He picked it up, tucked it under his arm, and left her house.

HE DROVE. ALL these cars around him, full of husbands and wives and kids, families on their way someplace or on their way home. On his right a man leaned over and kissed the blond woman beside him and when she cupped the back of his head, the way Rose did to Lewis, he averted his head. He didn't even have a pet fish at home to welcome him.

He stopped at a rest stop to get coffee, and then, in the car, he pulled out Jimmy's map and looked at it again. He had four days left of his vacation and he didn't want to be alone. He knew Rose needed to figure it all out herself, that she wanted to be alone, and maybe even she wanted to erase him, to start fresh, and maybe he couldn't blame her, but he couldn't do the same, not yet. Instead, he wanted to be with someone who was glad to see him, who had some idea what he was going through. He wanted to talk about everything that had happened until he understood it.

He got back on the highway, heading east until he saw the sign, BOSTON 67 MILES. Every time he had come here, it was because he felt he had to, because it was family, because she was his mother. He had been here many times, but he always ended up getting lost somehow, taking the wrong turn or missing it entirely, ending up in Auburn or Cambridge instead of Waltham. He stopped at gas stations, asking for directions, and then as soon as he was back in the car, he forgot the route numbers. "You've been here a million times, don't you know your way already?" Ava used to joke when he showed up late. "Maybe you do it deliberately." He looked up, and there, like a message, was the sign. ROUTE 128 WALTHAM. He wasn't lost at all. He made the turn.

It was night, and before he got to his old neighborhood, he passed Bell's, the café where his mother sold pies. The parking lot was crowded, and he was about to keep going when he saw his mother's car parked by the door. He pulled into the lot, driving around twice before he found a space, and then got out. A couple, laughing, walked into the café. He glanced at his watch. By now, Rose would be eating dinner.

He walked in. He swore he smelled cinnamon. The place looked the same as the last time he had seen it, all green plants and polished wood tables spread with red floral tablecloths. The clock was in the shape of a big mermaid with a switching tail that beat out the minutes. One of the two waitresses, her hair teased up into a bubble, a blue apron tied at her waist, smiled at him. Lewis had never seen so many pies. They were all lined up like trophies in a glass case, some with lattice crusts, and each one looked delicious. The waitress came over, her face expectant. "Come on, hon," she said, and led him to a booth.

"Is Ava here?" Lewis felt his voice fumble. "I'll get her," she said. "And I'll grab you a menu, too."

He sat in the booth, still dumbfounded by his surroundings, and then, there, in the back, like a mirage, was his mother. He could see her clearly now. Her hair was a storm of curls. She was talking to a man, who took her elbow and said something to her, drawing her close, so she blushed and laughed. He saw the sparkle in the man's eyes, the way he touched Ava's arm, but Ava's eyes were clear, focused on the table and not on him. She extricated her arm and reached for a plate. And then the waitress caught up with Ava and said something, pointing to Lewis, and that's when Ava turned, the plate in her hand. She stood there, staring at him. She looked confused, framed in the doorway and the light, as if she didn't know who he was or what to do. She walked to his table and slowly sat down. "I'm not dreaming, am I?" she said.

"What are you doing here?" he said.

"I'm working here. Full-time now. Bell's training me to be the manager."

"That's incredible!" He looked at her again, how relaxed she seemed, how happy.

"You'll have to meet her. I know I'm getting ahead of myself, but I have all these plans for baking evenings and hootenannies. I may even sell bagels here, imagine that!"

"The man you were talking with. Is he a boyfriend?"

Ava sighed. "What if he was?" she said quietly. "Would that be so terrible?"

"I'm sorry. I didn't mean anything."

"Well, he's not. I'm too busy to have boyfriends."

She leaned toward him, the way she used to when he was young, as if she wanted to scoop up every word. "Tell me everything. Where's Rose? How was the road trip?"

He had never really confided anything about his life to his mother before, but things had changed now. He wouldn't be talking to her about his father like a boy who wanted him back. He wouldn't be talking to her about Rose like Rose was just a friend. And when he looked at his mother, she wasn't the person she had been before to him, either. She looked so different, so calm. She didn't take her eyes from his face. "It didn't work out for Rose and me," he said.

"Some things just don't," she said. "No matter how much you want them to."

"Did you want them to with Dad?" He thought of that day when his father was supposed to show up and she'd sat out waiting with him, the two of them working their way through a bag of cookies.

She got a funny look on her face. "Oh, honey," she said.

He wasn't sure how to start, how to tell her. "Did you ever wonder what might have happened if he had come to get me?"

"He never did," she said flatly. "Do you know how happy I was when you turned eighteen? And you want to know why? Because then he couldn't come for you. Then it was over. You were an adult and he couldn't change his mind about custody again. Not anymore." She lifted up her hands. "Why are you doing this? Why are you spoiling a visit by talking about him? Do you know what it was like for me, on my own, terrified about money, worrying about you and him and you-and-him?"

He felt a flicker of old anger and tried to push it away. "What about what it was like for me? I just wanted my dad and you had all these boyfriends." A woman at the next booth glanced over, her eyes hooded, and he lowered his voice. "You had Jake."

"The boyfriends again. You're an adult now. Have you never been lonely?"

He thought of driving in the car here, how every once in a while, he'd think, if he just shut his eyes and then opened them, Rose would be in the seat beside him.

"You still blame me for your father," she snapped. "Isn't it time to give that up? I'm the one who took care of you, not him. I bought your clothes and your food, and I did it with my money, not his." She leaned across the table to him. "What has he ever done for you? Just tell me that." Her eyes flashed. "How am I wrong? Go ahead and tell me," she said.

He had gone over the story on the drive here. How he'd tell his mother about his reunion with Brian and how the whole visit had been like electric shocks. He could tell her how she had been wrong, how Brian had wanted him so much he had come back to get him, and that Jimmy had died because of it. He could tell her, too, how he knew suddenly, sitting in his father's living room, how right Ava had been all along. Brian wasn't worth her or him or any of them because he couldn't take responsibility, he didn't want to see himself in any light that wasn't shining. And Lewis could tell his mother the saddest thing of all, how and why Rose had left him.

If he told her, she'd be horrified and he knew she'd feel responsible for all of it, and what good would it do either one of them? She always knew she had married a jerk, but she didn't know he was involved in Jimmy's death, that he had ruined things between Lewis and Rose. Did she deserve that after all she'd been through?

"Did you see your father?" she finally asked.

He shook his head. "He wasn't at that address," Lewis lied.

He saw her shoulders visibly relax. She reached over and took his hand. "Look at me, getting so upset about the past," she said. "I'm too old for this." He noticed, then, the slight sag of her chin, a thread of gray in her hair. People were coming into her café, talking and laughing. The man who had taken her elbow was leaving. "I'm just glad to see you. That's all I care about. The rest is nothing," she said.

"I'm glad to see you, too."

She stood up. "Come on," she said. "I want you to taste my pie. Cinnamon plum and I guarantee it will knock your socks off."

He watched her get up, and his first inclination was to go help her, to make her sit down so he could serve her, but instead he sat back. When she returned with a red plate in her hands, silverware rolled into checkered linen, all he could say was, "I'm sorry."

"For what, honey?" She fussed over the table. She set the plate down, unfurling the napkin and handing him the fork. "Eat your pie," she told him, but it wasn't the same tone she used to get him to eat his dinner when he was a kid. No, this had pride in it. She waited while he took a forkful. Never had he tasted anything like this, the plum intense as a sparkle, a spice so mysterious that he couldn't place it. "Is it good?" She put her hand to her mouth, waiting, and when he shut his eyes and sighed dramatically, she laughed. "I need a second slice to make sure," he told her.

THAT EVENING, WHEN she was done with work, he followed her home in his car, making the turn onto Abbott Road, and then to Warwick Avenue again. It always looked the same and different, the suburban houses, the streets he had roamed with Jimmy and Rose. It was like a newsreel of his past unspooling toward him and he couldn't stop it. There it was, his old house, blue with white shutters and yellow flowers all around. Always the yellow flowers. Catty-corner across the street was Rose and Jimmy's house and a few houses down, the empty lot that had been Mr. Gallagher's.

Ava parked in the driveway and he pulled up along the curb. She sprang out of the car, giddily waiting for him to join her. "With the café, I'll be able to buy the house in a few years," Ava told him. "I told you I would. And I'll be able to fix it up more, too." She couldn't wait to open the door, to show him. "It might still smell a little like paint," she told him. "I just finished yesterday." As soon as he stepped inside, he felt disoriented. He touched the walls of the living room as if to ground himself. He remembered them white, but now they were a soft, soothing green, and she had a new darker green rug on the floor. "I splurged on that rug," she told him. "But it's so worth it, isn't it?" The kitchen that used to be yellow was blue, and there was a big white formica table planted in the center of the floor. "Just got it. I needed something bigger for baking," she said.

"It's really nice," he told her.

"I always knew it could be," she said.

THAT EVENING, THEY took a walk around the neighborhood. At first, all he could think about were the neighborhood patrol walks, the way the neighbors had peered out their windows, but tonight there were kids spilled out on the streets, biking, playing jump rope, hanging out. He didn't recognize any of them, though they all knew Ava. "Hi Ava!" they called.

"I test out my new pies with them by giving free samples," she whispered to him. "That's why they're so happy to see me. I keep them sugared up."

"It's got to be more than the pies."

"Well, maybe," she said. "I treat them like people, not just kids." She pointed out the houses, telling him who had moved and who had stayed. Bob Gallagher was gone, of course, but some of the old-timers were still there, including Debbie and Dick Hill. Debbie had taken a part-time job selling dresses at Grover Cronin's and had even started a consciousness-raising group. "There's a lot of new people, too," Ava said. "I'm now introduced as 'the woman who run the café.'"

He looked at her. She was still lovely, but there wasn't the shock of her anymore. When a woman came out of a house across the street, Lewis was surprised to see she was wearing the same black stretch pants Ava was, that her hair was as untamed as his mother's. The neighborhood women had all caught up to her, or maybe she was still forging ahead in ways he couldn't even imagine. Well then, good for her. "You're really brave," he said, and she smiled.

"What brought that on?" she wanted to know, but he just shrugged.

"I'll come visit more often."

"You're always here with me. Don't you know that by now?" she said.

◈ *Chapter Twenty-two* ◈

Three days later, Lewis was back in Madison, walking the halls of the surgical ward, his sneakers padding on the floor. He had returned with three of Ava's pies, which the nurses had already made short work of. "You tell your mother to move here," Elaine said. "I'll find her a job just so I can eat these pies every day." Already, he had been called to help lift a man from his bed to a gurney, the man thrashing against him, whacking Lewis in the chest and knocking the breath out of him. Lewis had cleaned up vomit in room 412, a young woman heaving into the sheets. He listened to Elaine snap at him for not draping a patient properly for a sponge bath. "Vacation is over, buddy," Elaine said. "Two weeks and you forget everything?"

He took an early lunch, going outside. It was always a surprise to be out in the fresh air.

He walked. He hadn't really been hungry since he had gotten back, but he forced himself to stop at a deli and get something to eat. His roast beef sandwich tasted chalky. His apple was spicy. No one at the hospital had really asked him about his vacation, and when in the nurse's break room he had offered, saying, "I saw my father for the first time in years," another nurse said, "I hope I never see my father. Let me tell you what he did to me, that stupid bastard . . . " But this time, Lewis couldn't focus the way he usually could on what the nurse was saying.

His eyes wandered to the door and the nurse finally said, "What's the matter, you sleeping?" and Lewis excused himself.

After lunch, he went back to work. The woman in 401 needed to be walked, but when Lewis went to get her, she scowled, shrinking from his touch. "Don't be so rough," she snapped. "Just hang on to me so I don't fall." All he had to do was escort her up and down the hall for ten minutes so her muscles wouldn't atrophy. Holding on to the tender skin of another person used to feel so intimate to him, but today, it just felt practical. He used to love to listen to his patients, to hear their stories, but this woman was complaining about how her daughter's kids didn't show respect, and Lewis tuned her out. "Tomorrow, I'll tell you about my grandson," she said. "He lives in Massachusetts."

"So does my mother," Lewis said, and with a start he realized it was one of the first true things he had told patients about his life.

He realized he was tired of making up his life, telling people stories. As the hallways stretched out in front of him, he saw he had all these people in all these rooms to talk to. He could march down the corridor to the pay phone and call his mother and she'd be delighted to hear from him, but it wouldn't kill the jumpy feeling. It wouldn't fill the hole. Ava had told him once that he could keep himself from getting lost if he just could pay attention to the signs and then he would know where he needed to be. But he didn't see any signs now. There was no place he wanted to be, except with the person who knew everything about him, the person who had been through it all with him. He wanted to be where Rose was and no map had directions on how to get there.

The next morning, he walked into Elaine's office and quit. "I want to take some time, figure out what I want to do in life," he told Elaine. To his surprise, she reached over and took his arm. "Don't go," she said. "You work harder than anyone else, and you're smarter and faster, too. I can't do without you." She studied him. "What will it take to keep you? Do you want a raise? I could see about getting you trained to draw blood. It might be a little difficult, but I could do it."

"I need to go," he said and she sighed. "I've been here long enough to know the doctors, which ones are good guys, which are not. Before you go, you see this one. Just in case."

"I don't need a doctor," Lewis said, but Elaine kept scribbling and then handed him a piece of paper. Dr. Mark Kawolski, it said. Lewis didn't even know him.

"He's a psychiatrist," Elaine said. "He'll swear and so will I that you are totally mentally unbalanced and can't go to Vietnam if you're drafted. He'll write you a letter."

"Why didn't you give me this before?" He looked at it astonished.

"I knew you didn't need it before. If you go off, I won't know that."

Impulsively, he reached across and hugged her, and when she pulled away, he saw her eyes were shiny with tears. "Don't make me have to find you," she said. "You keep in touch."

LEWIS DIDN'T HAVE a lot of money saved, but he wasn't worried. There were hospitals everywhere, and he could pick up work wherever he went, and he didn't really need all that much. He'd sleep in his car if he had to. If he got lonely, he could always find people who would talk to him. He knew he had that gift, but getting them to listen might be something else.

Suddenly, the world felt brimming with possibilities. If he wanted, he could take the SATs again and apply to college and this time, with a work record behind him, he bet he'd get in somewhere and they'd give him money. He thought of all the things he could be. Maybe he'd even go to medical school. He didn't have to make a final decision about anything in his life right now, but he was beginning to see the possibilities.

The next morning, he packed the car. He spread out Jimmy's map on the seat and tried to feel where he needed to go.

ALTHOUGH THE DREAMS stopped the day Lewis left, Rose was surprised to find she didn't feel any better without them. At least she had seen her brother in them. She popped Sominex every night, waking astonished that the world was still going on and there she was in it, not having a clue what to do next.

Rose arranged for her brother's remains to be sent to a local funeral parlor where she had them cremated. When they called her to pick them up, she was handed a small brown box, which she carried carefully. Anyone looking might have thought she was bringing home cupcakes from the bakeshop. She put the box in the living room, staring at it, trying to figure out what to do with it. Burial was out of the question. Her brother had been shut up underground in a small enclosed space for too many years. She wouldn't do that to him again. Jimmy needed to be out in the open, in the broad daylight, and the only thing she needed to figure out was where.

She loved Ann Arbor, all the parks and lakes. She wanted him someplace where she could always go and feel him there. She had to trust that she'd know the right place when she saw it.

It was something to do, these nights, walking around Ann Arbor, trying to scout out the perfect area. She walked by herself, her hands in her pockets, though she could have walked with the casual friends she had. One night, she had tried to call Lewis just to hear his voice, but he hadn't picked up, and she told herself, well, maybe that was a sign, part of moving on. It made her feel she had done the right thing, sending him away. Still, she felt lost and lonely. It wouldn't always feel this way, she told herself, or maybe she'd always feel as if a chip of herself was missing, and if so, then she'd just have to find a way to live with it.

She walked through Burns Park and the Bird Hills Nature area. She wandered by one of the ponds in Logan, circling around so many times, unsure, that a man fishing, finally turned to her. "Are you lost?" the man asked. He held up his fishing pole, and she saw the lure, glittering on the end of the line. She looked at him, considering. "Yes," she said, finally. "I believe I am." She let him give her directions out again, even though she knew her way. She walked deeper into the woods, her head down, her whole body expectant. In the end, she made her way to the Arb, walking until she got to a stream.

Here. Here was the place. When he was a kid, Jimmy loved jumping across the rocky streams in the woods behind their house. The place he talked most about visiting was California, where he could be by the water always. She looked around, feeling the sky around her, the breeze.

At school the next day, she asked for a personal day. "Again?" Peggy, the secretary said, tapping her pencil on the desk. "I'm scattering my brother's ashes in the Arb," Rose said. The words hung in the air and as soon as Rose said them, she wished she could take them back. Peggy stopped tapping. "You take the time you need," Peggy said quietly.

The next day, the box carefully placed in her backpack, Rose walked to the Arb. She didn't know anymore what she believed about death, but sometimes she thought, maybe if she finally put Jimmy to rest, she'd feel him alive again in some way. She'd sense a connection. Maybe he'd come back in her dreams in a better way, and she'd be ready to know him again.

She walked past Central Campus to Geddes Road to the lip of the Arb. The gravel path crunched under her feet. She reached up for one of the leaves on a tree, fingering it. Brady had taught her how to tell what a tree was just by the shape of the leaves, like it was the easiest thing in the world. She counted the ribs on it. Five. Maple. She still knew it. She let the leaves go. There was nothing to be afraid of.

Jimmy would never be alone.

She walked until she reached the first big clearing in the Arb. There were a few people, a boy wrapping his girlfriend up in a big blanket, a couple sprawled on the lawn kissing, a woman reading under a tree. No one was looking at her. She passed them, walking to the rocky stream.

She opened the box and took a handful of ashes out. She had thought it would be all dust, but there were chunks of bone here, a gritty weight in her palm. All she wanted to do was cup her hands over the ashes, hold him in her hands and not let go. I've got you, she had said, when he fell back against her in the bomb shelter in her dream. *I'll keep you whole.* She gathered more ashes. She held her arms out and opened her fingers, and there he was, sparkling in the air, floating down among the water and the rocks, and she wanted to grab him back. She could hear a bird in the tree. She sifted out more of his ashes, and by the time she got to the bottom of the box, she was crying. Now she knew where he was and she would be here with him when she could. She dusted her hands off on her coat and turned, tears streaming down her cheeks. She had wanted her grief to be over, to bury the whole experience along with her brother, but she might as well have swallowed the ashes because it all felt huge and immeasurable. By the time she got back to the main clearing, her sobs had stopped. She could feel how red and raw her eyes were.

The Arb was now empty. The woman who had been reading was gone. The couple kissing by the tree had vanished. It was just Rose alone under the warm sun in the silence, holding an empty box, but then, at the entrance, she saw a man, his hands in his pockets, not moving, watching her.

Lewis was standing there.

He wasn't moving and she stared at him, amazed, unsure how she felt. How had he found her here? She felt a breeze ruffling the edge of her skirt. Lewis took his hands out of his pockets and she saw that he had a map in his hand and she knew it was Jimmy's, the one she had thought she had thrown out. Imagine that. The guy with no sense of direction had come to find her, and while tracking the streets of Ann Arbor wasn't difficult, finding her here in the Arb was. Yet, he had done it.

There was a shadow stretched out like an arm across the lawn, hurtling toward her. It struck her then, as if she were suddenly flooded with light.

Here we all are together. In this beautiful, green forest, the Three Mouseketeers, she, Lewis, and Jimmy, finally, the one thing she had always wanted, only she hadn't expected it would be this way. She saw everything in front of her. A world that wasn't ever really safe. A lover whose presence still hurt her. A brother who was both with her and not. Then she thought of all the blood oaths they had ever taken. She thought of all the flashlight signals she and Lewis had blinked out across to each other when they were kids. S-O-S. S-O-S. *I'm here. I'm here.* That's what those lights said.

They had been so young then, nothing but kids. They had thought the whole world was theirs.

"Lewis." She called his name, but she couldn't move forward. Not yet. She waited to see what would happen next.

ACKNOWLEDGMENTS

I'm thrilled I get to say "thank you for changing my life" to the gods and goddesses at Algonquin, especially to my genius editor Andra Miller. Huge thanks to the amazing Bob Miller, Ina Stern, Elisabeth Scharlatt, Peter Workman, Michael Taeckens, Megan Fishmann, Kelly Bowen, Craig Popelars, Lauren Moseley, Brunson Hoole, Carol Schneider, Sara Rose Nordgren, Emma Boyer, Katie Ford, and the rest of the stellar team. I can never thank my adored agent Gail Hochman enough, and big thanks, too, to Jody Klein, Bill Contardi, Gabe Szabo, and Joanne Brownstein.

For research help, thanks to my two young, wonderful assistants, Madison Wilson and Robby Auld, and profound thanks to researcher Victoria Romero. Joe Flores gave legal help and hilarious stories of male nursing in the 1960s; police officers Peter Noonan and Al Loustalot (thanks to his granddaughter Victoria, too), were invaluable; and Kathleen Decosmo, Pat Carey, Amelia Quinn, Maggie Balistreri, Wendy Schwartz Kaplan, Loucille Fournier, and Mo Bordenca opened up the world of 1950s and 1960s nursing to me. Joseph Clark and John McHugh solved my forensics problems and I had delicious help about pie baking from master pastry chef Gale Gand. Thanks, too, to Jeff Clarke, Judy Cohen, Cara DeBeer, Gina Hyams, Bonni Miller, Linda Matlow, Eileen Oliver, and Caroline Muir.

For wading through drafts and offering insights: I have depended on Rochelle Jewell Shapiro, Leora Skolkin-Smith, Katharine Weber, Robb Forman Dew, Liza Nelson, Gina Sorell, Jane Praeger, Lisa Cron, Jeff Lyons, Jeff Tamarkin, Molly Moynahan, Jennifer Gooch Hummer, Jessica Brilliant Keener, Clea Simon, and Dori Ostermiller. For support and cheer: Victoria Zackheim, John Truby, Leslie Lehr, Linda Corcoran, Jo Fisher, Sarah McCoy, Amy McKinnon, Dawn Tripp, Jo-Ann Mapson, Elizabeth Brundage, Liz Flock, Peter Salzano, Sandy Novack, Sheila Weller, Helen Leavitt, Ruth Leavitt, Nancy Lattanzi, Kathy L. Patrick and the Pulpwood Queens, and Barbara Drummond Mead, whom I miss dearly. I would be remiss if I did not also thank my Facebook and Twitter friends who cheered me on as I posted about writing this novel.

I owe special thanks and love to Jodi Picoult for fairy-godmothering me, to Anne Lamott for her heart as big as Jupiter, and to Adriana Trigiani for her warmth and kindness.

And of course, to my partners-in-crime and the absolute loves of my life, Jeff and Max.

Is This Tomorrow

A Note from the Author

Questions for Discussion

A Note from the Author

In the 1960s, I moved from my grandmother's Brookline apartment to a new development in Waltham, Massachusetts. The suburbs! Our own house! My father never tired of telling me that "here was life." My sister and I could run around on our own, the schools were great, there was fresh air and sunshine. There were even spindly little trees planted, the promise of big leafy greenery to come. This new dream meant happiness, safety, community. Or did it?

I remember the thrill of roaming around solo, of going in and out of neighbors' houses whenever I wanted, because no one ever locked their doors. But there was some tarnish under the shine. When a black family wanted to move into the development, some neighbors started up a petition to stop them. My mother got the list of names and called every one. "Aren't you ashamed?" she accused, until the protest was dropped. There was the fact that we were the only Jewish family in a predominantly Christian neighborhood, and I often heard, casually, like the passing of party nuts, that we killed Christ, that we would be going to Hell. One friend even called me, weeping, to tell me she could no longer hang around with me, because her parents "didn't trust Jews."

But it wasn't just racism that permeated the neighborhood. People were terrified of Communists. A neighbor accused my mother of being "more than a little pink" because she was antiwar. We had duck-and-cover drills in school, cowering under our desks for protection against the atom bomb and the glow of radiation. We were all on alert, especially when a suspicious new family moved in: a divorced woman and her son and daughter. "She's had it once; she'll do anything to get it again," a neighbor said knowingly, and even though we kids weren't quite sure what "it" was, we had a good idea. She often sunned in her front yard in a bikini, at a time when all of our mothers wore modest one-pieces, and the tight dresses she wore to the backyard barbecues made all of the fathers want to dance close with her. Our parents warned us not to go into her house, because, they insisted, it was dirty or there was no food. Even worse, she worked, instead of making a nice home, cooking dinner, being a wife. She was unusual, and that was never a good thing.

The daughter—we'll call her Anna—was my friend, as was her brother, Roger. We kids liked Anna and Roger, but we knew early on that for a cookie, Roger would do your homework. For a pack of gum, Anna would show her panties. But that summer, something shocking happened. The wealthy family Anna babysat for wanted to adopt her, to take her away to New York, where they were moving, and Anna's mother said yes. Just like that her mother gave her up, and Anna vanished. Two days later, Anna's mother and Roger disappeared, too.

I never forgot them. I tried to find out what had happened to them, as a kid and as an adult, but I met dead end after dead end. When I started *Is This Tomorrow,* it was about that family, but like all fiction, it began to breathe and take on its own life, and it soon morphed into something else. I wrote about Ava Lark, divorced, Jewish, working, and beautiful, all of which made her a target in her suburban enclave. But unlike her real-life counterpart, she was devoted to her son, Lewis, who never forgave her for the yearning he felt for his absent father. The character who vanishes is Jimmy, Lewis's best friend, which somehow escalates the dislike everyone feels for Ava, and ruptures the neighborhood sense of safety, as Jimmy's unsolved mystery haunts and affects everyone for years to come.

I set the novel in the 1950s because the contrasts of that era stun me. Underneath that good life, the Eisenhower blandness, the wood-paneled rec rooms, the suburban idyll, was desperate anxiety about anything different, terror of Communism, unease about nuclear destruction, distrust of anyone even remotely unique and a need to attack them for it. The thing is, these facts, these attitudes, still seem to resonate today.

I never found out what happened to the real-life people who left without a trace, but I got to have closure with my fictional characters, solving their mysteries in ways that none of them—or I—ever expected. And through them, I was able to project a more hopeful, progressive, and truly accepting future.

Questions for Discussion

1. Why do you think Leavitt takes a child-vanishing story and sets it in the 1950s? What does the era add to the story? Would the story have had a different outcome if it were set in a different time frame?

2. The title, *Is This Tomorrow,* was the actual name of a lurid 1950s-era pamphlet about the threat of Communism, but the title works on other levels in the novel. Why else do you think Leavitt gave the novel that title?

3. So much of *Is This Tomorrow* is about what it means to be part of a community and how difficult it is to be an outsider. Who besides Ava and Lewis are outsiders? How does being an outsider affect both Ava and Lewis at work and in their relationships?

4. Cooking and the meaning of cooking figure in the novel, from the "meals men like" that Ava struggles with to her discovery that she has a talent for making pies. How does Leavitt show the changing nature of relationships, creativity, and male/female jobs in the novel, especially in the context of the 1950s, when women often didn't become professionals but married the people they wanted to be?

5. Leavitt's novel probes the directions our lives can take. Lewis and Jimmy have an actual map to guide them in future trips. Lewis has no sense of direction, and at one point Ava tells him to watch for and read

the signs and he won't get lost. What do you think are some of the important signs in Lewis's life, and how does Lewis follow or ignore them?

6. What are the very different ways in which Lewis and Rose cope with Jimmy's disappearance, and how is each way integral to their personality? Who do you think has the most difficulty coping and why?

7. What makes Ava so suspect in the neighborhood, and would those things be suspect in any other era?

8. Although the novel is set in the 1950s, what parallels do you see to contemporary life?

9. *It Is Tomorrow* is very much about fathers and sons and mothers and sons. How does Lewis's relationship with his father and with Ava change throughout the novel?

10. The novel explores the way we communicate. Rose feels she has an intuitive communication with Jimmy. She tells everyone about her brother, but she can't really listen to any disagreement about him. She also writes out her thoughts to Lewis in a journal. Lewis can really open up only to his patients. And even Ava hides things about his father from Lewis. How would the story have turned out differently if the characters could have communicated with one another without fear?

11. Why is being a nurse the perfect job for Lewis? And why does he begin to move away from it?

12. Why and how do all of the characters feel guilt in one way or another for something they could have or should have done?

13. At one point in the story, Lewis wants to tell Ava, "Don't be this person anymore" (page 183). What does he mean, and how do you think that question also refers to him?

14. Who does Leavitt lead you to suspect is responsible for what happens to Jimmy? How many different people did you suspect and why?

15. Ava asks at one point, about one of her boyfriends, "How had she missed the truth?" (page 311), which could apply to everyone in terms of what really happened to Jimmy. Why do you think people missed the truth?

16. Why do you think Leavitt jumped forward in time to show Lewis and Rose as adults? How would the novel have been different if the story had resolved while they were still children?

17. Why do you think Lewis chooses not to tell Ava what he knows about his father? What does this act show about Lewis?

18. How is the suburban dream blighted in the novel? What hints do you see of the 1960s era to come?

19. Ava's being Jewish marks her as an outsider, and yet she isn't a particularly observant Jew. How do you think the story would have changed if she were?

20. Leavitt has said that she always wants the endings of her novels to be never-ending, to be unexpected, and to make you continue to wonder about the characters' lives. Did the novel end the way you expected? What do you think happens after the last page, and why?

JEFF TAMARKIN

Caroline Leavitt is the author of nine novels, including the *New York Times* bestseller *Pictures of You.* A book critic for the *Boston Globe* and *People,* Leavitt is a senior writing instructor at UCLA online. Visit her at www.carolineleavitt.com.

Join us at **AlgonquinBooksBlog.com** for the latest news on all of our stellar titles, including weekly giveaways, behind-the-scenes snapshots, book and author updates, original videos, media praise, detailed tour information, and other exclusive material.

You'll also find information about the **Algonquin Book Club**, a selection of the perfect books—from award winners to international bestsellers—to stimulate engaging and lively discussion. Helpful book group materials are available, including

Book excerpts
Downloadable discussion guides
Author interviews
Original author essays
Live author chats and live-streaming interviews
Book club tips and ideas
Wine and recipe pairings

twitter Follow us on twitter.com/AlgonquinBooks
facebook Become a fan on facebook.com/AlgonquinBooks